The Sibyl's

Ember

X.K. Westwood

Dedication

For my parents - all four of you,
who gave me roots and the
courage to reach.

For the parents I borrowed through
love lost, who opened their homes
and their hearts.

For the teachers who carried me as their own,
teaching me how to shape light from silence.

And for the thread no one else can see – the one
that pulls me forward through every shadow.

Acknowledgment

To everyone who ever stood at the edge of something new and didn't know if they were allowed to step forward — this book was written for you and because of you.

To those who walked beside me, your belief carried me when I couldn't carry myself. Thank you for holding space for this story, asking hard questions, and letting me be honest.

To the friends who became family and the ones who let me be quiet when I needed to be, your love is threaded through every page.

To my editing team, April and Nora — your insight, patience, and faith in these words shaped them into something stronger than I could have imagined.

To the readers who find themselves in these characters, even in the smallest ways, thank you for trusting me with your time, your tears, and your hope.

And finally, to the boy I used to be — you made it. You're still here.

Content Warning

The Sibyl's Ember explores themes of grief, identity, religious control, and generational trauma. Within its pages, there are references to emotional and spiritual abuse, religious extremism, public shaming, implied child endangerment, and the complex dynamics of strained families. It also contains depictions of physical punishment under authoritarian systems, as well as the internal struggle of navigating queer identity in a world shaped by fear and silence.

This is a story about survival — about becoming, even when the world says you shouldn't. While light, love, and chosen family thread throughout, some chapters may be painful for those walking similar paths. Please read with care and take what you need to feel safe.

You are not alone.

— X.K. Westwood

Secret Path

For the ones who left

the path, who stayed

quiet to stay safe,

who asked the wrong questions at the wrong time.

For the ones who dared to wonder if they were allowed
to be more.

You were never lost.

You were lighting the way.

Sha'rein tal'vesh, dorai'len nar.

"A whisper given weight becomes a world undone."

— from Ven'al Shariel (Shadow of Names)

Prologue

Answered Prayers

The air was thick with sharp, resinous incense, undercut by the bitter weight of smoke.

Petra drew her shawl tighter as they crossed into the gathering hall, the murmur of the crowd thinning into a hush that settled over her like a fine layer of dust.

Despite the late hour, the temple breathed warmth; candlelight swayed and stretched across the stone floor, shadows shifting like slow tides.

She shifted Sol higher against her shoulder, feeling the small weight anchor her in the vast, waiting quiet.

Kellan's hand came to rest between Sol's small shoulders — light, but certain, as though the touch tethered them both to the only thing that mattered.

The old altar still carried Beryth's harvest glyphs, their edges softened by time, yet proud beneath the years. Faint veins of gold leaf clung stubbornly in the grooves, catching the slow dance of candlelight.

Over them, a new mark had been laid: a single eye, silver and unblinking, carved with unnerving precision. It gleamed against the weathered stone like a promise… or a warning.

Its lines were clean, almost lulling, a polished circle cradled by two crescent arcs, like a narrow path inked with deliberate care.

At the center, a small diamond-shaped pupil seemed harmless at first, just a mark, just a symbol. But the longer Petra looked, the more it seemed to contract, as if aware of her gaze… as if waiting.

It could have been a compass, a holy light meant to guide, yet something in its stillness made her throat close, as though it had already chosen a direction for her.

There was no warmth in it.

Kellan's hand rested lightly at the small of her back, his fingers a quiet heat through the shawl. He nodded in passing to a few neighbors, the miller, and old Laren with his stubborn hip, but said nothing.

Sol slept against Petra's chest, one small hand hooked in the fold of her collar. His weight anchored her; the slow rise and fall of his breath steadied her own.

She had been the one to ask Kellan to come. With so many trials behind them, and more pressing close, she knew they needed more than hope. They needed a miracle.

As Petra knelt, she felt Kellan hesitate beside her.

"You've been told the gods are waiting," Drevan said softly.

"That they are watching. That you must prove your worth."

His voice was smooth, not loud, not hurried, yet it wound through the silence like twine, drawing it taut.

"But what kind of god waits for you to beg?"

A shiver rippled through the room; somewhere, a voice whispered, truth.

"Elion does not wait. Elion does not sleep. Elion sees the innocent and moves."

Petra flinched, as if the words had struck skin.

Kellan didn't notice. His hand found Sol's back. He smiled down at their son and whispered:

"He deserves a god who listens."

Petra nodded, though her throat burned. She fixed her gaze on the flame and said nothing.

"I have seen the storm," Drevan said. "I have walked the blighted fields. The gods you begged for protection have turned their backs."

He paced the dais with slow, deliberate steps, the whisper of his robes against stone the only sound.

"But Elion—"

"Elion chose you."

"Not the nobles. Not the priest-kings. You."

He stopped at the edge of the front row, lowering his voice until the room seemed to lean toward him.

"Do you know what that means?"

Silence stretched long enough for Petra's breath to catch.

"It means you are not forsaken. Not forgotten," Drevan said. "You are the ones who will rise… if you choose the Path of Elion, the only true god."

When his gaze found hers, it held there, steady as a hand on her shoulder.

Or maybe she only imagined it.

Her arms tightened around Sol, feeling the fragile rise and fall of his breath. He stirred, a faint sound slipping from him, muffled against her chest.

"There is only one path to abundance," Drevan said, his voice softened now, almost coaxing. "Through Elion."

The silence that followed was absolute. Even the children had gone still, as if the air itself held its breath.

Beside her, Kellan exhaled, not in fear, but in something that felt like relief.

"Whatever path keeps him safe, Petra," he murmured. "That's the only one I'll walk."

Petra's stomach tightened, a slow, cold knot winding inward.

From behind them came a low whisper, "He's right."

And that, more than Drevan's words, more than the strange stillness, was what truly scared her.

She bowed her head, turning slightly away.

Candlelight danced over the altar's new symbol, and for an instant, she could have sworn the silver hid a living flame.

Somewhere beyond the temple walls, a lone crow cried into the night, its voice carrying like an omen.

No one moved. No one breathed.

She pressed her lips to Sol's hair and whispered— so faintly it was almost only a thought:

"If this will keep you safe… then let the old gods stay silent."

Chapter One

———

Letters and Lies

The cool morning air drifted through the chipped green shutters, thick with the scent of damp earth. Soltic pushed them open, gazing longingly at the distant fields. Mist curled over the hills, softening their edges like a half-forgotten dream.

He lit the candle on his writing table, its flame flickering against the worn wood. His pulse quickened as he reached beneath the loose floorboard and his fingers brushed Wyatt's latest letter—thin, familiar, cherished. But beneath it, something softer met his touch. A breath caught in his throat.

Beside the folded edges rested a length of pale blue ribbon, its silk frayed with time. Mira's, once tied in her hair when she twirled through the cottage, demanding princess braids and wildflower crowns. Soltic ran his thumb over the delicate fabric. It wasn't the only keepsake hidden there. The narrow space beneath the floorboards cradled a lifetime of small secrets, each too precious to leave exposed to the world.

He set the ribbon aside and placed Wyatt's letter in

the flickering candlelight. The ink had smudged where his fingers had lingered too long. Soltic traced the words again, imagining Wyatt leaning against his sheep, sunlit hair tousled, scribbling between distractions, pausing, perhaps, to laugh at something only he could hear.

Was it really only a week until Wyatt would be back in Oswynn? Hopefully, nothing would delay him.

The soft drum of rain against the old roof steadied his restless thoughts. He inhaled deeply, fingers tightening around the quill, and he began.

Dearest Wyatt,

I'm so relieved to hear you made it safely to Briarstead. Please be careful on your way back to Oswynn — the roads are meaner these days. Thom was ambushed past the bend near the eastern field. They took everything left him bleeding in the mud. He's lucky to be alive, but luck isn't worth much when there's no steel left to sell. Maris is holding the forge together best she can, but there's only so much one pair of hands can do.

Everything feels off…. Storms keep rolling in, the air thick even under the sun.

People move quieter, eyes wary like they're bracing for something they won't name. Maybe it's just my imagination. Or maybe we both know better, something is coming, and everyone can feel it.

I hate how far Briarstead feels. Even with your letters, it's like there's too much space between us lately. I miss you. I miss your laugh, your hands, the way you always knew how to pull me back when my mind ran too far ahead. I need you, Wyatt — more than I can say in ink.

Come home soon.

Yours in waiting,

Sol

Sol read his letter once more, ensuring the ink had dried before folding it carefully. He sealed it, tucking it into its usual hiding place. With a steady breath, he stoppered the ink and blew out the candle. He had to send it today—Wyatt needed to read it before leaving Briarstead.

Sol splashed cold water on his face before tugging on his breeches and tunic. Moving quietly, he padded downstairs, pulled on his cloak, and stepped into the misty morning. Mud squelched beneath his bare feet as he filled the bucket with feed. He chuckled as the drenched chickens flapped and squabbled, their ruffled feathers dripping in the steady drizzle.

He rinsed the bucket before filling it with fresh water, then carried it to the overhang near the kitchen.

Gathering an armful of wood, he stepped inside the warmth of the hearth a welcome contrast to the damp morning. He set the logs down, draping his cloak nearby.

His mother, Petra was kneading the dough, flour dusting her forehead. Sol kissed her temple in passing, the gesture familiar, comforting. He stirred the fire, setting the water to boil as the kitchen filled with the scent of rising bread.

"Good morning, Ma," he said cheerfully.

"Good morning, my dear. You seem to be in better spirits this morning," she said warmly.

"Ay, Ma, even the rain will not dampen my spirits today," Sol beamed.

"If I didn't know better, I'd say you were in love," she said lightheartedly.

Sol laughed. "It's nothing so serious. I am determined to enjoy this day."

"As you say," Petra teased, kneading the dough with practiced ease. "But while you're off enjoying the day, I'll need you to bring that sweet smile to the market. Elora has the fabric I ordered, and charm always gets a better deal."

"Ma, if you don't need me around the house, can I

spend some time at the market?" Sol asked hesitantly.

"Well, I suppose I can spare you. Not much to do with all this rain," Petra said, pressing a small coin purse into his hands. "Take Theo and Mira with you, and here, a few extra coppers for something sweet. Now, go wake the twins while I set the table."

Petra swatted Sol playfully as he headed upstairs. He pushed open the door to find the twins curled together in a tangle of sheets, their soft snores filling the room. At six years old, they had their own beds, yet every morning, they ended up nestled in the same one.

Sol filled their washbasin and placed a full pitcher on the dressing table. With a mischievous grin, he climbed onto the foot of their bed, bouncing lightly as he let out an exaggerated, ear-piercing crow, his best impression of a rooster determined to rouse the whole village.

"Wake up, you two! The sun has risen, and so must you!" he boisterously called.

The twins groaned and pulled the sheets over their heads.

Sol perched at the edge of the bed, reaching over to tickle them. "Well, I guess I'll just go to the market myself."

The twins, laughing and swatting at Sol's hands, suddenly froze, their eyes going wide.

"The market!" they squealed in unison, eyes lighting up with excitement. In a flurry of tangled limbs and laughter, they launched themselves from the bed, nearly toppling Sol in their eagerness to start the day.

"Wash your faces and comb your hair," Sol said adoringly, before adding, "Quick, my ducklings—Mama is setting the table now."

The twins darted around in a blur of activity and rushed to get ready. Sol stood there at the doorway, watching with a quiet smile. They were growing up too fast. For a moment, he simply stood there, soaking in their laughter, reveling in their carefree joy. Humming to himself, Sol made his way back to the kitchen, the scent of fresh bread filling the air. He kissed his father's forehead in passing and received a playful tousle in return, his wavy brown hair falling messily over his eyes as he chuckled.

"Sol, your cheerful demeanor is nauseating this morning," Kellan laughed.

"Oh, Da, you should be careful—it's contagious," Sol teased.

"Well, in that case, I shall take my breakfast in the

other room." Kellan started to stand, but Petra pushed him back into his seat.

"I will not be bringing your food anywhere other than this table, Father. So, you best stay put, or I'll let the twins have yours."

At that moment, the twins came tumbling down the stairs, laughter echoing through the cottage. Without hesitation, they flung their arms around their parents, wrapping their arms around them with boundless energy and the pure, unfiltered love of childhood.

"Good morning!" they said in unison.

Kellan stretched dramatically, smirking. "Not you two as well. Can't we enjoy this rain in peace?"

The twins wriggled in their chairs, barely able to sit still, their excitement spilling over in restless movements and barely contained grins.

"Daaaaaaa, Sol is taking us to the market!" Theo blurted excitedly.

Kellan smirked, casting a playful glance at Petra. "Well, Mother, it seems we'll have the house to ourselves, a quiet morning at last." He sighed dramatically, then threw her an exaggerated wink, his eyes twinkling with mischief.

Petra smiled at Kellan. "See, my dear, I still have a

few tricks up my sleeve."

Sol looked at his younger siblings and teasingly said, "If you two promise to be good, I might have a surprise."

Mira, cheeks full and eyes wide with curiosity, pouted. "No fair! You have to tell me! Tell me, tell me!" She huffed, swinging her legs beneath the table. "Keeping secrets isn't nice!" Her voice was muffled by the food she stubbornly chewed.

"Mira!" Petra scolded. "You know better. Don't speak with your mouth full. I don't need the neighbors thinking I raised barn animals."

"Sorry, Mama," Mira mumbled, swallowing quickly.

Kellan chuckled, glancing at Petra with a teasing glint in his eyes. "Now, Mother, I quite like our little heathens. But perhaps it's time they start sleeping in the barn." His laughter rumbled as he playfully ruffled Theo's hair.

Sol smiled to himself, thinking If they only knew the secrets I keep. Kellan had always liked Wyatt, but would he still, if he knew the truth? One day, maybe. One day, Sol wouldn't have to keep his love hidden beneath floorboards and prayers.

The warmth of the moment wavered, fragile as a candle's flickering flame. A quiet draft of doubt crept in, whispering reminders of what remained unspoken.

"Sol, where did you go?" Petra's voice pulled him from his thoughts. "Did you hear me?"

Snapping back to the moment, Sol nodded. "Ma, I'm sorry. Yes, we will get the fabric from Elora and pick up meat for stew. We will be back before midday."

Kellan's voice turned serious. "Make sure you're home in time for the afternoon prayer."

"Don't come complaining to me when your feet are soaked, and you're stuck with old lady toes," Sol teased, scooping Mira into his arms. She squealed, giggling as he tapped her nose, her laughter bright and carefree against the morning's lingering chill.

Wrinkling her nose at him, she pouted. "I do not want old lady feet!" But her playful grin betrayed her, even as Theo continued to jump from puddle to puddle.

The rain had passed, leaving the earth damp beneath their steps as sunlight warmed their backs. The path to town was familiar— unchanging trees, weathered fences. The twins chattered beside him, their voices filling the quiet spaces where his thoughts threatened to wander. He needed to be quick. But the letter pressed against his chest, tethering his thoughts to something distant yet certain. He traced its edges through his coat, its crispness grounding him. Sending it off made his steps lighter. As the inn came into view, he silently thanked Ysella Thornbrook for years of quiet loyalty.

A second mother in all but name. She never coddled him, never scolded him, yet her presence was steady. Her guidance was subtle, a steady hand on his shoulder, reminding him he was never truly alone.

The bell chimed as they stepped inside, its bright note slicing through the inn's quiet hum, stirring the air like a ripple across still water.

"Hello, Mum!" Sol called cheerfully.

"Is that my sunshine coming to brighten this dingy inn?" Ysella replied just as brightly.

The rich scent of fresh bread curled through the air as Sol led the twins to a table near the bar. Wood scraped against stone as they eagerly settled in, their excitement barely contained.

"Mead for the table?" Ysella called over her shoulder, a wicked grin tugging at her lips.

The twins erupted into giggles, their laughter bright and unrestrained.

"Aunty Thornbrook, Mama won't let us drink mead," Theo said regretfully.

"Is that so?" Ysella tapped her chin, pretending to mull it over. After a long pause, she let out a dramatic sigh. "Well, Mama isn't here… but I suppose Petra knows best. Alright then, juice and sweet rolls coming up—don't tell on me."

The twins squealed with delight.

Mira added quickly, "Sol said we have to be good or he won't give us the surprise."

Ysella placed three mugs of juice and steaming rolls glistening in hot butter on the table.

"Well, what is the surprise? How do you know it's even worth behaving for?" Ysella asked playfully.

Sol smiled, fingers absently tapping the letter in his pocket. There was a time when surprises had been simpler—just stolen sweets and harmless mischief, nothing heavy, nothing secret. He let the thought drift away like smoke, focusing instead on the eager faces before him, their joy a welcome anchor to the present.

"He won't tell!" the twins echoed in pitiful unison.

Ysella rested her hands on the twins' shoulders, her touch firm and reassuring. She cast Sol a knowing look before turning back to the little ones, her voice dropping to a playful whisper. "Listen carefully, my little darlings— never agree to a deal unless you know the stakes." Her grin widened, flashing her toothy smile as the twins giggled. Then, with a dramatic tsk, she turned on Sol, poking him in the chest in mock chastisement.

"And you—shame on you, leading them on like that!"

Sol grinned sheepishly, throwing up his hands in surrender. "Okay, okay!" he relented, his voice laced with mock offense, though the laughter in his eyes gave him away. He leaned in slowly, dragging out the moment just long enough to make the twins squirm, their anticipation bubbling over into restless giggles.

The twins leaned in, barely breathing, their wide eyes locked on him. Mira's curls brushed his cheek, soft as a whisper. Sol lowered his voice conspiratorially. "Mama said," he murmured, drawing out the suspense, "after we finish our errands, there'll be a few coppers for something sweet after supper."

The twins erupted with excitement in a cacophony of pleas.

"Hush now, my ducklings," Sol said, his tone playful yet firm. He knelt beside them, smoothing a stray curl from Mira's face. "You have to be good. Can you eat your rolls and sit still while Aunty Thornbrook and I talk?" He fixed them with a solemn, knowing look.

The twins nodded vigorously and tentatively started tearing their rolls.

Ysella wrapped Sol in a bone-crushing hug, squeezing the breath from his lungs before pulling back just enough to fix him with a stern glare. "You best not wait a whole week between visits, lad," she scolded, though the warmth in her voice made it impossible to take seriously.

Sol chuckled, smoothing out the wrinkles in his shirt where Ysella had crushed him. "I'm sorry, Mum," he said with a grin. "The storm kept us busy, too many fences to mend, too many chores piled up. I barely had time to breathe."

Ysella nodded, a knowing glint in her eye, before reaching out to tweak his nose. "You're off the hook this time," she chuckled.

Sol pulled the letter from his pocket, his cheeks burning. Avoiding her gaze, he murmured, "Mum, can you get this to Wyatt before he leaves Briarstead?"

"Now, don't you go getting shy on me!" Ysella teased, ruffling his hair before pressing a kiss to his cheek. "We've played this game for years, haven't we? And every time, I see the way you both glow with each letter, it's the sweetest thing."

Sol exhaled, only now realizing he'd been holding his breath. His thumb traced the letter's edge—just paper and ink, yet it carried the weight of something far more precious. It was silly, he knew. Just another letter. And still, his heart raced, and his cheeks burned with quiet anticipation.

"Yes, Mum, you're right," Sol said, his cheeks still a deep crimson. "I just get flustered."

"Scy!" Ysella called.

A familiar voice drawled from the back of the room, rich with lazy amusement. "Ysella, if this is more fixer work, you best keep it to yourself. You know I'm deathly allergic to honest labor—breaks me out in all sorts of complaints."

With a flourish, he pushed aside the green velvet curtains.

Ysella snorted, rolling her eyes before throwing an arm around him. "Scy, My buck, would you be so kind as to make sure my Shepherd gets this? You will need to make haste, as he will leave on the full moon." She squeezed his hip playfully.

"Yes, Mum, I can leave after lunch—on one condition," Scy teased, tilting his head with a grin. "I expect a proper goodbye."

Scy winked at Sol as he pinched Ysella. She yelped, swatting him away. "Get going, or you'll be saying goodbye alone."

Scy clapped Sol on the back, his touch firm, lingering just a moment. "You're a good one, Sol. Keep your chin up—don't let the world shake you." His smirk softened before, with a lazy stretch, he disappeared behind the curtain once more.

Ysella watched him go, shaking her head with a fond chuckle— then, for just a breath, her smile wavered. She turned back to Sol, her eyes softer now. "And your parents? How are Petra and Kellan?" Her voice held the weight of quiet concern.

"They are well. Mama needs fabric for mending the twins' clothes; they are growing like weeds. Pa and I fixed the fence," Sol said before adding thoughtfully, "I think he will want to buy three sheep from Wyatt."

Ysella nodded. "All seems to be in order. Are your folks still going to Elion's temple?"

Sol sighed. "Yeah, Mum. Three offerings a week, four prayers a day. Seems like it's never enough."

Ysella put her arm around his shoulders. "Well, it sounds like they are very devout. Have you noticed anything different about them?"

Sol shrugged. "Naw, we just spend more time praying."

Ysella kissed his cheek. "Sol, you are an amazing young man. Trust yourself. No one, not even the Keeper, can tell you who you truly are."

Sol chuckled, shaking his head. "You're impossible some days." But his words held nothing but warmth as he pulled her into a firm hug. Stepping back, he sighed. "We gotta get moving; we have to be home for the noon prayer."

Calling to the twins, "Come on, my ducklings, thank Aunty

Thornbrook."

With the final goodbyes, Ysella watched with a heavy heart as she watched the trio disappear into the bustling crowd. With a final sigh, she whispered a silent prayer for them in her heart.

The clouds meandered across the sky, softening the sun's relentless heat. Sol cast one last glance at Ysella, lifting a hand in farewell before grasping the twins' small fingers in his own. His brow furrowed. Ysella and Scy had always been kind, but something had changed—an unspoken warmth, a quiet protectiveness. It was a subtle shift.

The air was thick, and heavy with the promise of rain, pressing in like a held breath before a storm. The scent of damp earth clung to the wind, mingling with the distant tang of approaching rain. Theo's voice rose in excitement, Mira's laughter trailing after it, but Sol barely heard them, his thoughts were elsewhere.

Elion protect us, hold off a little while longer, he thought, glancing at the sky.

Elora's shop loomed ahead, its gaudy blue door and pink awning standing defiantly against the dreary sky. Normally, he wouldn't have minded stopping, but today, unease coiled in his gut. Instinctively, he pulled the twins closer, his grip firm. He cast them a warning glance, and they fell silent instantly.

Sol hesitated at the threshold. With a steadying breath, he forced himself forward, pushing past the gnawing doubt and stepping into the shop's dim, perfumed air.

"Welcome, young Ardens," said a pudgy older woman.

"Good morning, Aunty Elora," Sol said pleasantly. The twins, a step behind him, waved shyly.

"It's good to see you," he continued.

"Your mother has a few stacks of cloth waiting. It looks like it may rain soon — I'll wrap them in oil cloth," Elora said.

She studied him for a moment, then asked, "When is the Shepherd coming to Oswynn?" Her eyes swept over him, searching for something.

Sol tensed. "I'm not sure, Aunty," he lied. *But why?* The question had caught him off guard, and yet, something deep in his gut told him not to speak of Wyatt to Elora.

"I hope he arrives soon. I need wool," she said wryly.

"Still spending time with that shepherd, are you?" Elora asked, too casually. "I just always thought he'd find a girl by now — someone to settle him. Don't you think?"

"Maybe he's not looking," Sol said, too quickly. "Not everyone wants the same things."

He reached for the folded fabric again, but his hands didn't quite settle. The moment passed, but the heat in his chest did not.

Elora hummed, like that answer had told her something. "Mm. Well. You boys have always been close."

She reached for a strip of green linen, then paused.

"Well," she said, "the Keeper always leads hearts where they're meant to go."

Elora expertly wrapped Petra's order and as she handed it to him, her gaze lingered. "Be sure to bring the oilcloth to me at worship tomorrow evening,"

"Yes, Aunty. Mama will be grateful for your kindness," Sol said carefully, still forcing a smile.

"Elion the Keeper guide your path," Elora said, her voice firm, expectant.

"May we stay steadfast," Sol and the twins echoed—routine words.

Mira perked up. "Mama says the Keeper knows everything!"

Theo nodded eagerly, his excitement barely contained as he bounced on his toes. "That's why we have to be good, right, Aunty Elora?" His wide eyes searched her face, seeking both approval and reassurance in her answer.

Elora nodded matter-of-factly, her lips curved in a triumphant smile. "That is right, children." She leaned in, lowering her voice menacingly. "Remember, if you stray from the path, you will be cast into the void, so mind the teachings."

Sol suppressed a sigh, rolling his eyes. It was always doom and gloom with her. He forced a tight smile, nodding at Elora before making a quick retreat.

As Sol stepped outside, the air felt heavier, thick with something unspoken. He could still feel Elora's gaze pressing into his back, searching for something he couldn't name. A shiver crawled up his spine, but for what, Sol didn't know.

A damp breeze curled around him, cool against his skin, carrying the sharp, metallic scent of rain beyond the horizon. He adjusted the package in his arms, rolling his shoulders as if shrugging off the weight of something unseen, something lingering.

Elora had always been a little strange, always watching. But this… this was something else.

The scent of warm bread and honey drifted toward him, the sound of a woman's laughter spilling from the bakery window. Sol let out a slow breath, steadying himself before pressing forward. The weight in his chest remained, but as he stepped inside, it loosened— just a fraction.

The shop was warm, the ovens burning bright as always.

To the right, dried meats and sausages hung in thick ropes, their smoky scent rich in the air. On the left, today's baked goods were laid out in neat rows, their golden crusts catching the light.

The twins darted past Sol, their laughter ringing through the shop as they scrambled toward the row of sweets.

Hettie laughed. "Good morning, Sol."

"Good morning, Mum," Sol smiled brightly.

"Everyone loves Hettie's sweets," Rein said affectionately.

"Oh my, yes! And what do we have here?" Hettie cooed, placing a delicate piece of pink sugar candy into each tiny palm.

The twins looked up at Sol with big, pleading eyes but stayed silent.

Sol chuckled. "Of course, my ducklings, but do not get your clothes sticky."

The twins grinned, their eyes shining with delight as they carefully selected their prizes. With exaggerated reverence, they popped the sweets into their mouths, savoring them as if they were the last treasures left in the world.

"That is awfully nice, Aunty," Sol remarked.

Hettie clicked her tongue and handed him a piece as well. "Oh, pish posh. You deserve something sweet! Beryth knows you three don't have it easy with that battle axe—"

"Hettie! Now you mind your manners," Rein scolded.

Hettie sighed, her expression troubled. "I'm sorry, Sol. You know I care about you kids. But with Elion's cult growing stronger, his followers more brazen by the day… Oswynn feels darker. Heavy. Enough to make even the bravest consider packing up and leaving for good."

She rambled on, her words tumbling over themselves as Rein handed Sol the usual midweek meat package.

"—And did you hear about little Ansen? Bless his heart. A tail, if you can believe it.!" Hettie laughed, shaking her head.

The twins shifted impatiently, their fingers twitching at their sides. Their wide eyes darted between Hettie and the sweets, torn between curiosity and the irresistible pull of another sugary delight.

"Theo, Mira—what do you think? Apple bread or wild berry turnovers?" Sol asked, squatting down so he was eye-level with the treats.

The twins exchanged a quick, heated whisper, each trying to sway the other. But after a moment, they reached a silent truce and declared in perfect unison, "Apple bread!"

"It's Mama's favorite," Theo added proudly.

"Aunty, can we have a loaf of apple bread?"

"Of course, darlings. It's fresh this morning."

Hettie grabbed the loaf with a knowing smile, her

hands steady from years of practice. With effortless grace, she drizzled a warm, glistening glaze over the top, its sweet aroma filling the air.

The twins watched in silent awe, their mouths agape, as the warm glaze cascaded over the loaf, settling into a glossy sheen that promised pure, sticky delight.

Sol handed the payment for both the meat and bread to Rein, who counted out two copper pieces and handed them back.

Sol looked up, confused.

Rein huffed a quiet chuckle. "Hettie would never let me hear the end of it if I made you pay full price for her sweets."

"Thank you, Master Rein."

Hettie fussed over them, straightening their collars with gentle hands, brushing stray crumbs from their tunics, and tucking the packages snugly into their arms as if shielding them from the chill that lingered in the air.

She smiled wide, then wagged a flour-dusted finger at them.

"Now, you better hurry home—there's a storm blowing in."

A low rumble echoed through the darkening sky. Sol exhaled, tightening his grip on the package. The wind carried the thick scent of impending rain. Without a glance back, he guided the twins into the street, their footsteps lost beneath the rising storm.

Chapter Two

——

Beneath The Eaves

Pungent, woody incense stung his nose and brought tears to his eyes. His mother lit the white candles one by one, murmuring prayers like a lullaby to the past. His father approached and cradled the worn tome with silent reverence. The twins fidgeted but stilled beneath Petra's piercing glare. Sol stood motionless. Her presence grounded him as she stepped closer.

That familiar unease crept over him. He couldn't remember when it had started, only that it was stronger than ever. His father's voice, once a balm to his soul, now drifted past him. It was familiar yet hollow, no longer anchoring him the way it once did.

Elora would say something was wrong with him.

He recited the prayers anyway, and his voice was merged with the soft murmurs of the twins, who echoed each word with unwavering faith. He stole a glance at them—heads bowed, hands folded tightly, eyes closed in silent reverence. They were untouched by doubt or the weight he carried. Then, his gaze flickered to his father, forehead pressed to the floor, praying as if his very soul depended on it.

Sol swallowed against the dry, scratchy tightness in his throat, forcing down a cough that burned like embers. It lingered—thick, stubborn, unwelcome. He didn't dare clear his throat. His father's sharp glare had already found him, slicing through the incense-heavy air like a blade. It was a silent command to endure without breaking the fragile silence.

"Elion the Keeper, guide your path," Father said resolutely.

"May we stay steadfast," the rest of the family echoed in unison.

Sol waited for his father to make the first move before releasing some of the tension building in his stiff limbs. As Kellan stepped down from the altar, Petra hurried into the kitchen. The twins, buzzing with restless energy, bolted outside like tightly wound springs released.

"Father, thank you for sharing the Keeper of the Path's wisdom with us," Sol said hollowly.

Kellan rested a firm hand on Sol's shoulder, its weight steady and unyielding. Its warmth lingered, too long, heavy, and hard to ignore.

"Soltic, it is my duty to guide you as Elion, Keeper

of the Path, dictates. It's for the good of all. We know not all are ready for Elion's wisdom, but that will not deter us from living in light."

Sol forced a smile. "May we remain steadfast." He gently bowed his head.

Kellan lingered a moment longer, then finally lifted his hand from Sol's shoulder. Without a word, he turned on his heel and walked out, leaving the silence heavier than before.

Sol stood by the altar; his eyes were fixed on the delicate curls of smoke spiraling from the extinguished flames. The ritual was over, but its echo clung to the air. He shivered as an unseen breeze traced his spine and left a chill that felt more than physical.

He went to Petra as she chopped vegetables, dropping handfuls into the boiling water as she worked. Thunder rolled in the distance, he'd better hurry if he was going to feed the animals.

At the threshold, he paused and drew in a deep breath. The crisp, metallic scent of the outside air filled his lungs, sharp and grounding, like iron and earth—steadying the tremor he hadn't realized was there.

Sol mulled over Ysella's question…. had his

parents changed? He couldn't quite grasp it, but they had changed. He remembered being very young when his parents had laughed more, touched more, and felt unmistakably alive. Now, those memories slipped further away. In their place came prayer and ritual—steady, solemn, unyielding, slowly replacing the warmth and joy that once filled his childhood days.

The twins flitted to and fro, laughter trailing behind them as they darted around the barn. Sol followed at a slower pace, letting the crisp air soothe his racing thoughts and quiet the noise inside him.

Sol heaved the heavy wooden door open and slipped inside, the scent of manure mingling with stale hay.

"Good afternoon," Sol called as he entered the barn.

He greeted each horse slowly and lovingly. They nuzzled him for comfort, gently nickering and snorting. With his quiet greeting finished, he climbed into the hayloft. His fingers brushed worn wooden beams. As he worked, his thoughts drifted, soft and scattered, never settling long enough to bring him peace.

He hoped Wyatt would stay safe on the road. Bandits had always been a burden, but now their attacks came weekly. Fear clung to Oswynn's edges, which turned each journey into a silent gamble.

He envisioned Wyatt coming across the field with his flock in tow. A smile tugged at Sol's lips. Wyatt's big blue eyes lit up as their gazes met, his tousled blonde hair falling in wind-blown wisps across his dirt-smudged face.

A low rumble of thunder echoed in the distance, stretching across the sky like a warning. The storm crawled closer with each passing moment, its slow advance pressing on his chest like the weight of something inevitable and unseen.

He sighed, jerked from his thoughts by the pitchfork in his hand. He climbed down the ladder, laid fresh hay on the ground, and set out grain for them to eat. He did the same for the dairy cows and chickens.

The twins came sprinting as lightning split the sky, illuminating the old barn in a ghostly glow. Thunder followed, booming so loudly it shook his core. The horses panicked and reared with wild eyes before crashing their hooves back down onto the straw-covered ground.

The barn creaked as the storm raged outside. The twins shrieked as lightning flashed again, but Sol barely heard them. The air was thick and electric, yet eerily quiet.

He exhaled slowly, time stretching like molasses. Before the thought could form, he was already moving, gathering the twins, pulling them close, their small heads pressed against his chest as if he could shield them from everything.

Then, with a deafening crash, a heavy beam split from the rafters and slammed into the ground, right where they had stood seconds before. Dust exploded upward and filled the air as his heart thundered in his chest, stunned by how narrowly they had escaped.

His chest rose sharply, breath returning all at once. Rain slammed against the roof as the twins sobbed into his chest, their small bodies trembling. His ears rang with the aftermath. The calm had vanished. And yet, for one fleeting moment, it had felt like that fear, that chaos, had belonged to someone else entirely.

A teary-eyed Mira wailed. "Sol, you saved us. How did you know it was going to fall?"

That was a question he didn't know the answer to.

"Now go, run to the cottage before the storm gets any worse," Sol said with authority.

Mira whimpered, "No, Sol, please don't make us go by ourselves."

"Everything is okay, my ducklings, but I need you

to be brave. Tell Papa what happened. I need to make sure the animals are safe." Sol tried to reassure them.

Theo nodded grimly and extended his hand to Mira. His gaze was steady and unwavering. He didn't speak, but the quiet strength in his touch said more than words ever could at that moment.

Another flash lit up the sky.

"Okay, now run!" Sol shouted with a sharp urgency in his voice. The twins took off toward the cottage, their feet pounded the wet earth while Theo gripped Mira's hand tightly, pulling her along through the thickening rain.

Sol stood shakily. The twins had almost been crushed beneath the beam. The thought made him nauseous.

But how had he known?

He blinked his eyes and took a deep breath.

He dragged the ladder over and climbed up to inspect the damage. The beam wasn't load-bearing, at least from what he could tell. He hadn't heard even the faintest creak before it collapsed. *How could something so solid give way without warning?*

He pressed his hand against the splintered wood,

expecting the roughness, the cold—but it wasn't cold. Not exactly. It felt strange, as though the beam had fallen at the exact moment it was meant to. His fingers brushed over pockmarks near the break. Wood eaters. He realized they'd been at this for a while, a sharp unease crawling up his spine.

I'll need to tell Da, Sol thought, a knot forming in his stomach.

The heavy rain began to pound relentlessly against the roof, drowning out all sound except for the rush of his thoughts, chaotic and overwhelming.

He closed the shutters with a soft, steady motion, then moved the heavy beam as best he could. Once done, he crouched low and spoke softly to the animals, offering them grain from his hand to calm the nervous energy swirling around him.

He began a silent prayer to Elion. When the prayer failed to calm the gnawing anxiety deep within, he whispered another to Beryth, hoping for a sense of peace. Each word felt heavier, and his uncertainty grew with every breath.

He prayed to Beryth...

Suddenly, the sky opened up and unleashed a

torrential downpour. Sol sprinted toward the house, but the slippery mud made every step a battle. He slipped twice, feeling the cold earth beneath him, before finally managing to find his footing. Wiping mud from his eyes, he pushed forward, soaked and breathless.

He stood under the overhang, scrubbing off as much mud as he could before stepping inside. It had been two weeks of storms. The crops couldn't take much more.

He wrung out his shirt and breeches, water streaming from the soaked fabric. Stripped down to his undergarments, he stepped into the cottage, the warmth inside wrapping around him like a fragile comfort after the storm's relentless chill.

"Ma, it's really coming down now," Sol said, dripping onto the floor.

"You look half-drowned," Petra said, amused.

"Well, off to change with you! Don't just stand there."

Sol returned to the kitchen as the wind rattled the cottage walls, the scent of simmering stew curling around him. Running a hand through his damp hair, he sighed theatrically. "Ma, if the rain keeps coming up like this, I won't need to bathe 'til summer."

Petra smirked, tasting the broth. "Then perhaps we should send you to the sea and make a sailor of you."

Sol chuckled softly as he set the table, glancing up to see his family gathering quietly around him. The meal began as it always did— with bowed heads, whispered prayers, and Kellan's steady, comforting voice filling the air.

"Elion the Keeper, guide your path," Kellan intoned.

"May we remain steadfast," the family echoed.

Sol kept his head lowered for a moment longer. His heart was heavy with the effort. He willed the words to settle inside him, as they once had, but they passed over him. Hollow and weightless, offering no comfort.

He swallowed hard against the tightness in his throat, the lump that refused to budge. Reluctantly, he forced himself to eat, each bite tasting heavier than the last, the effort almost too much.

"Da, the barn has wood eaters," he said between bites. "It's holding for now, but we'll need a blessing on it."

Kellan didn't look up, his gaze fixed on something beyond reach. "The Keeper is above such trivial matters," he said with a light chuckle, his voice calm yet tinged with amusement. "You and I will see to it when the rain stops."

Sol hesitated. They had blessed the barn not three years ago for the same reason. Now it was foolish?

But he held his tongue. "Yes, Da," he murmured.

The twins chattered excitedly about their day at the market, and their voices were overlapping in a rush of enthusiasm. Their joy filled the space, a bright contrast to the quiet tension lingering in the room.

Petra smiled. "That was very kind of Auntie Hettie to give you sugar candy."

"It was yummy, and we didn't even get sticky fingers!" Mira declared proudly.

Kellan gasped in mock offense. "And my devoted children brought none for their beloved father?"

Petra scoffed, poking him in the ribs. "I'd say Father doesn't need any more sweets. Besides, they did bring us Hettie's apple bread."

Sol hurriedly cleared the table, quickly returning with the dessert. As Petra began passing out thick, generous slices, Kellan reached for the largest one, his hand halting mid-air when she swatted it away with a playful but firm look.

"You behave yourself, or you won't get a bite," she warned.

Kellan straightened with mock seriousness, folding his hands in an exaggerated gesture of obedience. The twins were eager to mimic him and followed suit, their eyes wide with playful solemnity.

The sight was too much for Sol and Petra, who both burst into laughter, the sound filling the room with warmth.

"Oh, I suppose I have no choice now, do I?" Petra sighed dramatically, passing out the slices. She claimed one with extra glaze before anyone could protest.

It was as it should be for a moment—laughter, warmth, the simple pleasure of sweets shared with loved ones.

Sol smiled, allowing the moment to envelop him like a familiar, comforting blanket. Yet, despite its warmth, something felt distant, almost surreal. It was as if he were standing on the outside, watching himself and his family from a place he couldn't quite reach.

He took another bite, and the apple bread was rich and sweet on his tongue. But it didn't warm him the way it used to.

"Alright, little ones, wash up for evening devotion," Petra cooed, with her soft and warm voice as she watched the twins trudge to the wash basin outside. Kellan followed closely behind, his presence a quiet comfort as if guiding them through the fading light.

She turned back toward the kitchen, her soft voice carrying over the quiet of the room. "Sol, darling, would you stay and help me for a moment?" she asked, her tone was gentle and calm.

Sol nodded, his fingers curled around the used plates as he moved toward her without hesitation.

She watched him in silence, her gaze steady but unreadable as he worked. After a long pause, she spoke in a soft tone, "Soltic, you are becoming a man," she said thoughtfully. "Before you know it, you'll have a wife by your side, children running beneath your feet."

Sol glanced up, meeting Petra's intense gaze. She watched him with quiet intensity as if trying to peer inside him, searching for something unspoken, a part of him she couldn't quite reach.

Sol nodded uneasily.

"It is your duty to lead your family and yourself down the just path. Do you understand?"

"Yes, Mama," Sol said tentatively.

Petra picked up a cloth, wiping the table in slow, deliberate strokes. Her movements seemed purposeful, matching the weight of the words she was about to speak. "I've noticed a change in you lately," she said softly but firmly. "You've been distant, and I see doubt in your eyes."

She let the words settle between them.

"There is no place for doubt, Soltic. Elion, the Keeper of the Path, is the only true god. In Him, you will find peace."

Sol's chest tightened as a wave of frustration and guilt surged within him. He opened his mouth to deny her accusations, but the words faltered on his tongue. "But Mama, I don't..." His voice trailed off, caught in the rawness of the moment.

"None of that," Petra interrupted, her voice sharpening slightly. "I want what is best for you and all of us. Do you understand?"

Sol swallowed. "Yes, Mama," he said quietly.

Petra cupped his face gently in her hands, and her thumbs brushed over his skin as she kissed his forehead softly. "You are a brilliant, kindhearted, and strong man," she murmured, her voice tinged with affection and something more profound. "I haven't spoken to your father about this yet, but tonight, after evening devotion, you will copy from 'The Keeper's Equality' to 'The Keeper's Bounty.' It's time you learn this."

Her grip tightened slightly. "Every word, Soltic."

Sol's pulse raced beneath his skin, each beat loud in his ears. Still, he managed a small, composed smile. "Yes, Mama," he said, voice quieter than he intended. "Thank you for helping me stay steadfast." The words felt both comforting and heavy, like armor; he wasn't sure he was ready to wear them.

"Good," she said simply. "Now hurry and wash up."

With that, she dismissed him.

Evening devotion began as it always did. Petra lighting the candles with steady hands, whispering prayers under her breath; Kellan stepping forward with practiced solemnity to take up the mantle before them; and the twins, restless as ever, twitching and shifting in their seats, their energy barely contained by the hush of reverence that settled over the room.

Sol settled into his usual place beside Petra and Theo, drawing in the curling tendrils of woody incense. He closed his eyes for a moment, silently commanding the scent to ground him—to press peace into his chest where doubt had begun to nest quietly.

Mama said she saw doubt in his eyes. The thought coiled in his stomach like a tightening rope.

But I've always been faithful—to the Keeper, to our family.

Since when did wondering, searching, or needing answers become betrayal? Since when did asking questions mean his heart had turned?

Maybe he had been distracted, Wyatt's absence, the storms rolling through, the lingering threat of bandits, the endless mending of fences...

Yes. That had to be it.

Because if it wasn't—

He clenched his fists, driving the thought from his mind before it could fully form.

For the first time, he truly listened to the devotion.

The words, meant to soothe, hung strangely in the air. Something about them felt wrong. Unsettling.

He closed his eyes, searching for the feeling that once anchored him, the steady warmth that used to bloom in his chest, the quiet certainty that everything was as it should be. But now, the silence pressed in, heavy and unfamiliar. He reached inward, but the comforting presence he once knew felt distant, like a memory slipping away.

But it didn't come.

Instead, the words sat on the surface of his mind, never reaching the depth where understanding should have taken root. They bounced around as if trying to break through, but never quite managed to penetrate the growing fog that clouded his thoughts.

Dizziness curled at the edges of his senses.

He focused on keeping his breath even and slow, terrified that any sharp inhale would betray him. His fingers gripped his knees tightly, a quiet anchor against the growing lightness in his head. The rhythmic pounding of his pulse in his ears was the only sound he could hear, louder than anything else in the room.

Kellan's voice pulled him back. "Elion the Keeper,

guide your path."

"May we remain steadfast," the family echoed.

Sol kept his head bowed a moment longer, the soft glow of the candlelight pressing gently against his eyelids. He focused on the warmth, letting it anchor him. Counting each breath, slow and deliberate, he tried to steady the restless flutter in his chest, grounding himself before facing what was next.

Mama was right. He just needed to try harder.

Sol stood quietly for a moment, and his gaze stayed on the twins as he kissed their foreheads gently. The soft touch seemed to linger in the air before he whispered goodnight to Petra and Theo. Their faces were warm with love and concern. With a heavy sigh, he took the tome in hand and ascended the stairs to his quiet room, the weight of both the book and his thoughts pressing on him.

Sol laid the tome on his writing table. The dim candlelight cast ghastly shadows around the room. The scent of burning wax filled his nose.

He unstoppered his ink.

Without hesitation, he began.

The Keeper's Equality

The only sounds in the room were the quiet

sputtering of the candle, the steady scratch of his quill, and the rhythmic cadence of his own heavy breathing. Though he knew the words by heart, he took his time writing them, the ink flowing slowly as he sought meaning in the familiar phrases. Each stroke of the quill felt deliberate as if searching for something beyond the words themselves, something lost.

Each word became a taunt.

He shook his head and took a deep breath.

Adjusting his grip on the quill, he began again.

The Keeper's Mercy

He etched the words carefully, searching, hoping.

The room started to spin.

His breath came in short, rapid bursts.

The quill slipped, slicing his fingertip.

A sharp sting. A bloom of red.

Without thinking, he pressed his finger to his mouth, the sharp, metallic taste of iron flooding his senses. For a brief moment, the raw tang grounded him, pulling him back into the present. But that brief respite quickly slipped away, leaving him as untethered as before, with only the echo of his own racing thoughts.

His pulse hammered in his ears.

He pushed back from the desk, shoving to his feet.

What was wrong with him?

Was he broken?

Could he find his way back?

His thoughts threatened to overwhelm him.

Then, his eyes flicked to the wooden floorboards beside the desk, the place where his treasures lay hidden.

His pulse slowed.

Wyatt... Deep blue eyes. A breathy laugh. Warmth, unshaken and real.

His breath steadied.

Ysella's voice echoed back to him...

Trust yourself. No one—not even the Keeper— can tell you who you truly are.

Sol swallowed hard and shook his head, forcing himself back to the task.

The Keeper's Bounty

The letters blurred again.

His hand moved on its own, finishing the last lines.

The words were there.
Perfectly copied.

As they should be.

Sol ran a thumb over the ink, smudging a letter.

The words were still hollow.

He exhaled, crept downstairs, and returned the tome to its place.

His limbs felt like lead as he dragged himself to the bed, each step an effort against an invisible weight pressing down on him. By the time his head touched the pillow, sleep had already claimed him, a welcome escape from the fatigue that gnawed at his bones.

54

Chapter Three

———

Storm Signs

The salty breeze teased his skin, rich with the scent of the sea— briny and clean, touched by the heat of sunbaked sand. Overhead, the sun hovered at its peak, erasing all shadows and cloaking the world in a stark, dreamlike stillness, as if time itself had drawn a breath and held it just for them.

It was the first time in weeks that there wasn't a cloud in the sky. The water sparkled like scattered diamonds, too bright to look at for long. Despite the twins' laughter and the gentle murmur of waves, something tugged at the edges of Sol's awareness, a subtle dissonance threading through the perfection of the afternoon.

It seemed like a perfect afternoon.

His mother stood on the shore, feet in the water, while his father chased the twins through the surf. Sol was knee-deep. He splashed at the water, laughing, but when he turned back toward his family, they seemed... *farther?*

He blinked against the sting, rubbing the salt from his eyes. The shoreline looked different, farther somehow. *Had the tide shifted that quickly, or had he simply lost track of time?*

"Come on, children, the tide is coming in," Kellan called. The twins took up spaces on either side of Mama.

A cold calm settled deep into Sol's bones, numbing thought and breath. Time stretched, elastic and endless, as if the world had slowed to watch what was about to unfold. And in that stillness, he understood that something had shifted. *He was in danger—real, inevitable danger.* Whatever force had set this moment in motion would not be undone.

And yet, he couldn't surrender to it.

He had to try.

He called out, but his voice barely carried over the distance.

The sand beneath his feet was gone.

He had been standing—hadn't he?

But now, his toes reached for something solid and found only shifting water. Beneath him, there was no ground, just an unsettling weightlessness, as though the ocean had quietly pulled the world out from under him.

Sol swam as hard as he could, but he couldn't close the distance. Papa was standing with his arm around Mama now.

"Come on, Sol, it's time to go," he called.

"Da, help me! I can't make it!" Sol cried, swimming with every ounce of strength he had.

He heard Mama's voice rise in prayer to Elion, tremulous and unyielding as she looked at him with sorrow-shadowed eyes. The harder he thrashed, the more fervent her words became—desperate, pleading, as if sheer will alone could save him.

The twins started crying.

"Sol, it's time to go!" Theo demanded.

"Don't you love us?" Mira cried.

"I do love you. I love you with all my heart!" Sol's voice was lost in the distance.

Even as his family called out to him, their voices trembled with urgency, but their bodies remained still, like monoliths carved from stone, silent and immovable.

Why didn't anyone move? Why didn't they come for him?

The water lay smooth as glass, unmarred except for Sol's desperate thrashing. Each stroke felt heavier than the last, and every time he looked up, the shore had slipped farther away like it was retreating from him on purpose.

"Please, Mama! — Papa! — I can't do this alone."

Mama's prayers rang in his ears, growing louder.

One by one, his father and then the twins faintly added their voices to Mama's booming prayer. His body screamed as he fought to reach the shore, coughing up saltwater.

When he looked up again, his family had blurred into a distant smudge on the horizon, faint figures swallowed by the vastness. Yet their voices lingered and echoed painfully inside his mind, growing more distant yet unbearably clear.

He couldn't swim anymore.

His limbs gave out, and he began to sink. His world turned black, his lungs burned, and his heart threatened to burst.

Sol's breaths came fast and uneven, trying to cough up seawater that was never there. His mother's prayers echoed in his ears, fading on a still breeze.

He tossed off the cold, damp sheets that clung stubbornly to his skin, breaking free from their oppressive weight. With a sharp jerk, he sat bolt upright, the sudden movement sending a dizzying spin through his head.

He was wet.

As if someone had dropped him, still dripping,

straight into his bed. The cold clung to his skin, sharp and unrelenting.

His vision steadied, though his eyes still flickered with a faint blur. He expected to see the familiar stretch of sand and sea, but instead, the peeling whitewashed walls and rough wooden beams of the ceiling gradually came into focus.

He staggered to his wash basin and swallowed; throat raw.

His reflection stared back at him, bloodshot eyes wide with fear, mirroring the pounding rhythm of his own heart, beating in uneasy time with his mother's fading prayer.

He forced slow, controlled breaths. The scent of the sea air gradually faded, replaced by the familiar, subtle warmth of the hearth. With careful movements, he splashed water on his face.

His reflection remained unchanged, hair still tangled and messy, lips parted slightly as if struggling to catch his breath.

He stared blankly, eyes glazed and unfocused.

Then, suddenly, overwhelmed by a flood of emotion, he broke down and cried. No sound escaped him.

No movement disturbed the stillness.

He was frozen, afraid to move, yet terrified to stand still.

His life was changing.

He lowered himself slowly onto the bed. It was dry beneath him, cool against his skin.

What was happening to him?

He loved his family fiercely. The thought of losing them stabbed through his chest like a jagged dagger-sharp, unrelenting, and burning deep inside. His emotions threatened to overwhelm him once more. His breath caught in his throat, and his vision blurred at the edges until his gaze fixed on the loose floorboard nearby, grounding him in the moment.

Slowly and carefully, he pried the loose floorboard free.

Settling onto the floor, his fingers trembled ever so slightly as he reached beneath and pulled out the letters. One by one, he unfolded them with deliberate reverence, reading each word as if it were a fragile secret entrusted only to him.

The warmth of Wyatt's words wrapped around him

like his favorite childhood blanket.

Wyatt's soothing voice filled his heart, calming its rapid beats.

He inhaled deeply, his eyes fluttering shut for a brief moment.

In that suspended breath, he could almost smell it, the rich scent of sun-warmed pastures, dusty country roads, and the lingering sweetness of Wyatt's embrace.

By the time he reached the final letter, the tightness in his chest had loosened, leaving him lighter, almost buoyant.

And yet, the sensation that this was more than a dream clung to him, persistent, undeniable.

Slowly, he got to his feet.

Sol followed Kellan into the barn, the floorboards groaning beneath their steps, a familiar welcome. Shafts of golden sunlight pierced the dusty air, casting long rays across the fallen beam like a spotlight on a forgotten scene.

Kellan ran a calloused hand over the splintered wood, his breath escaping in a slow, heavy exhale through his nose.

"My father used to say the gods don't stop storms from coming, but they teach us how to build strong roofs."

He tapped the beam.

"If you let a little damage go unnoticed, it spreads. By the time you realize the problem, it's too late."

Kellan shifted the beam, testing its weight.

"Faith's a lot like that."

"Granddad was very wise," Sol added thoughtfully.

Kellan's mouth tugged into a small smile. "That he was."

Sol took hold of the other end of the beam, and together, they hauled it out into the sunlight, boots crunching softly on the gravel.

At the doorway, Kellan reached for the ladder leaning against the barn wall. He tested its weight with a practiced grip, then anchored it with a solid thud before beginning his steady climb upward.

Sol stood at the base of the ladder, studying the worn rungs beneath his hands, his gaze tracking Kellan's steady ascent.

Above, Kellan moved with quiet precision, each knock along the rafters sending down a fine mist of dust that danced through the shafts of golden light.

"Good eye, boy. It's definitely the work of wood eaters," Kellan sighed, not looking down.

They moved methodically through the barn, weaving between old tools and dusty crates, pausing now and then to inspect the aged beams. Kellan tapped along the wood with the back of his knuckles, muttering under his breath, half calculations, half quiet conversation with himself.

"It's worse than I thought," Kellan said matter-of-factly. "We'll have to reinforce or replace most of these beams."

Sol hesitated.

He'd already brought it up last night—and been waved off with a grunt and a shrug.

But the collapsing beam had nearly crushed the twins. That wasn't something he could just let go. Maybe now, with dust still hanging in the air and the damage laid bare, Kellan would finally take it seriously.

Sol asked carefully, "Should we ask High Priest Drevan to bless against wood eaters?"

Kellan snorted, the sound echoing faintly through the rafters. "Blessings don't stop hungry bugs. This is a man's burden, we build what must be built and keep it standing. That's our part. Elion's part is greater than timber and wood eaters."

Kellan glanced down briefly, one brow arched in amusement.

"Or are you hoping High Priest Drevan's prayers come with a side of free labor?"

His voice was dry, but the jab landed.

Sol shifted his weight, eyes flicking toward the door as if calculating the distance, unsure whether to answer or escape.

"What if The Hand—"

He caught himself, but too late—the words already hanging heavy in the space between them. The air seemed to drain from the barn, thick with something unspoken, and Sol tensed instinctively.

Kellan's head snapped toward him, his gaze narrowing, jaw tight as a drawn bowstring.

"I mean... High Priest Drevan."

"Mind your tongue," Kellan said, voice low but absolute. "High Priest Drevan bears Elion's mantle — and you'll speak it with the reverence it deserves."

Kellan let the silence breathe, his gaze steady, before giving Sol a firm nod—final, but not unkind.

Sol nodded back, jaw tight. This wasn't the time to argue.

A flicker of warmth passed through Kellan's eyes. He stepped closer, gave Sol a once-over, and then ruffled his hair with a rough affection that made Sol's shoulders drop just slightly.

"At times, I forget you are still a boy."

He slung his arm briefly across Sol's shoulders, a quick, grounding gesture before gently steering him toward the door, guiding without force.

"Come now, we've got to inspect the fields."

They stepped out of the barn, the heavy wooden door groaning shut behind them with a reluctant finality. The dirt path beneath their boots was soft and yielding, still damp from the recent rain. A warm breeze stirred the air, brushing gently against Sol's face. He closed his eyes for a moment and savored the rare beauty of the first clear day in weeks.

He glanced at his father. Kellan moved with effortless confidence, each step deliberate, every decision sure and unwavering. Sol longed to feel the same — steady, certain, unshakable.

Then the wind shifted unexpectedly, carrying with it the faint, sour scent of waterlogged earth. The sharp, damp smell prickled at his senses, an unmistakable warning. That was not a good sign.

Pools of water stretched between the rows, glinting in the sunlight, reflecting the sky in broken patches. Kellan walked silently into the mud, his boots sinking slightly with each step.

Sol hung back a few feet, swatting at the relentless gnats and flies that swarmed around his face. Their high-pitched buzzing filled the thick, humid air, making it hard to concentrate. The sticky heat clung to his skin, adding to the oppressive stillness of the moment.

The mud sucked at his boots with every step, each one heavier than the last. In some sections, the stalks stood tall, their leaves tinged yellow and curling at the edges. Those might survive. But further in, plants leaned at sharp angles, their roots barely clinging to the softened earth, leaves blackened with rot creeping up from the base.

The sour scent Sol had caught on the breeze was stronger and thicker here. It mingled with the damp earth until it was impossible to tell where the air ended, and the rot began. It clung to the back of his throat, heavy and inescapable.

Whole rows had collapsed entirely, leaving behind only shattered stems half-buried in thick, clinging mud. In the low pockets where water stubbornly refused to drain, a lazy chorus of frogs claimed the flooded field as their new home.

Kellan plucked a browning leaf between his fingers and sighed deeply, the weight of the ruined field heavy on his shoulders. They trudged onward, mud clinging stubbornly to their boots, turning every step into a slow, exhausting struggle. Pausing, Kellan crouched low and held up a limp, broken stalk for Sol to examine.

"These are ruined. Isn't much we can salvage. We'll have to pray for guidance — Elion, Keeper of the Path, will have a lesson in this."

Kellan's hand closed around the ruined stalk, squeezing it with quiet fury. His fingers tightened, whitening as they dug deep into the fragile, crumbling stem. He crushed it completely with a sudden, sharp motion before hurling the remnants to the ground, where they scattered like forgotten memories.

"Elion's path is never without purpose," he

murmured, almost too softly for Sol to hear.

Sol's chest tightened with a mix of worry and determination, but he pushed forward regardless. "Da, there's still time to sow the vegetable garden," he said, his voice carrying a fragile hope.

Kellan exhaled slowly, eyes scanning the ruined field once more, the weight of disappointment settling heavily between them.

"Yes, Sol," Kellan replied, his voice softer. "But that's only a small step."

The shutters lay wide open, letting sharp sunbeams struggle to pierce the heavy gloom while an uneasy breeze stirred the stagnant air of the kitchen. The bitter scent of herbal tea permeated the small space, which was sharp. Sol's heart skipped a beat when his eyes fell on Elora, seated at the kitchen table, her smile faint, but hollow, never reaching her wary eyes.

Just what we don't need, Sol mused inwardly.

"Soltic, how wonderful to see you," she said, her words laced with a strain that masked something bitter.

"Auntie Elora, what a pleasant surprise," Sol

managed, forcing a smile that felt as fragile as glass.

Elora took a slow sip of her tea before turning her gaze to Kellan. Her voice was low and dry, tinged with a quiet disenchantment that hung heavily in the room.

"Still dreaming, I see," Elora said lightly, though her eyes were sharp. "Brother Kellan, I trust you've been diligent — before his doubt festers." Sol glared at her but caught himself before anyone noticed

"Elora, we were out in the fields," Kellan began, his gaze flickering briefly to Petra's before settling back, shadowed with resigned sadness. "Elion, Keeper of the Path, has handed us a harsh lesson. The damage is worse than we feared. We might salvage some crops," he paused, uncertainty tightening his throat, "but this harvest won't be enough to see us through the winter."

Worry passed silently between Petra and Elora, their eyes meeting briefly before darting away. Their faces darkened with a shared, unspoken dread, heavy and lingering in the stillness between them.

Petra rose, moved by both duty and despair and clasped her husband's trembling hands. Her gaze was steady, filled with fragile hope. "We've come through worse..." Petra said softly, her voice wavering at the end.

She kissed Kellan's cheek softly, her hand lingering against his face a heartbeat longer than usual, as if reluctant to let go. Elora then placed a tentative hand on his arm, her touch hesitant but seeking connection amid the heavy silence.

"Elion will lead you through this difficult journey. I believe there is a bigger plan at work," she said. "Elion is just, and all things come back to the light," glancing at Sol. Sol shifted from one foot to another uncomfortably. What was she implying?

"Ma, I'll plant the vegetables as soon as the soil dries. There's still time before the harvest," Sol insisted, fighting the despair building in his chest.

"Yes, dear, you're a good boy," Petra whispered, her voice trembling with a fragile mix of hope and fear. She reached out gently, brushing a stray lock of hair from his forehead as if grounding herself in the moment.

"Sol and I have plenty of work to do in the barn as well," Kellan sighed, the weight of his responsibilities evident. "I'll speak with High Priest Drevan at the temple after worship."

"He's a wise leader and can interpret Elion's signs better than we lay people," Elora stated firmly.

Elora stood and headed to the door.

"May the Keeper guide your path," she said.

"May we remain steadfast," Sol and his parents echoed, though each word carried a bitter uncertainty.

As Elora's footsteps faded into the quiet, a heavy silence settled over the kitchen. Sol felt the weight of unspoken worries pressing down on everyone, thick and suffocating. His father stared into his cup of tea, watching the steam curl upward in delicate wisps, vanishing just as quickly as their fragile hopes.

"I should check on the twins," Petra said finally, her voice cutting through the stillness. "They've been quiet for too long, and that's never a good sign."

As she moved toward the door, Kellan gently reached out and caught her hand. Their eyes locked in a silent exchange, a conversation without words, heavy with unspoken understanding, forged through years of shared burdens and quiet resilience. Sol watched quietly, sensing the depth of what passed between them, a bond only time and hardship could build.

"We'll be alright," Kellan said, his voice carrying a certainty that Sol wished he could believe.

Petra squeezed his hand gently, a silent promise

lingering in her touch before she slipped quietly away. Sol was left alone with his father, the shrinking kitchen suddenly feeling colder and more confined, a small space weighed down by heavy thoughts and unspoken fears.

Sol busied himself, clearing away Elora's teacup, each deliberate motion a fragile attempt to steady the swirling tempest of thoughts churning within him. From somewhere distant, his mother's gentle voice mingled with the twins' carefree laughter, drifting softly through the quiet house.

Kellan stood stiffly and, more to himself than Sol, said, "We must trust in Elion, the Keeper of the Path's wisdom." With that, he moved toward the altar. The familiar, calming scent of incense drifted through the dimly lit kitchen, blending softly with freshly baked bread's warm, earthy aroma. Beneath it all, the faint crackle of firewood whispered in the background, grounding the quiet ritual in homely comfort.

Sol slumped into the chair, heavy and defeated, his shoulders sagging beneath the crushing weight of their predicament. *What could they do? This wasn't Elion's will, it was misfortune, raw and merciless, like the sky had turned its back on them.*

Without the harvest, they wouldn't buy sheep.

They might have to slaughter a cow.

The thought twisted in Sol's gut, sharp and unwelcome, spreading a nauseating unease through his core. It coiled there, refusing to be ignored as if his body itself rejected the weight of what lay ahead.

Theo came rushing in, unaware of the inevitable hardships to come. He froze when he saw Sol in the kitchen, his hands hidden behind his back. Sol looked up and saw a mischievous, wide smile filling his brother's small, mud-streaked face.

"What do you have?" Sol asked, trying to grin; he didn't want to worry the little ones.

Theo stood still, rocking forward and backward defiantly. "Nuffin," he said, his eyes darting toward the door. Ribbit—a faint, strangled croak came from behind him.

"Stop right there!" Sol ordered. "Not another step until you show me what you have."

"NO!" Theo shouted, voice cracking with panic, and bolted forward.

Sol lunged after him, closing the gap in three long

strides. He seized Theo's arm and yanked him to a halt.

Theo thrashed in his grip, twisting and tugging with wild desperation, but Sol held firm, anchoring him with both hands, unwilling to let go.

Sol dropped to a crouch, leveling his gaze with Theo's.

"Enough," he said, sharper than he meant it to be.

Theo flinched, eyes wide, and stared at him in stunned silence. Slowly, his lip quivered, and tears welled up, blurring the blue in his eyes.

"Listen, my little duckling, I need you to behave. Mama and Papa need us to be extra good. Can you do that?" Sol said softly, wiping the tears as they streaked through the mud.

"Yes, Sol," Theo's voice was soft, but he kept eye contact. He slowly revealed a bright green frog between his hands. "Can I keep him?" he asked hopefully.

Sol laughed. "What would Mama say?"

"But I promise I'll take care of him," Theo whined.

"Theo," Sol said sternly but added gently, "Right now is not the time to try Mama's patience. Let this one go, and tomorrow we can catch more, and I will help you build a house for them outside."

"OK!" Theo said excitedly. Sol lightly swatted Theo on the butt and said, "Now hurry before Mama catches you."

Theo raced to the door and ducked below Petra's arm as she came in. "Supper will be ready soon. Clean up before you come back in, " she called after him. Mira followed Petra, carrying a basket filled with eggs.

"Thank you, love," Petra said, patting Mira on the head. "Be a good girl and get cleaned up. Make sure your brother doesn't dawdle!"

Petra busied herself at the hearth, chopping vegetables with more force than necessary, the knife's rhythmic thud a steady pulse in the silence. Sol moved quietly around her, setting the table with careful precision, one plate, one cup, each placed like a peace offering.

The tension in the room clung like smoke.

He hated seeing his mother like this, tight-lipped, shoulders stiff, eyes distant. It made him feel small and helpless, like a child again, watching something he couldn't fix.

"Mama," Sol said softly, "Everything will be okay. We have to trust Elion's Path." He couldn't meet his mother's eyes; the words were hollow.

Petra hugged him tightly, her arms trembling with a resolve that felt too thin.

"May we stay steadfast," she murmured, pressing a kiss to his temple. Then, more to herself than to Sol, she added, "Tonight, after supper, High Priest Drevan will guide us. He'll know what must be done."

Chapter Four

———

Smoke Gathers

The door slammed shut behind Sol, the sound cracking through the dark cavern-like distant thunder rolling over stone. A sharp echo lingered, swallowed gradually by the weight of silence. Candles lined the damp stone walls, their flickering light clawing at the rough ceiling above. Shadows stretched like grasping fingers, shuddering and shrinking with each of Sol's careful steps deeper into the chamber.

The sharp scent of woody incense curled into the air, mingling with heavy smoke from the hearth. It hovered above them, a lowhanging haze that dulled the distant chants and whispers echoing from deeper within.

Sol wanted to believe that something sacred still lingered in the cavern beyond Drevan's piercing gaze, beyond the ritual and smoke, something ancient and immovable, etched deep into the very marrow of the mountain. Not just memory, but presence. A force that had watched over them long before names were given to gods.

When he was younger, the candlelight had felt like a held breath, delicate, expectant, the hush before prayer like the stillness before something holy stirred awake. But now, the silence pressed in differently. It was thicker, almost suffocating, the kind that made him wonder not just if anyone was listening but if anyone had ever been.

Sol told himself the cracks were in him, not the stone. Yet the longer he stood there, surrounded by the weight of unmoving air and unanswered prayers, the harder that lie became to hold.

Sol felt impossibly small beneath the weight of it all, the vastness of the chamber, the suffocating silence, and the presence of unseen eyes he couldn't name but couldn't ignore. Mira and Theo stayed close, their tiny hands clutching his, damp with fear and trust, the only flicker of warmth in an air that felt carved from stone. They walked in unsteady silence, a step behind him, their presence a fragile comfort.

He stopped and turned to them, his fingers gently trailing through Mira's tangled hair before straightening Theo's crooked collar with practiced care. It had become a quiet ritual, this act of fixing and fussing, a small defiance against the chaos around them. A way to show they were still held, still seen, even as the world frayed at the edges.

The chants deepened, rising from murmurs to a low, rhythmic hum that pulsed against the stone walls and curled through the air like smoke. It wasn't just sound. It was a presence, steady and ancient, threading through the cavern's bones. Then came a hush, sudden and complete, as if the mountain itself had drawn breath and was holding it.

From the far side of the chamber, a figure emerged—tall and gaunt, draped in crimson robes that pooled around his feet like freshly spilled blood. The black trim shimmered in the candlelight, etching a stark silhouette against the rough stone as if the darkness itself had taken shape. His face was all hollows and sharp edges, his hands, pale, steady hands, curved around a silver staff topped with Elion's sigil.

Sol told himself to bow his head, to sink into the familiar rhythm of devotion—but in Drevan's presence, the gesture felt hollow. The chants, the candlelight, the rising smoke, everything was the same as every week before, yet now it seemed thinned, unraveling at the edges like fabric worn threadbare by time. Faith was supposed to anchor you, something to hold onto when the world felt uncertain. But tonight, it slipped through his hands, leaving only the sharp edges of doubt behind.

"Tonight, our humble village receives a rare blessing — noble blood joins our fold. Brother Mathren,

Baron of Caelwyth, and his wife, Sister Eryssa, Lady Greywell — long devoted to Elion in quiet faith — now stand among us in His light," proclaimed High Priest Drevan.

A ripple of whispers spread through the crowd as Drevan raised his hand, silently summoning figures from the cavern's shadowed edges. Baron and Lady Greywell stepped forward into the flickering light, clad in finery too lavish for Oswynn's humble halls. Their heads bowed just so, striking the perfect balance between measured humility and quiet pride.

Sol knew the name — everyone in Oswynn did. The Greywells ruled from Caelwyth, their estate tucked just beyond the village among the sunlit hills and fertile fields. They rarely entered Oswynn proper, never set foot in the market, and certainly never walked among the common folk.

Their wealth and devotion were the stuff of whispered tales— the kind Mira had once begged to hear before sleep, eyes wide with wonder and disbelief. But stories were safer at a distance. Standing here, beneath the cavern's dim, flickering light, their fine clothes seemed too rich, too out of place. And yet, despite their obvious difference, it was Sol who felt like the true intruder.

Lady Greywell's smile was practiced, her hands folded neatly in front of her, but her eyes—dark and unreadable—swept the room like someone counting the pieces on a chessboard.

Drevan's skeletal hand lifted once more, beckoning a third figure from the shadows.

Lady Alina stepped forward, and her head bowed with practiced grace, a pale lock of hair slipping loose over her shoulder like a strand of silk. Her face was finely sculpted, with delicate features as if carved from porcelain framed beneath a brow that held a mask of perfect stillness. She was taller than Sol expected, nearly eye-level with him, though her slender frame and lowered gaze made her seem smaller, as though she had spent her whole life learning to occupy less space.

Drevan's voice cut through the smoke and whispers. "Lady Alina Greywell, devoted daughter of Elion, offered in faith and loyalty to our Keeper's will."

She was introduced simply as Lady Alina—no Sister yet. In the Keeper's eyes, faith was neither inherited nor granted; it had to be chosen. Earned.

The murmurs stirred again, softer this time, curiosity edging out reverence.

When she reached her parents' side, she lifted her chin just enough to meet the crowd's expectant gaze— then, for a fleeting heartbeat, her eyes found Sol's.

Her eyes were green—clear and bright—but carried weight far beyond their color, the look of someone who had been told her fate long ago and had since ceased to question it. There was no malice in their depths, only quiet acceptance, and beneath that, something softer, more elusive, something Sol couldn't quite name or understand.

After the final prayer, Drevan descended from the altar, his robes whispering softly against the stone with each measured step. He moved like a hunter, never rushing, never announcing his approach— closing the distance with the quiet, unerring certainty of something that already knew exactly where its prey would flee.

"Brother Kellan," Drevan said, his voice a thread of silk through the smoke, "Sister Elora has already spoken to me of the signs."

Kellan's brow lifted ever so slightly, but there was no flicker of surprise, no hint of offense at being preempted. Sol knew his father well enough to recognize the quiet acceptance settling into his expression: the understanding that Elora's faith came at a price, and part of that price was her unshakable habit of speaking first.

It should have been nothing. Elora had always pushed to be noticed, her voice perpetually a step ahead of the others. But now, there was something different, something sharper lurking beneath her usual sweetness. Sol couldn't quite place it, yet it left the back of his neck prickling like the uneasy stir of a distant storm, still too far off to see but close enough to feel.

A soft hum—almost a purr—escaped Elora's throat, her shoulders squaring under the weight of Drevan's acknowledgment. Her chin dipped just slightly, her hands folded in front of her, the picture of modest piety wrapped around barely contained pride.

"It is a blessing," Drevan continued, "to have such vigilant devotion among us."

Kellan offered a thin smile in return. "Of course, High Priest."

Drevan's smile barely shifted, a mere suggestion at the corners of his mouth, but his gaze flicked, sharp and deliberate—to Sol. "Perhaps Lady Alina and young Soltic might become acquainted while we attend to… more delicate matters."

Sol's stomach sank, resentment curling low and slow in his chest. Of course. The men would talk about the land — the fields, the wood eaters, the beams sagging under time and weather. They would speak of his home, carve decisions into its bones, and he wouldn't be invited. Again.

He knew better than to protest. That wasn't how things worked. But it didn't stop the bitter taste from rising in his throat. He forced his shoulders to stay loose, schooling his face into something neutral. If he had to endure being pawned off, he wouldn't give them the satisfaction of seeing him bristle.

The women drifted into the shadows, Elora's voice trailing behind them, curling through the air in smooth, familiar tones like a ribbon loosed in the wind.

Kellan followed Drevan and Baron Greywell, their footsteps receding into the deeper dark, vanishing into the stone-veiled recesses of the cavern.

That left Sol beside Lady Alina, both of them standing at the edge of it all — not participants, but afterthoughts, like half-forgotten pieces left behind once the real game had begun.

For a heartbeat, the silence stretched between them, taut and uncertain, as if the air itself waited to see who would speak first.

With a gentle tilt of her head, Alina gestured toward a small alcove near the entrance — candlelit and carefully arranged, like a stage waiting for its players.

Sol followed without a word. The air inside was too warm, the candlelight too sharp, the silence pressed in too close. The distant crackle of torches echoed faintly through the chamber, but rather than soothing, it only made the quiet between them feel denser, more aware of itself.

Sol stood beside Lady Alina, hands awkwardly clasped behind his back, shoulders held in a tension that bordered on rigid. She stood close—not too close—but just near enough for him to catch the faint trace of something floral and unfamiliar, a perfume that felt foreign as it belonged to a life lived behind silken curtains and quiet servants, far from anything he'd ever known.

She smiled, the kind of smile Sol imagined she'd rehearsed more than once, wide enough to be welcoming, carefully softened to pass as effortless. It should have eased him. It probably did for most boys.

"You're awfully quiet," she said, her voice light, conversational.

"I was warned you'd be shy."

Sol's brow creased, his gaze snapping back from

the distant flicker of torchlight. "Warned?"

"Oh, you know." She gave a casual shrug, her fingers tracing a slow line along the stone wall beside her. "Elora has quite the imagination."

"Does she?" Sol said, his polite smile tightening slightly.

Alina tilted her head, studying him the way someone might regard a half-finished painting, weighing whether it was on the verge of becoming something beautiful or if it had already veered irreversibly off course.

"She also said you were clever." Her smile curved at the edges, a touch playful. "I was hoping you'd have something clever to say."

Sol's mind was still too tangled in the thought of Elora feeding rumors about him to a noble girl even to try. "I'm not sure I'm in the mood for clever."

"Oh." Her brows lifted slightly, her smile still intact but thinner at the edges. "That's a shame. Boys usually like trying to impress me."

The silence stretched too long, not quite comfortable, not quite tense—hovering in that uncertain space between politeness and unease. Then Alina exhaled softly, her fingers drifting over the embroidery on her sleeve as if seeking something familiar. The sound was small, but it tugged something loose in Sol's chest.

"I'm terrible at this," he muttered.

Alina glanced at him, one brow arched. "At what?"

"At..." He exhaled sharply, frustration rising before he could catch it. "At this. The... polite little dance we're expected to perform. All the pretending."

Alina's smile wavered, revealing a flicker of something quieter beneath. "I hate it too."

The confession landed softly between them; a pebble dropped into a still pond. Sol turned his head, studying her more closely — the perfect lines of her dress, the smooth braid over her shoulder, the posture trained into her bones.

But it was her eyes that held him—not their color, nor their brightness, but the quiet tiredness beneath them: the kind that comes from being seen the wrong way for so long that you forget what it means to be yourself.

"Do you want to get out of here?" she asked, her voice quieter now, almost conspiratorial. "It's cooler outside."

Sol didn't hesitate this time. "Please."

She led the way, slipping silently through the narrow entrance into the cool night air. The sudden shift— from the heavy weight of incense and candle smoke to the crisp, sharp scent of earth, hit Sol like a splash of cold water. He hadn't realized how tightly his chest had been clenched until the tension began to ease, leaving behind a hollow calm he wasn't sure he was ready to face.

The stars hung brightly above them, scattered wide across the vast, dark sky, the only silent witnesses to their quiet retreat. They stood close, shoulders nearly touching, the cool night air wrapping around them like a fragile comfort. For a long moment, silence stretched between them, heavy but not uncomfortable. Then Alina let out a slow breath, soft and steady. "Better."

Sol nodded. The silence between them no longer needed to be filled.

He glanced at her — really looked. Not as the baron's daughter, not as a rumor wrapped in silk. Just a girl beneath the stars, her pale braid catching the moonlight, her eyes reflecting more than they revealed — and for the first time, he noticed the quiet beneath her composure.

After a moment of stillness, she leaned in just slightly, the faintest movement that barely disturbed the quiet night. Her hand reached out gently, brushing lightly against his where it rested on the low stone wall between them, a touch so soft it felt almost accidental, yet it carried a quiet intention beneath its delicate weight.

He stretched his arms out in front of him, breaking the contact. Not a rejection, not precisely, but something in him recoiled before he could name it.

Alina didn't pull back. Instead, she held her gaze on him sideways, a subtle, unreadable flicker dancing just beneath the surface of her eyes, something hesitant, guarded, and quietly defiant all at once.

"What?" he asked, his voice softer than before.

She smiled, though her eyes stayed still, "Nothing."

The silence that followed was comfortable, the weight of expectation left somewhere behind them in the cavern. They stood, two souls positioned like pieces on a board, who had slipped free — if only for a moment.

Sol glanced at her from the corner of his eye, and for the first time, she was no longer the baron's daughter or someone he was meant to impress. She was simply Alina, standing beneath the vast canopy of stars, her pale hair silvered by the soft moonlight, her green eyes catching every glimmer like scattered gems.

She was beautiful, but not in the way he had

expected. Here, away from prying eyes and careful scrutiny, she felt more real, more tangible, and that made it harder to meet her gaze. What stirred inside him wasn't desire, exactly, yet it tugged at something deep, pulling him all the same.

Alina caught him looking and grinned. "What?"

Sol shook his head, the corner of his mouth quirking up.

"Nothing."

"Liar." She bumped her shoulder lightly against his, playful but careful like she wasn't sure how much weight this moment could hold.

"Come on, Soltic Arden — say something clever."

Sol exhaled through his nose, shaking his head. "You'll be waiting a while."

Alina laughed again, the sound trailing behind them into the night—a flicker of warmth, fragile and bright, cutting through the surrounding darkness.

The hush of the cavern settled heavy around them. Though the ceremony had long since ended, the air still lingered thick with smoke and something unspoken, an invisible weight that neither dared break.

Clusters of villagers lingered near the cavern walls, their voices hushed and wary, eyes moving toward the shadowed corners where nobility and faith had quietly collided tonight.

As Sol passed, a whisper slipped through the hush — low, fervent, and far too close:

"The false gods hide in shadow, but Elion will burn them out."

He didn't look back. Yet the words lingered, clinging to his lungs like stubborn ash.

No one noticed their return, silent as shadows slipping through the night. Still, Sol felt seen—marked in a way that words alone couldn't capture.

Mira's eyes caught him for a heartbeat, and her brow furrowed slightly, a question she didn't ask. She stayed close to Petra, her hand wrapped tightly in their mother's. She was too young to fully understand the undercurrents but old enough to know something had shifted.

Elora stood near the front, hands folded neatly at her waist— the very picture of quiet grace. Her smile never wavered, yet Sol's gaze slid over her, catching the moment her eyes found his. The smile remained, but beneath it stirred something else—not suspicion, nor quite satisfaction, but a quiet knowing that tightened Sol's skin like stretched leather.

The crowd drifted apart soon after, spilling into the cool night in twos and threes, their voices low and careful. Sol followed his family down the worn path toward home, the stillness between them filled only by the shuffle of footsteps over dirt and stone. His mother walked ahead with Mira; her arm curled protectively around her daughter's shoulders. Theo lagged slightly behind, eyes half-closed with exhaustion, every step heavy.

Kellan walked beside Sol, close enough to touch yet somehow just out of reach, his thoughts too deep, too distant for words. Sol opened his mouth once, then again, a fragile thread rising to his lips— not a question nor a challenge, but something lingering, unspoken.

Did you know they'd be here?

Why her?

Does it matter what I want?

But the words curled tight in his throat, brittle and half-formed, and he swallowed them like dry leaves caught in a restless wind.

It wasn't the first time Kellan had closed the door like that. Sol could count the moments his father had truly invited him into real conversation on the one hand—and none had ever touched the things that truly mattered. Fields and weather, tools and prices, those were safe topics, rehearsed and impersonal. But the moments that shaped their family, the quiet decisions that bent the future? Those belonged to Kellan alone.

Sol had thought, once, that it would change when he got older.

It hadn't.

Kellan's hand lifted slightly—a half-gesture, caught between intention and hesitation as if he meant to clap Sol on the shoulder or smooth the back of his hair like he used to when Sol was small. But the moment slipped away, his hand falling back before Sol could even be sure it had happened.

When they reached it, the house was dark, save for the faint orange glow of banked embers in the hearth. Petra murmured something to Mira and Theo, ushering them toward their shared room with the gentle press of her hand between their shoulders. Sol lingered near the door, the cool air curling against the back of his neck, reluctant to step fully inside.

Kellan was already settling into his chair by the hearth, boots scuffed and kicked off, fingers tracing slow circles over the worn wood of the armrest. His eyes gazed distant—not troubled, not quite—but drifting somewhere beyond Sol's reach.

For a moment, Kellan's gaze flicked toward him. The kind of glance that might have once led to a question, an invitation to sit, to share whatever was tangled between them. But whatever passed through Kellan's mind faded before it reached his mouth.

Sol leaned against the doorframe, words poised on his tongue—half-formed, fragile, too delicate to break the silence.

"What did he want?" Sol asked finally, his voice soft enough not to wake the others.

Kellan's fingers paused for a breath before he resumed the slow circles. "Nothing that concerns you."

There was no bite in it, no anger — the gentle certainty of a door quietly closed.

Sol swallowed against the tightness in his throat. "But—"

"It's late," Kellan said, softer this time like that was meant to make it easier. "Go to bed, Soltic."

The conversation was already over.

The fire had burned low by the time Sol crawled beneath his blanket, the house wrapped in the soft hush that came after long prayers and longer silences. Mira's soft breathing drifted from the next room, a steady rhythm Sol tried, and failed, to match.

Sleep didn't come easily—never did after temple nights. But this time, it wasn't the familiar weight of prayers or the echo of half remembered chants pulling at him.

It was Alina's laugh.

The way her shoulder had nudged his, light and natural like they were just two people standing under the stars instead of pieces on someone else's board. She was beautiful, that much was obvious. But it wasn't just her face he couldn't shake. It was how she slipped so effortlessly into everything, like she'd been born knowing exactly when to smile, the right words to say, and how to move through the world without stumbling over her own doubts. It wasn't fair. It wasn't her fault. Yet still, something twisted in his chest all the same.

It was Elora's smile, too. That knowing curve of her mouth, the certainty in her eyes that Sol couldn't shake. As though she could already see the shape of his life, and no matter which way he twisted, she would always be standing at the center of it.

And it was Kellan. The quiet way his father shut him out—the gentleness of it somehow sharper than anger. Sol wanted to believe it was protection, that whatever Drevan had said wasn't meant for him to carry. But a colder thought whispered beneath it all: maybe Kellan simply didn't see him as someone worth including. Maybe Kellan didn't see him as someone worth bringing in.

And finally, it was Wyatt. The ache of his absence, the memory of his hands—rough and sure, and the way Sol had never had to wonder who he was when they were alone. That was the difference. With Alina, there was always a question. With Wyatt, there had only ever been an answer. He lay awake, tangled in all of it — the strings between who he was and who he was supposed to be pulling tight enough to leave marks.

Chapter Five

———

Where We Leave Our Names

The path to the blacksmith was worn smooth by time and rain, the earth still pliant enough to bear the memory of the storm. Sol's boots left faint impressions behind him, shapes in the mud that said he'd passed through. That he still existed.

Walking had always been like this for him, not just a way to get somewhere but a means of staying ahead of the thoughts that pressed in too hard when he stood still. It wasn't about the distance. It was about movement, about keeping the noise behind him. Out here, under the vast sky, with the air moving around him and the ground shifting beneath his feet, it was easier to believe he might belong to something. That the ache might quiet if he just kept moving.

In. Hold. Out.

He didn't even notice it at first, the way his breath fell into step with his feet, forming a quiet rhythm he'd trained into himself over time. Not on purpose. Just a habit that had become a tether, something steady to hold onto when everything else threatened to pull him apart.

His fingers trailed through the tall grass at the path's edge, the blades bending toward him like they remembered his touch. *How many times had he walked this road alone, carrying the same quiet weight in his chest, waiting for something to shift?*

Most days, it didn't. Most days, walking was just walking, and thinking was just thinking, and the knot inside him stayed where it always did, tight and quiet, tucked just beneath the surface. He carried it like a stone in his chest, familiar and mostly dull, only noticeable when he pressed too hard on the wrong thoughts.

The blacksmith's shop loomed ahead, its silhouette blurred by the steady curl of smoke rising from the chimney. The air was thick with the scorched tang of burning coal and the sharp bite of hot metal, a scent that clung to the back of the throat. A fine layer of soot coated the windows and doorframe as if the forge couldn't help but leave its signature on everything it touched, claiming the space and marking it as its own.

"Maris! Hello?" Sol called into the open doorway; his voice was swallowed slightly by the low roar of the forge.

A moment later, Thom limped out from behind the anvil, wiping his hands on a soot-streaked rag, his broad face splitting into a grin. "My boy!" he boomed, voice rough with warmth. "It's good to see you!"

"Thom!" Sol's smile faltered a touch. "Should you even be up?"

"No," came a sharp, familiar voice, and Maris stepped into view, arms full of wood for the forge. "He's too stubborn to stay in bed, and I'm too tired to fight him anymore."

She nudged a chair toward Thom with her knee, and despite his half-hearted grumbling, he sank into it with a theatrical groan. "I'm not helpless, you know," he muttered, though the glint in his eye said otherwise.

"No one said you were," Maris replied, depositing the wood beside the hearth. "But if you fall into that forge, I'm not pulling you back out."

Sol laughed, the sound catching in his throat, warmth blooming in his chest. For all the tension that had threaded through the village of late, this place remained stubbornly familiar, sootcovered, clattering with noise, and defiantly alive.

"I'm glad you're up," Sol said honestly.

"Up, but under ruthless command," Thom grumbled, settling a battered set of bellows across his lap. "My foreman's a tyrant in lace."

"Lace, is it?" Maris swatted the back of his head with a sootsmudged rag. "You're lucky I haven't packed up my tools and let the forge eat you alive."

Sol smiled. They bickered like family, all sparks and soot, but underneath, it ran something solid. A rhythm. They moved around each other with the quiet fluency of people who hadn't just stayed but belonged.

And for a moment, it made something pull tight in Sol's chest—a longing without a name, sharp and sudden. Not envy, not quite, but a wish so old it felt like it had always lived inside him. The ease between them, the quiet certainty of belonging, stirred something unspoken, something he didn't know how to reach, only feel.

"How's he really doing?" Sol asked quietly, catching Maris's eye while Thom fussed with the bellows.

Maris's smile softened. "Better than he was. Worse than he says. But he'll be all right."

She shifted, fingers tugging at the frayed edge of her apron, eyes flicking up just once. "Have you heard from Wyatt?"

The smile that spread across Sol's face was immediate, unguarded. "A few more days. I've sent a letter to Briarstead," saying it aloud lit something warm inside him — something that had nothing to do with the forge fire.

"I'm sure he'll like that," Maris said, though the words came slower this time, her gaze snagging on the open door. Her fingers tapped once, twice, against the bench—restless, searching.

"You did tell him about the bandits, right?"

"I did," Sol said, though the familiar weight of worry settled in again. "We're all grateful Thom's going to be okay."

"Grateful but not cautious enough," Thom muttered, easing himself to his feet. "Are you here for a chat, or did your father send you with a list?"

"Oh, right." Sol fished a crumpled slip of paper from his pocket. "Wood-eater damage. We need replacements for some of the barn beams."

Thom took the paper, gave it a cursory glance, and passed it off to Maris with an exaggerated groan. "I'm far too delicate for paperwork. Be a good lass and take care of this order for me, would you?"

Maris snatched the paper with a roll of her eyes. "I'll give you fragile."

While Maris moved to gather the materials, Thom eased himself back onto the stool with a grunt. "Let me know when the repairs are done. I'll come down and bestow a proper blessing, something worthy of my station."

Sol hesitated. "I… don't think Papa wants a blessing."

Thom's brow lifted. "Not even Beryth's?"

Sol didn't answer. Anything he said would've sounded too much like doubt—and doubt had no place in a house already holding itself together by threads.

The silence that followed wasn't sharp, but it stayed just long enough to press at the edges of something unspoken.

Maris returned, her arms laden with a bundle of tools, a box of nails clinking softly with each step, and a rough coil of twine slung over one shoulder. Sol took the load with a nod of gratitude, adjusting the uneven weight in his arms as if reacquainting himself with an old burden.

"Thanks," Sol said and meant it.

As he turned to leave, a butterfly flitted past, its pale wings slicing through the soot-thick air like a quiet blade. For a moment, it hovered there. Too still. Too deliberate.

And just like that, the clamor inside him fell away.

It didn't speak. Didn't offer a vision. Didn't need to.

But the knowing sank deep, steady, unmistakable.

Wyatt was coming.

Today.

Sol didn't know how he knew — he just did. The certainty sat in his chest like a spark catching dry tinder.

With the bundle clutched tight in his arms, he broke into a run. He didn't hesitate. He knew exactly where to find him.

Over fences, he flew, feet barely skimming the earth, the ground rising to meet him as if it knew exactly where he was meant to land.

The sun hung high, the sky stretched thin with light, and the scent of sun-warmed grass filled his lungs, sharp, sweet—like the closest thing to freedom he'd tasted in weeks.

At the top of the first rise, Sol skidded to a halt, chest heaving, sweat prickling down his back. Gold and green fields rolled out before him, all familiar — except for the figure standing at the pasture's edge. They didn't belong there.

Sol wiped his forehead with the back of his hand, leaving a dark smear across his brow, but his gaze never wavered from the stranger. Too still. Too at ease. Not a farmer. Not a neighbor. And definitely not Wyatt.

He stepped forward, legs heavy from the run, mind racing to make sense of who it might be and why they'd come here, now, to this place.

Maybe they had news.

Maybe they'd seen Wyatt.

The figure shifted, weight rolling lazily to one side, and Sol caught the flicker of a grin, all sharp angles and effortless charm like the whole world was a joke only he knew the punchline to.

"Fancy meeting you here," Scy drawled, arms crossed, his posture at complete odds with the tension buzzing under Sol's skin.

Sol blinked, still catching his breath, still trying to switch gears. "What—what are you doing here?"

Scy stepped closer, reaching out uninvited to straighten Sol's collar, brushing dirt from his shoulder with exaggerated care, then licking his thumb to scrub at the soot on Sol's face.

"What am I doing here?" he said, pinching Sol's cheek hard enough to be obnoxious.

"Same thing as you, lad. Chasing sheep."

Sol batted his hand away, face flushing hot, but his heart was still thudding — part from the run, part from the hope that refused to die.

Scy's grin softened, just barely — and for the briefest moment, so fleeting Sol couldn't be sure he hadn't imagined it, his gaze flicked toward the pasture.

Toward the place where Sol and Wyatt always met.

"But don't mind me," Scy said, stepping back. "I've got to get back before Ysella decides my ear would look better notched." He gave a lazy salute, turned, and strolled off.

And as Scy slipped into the shade, another figure stepped into view—familiar, steady, and utterly his.

Wyatt.

Sol's body moved before his mind could catch up, feet pounding over the earth, his heart drumming out the rhythm of Wyatt's name with every step. The ground barely touched him; the fields blurred into streaks of green and gold until strong, steady arms caught him, lifting him clean off the earth and spinning him once, twice, before his boots found solid ground again. They stood there, clutching each other as if letting go might shatter something sacred.

Their hands locked tight, no hesitation, no apology.

"You've gotten taller," Sol gasped, breath hitching with a laugh. "When did that happen?"

Wyatt grinned — wide, familiar, breathless. "You got scrawnier."

Sol swatted his arm but didn't let go. "You're an ass."

"I know," Wyatt said, laughing as he bumped their foreheads together. "Gods, Sol. I missed your voice."

"You could've written more."

"I did," Wyatt said, eyes shining. "Just not letters I could send." That quiet settled between them—soft, not heavy.

Then Wyatt's hand rose, brushing away the tear Sol hadn't meant to shed. His voice lowered, warm and certain.

"Oh, my soul," he whispered, tilting Sol's chin up to meet his gaze. "You're still the only thing that ever felt real."

Sol's breath caught, and when Wyatt kissed him—firm, searching, reverent, Sol rose into it without hesitation, the world dissolving into heat, grass, and the steady thrum of being truly seen.

When they finally pulled apart, laughing breathlessly into each other's mouths, they collapsed into the grass like boys who'd just survived a storm—wild, exhilarated, and desperately grateful for the moment they still had.

The sheep drifted closer, bleating softly as if they belonged to this fragile moment. Wyatt scratched one gently behind the ear, his other hand still tangled with Sol's, fingers lacing together with quiet certainty.

"You're quiet," Wyatt said, voice low enough not to break the fragile peace between them. "Even for you."

Sol's fingers curled into the grass, dirt cool beneath his palm. "Just thinking."

"Dangerous habit," Wyatt teased, though his smile didn't quite reach his eyes. "Want to tell me what about?"

Sol didn't answer right away. How could he? How could he explain the weight pressing in, the barn's empty shadows, the wide fields stretched silent under an uncaring sky, the hollow quiet at dinner, and the way his father's prayers had started to feel like a yawning void swallowing everything he once believed in?

Instead, he leaned heavily against Wyatt's shoulder, surrendering his weight and the unspoken heaviness he carried. "Later," he whispered, voice rough with everything he wasn't ready to say.

"Later," Wyatt echoed, soft as a promise.

The sheep wandered off, their soft bleats fading into the gentle hush of the afternoon. The air softened around them, warm and still, and they sat together, there was no need to fill the silence. Here, with the sun settling warmly on their faces and the whole world paused like a breath held in time, there was no Path, no faith, no fear.

Only them.

"You're early," Sol said, his voice muffled against Wyatt's shoulder.

"Couldn't stay away." Wyatt's voice was quiet,

meant only for him.

Sol's fingers curled tighter around Wyatt's, anchoring himself in the solid warmth beneath his skin. Wyatt's thumb traced a slow, deliberate circle against Sol's palm, comfort offered without asking, reassurance given without a single word spoken. In that small, steady touch, Sol found a quiet refuge, a silent promise that he wasn't alone.

The silence that followed wasn't awkward or heavy, and it was the kind they'd always shared, a gentle pause stretched wide between them, filled with everything they didn't need to say. In that quiet space, their connection spoke louder than words ever could.

Finally, Wyatt leaned back to catch Sol's gaze, his smile tilting into something softer. "Are you gonna let go, or am I carrying you home?"

Sol laughed and kissed Wyatt's cheek before holding up the forgotten package. "I have to get this back to Da."

Wyatt squeezed Sol's hand. "I was going to surprise you, you know. But here you are."

Wyatt rose slowly to his feet, then gently pulled Sol up beside him, never once releasing his hand. His voice was soft but steady. "How'd you know I was here?"

Sol hesitated, his words tangling awkwardly. "I… don't know. I just—" He stumbled, cheeks flushing. "I guess I felt you coming."

Wyatt's laugh was bright and easy, his free hand tousling Sol's hair. "You're such a strange little thing."

Sol grinned despite himself and swatted Wyatt's hand away with a teasing flick.

"I'll walk you home," Wyatt said, his voice softening again, a hint of a smile in his tone. "But we should probably stop by Ysella's first, tell her I'm back before she gets creative with that wooden spoon."

"That spoon really hurts," Sol muttered

Still, hand in hand, they started down the path together.

The spell of their private world cracked the moment Sol and Wyatt stepped into the yard. It wasn't harsh, no sudden jolt or jarring break, but a quiet slipping back, like reality settling softly into place. Around them, the familiar sounds of home unfurled: the gentle cluck of hens wandering too close to the porch, the creak of the gate swinging slowly in the breeze, and the distant murmur of a day unfolding beyond their bubble. The twins' shrill and bright laughter a moment before they came charging around the side of the house.

"Wyatt!" Mira shrieked, her bare feet kicking up little dust clouds as she ran full speed at him.

"You came back!" Theo shouted, grinning widely.

Wyatt barely had time to brace before Mira and Theo barreled into him, arms locking tightly around his waist, their legs swinging wildly as he hoisted them up like sacks of grain. He rocked back with a hearty laugh, swinging them side to side, their joyous laughter spilling upward into the open sky—wild, untamed, and free. Finally, with exaggerated theatrical care, he set them down, grinning as they scrambled to their feet.

The noise pulled Petra from the kitchen, her apron dusted with flour, cheeks flushed from baking. Her smile spread wide and bright as she called out, "There's my handsome shepherd!"

She caught him in a tight hug, her hands trembling slightly as they smoothed over his hair, like she needed to convince herself he was real, that he was truly here.

Kellan followed her onto the porch, quieter, but his

smile was still warm. "Good to see you, lad."

The table was set simply—crusty bread, sharp cheese, thin slices of herbed pork, and bowls of preserved fruit glistening with syrup. Sol took his usual seat beside Wyatt, close enough that their knees brushed gently beneath the worn wooden table.

Kellan's voice rose in the familiar blessing, slower and more deliberate than usual, each word heavy with a weight it hadn't carried before, a solemn grace that settled over them all like a whispered prayer.

"May Elion guard the work of our hands, May the Path ahead remain clear, and may we walk in step with the Keeper, trusting all we have is enough."

Petra's fingers twisted tighter in the rough weave of her apron, betraying a tension she tried to hide. Sol kept his gaze low, feeling the words slip past him—not cruel, exactly, but distant like they were meant for someone else.

The blessing ended, and for a moment, the silence held, like a held breath no one knew how to release. Then Petra clapped her hands, bright and too quick. "Eat before it's cold."

The conversation resumed, lighter now, but Kellan's gaze lingered a moment too long on the closeness between Sol and Wyatt— not suspicion, exactly, but a quiet unease that settled beneath his calm exterior.

Later, after the meal had settled and the twins ran wild through the yard, Wyatt and Sol drifted toward the porch. The sun hung low, gilding the fields in molten gold, its fading light softening every edge, bathing the world in a gentle hush.

The sun hung low, spilling gold across the fields and turning the edges of the grass into flames. The air smelled like earth warming after rain, soft, a little damp, and filled with the quiet hum of life settling down for the evening.

Sol leaned into Wyatt's shoulder, and this time, Wyatt didn't shift away. His arm curled around Sol's back, fingers slipping through the belt at Sol's hip, casual, instinctive, the kind of touch they could risk out here, with no eyes but the setting sun and the wind in the grass. It wasn't a claim. It was a tether. A silent promise that said: I'm here. I came back for this.

Sol's gaze drifted toward the fields, where the tall grasses rippled in the hush of twilight, and the distant tree line softened to a smudge of shadow against the sky's last gold. Everything felt farther away now — quieter like the world itself was exhaling.

"It's not so bad sometimes," he said quietly.

Wyatt's thumb moved in slow, thoughtful circles against the worn leather at Sol's waist, not rushing, not needing anything, just there. The quiet pressure of it sank deeper than words, a small, steady reminder that they were still tethered, still real, in a world that had threatened to forget them.

"It's beautiful."

"You've always made it look easy — fitting in here," Sol said too casually.

Wyatt huffed a soft laugh. "Only because you're here."

Sol's smile flickered — there, then gone.

"Flatterer."

"True, though." Wyatt tipped his head back, eyes half-closed, basking in the last stretch of sun.

"The fields, the sky, even the smell of the animals — it's fine, I guess. But it's never meant anything without you."

The words sank deep, heavy, and sweet all at once — settling somewhere behind Sol's sternum like a swallowed stone wrapped in honey. He wanted to hold onto them, tuck them into the quiet parts of himself where nothing else could touch them. But there wasn't room. Not with everything else pressing in behind his ribs — the ache, the fear, the things he hadn't named yet, all crowding the space where comfort might've lived.

"We should go inside," he said, though he didn't move.

"We could stay a little longer."

"We shouldn't."

Wyatt's fingers curled tighter in Sol's belt, tugging him closer.

"But we could."

For a single breath, Sol let himself want it, the warmth, the stillness, the quiet claim of being held. Just one moment suspended in sunlight, like maybe the dark couldn't find him if he stayed still enough.

Then, with a breath that trembled just slightly, he straightened, his fingers curling gently around Wyatt's. He drew the other boy's hand from his waist — not a rejection, but a retreat. A quiet goodbye to a second he couldn't afford to keep.

"We'll have time," Sol said.

The words felt thin in his mouth.

Wyatt didn't argue. He only smiled — that quiet, steady smile that never asked for anything, never needed to. The kind that always landed in Sol's chest like an anchor and a promise all at once. A smile that said: I see you. I'm here. That's enough.

They walked together, the space between their hands humming with silence…tender, uncertain, and full of things left unsaid.

Chapter Six

———

Silk Bound Faith

Two days had passed since Wyatt's return, and Sol had spent every hour grasping at slivers of time, chasing glances across the barn, fingers brushing too long when they handed off a tool, knees bumping under the table and lingering like a secret. Their moments were stitched into quiet corners, a shared grin beside the well, a whisper traded when no one was watching — fleeting, fragile things that somehow felt more real than anything else in the day.

The afternoon hung heavy, thick with heat that pressed deep into the earth and shimmered in the air, warping the edges of the day. Mud from the last storm clung to the yard in cracked, uneven patches, flaking like old paint under the weight of the sun. Kellan and Sol had finally called it, the barn repairs dragging well past what they'd planned, sweat soaking their collars, hands scraped raw, every beam a small battle against time and splinters. It was tiring work that left limbs slow and heavy, but Sol was grateful to sit, letting the weight of the day settle over him. There was still time before supper.

The knock barely registered.

It wasn't loud, more a suggestion than a summons, the sound of someone clearing their throat at the edge of a thought. The kind of knock that didn't ask if you were home, it presumed you were waiting, breath held, expecting it all along.

Sol wiped his hands against his tunic, the motion automatic, but his mind was already tilting under the wrongness, curling at the edges of the moment. That familiar twist low in his gut, the one that came before something broke, before the world shifted under his feet. He opened the door.

There was no threshold, no drawn breath, no moment of decision. No weighing of welcome or refusal, just the quiet surrender of a hand on the latch and a world already shifting.

Elora stood on the step, her plain navy-blue dress pressed to rigidity, every seam sharp with starch. Her hair was yanked back so tightly it seemed to strain her skin; the knot at her nape wound like a trap. Sol had the absurd thought that if someone ever untied it, she might unravel entirely, not delicately, but in harsh, frayed threads. Her smile stretched thin across her face, not warm but tight, like a lid screwed down over something brittle and bitter, barely holding it in.

"Well, don't just stand there," she said tartly, stepping forward as though the space was already hers. "Invite us in."

Us?

The word barely formed before Sol's gaze slipped past her shoulder.

 Lady Greywell stood behind her, the hem of her traveling gown just brushing the packed earth, delicate embroidery catching threads of sunlight, elegant and deliberate, a sharp contrast against the scuffed floorboards. She stepped inside without pause, the air seeming to part around her as if the world itself had been waiting to shift and make space.

Beside her stood Lady Alina, hands clasped tightly at her waist, the slightest tremor betraying nerves before she forced them still. Her dress, soft sky-blue, embroidered with pale flowers and edged in the unmistakable Eye of Elion, was undeniably lovely. But it didn't belong here. It belonged somewhere untouched, with polished floors and space between the door and the table, space to breathe, move, and not feel so out of place.

He didn't move so much as drift aside, his body reacting before his mind could catch up. Nobles didn't come through this door. Not into the kitchen where flour dusted the table, stew simmered over the hearth, and the back door stood open to catch whatever breeze the day offered.

The kitchen was a place of calloused hands and bowed heads, meant for work and prayer, not for women whose shoes had never once kissed the raw skin of the earth.

"Such a cosy home," Elora declared, stepping inside before the door had fully opened, her voice drifting through the room like an overly sweet perfume meant to mask something far more sour beneath. Her gaze swept the table's worn wood, the chipped chairs, and the faint scorch mark near the hearth, a stubborn reminder of last autumn's kettle mishap.

"I've told High Priest Drevan so many times how this family is a shining example of devotion," she said. "It's only right that Lady Greywell sees for herself."

Sol stayed near the door, his hand still resting lightly on the latch even though it had swung wide open. His heart lagged behind, slow to catch up, but his stomach had already plummeted, sinking into that leaden certainty that always settled just before everything shattered.

Nobles did not come to their door.

Not for kindness.

Not for anything good.

The kitchen was too small, too worn, for visitors like these.

The Ardens had only one table, its surface worn smooth from years of elbows and cutting boards, the edges nicked and scuffed from Theo and Mira's restless games. There was no formal parlour, no sitting room to veil the roughness of their lives. Here, guests sat where the family sat, shoulder to shoulder, with no space left for pretense.

Still clutching her apron, Petra motioned toward the table with practised instinct, her smile wavering at the edges. "Please, you must sit," she said, her voice pitched just a shade too high, cheer stretched thin over something brittle beneath.

Lady Greywell lowered herself gracefully onto one of the rough-hewn chairs, making it look deliberate, a woman who could turn condescension into kindness. Alina followed a step behind, her hands briefly brushing the seat of her chair as if she were checking for splinters before she sat.

Elora sat without waiting to be offered, sliding into the chair nearest the hearth, the one Kellan usually claimed, its legs worn uneven from years of habit.

Sol stayed standing near the door, the latch still under his hand, as if keeping some small connection to the outside world would hold him steady. Kellan, silent as stone, settled against the wall, arms folded loosely across his chest, not defiant, but steady, watchful, like a man gauging the weight of what had just stepped uninvited into his home.

Petra poured water into their only matching set of cups, a wedding gift from her sister, used only on feast days or when the High Priest came to call. She set them on the table with care as though fragile glass could make the room feel more dignified.

Lady Greywell took a cup without a word, her fingers gliding along the rim as she turned it slowly in her hands. The motion was measured, deliberate, less about the cup and more about letting the silence stretch, heavy and expectant.

"It's rare for Sister Eryssa to visit homes beyond the village square," Elora said, her voice honeyed with practiced warmth. "But I told her your family was worth seeing firsthand. After all, true faith shines brightest in the humblest places."

Petra smiled at that, though her fingers twisted the corner of her apron into a tight knot.

Sol caught the glint in Elora's eyes as she spoke, Sister Eryssa. She lingered on the title, savouring the power it lent her, the subtle reordering it suggested. It wasn't disrespectful, not quite. Just a quiet reminder that even Lady Greywell bowed to the same god. And Elora? She was the one holding the prayer book.

"We are honoured, of course," Petra said softly. "Our home isn't much, but we do our best to keep it… welcoming."

"Welcoming," Elora echoed, her gaze drifting over the room with slow, deliberate ease. "And faithful. That's why we're here, after all, to reaffirm the bonds between those who walk the Keeper's path.

A family as steadfast as yours deserves to be seen. And remembered."

Sol couldn't tell if it was a compliment, a warning, or both at once.

Lady Greywell spoke, at last, her voice low and deliberate, each word laid with the precision of a stone in a wall. "Faith is the foundation of all strong homes. Without it, nothing stands. Nothing lasts."

Petra nodded quickly, the motion too eager. "Yes, of course. We're grateful for Elion's blessings every day."

The words rang true on the surface, smooth and proper, precisely what was expected. But even Sol could hear it: the tremor beneath, the hush of hope threaded through the syllables. A quiet, desperate prayer that saying the right thing might somehow make it so.

Sol's fingers twitched at his sides, itching for something to do, but there was nothing to hold onto. Nothing to steady himself. The air was too thin like the walls were pressing in.

Lady Alina hadn't spoken. Her gaze flicked to Sol, fleeting and unreadable, before dropping. Her hands folded tightly in her lap, fingers interlaced so firmly her knuckles stood out white against her skin.

The silence edged in, poised to swallow them whole, thick, waiting, inevitable. But Elora never let the silence linger. She devoured it before it had the chance to settle.

"And of course," Elora said, her smile razor-thin and sharp enough to cut, "faith grows strongest when families stand together— especially when the time comes to weave new bonds between old houses."

Petra's smile didn't quite hold.

Sol's stomach tightened.

Lady Greywell's smile softened, careful, practised, but undeniably warmer than Elora's. "In times like these, strong families build strong villages. And strong villages, in turn, build strong faith." Her words were all polite, with soft edges and open hands, a deliberate offering of peace.

But Sol could feel the shape of the noose tightening all the same.

Elora's voice began to settle into its usual rhythm, the singsong performance of faith and community, her words as polished as the prayer stones the children carried to the temple. But it was Lady Greywell's voice, soft and steady, that cut through it.

"The storms have been unkind this season," Lady Greywell murmured, her fingertips tracing slow circles along the rim of her cup. "I noticed it on the ride here, fields still soaked, the soil stubbornly clinging to the roots."

Petra's smile flickered, her grip tightening on her apron. "We've managed," she said quickly. "The men have worked hard to repair the barn after the worst of it."

"As devoted families do," Lady Greywell agreed, her voice warm but the light in her eyes cold and distant.

"Yet devotion alone won't keep a field from flooding, nor can faith coax the earth to yield what it no longer holds."

Sol's stomach knotted, but he said nothing. It wasn't untrue. The lower field still held water like a cupped hand, the edges of the grain already browning where roots had sat too long in the muck.

"Faith is not about ease," Kellan said, calm but cautious. "We know that better than most."

"Of course," Lady Greywell said smoothly, her voice polished with practised ease. "That's why it falls to those of us blessed with more to ensure the faithful are never left to bear their burdens alone."

Petra's lips parted, startled by the offer she thought she had heard, but Kellan's hand on her arm stilled her response.

"That's generous," Kellan said cautiously. "But the Ardens don't take charity."

"Oh, no," Lady Greywell said, her smile softening as her voice dipped into something almost maternal. "Not charity—support. Between those who walk the same path, who serve Elion. Surely there is no shame in accepting the hand of a fellow believer."

Sol's skin prickled beneath the weight of Lady

Greywell's gaze. Though her eyes never shifted from Kellan, it was Sol who bore the full force of her attention. There was no threat in her voice, no hint of obligation, only a promise wrapped in silk, the kind you couldn't refuse without risking offense.

"Faith isn't measured only by how we pray," Lady Greywell continued, her voice steady but layered with meaning, "but in how we care for one another. There are… subtle ways the faithful can demonstrate their devotion when the moment calls for it."

The silence following her words stretched thin and cold.

Kellan's jaw tightened, but he gave a slight nod — the kind a man offers when he knows he's stepping into something he can't refuse but doesn't dare accept too quickly.

"Your kindness is noted," Kellan said carefully. "We are, as always, grateful for Elion's favour."

Lady Greywell's smile deepened, sharp with certainty, like a woman who had already glimpsed the outcome and now merely waited for the players to take their places.

"We'll speak of it another time," she said, as though

it was already decided. "For now, let's simply enjoy the company of the faithful."

The conversation shifted after that, not through words, but in the quiet reshuffling of bodies and glances, the subtle choreography that always unfolded when unspoken truths were about to surface.

Elora pressed her palms together with a smile, the gesture too rehearsed for the weight in the room.

"Sister Eryssa and I would be honoured to speak privately with Brother Kellan and Sister Petra," she said as if the notion had only just crossed her mind, light and pleasant in tone yet unmistakably rehearsed.

There was no asking. Not really. The decision had already been made, even if no one had spoken it aloud.

Petra's smile trembled on the edge of breaking, but she stood anyway, her hands trembling as they smoothed the creases in her apron. Sol's chair scraped softly against the floor as he rose, his face carefully composed, but Sol caught the tight line at the corners of his father's mouth, the quiet resignation of a man who already knew he'd lost the argument yet still braced himself to measure how deep the wound would cut.

"Soltic," Lady Greywell said, her voice still soft,

still sweet, but with the weight of expectation under every word, "perhaps you and Lady Alina might take a short walk. It's such a lovely afternoon."

It wasn't.

Sol hesitated, glancing toward Kellan, but his father gave a slight nod. There was nothing to do but comply.

Alina rose a moment later, hands smoothing the front of her skirt, though there wasn't a wrinkle to be found. Her smile was polite, practised, and not quite effortless. Beneath it, something flickered: a brief tremor of uncertainty, the same hint Sol had seen at the temple. Only now, without the weight of the crowd, it was sharper, more naked.

They stepped outside, the door closing softly behind them.

For a few heartbeats, neither of them spoke.

The yard felt smaller with her in it, like her presence drew the edges inward, tightening the air itself. Every sound rang sharper, every movement more vivid, heightened by the stark contrast between her and the bare, honest earth beneath their feet.

They walked toward the vegetable garden, silence stretching between them, taut but not unkind. Both were too aware of the walls they'd left behind and the words that hadn't followed them out.

"You don't have to entertain me," Alina said after a while, her voice low but not unfriendly.

Sol glanced at her, caught off guard by the candour in her tone. "Is that what this is?"

Her mouth curved into something almost like a smile, the kind you start and think better of. "That's what it always is."

There was no bitterness in it, no edge, just plain fact. Sol wasn't sure if that made it easier to bear or somehow worse.

They reached the edge of the garden, where the rows still listed unevenly from the storms. Leaves sagged with browned edges, the soil beneath them dark and bloated where water had lingered too long. Alina paused, her hands clasped loosely before her, gaze steady but unreadable.

"She didn't tell me much," Alina said softly. "Only that your family was… important."

The word sat wrong, like a prayer spoken in the wrong cadence.

"Important?" Sol echoed.

Alina shrugged, her gaze drifting toward the distant tree line. "She says things like that often. It usually means there's a plan, and I'm not part of it."

Alina stood still, her fingers curling gently in the fabric of her dress, shoulders held a touch too straight. Her breath hitched once, barely, but she steadied it. And Sol knew.

It wasn't logical. It wasn't a feeling he could name. It was the same quiet pull that sometimes drew him outside just before a storm broke.

This wasn't trust earned or even understood. It was trust recognized, like catching the shape of something familiar in the dark.

She wasn't his ally. Not yet.

But she wasn't his enemy either.

The door creaked open behind them, and Elora's voice followed, too bright, too smooth for whatever shadows were still shifting inside.

"We should go back," Alina said quietly.

The adults were still speaking in the kitchen when Sol and Alina returned, but the tone had changed.

The edges had thinned, silences stretching longer between every sentence. Petra's smile was courteous but faltered at the corners, held together by habit more than warmth. Kellan stood with his arms loosely crossed and weight settled, the stance of a man preparing to weather whatever came next.

Elora was all bright, her voice smooth as honey. "It's always such a joy to visit a home so devoted to the Keeper's light," she said, rising from her chair with the practised grace of someone who always decides when a visit ends.

Lady Greywell stood beside her, slower now, each movement measured and deliberate. "It's clear your family understands what it means to be faithful," she said, her gaze sweeping over Petra and Kellan with the same gentle weight she'd worn all afternoon, kindness as armour, every smile a sheath concealing something sharper.

"We are blessed to have a home," Petra said, her voice soft, "and to be able to raise our children in the light."

"Blessed indeed," Lady Greywell agreed softly. "And when blessings are shared, between families, between generations, they only deepen, growing stronger with each passing hand."

The meaning in her words hung heavy in the air, too light to be a threat, yet too deliberate to mean nothing. Kellan's hands curled into fists at his sides, though his smile remained carefully in place.

"There will be opportunities," Lady Greywell continued, "for families like ours to stand united in faith, purpose, and legacy." Her eyes flickered to Sol for a heartbeat, sharp and deliberate. "And when that time comes, I have no doubt the Ardens will choose wisely."

The room felt smaller with each word, the kitchen shrinking around Sol's shoulders.

Petra's hands clenched the fabric of her apron, twisting the hem into a tight knot between trembling fingers, yet her voice held steady. "We're honoured to walk the path."

"Of course, you are." Lady Greywell's smile didn't falter, not even for a breath. "And we'll be sure to visit again soon."

Elora clapped her hands once as if the matter were already settled. "The Keeper's light shines brightest on homes like this," she said, her voice tipping toward sing-song.

The words stuck to Sol's ribs like something bitter.

Kellan opened the door, and the Greywells stepped into the fading afternoon light. Alina lingered a step behind, her gaze flickering to Sol before she crossed the threshold.

A shared glance between two souls who knew they'd both been measured for a fate neither had chosen. A moment reserved for those standing at the edge of the same storm, waiting for the sky to break.

Elora was the last to leave, her fingers brushing briefly against Sol's sleeve as she passed, a touch so light it could have been accidental. Or it might not have been.

She lingered just long enough to make him wonder, her smile soft and tender, like the gentle sweep of a stray hair from a beloved child's brow. A touch meant to soothe or to quietly remind him whose hand would shape the path ahead.

"May the Keeper guide your path," Elora said, her voice low and almost fond, as though this was her blessing to give.

"May we stay steadfast," the family echoed, each word laden with a resignation too deep to conceal. They clung to the phrase, desperate for meaning, even if they no longer knew what it was.

Lady Greywell's voice lifted in reply, unnervingly bright. Her joy was so effortless it left no room for refusal. Her faith was a door already locked behind them.

The door closed at last, leaving only thick and expectant silence in their wake.

The kitchen was unchanged from that morning, the same worn table, the familiar hearth, the lingering faint scent of stew, yet everything felt different now. The house seemed to have shifted, silently making room for an unbidden presence none had welcomed.

Sol stood near the door, his fingers resting against the latch, his mind still circling Lady Greywell's words, a promise shaped like kindness, a future shaped like a snare.

Kellan exhaled slowly and low, the kind of breath a man draws when he knows he can't stop what's coming, only brace for the inevitable break.

"We'll talk later," Kellan said quietly, walking out the door into the yard.

Petra lingered a moment longer, her hands twisted tightly in her apron, shoulders bowed beneath the weight of unspoken words.

Sol remained still.

He stepped into the yard, the air heavy, steeped in

the kind of silence that usually came before rain.

But there were no clouds. No breeze. Only the bright, indifferent sky stretched vast and endless overhead.

A single feather drifted down, cutting through the stillness like a blade.

It landed at his feet, long and dark, a hunting bird's feather, glossy as ink. No hawk circled above. Sol looked up anyway, but the sky was empty.

He knelt, fingers closing around the feather's shaft. It was too heavy for what it was, the weight of it settling into his palm like something meant to be.

In. Hold. Out

He let the feather fall, watching it settle against the dust.

Behind him, the house loomed quiet, its windows dim and shuttered. Ahead, the road stretched wide and uncertain. And in the space between, neither here nor gone, Sol stood alone beneath a sky too still, with the storm, whatever shape it would take, still on its way.

Chapter Seven

———

No Saints at the Table

A warm summer breeze drifted through the open kitchen door, carrying with it the earthy scent of freshly cut grass and sun-warmed soil. Golden sunlight poured across the worn floorboards, highlighting the scuffed edges of old chairs and catching in the curls of steam rising from a simmering pot on the stove. Porridge bubbled gently, filling the room with comforting warmth.

Sol sat quietly, allowing the gentle hum of his family's conversation to wash over him as Petra laid a warm loaf of bread on the table, arranging bowls of porridge beside neat slices of apple and wedges of cheese. Kellan took his place at the head of the table, his broad shoulders silhouetted against the glow of the morning light.

Kellan bowed his head, his familiar, husky voice steady as he brought the morning prayers to a close.

"When Elion, Keeper of the Path, lights our way, may we have the strength and courage to follow. May Elion, Keeper of the Path, guide us." Adding more reverent decree than request.

"May we stay steadfast," the family echoed softly.

Sol's breath caught, sharp and sudden, as heat surged up the back of his neck and bloomed across his cheeks. Beneath the table, he clenched his fists, knuckles pressed white against his thighs.

He didn't understand what exactly was his father expecting of him? Things had felt almost normal for days, aside from Kellan and Petra's hushed conversations and the way they always fell silent whenever Sol or the twins walked into the room.

Mira glanced up, her brow creased with concern. "You don't look so good, Sol."

Sol forced out a breath and managed a faint smile. "Just tired," he said quietly. "Didn't sleep well, that's all."

Theo lit up. "There are five frogs in Fort Hop-a-lot now!"

Kellan smiled gently. "Are you keeping their pond filled?"

"Yes, Papa! It's the best home," Theo said proudly.

Petra cut in before the plea could form. "Frogs belong in Fort Hop-a-lot," she said gently but firmly. "Not in the house."

Sol caught a brief, unreadable glance from his

father before Kellan turned back to his porridge, stirring slowly.

Petra's voice broke the silence, calm and deliberate. "We'll all be visiting the Baron's estate tomorrow for afternoon tea."

"Us too?" the twins exclaimed, wriggling with excitement.

"Yes, you two, too," Petra laughed warmly. "The Baron wishes to meet the whole family." Her eyes met Sol's directly, gentle but full of meaning, adding, "Baths for everyone tonight, and I'll be scrubbing behind your ears. We must all look our best. Bring me your temple clothes. So, I can wash them properly."

Sol felt his stomach twist. What had their humble family done to attract such interest from the Baron? The barn repairs, the sudden attention—Elion's touch, once a source of comfort and quiet guidance, now felt like a tightening grip around his chest.

The twins peppered Petra with questions faster than she could keep up. Was the Greywells' house truly enormous? Would there be sweets? Was it true that nobles wore only silk?

Kellan's voice gently interrupted, stern but not

unkind. "You must always say no twice if they offer anything. You'll stay quiet unless asked a question directly. Do you understand?"

Mira, suddenly uncertain, asked meekly, "But why, Papa?"

Kellan sighed softly, his shoulders sagging. "These are simply the rules when visiting nobles."

The twins nodded solemnly, their wide eyes reflecting a quiet, uneasy acceptance.

Sol chose his words with care, forcing down the bitterness threatening to creep into his voice. "Da, what have we done to earn such esteem?"

Kellan's expression softened slightly, but his voice held steady.

"When Elion casts his blessed light upon you, you do not ask why. You give thanks, and wait patiently for his path to be revealed."

Sol dropped his gaze, swallowing painfully against the lump in his throat. The room felt too quiet, too still, as if holding its breath alongside him.

"We are highly favored," Mira whispered reverently, eyes glistening with pure devotion.

Petra reached discreetly beneath the table, her fingers brushing lightly against Kellan's. Their hands met for only a moment, just a brief touch, but it was enough. A quiet exchange passed between them, unseen by the children, steadying them both with its familiarity and silent understanding.

Gradually, the conversation drifted back into lighter territory, the twins cautiously resuming their excited chatter. But Sol couldn't shake the way his parents kept glancing at each other — not panicked, just… braced. Like they'd already said something in silence that he hadn't been invited to hear.

As the family's conversation settled into its familiar rhythms, soft laughter, overlapping voices, and the clink of cutlery, Sol pushed away his half-eaten porridge. The food sat heavy in his stomach. He glanced toward Petra, searching her face for something unspoken, unsure whether he wanted comfort or answers.

"Ma," he said softly, catching a brief lull in the conversation, "I promised Ysella I'd help her at the inn today. She asked if I could stay for supper afterward."

Petra blinked, then offered him a steadier smile. "Of course, love. Just don't be too late getting home."

Sol stood, the scrape of his chair loud against the worn floorboards, grateful for the excuse to leave the heavy air of the kitchen behind. At the threshold, he paused and looked back. His family sat in easy conversation, their voices warm and familiar, yet they felt oddly distant, like echoes from another room. A hollow ache stirred in his chest. He shook the feeling off and stepped into the waiting sunlight, letting the warmth wash over him like a quiet reprieve.

Walking the worn path toward Ysella's, Sol felt a storm of thoughts churning in his mind. Why had their quiet lives become so entangled with nobles and unseen forces? Had they truly earned Elion's favor, or had something else taken notice? The questions spun faster with every step. Prayers that once felt like guiding stars now seemed clouded, tangled in doubt, their comfort unraveling into uncertainty.

He kicked a small stone along the dusty road, watching it skip and roll ahead.

In. Hold. Out.

The breath came without thought, rising and falling in quiet rhythm, matching the steady cadence of his footsteps, a pattern carved deep into him, instinctive and anchoring, meant for moments like this when the world felt too large to name.

With each step, the weight he carried from home began to ease as if the road itself were gently drawing it from his shoulders. The soft murmur of voices and the familiar clink of mugs floated on the breeze, mingling with the warm, inviting scent of fresh bread and spiced stew. Ysella's inn had always been more than a place to eat, it was a quiet refuge where troubles could be set aside, if only for a little while, and exchanged for the comfort of a hearty meal and the balm of shared laughter.

Sol exhaled, his shoulders loosening as the familiar, lively bustle welcomed him.

Stepping inside, Sol was greeted by the cozy din of the inn, laughter weaving through bursts of conversation, the clatter of tankards, and the comforting scent of hearth smoke and stew. Ysella spotted him almost instantly, wiping her hands on her apron as she waved him over with a grin that could melt winter frost. "There's my favorite helper!" she called, her voice bright with fondness. "And just in time, too, I've got a mountain of things that won't move themselves."

"Always," Sol replied warmly, accepting the brief, firm squeeze she gave his shoulder. "What do you need first?"

Ysella swept a damp strand of hair from her flushed face, her sleeves dusted with flour and the energy of the morning rush still clinging to her. She nodded toward the back with a tilt of her chin.

"New shipment just arrived, think you can handle stacking and sorting the crates? They're cluttering up my storeroom like lost sheep."

"Of course, Aunty. I'll get right to it." Sol quickly headed to the back room.

In the cool, dim hush of the storage room, Sol was pleasantly surprised to find Wyatt already at work, muscles straining as he eased a heavy crate onto one of the rickety wooden shelves. A mischievous grin tugged at Sol's lips. Moving with practiced stealth, he crept forward on quiet feet and, with a swift motion, covered Wyatt's eyes from behind. Wyatt spun around with a startled laugh, immediately pulling Sol into his arms and kissing him fiercely.

"Took you long enough," Wyatt teased softly, resting his forehead against Sol's. "I was beginning to think I'd finish before you even got here. I've missed you."

Sol leaned into Wyatt once more, savoring the

warmth of another soft kiss as he slipped his arms around Wyatt's neck, letting them rest there with quiet ease. "I missed you more," he murmured against Wyatt's lips, the words low and earnest. With the contact, the tight knot in his chest, the one he'd been carrying all morning, began to ease, loosening thread by thread.

A sudden low whistle sliced through the quiet, snapping their moment in two. They sprang apart, hearts racing, hands fumbling to smooth clothes and regain composure. At the doorway stood Ysella, arms crossed and grinning like a cat who'd found the cream.

"Tsk, tsk," Ysella said with a mock scold, folding her arms across her chest as her eyes danced with amusement. "I come back to offer lemonade like the generous soul I am, and what do I find? My best helpers sneaking kisses instead of stacking crates."

"I, um...we—we were just—I mean..." Sol stammered helplessly, his face turning beet red.

Ysella lifted a hand, stifling a laugh as her grin widened. "Save it, my sunshine," she said, her tone rich with affection. "I'm not here to scold—well, not just yet."

Wyatt broke first, laughter bursting from him in sharp, breathless peals as his shoulders shook. Ysella followed instantly, her warm, full-bodied laugh echoing through the storage room like sunlight through clouded glass. Sol held out a moment longer, but then he gave in, laughter spilling from him in helpless waves. The release felt good—wonderful, even—to laugh so freely again.

Ysella stepped forward and looped an affectionate arm around each boy's shoulders, drawing them in with a squeeze that was equal parts comfort and mischief. Her voice dropped to a tender murmur. "I'm truly glad you two found each other. You're good together— better, even." She gave them both a sideways glance, one brow arched in playful approval. "Now, I'll fetch that lemonade—you're clearly thirsty—but finish this work. When you're done, I'll have a nice hot meal waiting for you both."

She turned toward the door, tossing a wicked grin over her shoulder. "And no dessert before dinner!" she called, her voice dripping with mock scandal. With a gleeful cackle, she vanished down the hallway, laughter echoing behind her like a fading drumroll.

Sol and Wyatt burst into laughter once more, their voices rising in unison, bright and unguarded. The joy of the moment swept through them like sunlight breaking through storm clouds, scattering the last traces of tension into nothingness.

They slipped into their familiar rhythm with ease, moving around each other in a quiet, practiced dance as they worked, restoring order to the cluttered storage room. The air was thick with the scent of aged wood and the dusty traces of seasons long gone, underscored by the faint hum of laughter drifting in from the dining hall.

"So," Wyatt began casually, glancing sideways at Sol as he lifted a heavy crate onto the shelf, "how was breakfast? You've seemed a little distracted."

Sol hesitated, stacking a sack of grain with deliberate care as he searched for the right words. "Baron Greywell's asked to see us tomorrow," he said slowly. "The whole family."

Wyatt paused mid-motion, brow furrowing slightly as he turned fully to face Sol. "Why the sudden invitation?"

Sol shook his head, his voice barely above a whisper. "I don't know. Da says we're favored, but it doesn't feel right. First, the ladies show up unannounced—Elora, of all people. Then the Baron sends men to fix our barn, and now we're invited to tea? It's too much, too fast."

He exhaled hard, frustration tightening his throat.

"Something's off."

Wyatt rested a steady hand on Sol's shoulder, his

touch warm and grounding. "Maybe it's just some kind of honor," he said gently. "You know how nobles are, always sticking their noses in places they don't belong."

Sol met Wyatt's warm gaze, managing a faint smile, though doubt still lingered in his eyes. "I hope you're right."

They continued working in companionable silence until, at last, Sol finished sweeping the now spotless storage room. He stepped back, broom in hand, and studied the rickety shelves with a thoughtful frown, and his brow furrowed in quiet concern. "We should fix those shelves soon, I don't know how long they'll stay standing."

Wyatt leaned playfully against the doorway, a teasing grin spreading across his face. "Trying to impress Ysella?"

Sol laughed softly, a genuine warmth rising in his chest as a flush crept up his cheeks. "Maybe," he admitted, a small smile tugging at his lips. "She's always been kind to me."

Wyatt nodded, his smile fading into something quieter, more sincere. "Aye, I owe her more than I'll ever be able to repay." His gaze lingered on Sol, affection unmistakable in his eyes. After a comfortable pause, he let out a theatrical sigh and stretched his arms overhead. "I'm starving, let's get cleaned up."

As Sol moved to pass, Wyatt gently caught his wrist and pulled him close. He leaned in, slow and sure, pressing a soft, lingering kiss to Sol's lips. Sol melted into it, the warmth blooming in his chest, chasing away the last of his doubts.

"I'm glad we found each other, too," Wyatt murmured, his voice barely above a whisper, fingers brushing tenderly along Sol's cheek.

The quiet intensity in Wyatt's gaze sent a comforting shiver down Sol's spine. Sol returned the look with a soft smile, the heaviness in his chest lifting at last. Wyatt gave his hand a gentle squeeze and led him into the fading afternoon light toward the wash basin.

Outside, cool water splashed over their hands, washing away dust and worry alike. The air was softer as evening approached, carrying birdsong's distant, soothing call. Sol glanced at Wyatt, who met his eyes and offered an easy, reassuring smile. For a moment, standing together beneath the vast, tranquil sky, Sol allowed himself to truly breathe, each inhale grounding him, steadied by Wyatt's quiet presence.

A small table had been set off to the side, two chairs waiting like an invitation. Ysella approached with two generous bowls of stew and a basket of warm bread, the scent rich and comforting. She paused, eyeing them both with playful suspicion.

"Did the storeroom survive you two?"

"Better than survive," Sol said, smiling for real. "We even swept and carried the crates out."

Ysella chuckled warmly as she set the bowls down, the aroma of stew curling into the air. "Good lads," she said with fondness, giving Sol's shoulder a gentle squeeze. "Eat up, you've more than earned it."

As they began to eat, Sol noticed a subtle change in the inn's atmosphere. Conversations dipped into hushed murmurs, villagers leaning in, their voices low and eyes darting toward the door or each other with cautious glances.

Before Sol could wonder further, Scy appeared beside them, dragging over a chair and balancing a plate of roast pork precariously on top of his mug of mead. "This looks like a cozy spot, hope I'm not crashing the party," he said with a grin before pulling Wyatt into a playful headlock and tousling his already messy hair.

Wyatt laughed, struggling to break free. "Fine, yes, please join us, Scy!" Once released, he tried fruitlessly to smooth his tousled hair.

"That's better," Scy teased, stuffing pork into his mouth. "Don't worry, Wyatt, you're still dashing. Although your hair was already begging for table scraps."

Wyatt shook his head, chuckling softly, then leaned forward, his voice growing serious. "What's got everyone whispering tonight, Scy?"

Scy paused, his gaze sweeping the tavern with a quick, wary glance before he leaned in, lowering his voice.

"Word out of Briarstead, rumor has it the Baron's planning to outlaw the worship of any gods but Elion."

Sol coughed sharply, nearly choking on his stew. He forced down the mouthful, eyes wide as he struggled to find his voice.

"He can't do that, can he?"

Ysella had stepped closer without anyone noticing, her presence quiet but steady. She let out a weary sigh, the kind born of long days and longer memories. After a glance around the room, making sure no one unfamiliar was within earshot, she lowered her voice and said quietly,

"He's a Baron — there's plenty he can do. And some folks are saying he plans to raze the old shrine to Beryth outside town."

Wyatt's voice dropped, edged with disbelief.

"Raze the shrine? People won't stand for that."

"Maybe not openly," Ysella murmured, her voice barely above a whisper. "But people are frightened. After the bandits struck the trade road again last week and killed two men hauling grain, there's been talk. Loud talk. Folk says we've strayed too far from Elion, that the attacks are punishment for our divided faith."

Sol's appetite vanished. The stew turned to paste in his mouth, its warmth drained to ash. He gripped his spoon tightly, knuckles pale, as a knot twisted deep in his gut. All his life, he'd believed that faith and devotion were enough—that they meant something. But now? The thought of that being stripped away, of the land itself being made to forget, was like a shadow settling over his soul.

He looked up at Ysella, needing something solid.

"What about you? Do you think it's true?"

She hesitated, a flicker of pain in her eyes.

"I don't know, lad. But even if it's talk, the Baron's

influence is growing. And wherever he steps, Drevan and his followers are right behind him."

Scy scoffed, leaning back with a grimace.

"I don't like it. That wolf in sheep's robes—the Hand will stop at nothing to swell his flock. And the Baron? Just another blind lamb being led to the slaughter."

Ysella shot him a sharp look and elbowed him gently.

"No offense to your faith, Sol. Some good people follow the Keeper — your folks included."

Scy shrugged, voice dropping to a hush. "Still... you hear things. Folks in Market Hill say Drevan doesn't sleep anymore—just paces the temple halls at night, whispering to something that never answers."

Sol blinked, unsettled.

"That's just gossip." Scy didn't argue. He leaned back again and muttered, "Gossip's got teeth, sometimes."

"Maybe," Ysella murmured, her voice sinking even lower. "But I trust rumors more than I trust that man." She placed a warm, grounding hand over Sol's, her gaze steady.

"I didn't mean to spoil your evening, love."

"No," Sol replied softly, forcing a faint, grateful

smile.

"Better to know."

Wyatt's hand came to rest on Sol's shoulder, steady and warm. "We'll figure this out — no matter what happens."

Sol nodded, drawing comfort from Wyatt's quiet certainty. They turned back to their meal, their conversation low and tentative, reaching for some semblance of normalcy. But the unease remained, thin as smoke, clinging to the edges of their thoughts, refusing to dissipate.

As they finished eating, the inn slowly reclaimed its usual, comforting rhythm, the clink of cutlery, the low murmur of voices, but hushed whispers still lingered in the corners, like shadows unwilling to retreat.

Sol set down his spoon, the movement slow.

"It's getting late. I should head home."

Sol hesitated, his eyes drifting toward the shadowed road just beyond the doorway. The unease in his posture didn't go unnoticed.

Before he could voice a single thought, Wyatt reached out and touched his arm, a silent gesture of reassurance, steady and sure.

"I'll walk you," he said gently, a smile pulling at the corner of his mouth. "You shouldn't have to face the dark alone."

Sol let out a quiet breath, a wave of relief loosening the tightness in his chest. "Thank you," he murmured, the simple words carrying a weight of emotion that reached far beyond mere gratitude for the company.

They rose from the table in quiet unison, Wyatt's hand resting gently at the small of Sol's back as he guided him toward the door. With soft nods of farewell to Ysella and Scy, who returned their goodnights with warm smiles, they stepped out into the hush of the moonlit evening, the air cool and crisp against their skin.

Sol glanced up at the stars, breathing deeply. Beside him, Wyatt matched his pace, steady and calm. Despite everything they'd heard tonight. Sol felt profoundly grateful to have Wyatt by his side, grounding, comforting, and reminding him he wasn't alone.

The sounds of the inn fell away behind them as they stepped into the quiet night. Overhead, the stars stretched across the sky in a dazzling sprawl, brilliant and sharp against the velvet dark. They walked in easy silence toward Sol's house, their footsteps muffled by the soft dirt path, the cool night air gently easing the weight left by the evening's conversation.

At the edge of the pasture, Wyatt slowed his steps, then gently nudged Sol's shoulder. With a small, knowing smile, he tilted his chin upward, directing Sol's gaze toward the stars that shimmered above them like scattered silver.

"See that cluster there? Looks like a crooked bird?"

Sol squinted. "That's… barely a bird."

"That's Filch's Constellation," Wyatt grinned. "Greatest thief that ever lived. Want to hear how he stole godhood?"

Sol exhaled through his nose. "I don't think I have a choice."

"Correct."

Wyatt stretched, letting the hush of night settle around them like a blanket.

"Kieroth wasn't born a god," he said quietly. "He was just a man with a silver tongue and no sense of limits. A liar so smooth he could convince a lock to open itself. And one day, that wasn't enough. He decided he deserved a seat among the gods, and so he set out to steal it."

"And because he was Kieroth… he did."

"He snuck into the heavens, dodged celestial guards, and crashed a feast meant only for the divine. He ate their fruit, drank their nectar, gave bad advice on love, and no one questioned him — because he walked in like he belonged."

"All night, he blended in. Until Saelreth, the God of Order, narrowed his eyes and asked, 'Wait… who invited him?'"

"At that moment, Kieroth might've not talked his way out — except his very unreliable magpie, Filch, was busy stealing everything not nailed down."

The Moon Goddess's favorite ring dropped into a wishing well, much to Liraeth's eternal displeasure.

A handful of stars—returned after someone realized they were actually hot.

The Book of Divine Laws, complete with annotations, marginal doodles, and a definitive list of who actually counts as a god. "So, when they demanded proof Kieroth didn't belong…"

Wyatt shrugged.

"There wasn't any. Because Filch ate it."

"Well, most of it. He left the pages about divine poultry law. Which helped no one."

"And just like that, the gods had to let Kieroth stay. He tricked them not with lies but by making the truth too inconvenient to find."

"They threw Filch into the stars for the trouble. That's why he looks crooked."

Sol stared up at the faint, crooked shape in the sky. His lips twitched.

"That's absurd."

Wyatt stretched lazily. "It is. But wouldn't it be the greatest trick ever played?"

Sol exhaled, still smiling. "Maybe."

Above them, Filch's stars twinkled knowingly.

They walked in easy silence, the night air cool against their skin, carrying the scent of grass and distant hearthfire. The path ahead stretched pale and silver under the moonlight while the gentle chorus of crickets filled the hush between their steps.

When they reached the fork where Wyatt would turn back, he slowed to a stop, his gaze drifting toward Sol with a quiet weight behind it.

"You sure you don't want me to walk you the rest of the way?"

Sol shook his head, offering a small, tired smile. "I'm fine. It's not far."

Wyatt studied Sol's face for a long moment, his eyes searching for something unspoken. Then he exhaled softly through his nose, the sound threaded with reluctance as if releasing the night one breath at a time. "Alright," he murmured, voice low. "But don't go disappearing into that head of yours on the way home."

Sol huffed a quiet laugh. "No promises."

Wyatt stepped closer, hesitating only briefly before reaching out. He brushed his fingers along Sol's wrist before lacing them together and giving a gentle squeeze. Whatever happens tomorrow," he said softly, "you don't have to face it alone."

His thumb brushed lightly against Sol's knuckles before letting go as if reluctant to lose the touch completely. "I mean it."

Sol swallowed hard, a quiet breath catching in his throat as warmth pooled in his chest, tender and aching all at once, like the echo of something precious he didn't yet know how to name.

"I know," he said, and he truly believed it.

Wyatt leaned in and pressed a kiss to Sol's temple, brief, lingering, and filled with the kind of quiet understanding that needed no words. He held Sol's hand a moment longer, as if reluctant to break the connection, then gave it a gentle squeeze before turning away, his steps slow as he headed down his own path home.

Sol watched Wyatt disappear into the shadows, his figure swallowed gradually by the quiet night. Only when the path was empty did Sol turn toward his own house, releasing a long, steady breath. The stillness felt heavier now, but he walked on, each step a quiet act of resolve.

He let the stillness settle, but the day's weight pressed heavier now that he walked alone. The warmth of Wyatt's hand lingered, even as the night pressed in around him. But ahead, past the road home, loomed the Greywells' estate, waiting.

Above him, Filch's stars winked in crooked silence. He wasn't sure if it was a comfort or a warning.

Chapter Eight

———

Echoes of the Lost

Sol stood still, eyes fixed on the winding road ahead, where the summer sun retreated behind a veil of thick, bruised grey clouds. Far off, a carriage surged forward, its wheels carving through the dry earth, sending up a storm of dust that curled and danced in its wake. The rumble of its approach thudded faintly through the ground, growing louder with each turn of the wheels on the narrow dirt path.

"Ma!" Sol called into the house. "The carriage is up the road."

His reflection shimmered in the windowpane, suspended between light and shadow like a ghost lingering at the threshold. For a heartbeat, he met his own eyes, his lips drawn into a thin, unreadable line. Then, with a breath too quiet to be called a sigh, he turned and stepped inside just before the rising dust cloud brushed the doorway.

Outside, the carriage screeched to an abrupt halt, its wheels skidding over loose gravel with a harsh grind that broke the hush of the afternoon. The door swung open a beat later, and a tall, impeccably dressed footman descended with the kind of fluid precision that spoke of long-rehearsed grace. His face was strikingly handsome in a way that belonged in a noble house, not on a quiet farm road. He swept into a deep bow, posture crisp and rehearsed.

"I trust I'm not intruding," the man said, his voice smooth as polished glass yet cool with detachment. "I've been sent to escort the Ardens to my master's estate, the Baron awaits."

Sol rolled his eyes before he could stop himself. What a farce.

The footman caught the gesture, his gaze flicking over Sol with a polished sort of scrutiny, polite but assessing. Sol quickly smoothed his expression into something closer to indifferent, the practiced mask of someone used to watching rather than speaking.

"Thank you," he said stiffly. "Please allow us a moment to prepare."

The footman merely inclined his head and stepped back, moving with the quiet composure of someone long practiced in the art of waiting.

Behind him, the house stirred to life, fabric whispering, boots scuffing over wooden floors, and the soft clatter of last-minute adjustments echoing through the hall. Sol turned just in time to catch Kellan fussing over Theo's tunic, fingers battling an unruly curl that refused to stay flat. A pace behind, Petra stood with her hands clasped, her expression composed with deliberate care.

"Theo, Mira," she said evenly, "remember what we talked about. I don't want any trouble."

"Yes, Mama," the twins chorused, though their wide eyes sparkled with restless energy.

Kellan pressed a kiss to Petra's forehead, a rare offering of tenderness that passed like a shadow. "Come now, Mother," he murmured. "They will do us proud."

It wasn't reassurance. It was a command.

The road blurred past, flanked by miles of struggling fields stretched beneath a restless, brooding sky. The Ardens were not alone in their hardship. The unnatural storms had carved their scars into every farm along the way, crops left to wither under too much rain and too little sun.

I wonder who else has earned Elion's favor, Sol thought, bitterness curling sharp and quiet beneath the surface as he watched the wasted landslide past.

The twins, blissfully unaware of the weight bearing

down on the adults, chattered with bright enthusiasm, their energy a fragile shield against the thickening silence. Their wide-eyed wonder at the changing scenery, fields giving way to clipped hedgerows, then to looming iron gates, kept Petra from wringing her hands and stayed the deepening line in Kellan's brow.

Even Sol, lost in his own brooding, found himself drawn out by their boundless excitement.

But then, as the Greywell estate emerged on the horizon, the twins fell silent.

The gardens were impossibly pristine, rows of roses sculpted into careful arches, fountains spilling crystal-clear water into stone basins. Beyond them, the manor rose like a fortress. Its many chimneys reached toward the sky, its pale stone façade unyielding, watchful.

Inside the carriage, Kellan's voice dropped to a low murmur.

"Sol, this meeting is important."

Sol turned to face him, locking eyes with his father's steady, unreadable gaze.

"The Baron can raise us or ruin us," Kellan said, each word measured and heavy. "Save your dreaming for the fields."

Sol swallowed hard against the blade of his father's tone. There was no room left for argument.

Their eyes locked for a moment, long enough for Sol to feel the full weight of his father's faith, fear, and expectations pressing down on him like a stone laid across the chest. Heavy. Unyielding.

Impossible to ignore.

"Yes, Da. Of course."

Kellan exhaled, then bowed his head. "Elion the Keeper, guide our path."

"May we stay steadfast," they all murmured in unison.

The carriage began to slow, the wheels crunching over the gravel drive in a steady rhythm that echoed through the hush. The moment they came to a stop, two finely dressed attendants stepped forward without hesitation, opening the doors with the smooth, efficient grace of a long-rehearsed routine.

Inside the manor, the world shifted.

The Ardens were led through towering wooden doors, their surfaces dark with age and heavy with carved sigils of Elion. The symbols spiraled in intricate patterns across the oak, sacred prayers etched so deeply into the grain they seemed meant to outlast time itself.

Sol's boots echoed sharply against the marble floor, each step swallowed by the hush that clung to the air, thick with incense, beeswax polish, and something older. High above, vaulted ceilings arched like the ribs of some great, slumbering beast, while golden light filtered through tall, arched windows, casting shifting patterns across the stone beneath his feet.

And then, the receiving hall—

A room filled with opulence unlike anything Sol had ever seen.

Rich reds and golds draped the furniture in regal layers, their textures catching the light like fire. Heavy curtains, thick as cloaks, pooled against the polished floors in silent folds. At the far wall hung a great tapestry depicting Elion's sacred path, its intricate threads of silver embroidery shimmering with every breath of air.

It was beautiful and powerful. It was meant to impress, to humble.

Sol forced his shoulders back, forced his face into something unreadable.

Whatever came next, he would not shrink beneath

it.

The twins stood locked at Sol's sides, their usual energy smothered into an uneasy, unnatural meekness. Even Mira, who could never resist a question, not even in the most serious moments, remained silent, lips pressed into a thin line. They felt it too, the weight in the air, thick and unspoken, pressing down like a held breath.

Kellan stepped forward, his posture squared, as if sheer presence alone might shield his family from whatever lay ahead. Behind him, the Ardens stood frozen, wide-eyed, and rigid, like deer poised to bolt, suspended in that fragile breath between fight or flight. Then, the doors at the back of the room swung open.

A small, wiry man entered first, his plain robes unadorned, marking him clearly as a servant or steward. He moved with quiet precision, stepping to the side with practiced deference, head bowed low as he made way for the man who followed.

Baron Mathren Greywell.

His presence filled the space before he even spoke, though it wasn't his height or his build that commanded it, it was the stillness, the way the room seemed to shift to accommodate him.

The Greywell ladies entered a moment later, and their footsteps hushed as they stepped into the golden light spilling through the high windows. The sunlight caught on Lady Alina's gown, the fabric rippling as she moved, shimmering like water in motion, lending her an ethereal, almost angelic presence.

Sol gritted his teeth.

"Won't you please sit?" Baron Greywell gestured to the finely upholstered chairs arranged before him.

Lady Greywell, however, had no patience for formalities. With the kind of effortless grace that needed no announcement, she swept past her husband without so much as a glance and made her way directly to Petra, her focus sharp, her stride unerring.

"Oh, how wonderful to see you," she cooed, her voice sweet as spun sugar, taking both of Petra's hands in hers. She leaned in, lips brushing each of Petra's cheeks in turn, a gesture that shimmered with charm but rang hollow, more performance than genuine warmth.

"Please, make yourselves comfortable."

"Thank you for your generosity," Petra replied modestly, inclining her head in respect.

Sol remained standing, the weight of the room

settling over him like a second skin, every gaze a quiet pressure against his back. He was just about to move toward his seat when Alina's voice rose, clear, composed, and unmistakably intentional.

"Soltic," she said, with a hint of invitation curled into the formality, "I'd like to show you the estate if that's agreeable?"

For half a heartbeat, he hesitated, caught between the weight of every eye in the room and the smooth command beneath her question.

Excluded. Again. The word struck like a bruise already forming.

His jaw tightened, but he forced the tension from his shoulders before giving a formal bow.

"It would be my honor, Lady Alina."

The words felt hollow, a formal courtesy stretched too thin, but he knew better than to refuse.

Without waiting, Alina turned and led Sol back through the same grand doors they had entered, her steps measured and unhurried, every movement precise. Behind them, the conversation in the hall softened, unraveling into distant murmurs like a tide pulling back.

"Apologies for pulling you away, Soltic," Alina said, dry amusement coloring her voice. "This was my mother's idea. 'Be agreeable, Alina.'" She mimicked the phrase with a long-suffering sigh.

Sol raised an eyebrow. "Agreeable?"

Her lips twitched — not quite a smile.

"I won't pretend to know my mother's mind… but it feels like something else is in motion."

They turned into an inner courtyard, where the low burble of an ornate fountain filled the air with a gentle, rhythmic hush. Carved stone archways lined the walls, their weathered edges softened by creeping vines and clusters of pale blooms. It was quiet here, secluded, cloistered, a space tucked deliberately away from prying ears.

Alina sat on the fountain's edge and motioned for Sol to join her.

"We can speak freely here. This part of the estate is away from the main hall — only family comes here."

Sol sank into the seat with quiet relief. It was rare, these days, to feel even a flicker of ease.

"What have you heard?" he asked, his voice low, edged with suspicion that hadn't yet hardened into accusation.

Alina hesitated, the silence stretching between them like a held breath.

"Not as much as I'd like. My mother has been… quiet lately."

She exhaled softly, lowering her gaze to the hem of her sleeve, her fingers brushing the delicate fabric with the absent-minded care of someone retreating inward.

"I do know the recent murder of a farmer has everyone on edge."

Sol's posture stiffened.

"Who was murdered? When?"

"A day or two ago. I don't know their name."

Her voice was careful. Almost apologetic.

Of course, she doesn't know, Sol thought, bitterness curling through the words like smoke.

Just another poor farmer. Another nameless loss in a ledger no one reads.

"There are rumors," Alina added cautiously, "that the attacks are growing more… selective. Not random, like they once were." She hesitated. "But I'm sure it's just talk."

Sol's heart beat faster.

"That makes eleven attacks in less than a month." He shook his head, frustration simmering just beneath his words.

"They're only getting worse."

Alina nodded. "Aye, they are."

She looked toward the vine-covered archways before speaking again.

"High Priest Drevan says they're punishment for the village's… indiscretions."

Sol's breath caught.

"Is it true," he asked carefully, the words measured like stones across the water, "that your father plans to raze the old gods' shrines?"

Alina exhaled through her nose.

"Let's just say the servants have been whispering carefully," Alina replied, her voice quiet but steady. "I trust a few, but none have heard it from my father's mouth."

Sol's jaw tightened, a flicker of frustration passing over his face before he turned away, eyes narrowing on the far wall.

"That's not right," he said, voice low. "The farmers

have every right to worship as they please—"

Alina's expression gave nothing away, smooth and unreadable, but her voice softened, calm and deliberate, like someone choosing every word with care in a room full of listening walls.

"I never said I agreed with him."

Sol exhaled sharply, raking a hand through his hair. "My apologies, Lady Alina. It's just… disheartening."

She isn't my enemy.

Her features eased.

"Just Alina, when we're alone. Please."

Sol blinked.

"It's refreshing," she said, tilting her head slightly, a trace of amusement in her eyes, "not having to put on airs with you."

A slight grin tugged at his lips, reluctant but real.

"Sol. Not Soltic."

She raised a brow.

"My parents only call me Soltic when I'm in

trouble," he said, a quiet laugh escaping him. "Well… and Elora."

At the name, Alina made the sign against evil, her lips twitching in a smile she tried, and failed, to suppress.

"Well then, Sol," Alina said, one brow lifting with mock innocence, "Elora tells me you spend quite a bit of time at the inn.

Don't you have enough work waiting for you on the farm?"

Sol smirked.

"We've had a bit more free time lately… courtesy of your father's help."

He let the grin linger a moment before finally admitting,

"And… it gives me an excuse to see Wyatt."

"Wyatt?" Alina's voice was soft, touched with something like concern.

"The Thornbrook boy? The shepherd?"

Sol couldn't help but smile.

"Yes. Wyatt Thornbrook."

The name itself felt like a kind of warmth.

"His aunt Ysella runs the inn. Only she and Scy

truly understand how deeply our feelings run."

Just saying his name settled something in Sol's chest like breath finally drawn to its full depth, steady and sure after a long time held.

He tilted his face toward the sky, letting the golden light wash over him like something half-remembered.

Wyatt appeared in the quiet behind Sol's eyes, not summoned but simply there, like sunlight slipping through a cracked door.

His easy smile. The way light always seemed to find his hair. That quiet, anchoring steadiness Sol clung to whenever the world began to tilt.

Wyatt didn't fill the silence, and he made space within it. And that space felt like breath, like stillness without weight.

Alina said nothing. Her expression remained unreadable, carved from something softer than stone but just as closed.

"Sol," she asked gently, "who knows about your feelings for Wyatt?"

Still wrapped in memory, he barely registered the shift in her tone.

"Not many," he admitted with a dreamy sigh.

"It's not a secret. We just haven't told my family yet. But Wyatt and I… we've never hidden it."

Alina exhaled, slow, deliberate. Then, without a word, she reached out and rested a light hand on his lap, perhaps to ground him… or maybe to steady herself. Sol couldn't tell.

But he barely felt it. His thoughts were still with Wyatt, distant and quiet, like a name half-whispered in a dream.

"He's handsome and strong," Sol said quietly, then paused, searching for the right weight to give the truth.

"But that's not why I love him. It's the way he listens. The way he stays steady when everything else feels like it's falling apart."

He exhaled slowly as if just naming it, saying it aloud, brought some of that steadiness back into his chest, quiet and anchoring. "With him, I don't have to explain who I am. I can just… be." A soft smile played on his lips as the memory unfolded.

"I remember when we first truly got to know each other," he murmured.

"I had just returned from visiting my uncle and aunt in Nazareth after little Calla was born. I already knew him, of course, everyone in the village knows Wyatt, but that night, crossing the pastures, I stumbled upon his campfire glowing in the dark like it had been waiting for me."

His gaze turned inward, lost in the glow of something sacred.

"I asked if I could share the warmth."

The words were simple, but their weight held so much more.

"We talked all night. We had more in common than either of us expected. And now… it's been three years, and I can't imagine him not in my life."

His voice trailed off, thick with love, the kind that doesn't blaze like fire but holds steady like earth, quiet and enduring beneath everything else.

Alina sat very still. When she finally spoke, her voice was careful, low with something unspoken. "Sol…" She paused, the silence stretching, her next words chosen like steps through fragile glass.

"Do you know what Elion teaches about love like yours?"

Sol blinked, finally pulled from his thoughts. His gaze drifted down to meet hers, confusion flickering across his face.

"Love," he said, as if the answer was obvious, "is what Elion wishes for all his children."

"As a river must flow to the sea, and a tree must bear fruit, so too must love follow the path set forth by the Keeper."

Alina's voice was quiet, almost reverent, the words spoken from memory, not belief. She kept her gaze lowered, not meeting Sol's eyes.

"That which does not serve His will is a corruption, a twisting of what was meant to be whole. It shall be cut away, lest it rots the branch."

The silence that followed thickened, pressing in like a weight on his chest.

Sol was on his feet before he even realized he'd moved, the surge in him sudden, like breath breaking the surface.

"Our love is not corrupt," he snapped. "We can care for our family, work the land better than most—"

His mind was racing, grasping for logic, for

something to prove her wrong.

"Sol…" Alina started her tone carefully measured.

But he wasn't listening.

"Lady Alina," he said, his voice quick, edged with urgency. "Wyatt and I can serve the Keeper. We are faithful. That hasn't changed."

Alina exhaled slowly, her head shaking once. "I'm only telling you what is taught," she said quietly, almost apologetically.

"Love is beautiful, but the devout will not look kindly on this." Sol felt dizzy like the ground was shifting beneath him.

"My parents will love me no matter what," he said, the words defiant but hopeful. "They love Wyatt, surely they'll accept us."

Alina paused, her silence stretching into something heavy. When she finally spoke, it was with the weight of something deeply personal, something carried for a long time.

"I have no doubt they love you, but…" she swallowed, "if they wish to remain in the Keeper's favor, they will follow His will."

Her voice grew even softer. "I had an uncle who loved a man."

Sol's chest tightened.

Alina inhaled slowly, steadying herself.

"His name was Alaric. He was Baron then — the title was his."

"There were... tensions in the house when it became known." She looked away, her voice low.

"I cannot prove what happened, but his lover was murdered before his eyes."

Sol's breath caught.

"My Uncle leapt from the estate's tower observatory that night."

"My father assumed the barony shortly after his death was announced."

The silence that followed was thick, stretching between them like something fragile and unspeakable.

Sol's eyes burned. The weight of her words settled in his chest like lead, cold and unmoving.

"Alina..." his voice cracked. "Why are you telling me this?"

She reached out, fingers cool but steady, and placed a hand over his.

"Because you are my friend. And I want you to be safe."

Sol clenched his jaw, his hands curling into fists at his sides.

"Do you think your uncle was bad? That he deserved to be 'cut-away' like rot?"

Alina flinched, her shoulders tightening as a flicker of hurt crossed her face and vanished.

"How could you think that of me, Sol?"

The guilt came swiftly, sharp, and undeniable. He hated how easily his hurt twisted into accusation, how reflexively he reached for blame when all he wanted was understanding.

"This is just… hard to take in." His voice was quiet now, defeated.

Alina watched him carefully, her expression unreadable, as if weighing something unspoken. Then, without a word, she rose with quiet purpose and motioned for him to follow.

"To show you my heart, I need to show you

something."

Sol nodded, numb, his mind racing.

He followed her into the depths of the estate, each step echoing with the uneasy sense that he might never see the world quite the same again.

They walked in silence too heavy to be called peaceful, the weight of unspoken truths pressing between them like walls.

Sol's mind still reeled from their conversation in the courtyard, the doctrine, the warning, the quiet threat braided into Alina's careful words. His breath stayed shallow, his thoughts running in tight, anxious circles.

When Alina finally stopped, they stood before a large door, its presence looming with the promise of something more.

She glanced down the hallway, checking for watchful eyes before guiding him inside.

It was her chambers.

Soft pastels bathed the room in gentle light, spilling across the walls like a whisper of spring — a strange, almost jarring contrast to the cold still clinging to Sol's chest. The warmth in the room felt borrowed, distant, as though it hadn't been meant for him.

The walls were refined and elegant, but his eyes caught immediately on the mural stretching across one side of the chamber:

A ship with unfurled sails, Elion's sigils emblazoned in gold across the canvas, dominated the wall like a silent decree.

Sol exhaled sharply. The mark of the faith turned his stomach, coiling in his gut like a knot. Behind him, Alina barred the door, her movements quick, purposeful, as if to keep something out. Or in.

Without hesitation, she crossed the room to her wardrobe, slipping a slender key from seemingly nowhere.

Sol watched as she stepped onto her dressing table, hands steady as she unlocked a narrow, hidden door near the top of the wall.

With practiced ease, she reached inside and drew out a stack of wellworn books, their bindings softened and frayed with age. She held them close as if afraid the light might harm them — or the world might see.

She climbed down with practiced care, then crossed the room toward the bed.

Sol hesitated before following, heart thudding

beneath his ribs like a warning drum.

She laid the books before him, her quiet treasures unfurled across the plush blankets, fragile as memory.

For a long moment, neither of them spoke. The silence pressed in, thick with meaning.

Sol inhaled sharply, the weight of it settling behind his ribs. He knew this wasn't just hidden knowledge, and it was a secret too dangerous to name, one she could never afford to be uncovered.

"This is what I wanted to show you," she said softly.

Sol swallowed hard. His fingers twitched at his sides as if his body already understood what his mind wasn't yet willing to accept.

He sat down slowly, eyes drifting across the covers.

Some of the books looked innocuous, worn records of history, dusty treaties, but others… others pulsed with danger. Heresy dressed as scholarship. A blade turned inward, aimed at the very heart of the faith.

The Wars of the Valley Kings.

The Crooked Path: A Study of Lost Faiths.

The Mirror and the Flame.

Then his gaze landed on a title that made his breath hitch.

The Lies of the Keeper.

Sol's stomach dropped, a cold, twisting sensation settling deep in his gut.

His hand hovered above the book, fingers outstretched but trembling. He didn't touch it. Couldn't.

Across from him, Alina let out a quiet sigh, but she didn't flinch. She simply waited, still and steady.

"I don't deny the Keeper's place, Sol. I only seek to understand."

Sol tore his gaze from the books, his chest tightening. "Why?"

She met his eyes, steady but laced with caution. "Because the world is wider than one god," she said softly, each word deliberate.

Sol shook his head, heat rising up his neck and flooding his face. "This is heresy." His voice cracked with disbelief.

Alina's lips pressed into a thin line, but her voice held. "Only if one refuses to believe there is room for more than one truth."

That stopped him.

She watched him closely, her gaze unwavering. "I follow the Keeper, Sol. I always have," she said, her voice steady with conviction. "But I do not believe he is the only light that ever burned."

Sol's jaw tightened, his breathing shallow, as if her words had knocked the wind from his chest.

His eyes drifted across the spread of books once more, aged bindings, cracked spines, ink-heavy titles steeped in rebellion. But something smaller, half-tucked at the edge, pulled at his attention.

A slender volume, its cover is worn soft by time and touch.

Unlike the others, it didn't bristle with doctrine or cry out in defiance.

It simply… waited.

The Longing Letters.

Sol tilted his head, his fingers brushing the worn spine.

"This doesn't seem like the others."

Alina stilled.

For the first time since bringing him here, her

expression wavered, something tender breaking through the practiced composure.

She reached for the book, fingertips brushing the faded gold lettering as though afraid to press too hard.

When she spoke, her voice was low, measured.

"It belonged to my uncle."
Sol frowned.

"The one who—"

"Yes."

Her voice didn't break, but it folded in on itself, quiet and close, like something wrapped in memory.

She hesitated before opening the book, her fingers trembling slightly as she flipped through the fragile pages.

Sol caught glimpses of delicate, aching lines, poetry threaded with longing, with grief, with love too carefully hidden to name aloud. "He didn't write it," Alina murmured.

"But he returned to it often. I think it made him feel less alone."

She shut it gently, her fingers resting on the cover a moment longer.

"I keep it because I don't want to forget him."

Sol didn't know what to say.

For all the knowledge she'd entrusted him with tonight, this felt like the most fragile secret of all, something sacred and sorrowful, cradled in silence for years.

Alina finally closed the book with gentle finality, her fingers lingering for a moment on the worn cover before she rose to her feet.

"Come. There's more I need to show you."

Sol hesitated, then followed — but his gaze lingered on the book.

The Longing Letters.

The title trailed after him like a half-remembered dream.

Chapter Nine

A Razor's Edge

Sol drew his cloak tighter around his shoulders, though the sun hung bright overhead. A sharp, unnatural chill crept up his spine, prickling beneath his skin. The air felt wrong, too still, too quiet. No breeze stirred the trees. No birds called from the branches. Only the dry crunch of gravel beneath his boots marked his passage.

A single feather drifted lazily across his path, turning slowly in the still air.

Sol frowned and glanced upward. Nothing, no wings, no shadows, not even the distant caw of a bird. Just sky. Empty and silent.

Sol bent to pick it up. The feather was heavier than it should have been, its weight strange in his hand. His fingers brushed along the stiff rib, dark brown, almost black, the texture unsettlingly familiar, like something half-remembered from a dream or an old story. The instant his gaze flicked back to the path—

The ground was gone.

The wind tore at his clothes, cold and wild, as the

world blurred beneath him in a dizzying sweep. His breath caught, not in fear, but in something raw, electric, and impossibly alive.

He was flying.

For a heartbeat, thought vanished, no past, no future, only the rush of air and the sky beneath his skin.

No weight dragging him back. Just endless sky.

No breath catching in his ribs like it so often did when the world felt too close.

The sky held him.

A laugh—his own—escaped before he could stop it.

It felt impossible. It felt right.

Fields unfolded beneath him in waves of green and gold, soft and endless. Even from this height, the storm's damage was evident, drowned patches of crop, fences splintered and sun-bleached. But the land still breathed. It would hold. They would survive the winter. That much, he knew with quiet certainty.

Then, the old pond, he skimmed low over the water, the surface rippling beneath him.

He turned toward the village.

That's when he saw it.

A thin coil of smoke, rising dark and slow against the clear morning sky. Not from a single chimney. Not from cooking fires.

Thick, black plumes rose into the sky.

His heart slammed against his ribs.

No.

Not the village.

He flew harder, the wind screaming in his ears, tearing at his cloak as panic surged in his chest. He had to reach Wyatt and Ysella. They had to be safe.

But as he neared the outskirts of the village, the smoke thickened, choking, blinding. The world blurred into gray. Then, through the haze, the fire revealed itself, sharp tongues of flame cutting through the fog like knives of light.

Hettie and Rein's shop—gone, engulfed in fire.

The blacksmith's forge—billowing smoke from every window.

The herbalist's hut—burning from the inside out.

Sol's stomach twisted into a knot. *Where were the*

villagers?

He dove toward the inn, his last, desperate hope, heart pounding like a drumbeat in his ears. But before he reached it, something strange caught his eye.

Elora's shop.

It stood untouched amid the chaos, pristine and whole, as if the flames had simply passed it by.

Not just untouched, it looked larger than before, impossibly
so. The wooden sign above the door gleamed as if freshly varnished, catching the light with an unnatural sheen. Even the paint looked newly applied, every line crisp and unblemished, as if time itself had passed it over.

And there, standing outside the shop…Elora.

She was waiting. Her eyes locked onto him.

And she smiled.

Something yanked him downward.

The sky tore open above him, and Sol plummeted through the blazing roof of the inn.

Smoke surged into his lungs, thick and bitter. The heat should have scorched him, but instead, he was freezing, his skin clammy, his breath clouding like winter air. It felt like the fire raged in another world entirely, close enough to see but not feel.

His voice cracked with panic.

"WYATT! YSELLA! SCY!"

No answer.

He staggered forward, coughing violently, each breath a battle against the smoke clawing at his throat. Tears streamed down his sootstreaked face, carving raw paths through the grime. The air was thick, blinding, suffocating, every step a guess.

He lurched into the storage room.

Empty.

No sign of them.

Where were they?

His hands trembled violently as he forced himself forward, shoving splintered beams and smoldering debris aside. The flames licked around him, but still the heat didn't touch him. Instead, he felt a hollow ache, like the air itself had been stripped of something vital, something sacred that was no longer there.

Sol staggered into the city center…And froze.

His breath caught. His knees buckled.

There they were.

The villagers.

More than half the town, strewn across the dirt, silent, still, unceremonious. Their bodies lay twisted and lifeless, scattered like broken dolls abandoned mid-play.

The world tilted. His knees nearly buckled. Vision swam.

Elion protects us—No.

This was not Elion's doing.

This was The Hand.

This was High Priest Drevan's work.

Sol's hands curled into trembling fists, nails biting into his palms. His breath came in shallow gasps as he squeezed his eyes shut— he couldn't look, couldn't breathe, couldn't bear the weight of what lay before him. His voice broke, thin and cracked, barely more than a whisper. "Beryth… I beseech you…"

His knees gave out, collapsing into the dust, and he knelt among the dead. The sky yawned above him—vast, empty, and merciless—offering no comfort, no answers.

The silence that followed pressed down like a shroud, thick and unrelenting, the kind that made the world feel hollow.

And still— Elora stood nearby.

Smiling.

She had been waiting for this.

Sol woke with a gasp, heart hammering in his chest.

The room was stifling.

He kicked free of the twisted blanket and lurched to the window, flinging it open with trembling hands. Cool night air rushed in, slapping his sweat-damp face, but it barely slowed the frantic rhythm of his breath. His chest heaved. His hands wouldn't stop shaking. It felt like his body didn't know where it was, still in the dream and the fire.

Too much.

The village in ruins. The flames licked at the walls. The faces of the fallen. The silence that followed, deeper than death. And worst of all, no answers. Nothing but questions, piling on top of each other, pressing like weight against his ribs.

His head dropped into his hands.

The sounds of the night drifted in through the open window, the gentle rustle of leaves in the breeze, the distant, mournful call of an owl, the steady, rhythmic chorus of crickets. It was the same symphony as always, soft and familiar. The world outside felt untouched. Unchanged. As if it hadn't seen the fire, hadn't felt the loss. As if it had simply moved on.

A dream. Nothing more.

He exhaled, slow and measured.

Just a dream.

Then his gaze landed on the desk.

And there it was.

The feather.

Sol froze, heart thudding once, hard, loud, then again, faster. He stared at it, dread curling slowly in his gut. He hadn't brought it inside. He was sure of it. He'd left it on the path, he remembered that. Yet there it sat, perfectly still atop the wooden surface, like it had always belonged there. But it didn't. It shouldn't. Something was wrong.

His pulse thrummed at the base of his throat as he rose, feet moving without thought. He reached for it, he ran a fingertip along the edge, just as he had before, waiting, expecting…Nothing.

The ground didn't fall away.

His feet remained planted.

His breath eased.

A hoarse laugh escaped him, shaky, brittle, and far too hollow to be real. "I guess it's not magic," he murmured, but the words fell flat, as weightless and unconvincing as ash. He stared at the feather in his hand a moment longer, half-expecting it to twitch, to vanish, to prove him wrong.

But it didn't. It just lay there, quiet and ordinary, and entirely out of place. With a slow breath, he set it down, the gesture feeling more like surrender than dismissal. It was still early. And he wouldn't sleep again, not with his thoughts clawing around in the dark. He might as well get started.

Sol hurriedly washed his face, the cool water doing little to clear the lingering weight of his dream. He dressed quickly, needing to feel the morning air on his skin, to remind himself of what was real.

Stepping outside, Sol was swallowed by the hush of low hanging fog, curling in dense, ghostly ribbons across the yard. The air was damp and cold against his skin, muffling sound and softening the edges of the world. Dawn had only just begun to bleed into the sky, a pale, uncertain light stretching over the horizon. Still, the chickens were already stirring, scratching, clucking, pecking at sluggish insects too cold to flee, their small routines oblivious to the weight pressing on his chest.

He reached for the feed, scattering it absently. A handful remained in his palm, and he let the birds peck at it, their beady eyes darting.

Then, sharp pain.

"Lucky," he muttered, pulling his hand back as the old flock matriarch latched onto his flesh instead of the grain.

His fingers throbbed, the skin flushed red but unbroken, stinging with each pulse. He drew in a slow breath and let it out even slower, grounding himself in the sharp, physical ache, something real, something he could hold onto.

Then, just beyond the curtain of mist, something moved.

His gaze snapped up.

Kellan.

His father was already far down the road, each step measured, purposeful, as if chasing something only he could see.

Sol parted his lips to call out, but stopped. The sound caught in his throat, silenced by the weight of the morning and the sleeping house behind him. There was no reason to wake the twins. And no reason to invite more of his father's silence.

He could chase after him. If he ran, he'd catch up easily.

But what would he say?

And more importantly…*what would his father say back?*

Kellan had been distant. Silent. The questions always outnumbered the answers.

Sol sighed. Instead, he bent to gather tinder and firewood, bringing it inside to stoke the hearth.

The house was quiet.

His mother should be up by now.

Petra was never one to stay in bed when the sun was rising.

Sol crouched near the hearth, coaxing the embers

until they flared to life, casting soft orange light across the quiet kitchen. The crackle of kindling masked the sound of approaching footsteps, and he didn't notice them until a warm hand settled gently on his shoulder.

He tensed, only for a breath, before recognizing the touch.

He looked up into his mother's kind, weary eyes.

"You're up early," Petra said softly, her smile gentle.

"I couldn't sleep." Sol hesitated, then asked, "Where is Da going this early?"

Petra's smile faltered, just for a heartbeat, before she smoothed it back into place.

"He's meeting with High Priest Drevan," she said, her voice calm. Too calm.

Sol watched her closely, waiting. Hoping for more, an explanation, a reason, anything to make sense of it. But she offered nothing. No flicker of hesitation. No invitation to ask.

Then, without another word, she turned back to the stove, the conversation sealed shut like a pot lid.

Sol clenched his jaw. "Mama, what is happening?"

Petra stilled, but only for a breath.

"Everywhere we go, we're being watched," Sol continued, voice rising. "The Baron has repaired our barn, and somehow we can afford quality meat and vegetables? Are we just pretending that's normal?"

She turned then, eyeing him carefully, measuring, deciding.

"Darling," she said at last, "it's… complicated. Not all of Elion's plans have been made clear to us."

Complicated.

It was the word his mother always reached for when she didn't want to explain, when the truth was too jagged to speak aloud.

A shield wrapped in softness. A way to say enough without saying why. Because some answers only led to more questions. And some questions were safer left unasked.

Sol scoffed. "We're being paraded around like High Priest Drevan's prized pigs."

The words hit like a slap, sharp, uninvited, and echoing louder than they'd been spoken.

Petra's expression hardened in an instant, the

warmth draining from her face as if a door had slammed shut. Her spoon tapped sharply against the bowl, an accidental punctuation in the heavy silence that followed.

"You will watch how you speak to me," she said, low and cold, each word deliberate as a blade.

She never raised her voice. She didn't need to.

"The Path may not be clear," she continued, "but we have faith."

Faith.

The word felt hollow.

Sol drew a slow breath, struggling to steady himself before the words he wanted to say came out too sharp and loud. Instead, he lowered his gaze, his jaw tight, and moved to put water on to boil for porridge, something to do, something to hold.

Then, without a word, he slipped out the door.

The morning air hit him like a slap, cold and bracing, but it wasn't enough. He needed something that could match the ache beneath his skin.

Without thinking, his fist slammed into the wooden fence.

A sickening crack.

Pain surged up his arm, white-hot and immediate. At least it was real. He recoiled, regretting it almost immediately, blood welling over his skin.

He flexed his fingers, savoring the sting.

At least he could still feel pain, anger, something real beneath the fog.

By the time he'd wrapped his swollen hand and stepped back into the kitchen, breakfast was already laid out. The house was thick with the familiar scent of morning: warm porridge, fresh bread, a trace of herbs from the hearth.

It should have been comforting. Instead, it felt like a memory trying too hard to be present.

It wasn't.

Petra sat, composed, her voice bright as if nothing had happened.

"Sol, would you do us the honor of blessing this meal?"

Sol swallowed.

"Of course, Mama."

The words sat like stones in his mouth, thick, heavy, unwilling to move.

He folded his hands and bowed his head, but the prayer dragged behind his breath, sluggish and strained. Each word caught in his throat, less like devotion and more like a duty he couldn't quite fulfill.

"Elion the Keeper, guide your path," he said, his voice hollow.

"May we stay steadfast," Petra and the twins echoed.

Their voices were full of certainty.

He felt like a lie.

They ate in uneasy silence.

Even the twins, usually a whirlwind of giggles and bickering, sat quiet and still, nudging their food in small, distracted circles. The silence stretched between them all, unnatural, weighty.

Sol kept his gaze fixed on his bowl, swallowing hard past the knot in his throat. His knuckles throbbed with every subtle movement, the dull ache a welcome anchor. It was something real, something sharp to hold onto amidst the thick, stifling quiet pressing in from all sides.

He cleared his throat. "Mama, I'm going to help

Wyatt with his flock today."

His voice was careful, measured, like each word had been weighed before speaking. Petra's spoon froze midair, hovering over her bowl. She looked up and studied him, too long and too intently, as if trying to read the spaces between his words.

Sol was the first to look away.

When Petra finally spoke, her voice was flat, too even, too practiced, like a line she'd rehearsed.

"Sol, you spend a lot of time with that shepherd."

That shepherd.

The words hit like a splash of cold water, jarring and sudden.

Sol's pulse quickened, pounding in his ears as his mind flashed to his conversation with Alina, the warning laced beneath her polite phrasing, the caution in her eyes.

He shifted in his seat, schooling his voice into something casual. "Mama, we've been friends for years."

"Yes, that is true," Petra murmured, stirring her porridge slowly. "But I think you need to make more friends."

Sol tensed.

"Lady Alina and you seem to get along very well," Petra continued.

Sol's response came too quickly. "She's nice. We get along fine."

His chest tightened, as if the air itself had thinned, leaving him to breathe through a narrowing gap.

Petra tilted her head ever so slightly, studying him with calm intent. "Yes, she is a devout young woman. You could learn something from her."

Sol forced his expression to remain neutral, every muscle in his face held carefully still.

If only she knew.

"Yes, Mama. I think she is very smart and grounded."

Petra's smile was warm, but there was a tension beneath it, something coiled and quiet, like a wire pulled taut.

"And she is charming," she added, her tone light, almost offhand, but too carefully measured to be innocent.

Sol felt his throat tighten. This wasn't just a passing comment.

It was pressure, soft, but unmistakable.

"She is the kind of girl you should get to know."

The words dropped into the space between them, and Sol could feel the walls closing in.

"Yes, Mama."

The words tasted unfamiliar, unsettling, but he said them anyway, forcing each one past the weight in his throat.

Petra held his gaze a moment longer, searching for something behind his eyes. Then, at last, she gave a single, measured nod.

"Sol, you may go help Wyatt," she said at last; her voice deliberate. "But be home in time for supper."

The finality in her tone struck him like a closed door—firm, unyielding. Sol exhaled slowly, realizing only then how long he'd been holding his breath.

"Thank you, Mama," he said, the words quiet but steady.

He pushed back from the table with deliberate care, every movement measured. But inside, his thoughts were a blur, whirling faster than he could contain.

Petra's words were not just suggestions.

They were orders.

And Sol wasn't sure how much longer he could follow them.

The sun hung low on the horizon, casting long golden rays over the fields, but the warmth was already beginning to swell against his skin.

Sol moved without thinking, his feet finding their rhythm even as his thoughts spiraled.

Breathe in...hold...breathe out. The pattern was all he had, something to anchor him as the rest slipped out of reach.

In. Hold. Out.

The rhythm steadied him, just enough to keep moving. But beneath the surface, his thoughts spun wild, twisting into knots he couldn't begin to unravel.

What would Wyatt say when he found out?

And what could they possibly do against something this big?

IN. HOLD. OUT.

He cast a wary glance over his shoulder, the hairs on his neck prickling with unease. Still, he pushed onward, each step slower than the last. When he reached the edge of the pasture, he paused, scanning the horizon with narrowed eyes, searching for, he wasn't sure what, only that something felt off.

Then—there.

Wyatt, leaning against a tree, his flock grazing lazily nearby.

IN. OUT. HOLD.

We'll figure it out. Together.

Wyatt straightened the instant he spotted him, pushing off the tree in one smooth, practiced motion. His long strides ate up the space between them, purposeful and fast.

Sol's breath caught in his throat. He darted a glance around, no villagers, no distant eyes peeking through shutters. Only them.

Relief loosened something profound in his chest, warm and unexpected.

Wyatt stood before him now, only a few paces away. Sol tried to speak, but his voice failed.

Tears welled in his gray eyes, then spilled over.

Wyatt hesitated only for a second before pulling Sol into a tight embrace. His arms wrapped around him with the fierce certainty of someone determined to hold him together.

Sol clung to him.

Wyatt's fingers threaded gently through Sol's hair, each pass deliberate and soothing. His other hand moved in slow, steady circles between Sol's shoulder blades, anchoring him with quiet comfort.

"Shhh, shhh," Wyatt whispered against his temple, his breath warm. "Come now, my love. Breathe with me, just one deep breath."

Sol melted into him, finally feeling the comfort he had longed for.

They stood there, silent but whole, Wyatt shielding him, protecting him from a faceless threat neither of them could yet name.

At last, Sol's storm-gray eyes met Wyatt's deep brown ones.

"I love you," he whispered.

Wyatt cupped Sol's face gently, his thumb brushing the lingering dampness from his cheeks.

"I love you, too," he said, his voice warm. "But you don't need to cry."

Wyatt's smile was small but unwavering, reassuring

in its quiet certainty. Sol hesitated, fingers curling tighter into Wyatt's sleeve as if afraid to let go.

His breath hitched, shaky and uneven, the fragile calm already slipping through the cracks. When he finally spoke, his voice was soft, trembling, barely more than a whisper carried by the wind.

"Wyatt… we're in trouble."

They sat beneath the tree, the soft rustling of leaves overhead doing little to quiet the storm in Sol's mind.

The words tumbled from Sol in a breathless rush, a torrent of tangled fears, fragmented truths, and unspoken doubts, flooding the space between them.

He told Wyatt everything.

Everything except Alina's library.

Wyatt listened without interrupting, his arm still draped protectively around Sol's shoulders.

When Sol finally fell silent, Wyatt let out a slow, measured breath, the weight of it carrying unspoken thoughts.

"I'd heard whispers of those teachings before," he said quietly. "But I never thought they'd take them this far. I didn't want to believe it."

Sol pressed his face into the crook of Wyatt's neck, his voice muffled but raw.

"I… I was taught to trust Elion. Never question His teachings. But this-this is wrong."

Wyatt let out a heavy sigh, the sound full of quiet concern.

"It must've been hard for Lady Alina to tell you," he said gently. "Do you trust her?"

Sol sat up abruptly, turning to face him, his movements sharp with certainty. His gaze locked onto Wyatt's, steady and unflinching.

"Yes."

There was no hesitation.

"I can't explain it. I just… know I can. We can."

Wyatt held his gaze for a long moment.

"But how?"

Sol shook his head, frustration bubbling up.

"I don't know," he said, too loudly. Then softer:

"It's like…" He faltered.

"It's like when I knew your uncle had died, before you ever said a word. Or how I sensed that letter I sent last winter would never reach you."

His voice softened, dropping to a hush.

"I didn't figure it out, Wyatt. I just… knew."

Wyatt studied him for a long moment, his expression unreadable, guarded, but not cold. Then, with deliberate gentleness, he reached forward and tucked a few stray strands of hair behind Sol's ear, his fingers lingering just a second longer than necessary.

"Okay," he murmured.

"Okay?" Sol blinked.

Wyatt smiled just a little, soft and knowing.

"You know I trust you," he said. "It's just… You seem to know things more often now. It's unnerving."

Sol stilled.

How did he know?

The barn. The feather. That quiet pull of something just beyond the veil.

It had always been there, whispering beneath his skin, humming low like a thread woven through his bones.

"Sol," Wyatt said softly, shifting onto his knees in front of him, his voice grounding the moment like a lifeline.

He took both of Sol's hands in his own.

"No matter what happens…" His voice was steady, unshaken.

"I will be by your side."

Sol kissed Wyatt gently.

Wyatt kissed him back fiercely, as if their connection alone could solve all their problems.

They kissed again, longer this time, deeper, until Wyatt's hand slid behind Sol's head, his fingers threading through soft hair, pulling him closer with a quiet urgency, as if letting go was no longer an option.

Their hands moved with practiced familiarity, not driven by desire but by the aching need for reassurance, for something steady in a world that no longer felt still.

For something real to hold onto.

They pulled apart slowly, their breath still mingling in the charged space between them. Sol lingered in the closeness, the world momentarily held at bay. Then he let himself lean in fully, resting his forehead against Wyatt's shoulder, drawn to the steady rhythm of his breathing, the quiet, living proof that he wasn't alone.

For a moment, the world was quiet.

A fleeting calm.

The afternoon passed in wordless ease.

They led the sheep to the old fenced-in pasture, the animals bleating softly as they clustered together. Sol leaned against the weathered wooden slats, watching Wyatt move among them with practiced ease. The calm settled for only a moment…Then Sol froze.

A figure stood just beyond the bend in the road, half-obscured by the hedgerow. Motionless. Watching.

His heart seized.

Elora.

His breath hitched as she moved toward them, her gait unhurried, deliberate.

"Good afternoon, Aunty Elora," Sol greeted, forcing his voice to steady.

"Soltic." She nodded, her gaze sharp. "You're quite good at handling sheep."

"He's a natural," Wyatt said brightly, vaulting over the fence to stand beside him.

"Yes, it seems he is." Elora's lips curved into

something not quite a smile. She turned to Wyatt. "You're lucky to have a friend like Soltic."

Friend.

The word landed like a blade, sharp, deliberate, spoken as if it carried a bitterness she could barely stomach.

Wyatt stepped forward, placing himself just in front of Sol, a quiet shield. Unshaken, he lifted his chin. "Yes, ma'am. He's one of my closest friends."

"You two looked rather cozy in the fields," Elora mused. "Not a care in the world."

She turned as if to leave, but something in her posture lingered, rigid, unresolved, like the final chord of a song left hanging in the air. Then, without facing him, her voice dropped, low and pointed over her shoulder.

"Elion the Keeper, guide your path, Soltic Arden."

Low. Inevitable. A promise, not a blessing.

How much had she seen?

The words slithered down Sol's spine like ice.

His own response came automatically, his voice distant, numb.

"May we stay steadfast."

Elora lingered for only a breath longer, her presence sharp and unsettling even in silence, then, without another word, she disappeared down the path.

The instant she was gone, a sick twist knotted in Sol's gut.

Wyatt didn't miss a beat. He took Sol's hand firmly and pulled him between two nearby buildings, into the sheltering shadows.

Before Sol could protest, Wyatt wrapped him in another tight, protective embrace, peppering his face with soft, reassuring kisses.

"We'll face whatever comes," he murmured against Sol's temple.

"Together."

The walk to the inn was brief, the sun already skimming the horizon in hues of amber and rose.

Sol knew he needed to get home.

But as they reached the creaking steps of the old, whitewashed porch, they found Scy lounging casually against the railing, his signature toothy grin firmly in place, like he'd been waiting for them all along.

"My lads, just in time." He spread his arms wide. "Ysella's got something special cooked up."

Sol sighed. "Sorry, Scy, I have to get back before supper."

Scy's eyes flicked between them, sharp as ever.

"Well, more for me then." Scy studied them both a moment longer, that ever-present smirk curling at the edges of his mouth. "You two look like you've seen a ghost."

Wyatt glanced at Sol, hesitation flickering in his eyes before he answered. "It's… complicated."

And it was.

Everything was complicated.

His family. His faith. His future.

Once, the word had just meant a puzzle to solve, something distant, manageable.

Now it sat heavy in his chest, the weight of choices he didn't yet understand and consequences he couldn't outrun. Complicated no longer felt small. It felt endless. Now it just made him tired.

They said their goodbyes, but as Sol turned to leave, Scy's grin widened.

"Oi—wait a sec," he said, vaulting over the railing like it was nothing.

Before Sol could blink, Scy shoved a sealed envelope into his hand with a flourish.

"Almost forgot, gift from your favorite noble house," he said, grinning like a cat with a secret.

He rocked back on his heels, arms folded, clearly savoring the moment and whatever reaction might follow.

"Told me it had to reach your hand tonight. Which is dramatic… and probably not good."

The smirk deepened.

"Complicated."

Sol hesitated, his grip tightening around the envelope. It felt heavier than parchment had any right to, weighty not with mass, but with meaning. There was no name, no crest, only the seal he knew too well. His breath caught, shallow and uneven, as a cold certainty settled in his chest. Whatever lay inside, it wasn't kindness. With a slow, deliberate motion, he broke the seal and unfolded the paper, bracing himself for the words to come.

Soltic,

We have to talk. Come to the inn at midday tomorrow.

Tell no one.

—A

Chapter Ten

Noose and Nail

The afternoon air was thick and humid, the final whispers of rain still veiling the fields in a soft shimmer. Sol paused at the threshold, knocking thick mud from his boots with the heel of one foot. The scent of wet earth clung to him, mingling with the musty warmth that drifted in through the open door.

At the table, Petra sat quietly, cradling a steaming cup of tea between both hands. The fire had burned low, embers glowing faintly beneath the newly laid logs, still untouched by flame, as if waiting. The silence in the room was not unfamiliar, but this time it held weight, thick and deliberate. It felt like something had settled. Or was about to shift.

Sol rolled his sleeves up, shaking off the lingering dampness.

"Mama, it's a hot one." His voice came out light, casual.

Petra hummed softly in reply, her gaze never leaving the fire. She turned the cup slowly in her hands, fingers tracing the rim in a motion more thoughtful than idle.

"Sol," she said at last. Her voice was as steady as ever, but there was a tension beneath it, subtle, unfamiliar, and sharp enough to catch.

"Come sit with me."

He paused, the space between them stretching for a beat, before lowering himself into the chair across from her.

Then she looked at him, really looked at him, as if searching his face for something long buried or newly revealed. Her eyes lingered, quiet and unreadable.

"Elora spoke to me last night," she said.

Sol kept his expression neutral, forcing his shoulders to remain loose. "Oh?"

"She mentioned she saw you in the pasture with Wyatt. That the two of you seemed… close."

Petra's voice remained light, almost conversational, but Sol heard the weight beneath it, the same quiet gravity she carried when asking after the harvest, already knowing the fields were dying.

He drew a steady breath. "Of course, we are, Mama. You've always said he's like a twin separated at birth."

"I have," she said softly. Her gaze didn't waver. "But I've seen something shifting in you. Even before Elora spoke, I felt it."

She didn't elaborate, just watched him for a long moment before letting out a quiet breath.

"That's why I asked you to spend more time with Elion's word, you've been restless lately, Sol."

Sol began to speak, but Petra raised a hand, not to silence him, but to hold the space steady, as if the air between them might shift too suddenly and unbalance it all.

Restless.

The word curled in his chest like smoke—thin, clinging, impossible to swallow. He wanted to laugh, to shrug it off, deny it. But something in her voice turned his stomach.

She wasn't accusing. She wasn't angry. She had simply seen too much.

"I'm not asking for an answer," Petra said, her voice gentle as ever, yet it left no room to run.

"But I think a walk might help clear your mind. Let

the Keeper guide you — quietly, if He's willing."

The Keeper's path. Sol forced himself to nod. The words hadn't landed like a command, but more like a hope. She wasn't pressing, not exactly. Just reaching, gently, for the only truth she still believed in.

"Yes, Mama."

She reached across the table and, in a rare gesture, her fingers brushed lightly against his wrist—brief, warm, and gone before he could respond.

"Good." A small smile flickered at the edges of her lips, though her eyes remained searching.

"Go on, then. Before your father finds something for you to do."

Sol rose, smoothing his hands over his tunic—a small gesture to ground himself. "I won't be long."

Petra's eyes flicked toward the fire. "Take as long as you need."

With that, she turned back to her tea, and the moment folded shut as softly as it had opened.

Sol stepped outside, his body already in motion before his mind could catch up. The sun hung high, too bright, too still. He barely felt the warmth on his skin. His feet found the road to the inn, his path certain, his thoughts tangled.

He wanted to see Alina. But he knew she did not bring good tidings.

When he arrived, the inn was quiet, not the usual lull between guests, but a stillness that felt suspended, as though the room itself were holding its breath.

Behind the counter, Ysella arranged the glasses with deliberate care, her movements precise, almost too careful, like the clinking of glass might disguise something unspoken.

Sol managed a smile. "Good day, mum." His voice barely reached the space between them.

Ysella didn't hesitate. She came around the counter with purpose and wrapped him in a fierce hug.

"Oh, my Sol."

His breath hitched. He fought the sting in his eyes, pressing his forehead briefly to her shoulder before straightening.

"Wyatt told you?" His voice was rough, barely above a whisper.

Ysella leaned back just enough to meet his gaze, her

eyes shadowed with something too dense, too layered for words.

"It's complicated," she said at last, her smile faint and sorrowful, the kind that knew too much.

Sol let out a sharp breath. "Everything is."

"My dear, life is very complicated. And it seems you're in for more." She cupped his face briefly, a quiet promise in her touch. "But we are here for you."

Sol swallowed hard and nodded. "I know, Mum."

Ysella's lips pressed into a thin line, her fingers tightening briefly against his arms. "We will stand beside you. Nothing is going to harm you or Wyatt."

Her voice held steady, but the emotion shimmered just beneath, barely restrained, almost breaking.

A soft rustle of fabric drew Sol's gaze toward the green velvet curtain near the back of the room.

Wyatt stepped out slowly, his gaze locking onto Sol's. He didn't speak, not at first. He just looked at him, quiet and steady.

"You alright?" he asked, voice low. Sol gave a small nod. "I don't know."

That was enough.

Wyatt stepped forward, paused for a heartbeat, then pulled him into a quiet embrace, not to fix anything, but simply to say: I'm here.

Sol let his chin rest lightly on Wyatt's shoulder. The space between them stilled, their breath settling into the same rhythm.

Neither of them said a word.

Ysella cleared her throat, her voice deliberately casual. "Not that I want to interrupt, but you have a visitor who has been patiently waiting."

She motioned toward the hallway. "Last room on the right."

Sol straightened, running his hands down his sides in a slow, grounding motion. He wasn't sure what he expected, only that something in the air felt…off. Uneasy.

Maybe Alina had more than whispers and wary glances to offer, something solid, something clear, in a village where even the ground seemed to shift beneath them.

He turned to Wyatt. "Are you coming?"

Wyatt hesitated. For a heartbeat, Sol thought he might refuse.

But then he nodded, falling into step beside him.

They moved down the dim hallway, floorboards groaning beneath each step. The only sound between them was the slow, steady draw of their breath.

At the final door, Sol's hand hovered over the worn brass handle. His fingers flexed, uncertain, suspended in thought.

Sol inhaled deeply, grounding himself in the quiet comfort of that touch. Then, with a final breath, he pushed open the door.

Alina was inside, pacing, restless energy coiled tight beneath her movements. She looked up as they entered, her face flooding with relief. "Sol, I've been worried sick."

She crossed the room quickly and embraced him, the hug brief but fierce, before stepping back to take in Wyatt with wide, searching eyes.

A genuine smile crossed her face. "You must be Wyatt—the wayward shepherd."

Wyatt bowed carefully. "It's an honor."

Alina scoffed. "None of that. We're meeting in a dark room, in secret. I don't think formalities apply."

Wyatt chuckled, tension easing slightly. "I suppose you're right."

Alina turned to Sol, a teasing glint in her eyes. "You never mentioned your paramour was so devastatingly handsome."

She laughed, light and unapologetic. "Truly, I applaud your taste."

Wyatt laughed, the sound easy, while Sol's cheeks flushed with heat.

It was strange, having their relationship acknowledged so openly by someone outside of Ysella or Scy. Disorienting, even.

But then Alina's smile faded, her expression sharpening in an instant. The silence that followed stretched long and thin.

Sol's stomach twisted. "What was so important that we had to meet in secrecy? What have you learned?"

Alina hesitated—a rare, almost jarring thing.

Sol's fingers curled into fists. "Alina. Just say it, please."

She drew in a sharp breath. And then, in one breath….

"They're announcing our engagement at temple worship this week."

The words tumbled out of her, as if speaking them quickly might dull the edges.

Sol stared, unblinking.

Then he laughed—a short, breathless sound.

But her expression didn't change. If anything, it darkened.

His breath caught. "You're joking."

Alina looked away. She couldn't meet his gaze. "Sol, I heard them talking. My parents, your father, High Priest Drevan. Yesterday morning."

She hesitated, voice quieter now.

"He said Elion spoke to him in a dream. Claimed the match was divinely ordained, that it would strengthen the community. That your family, being a pillar of faith, would ensure that faith endures by joining with nobility."

Sol didn't speak. He just stood there, the words hanging in the air like smoke, trying to feel anything but the slow, cold weight settling deep in his chest.

"But we aren't engaged," he said, voice flat. Then, sharper: "Did you agree to this?"

Alina's hands curled tightly into the fabric of her skirts. "I wasn't asked."

Her voice was quiet, barely more than a breath. Small, but steady.

"As a noblewoman, my choice in marriage will never be my own."

A terrible silence fell between them.

Sol swallowed hard, lowering his head. "I'm sorry."

"But I swear, I'll keep your secret."

She hesitated, her voice more controlled now, though still brittle at the edges.

"If they believe the match is real… Wyatt could come to the estate. It wouldn't raise suspicion. And it might buy you both some time, some safety."

She wrung her hands, trying to sound hopeful—and almost succeeding.

"You'll have a title. Land. Your family will be taken care of."

"This isn't right."

The words came sharp and furious, but not from Sol.

Wyatt.

His voice cracked as the strain broke through.

"People aren't pieces on a board. You shouldn't have to go through this. Either of you."

Alina let out a soft, bitter laugh. "That's noble of you," she said, pressing a hand to her chest, mocking the word. "But that's all our lives are — land, titles, alliances. My father doesn't see me as a daughter. He sees leverage."

Sol's hands trembled. He felt cold. Hollow.

His voice barely rose above a breath. "We don't have a choice, do we?"

Alina's face softened, but there was no comfort in it.

"I wish I could say otherwise. But the path was never ours to choose."

Sol exhaled sharply. "I see."

"There's more."

Sol's head snapped up.

Alina grimaced. "They're planning a proclamation before the Fall Harvest. Beryth's shrines will be torn down, replaced with monuments to Elion."

He went still. "No."

Alina swallowed. "He won't ban the other gods

outright. Not yet. But he'll make it harder to worship them."

Sol's breath hitched, shallow and fast. "I can't keep that secret. They have to know — the villagers, they need time. Time to hide what they can."

"That's why I'm telling you," Alina said, her voice steadier now. "They'll have to be careful, but it can be done if they move before the proclamation."

The words should have brought Sol relief. Instead, a crushing sense of helplessness settled over him.

His knees gave out, and he sank onto the edge of the bed.

Wyatt was beside him in an instant, arms wrapped around him, firm, steady.

A silent promise.

Then Wyatt turned to Alina, his voice lower now, but no less weighted.

"Is there more?"

Alina looked at them — two boys with the ground shifting beneath them.

A single tear slipped down her cheek before she could stop it. She didn't wipe it away.

"I won't tell anyone," she said, her voice thick. "Whatever happens, your secret is safe with me."

Alina managed a small, dry smile. "At least we're still friends."

Sol's throat tightened. He reached out and gave her hand a single, steady squeeze.

Wyatt's voice was quiet. "Thank you, Alina."

She rose, smoothing the front of her dress, a motion more habit than grace.

"I should go. If my mother notices I'm gone too long…"

Sol and Wyatt began to rise, but she lifted a hand.

"No. Stay," she said gently. "Take the moment."

She turned and slipped through the door without a glance back.

Her absence hung heavy, like a breath held too long.

The air thickened around them.

The walls seemed to close in.

They stayed rooted, holding tight. Holding on—

to each other, to silence, to all the words left

unspoken.

A soft tap came at the door.

Sol blinked, disoriented. The sun hung low in the sky. *Had they fallen asleep?*

The door creaked open, and Ysella slipped inside. She settled quietly beside the bed, hands folded in her lap, watching them with a gentle, watchful concern.

"I heard raised voices," she said softly. "And then crying. I wanted to give you time."

Sol shifted against Wyatt, his body stiff from restless sleep. Wyatt stirred but didn't pull away, his fingers found Sol's, squeezing once with quiet reassurance.

Ysella tilted her head, eyes searching. "Is it as bad as all that?"

Sol swallowed hard. "I am to be married, to Lady Alina."

Wyatt exhaled sharply, his grip tightening, too raw to speak.

Ysella froze. Her lips parted, but no words came. She looked away, toward the window, gathering herself in the silence.

Finally, she spoke. "Sol. Wyatt. We will figure this out." Her voice was steady, but her eyes shone with something too close to fear.

"The answer is just out of reach right now, but it will come. I promise."

Sol nodded weakly, desperate to believe her.

Ysella sighed and rose. "You need supper. No one thinks straight on an empty stomach." She paused at the door, then glanced back.

"Come now. This is not the time to lose faith."

Faith.

Sol bit his lip hard.

It always came back to that, didn't it?

They followed Ysella out, each step through the inn sinking like quicksand beneath their feet.

The air hung heavy with silence. A few villagers picked at their meals in near-whispers, the weight of something unspoken pressing down on them all.

Sol and Wyatt settled into their usual corner table, the worn wood familiar beneath their hands. Ysella returned moments later, carrying a roasted chicken and two tall mugs crowned with frothy foam.

Sol eyed his drink warily, fingers lingering on the rim as if questioning what it might dull, or reveal.

"Oh, you two can do with something stronger than juice," she said, managing a smile, just enough to lift the edge of the moment.

Sol took a bold gulp, then immediately choked, sputtering ale across the worn table. Wyatt and Ysella burst into easy laughter, the sound warm and genuine.

Sol coughed, wiping at his mouth with the back of his hand. "People actually like this?"

Wyatt grinned, a teasing glint in his eye. "You'll get used to it, eventually."

Ysella's smile faded as she sat. "Now—start from the beginning."

Sol tried. He really did. But his throat tightened, words caught like stones he couldn't swallow.

Wyatt took up the story in his stead, his voice steady as he laid it all bare.

When he finished, Ysella sat back, pale and shaken.

Without a word, she reached for Sol's mug, drained it in one long, trembling pull, then set it down with a heavy, final thud.

"You are to marry into the Greywells." Her voice was quiet, almost distant. "And the Baron is going to destroy our temples."

Sol nodded numbly.

Ysella exhaled slowly, the weight of the moment heavy in the air. Then, with a low, fierce growl, she seized both their wrists, pulling them close.

"This is not over, my lads. Not even close."

The inn door slammed open just then.

Scy strode in, soaked through from the relentless rain, his expression as grim as death itself.

He didn't greet anyone. Didn't offer a smile.

He strode behind the bar, grabbed two mugs of ale, then sat heavily at their table.

One mug slid to Ysella. He downed half of his before finally speaking.

"Orin Marsh."

A heavy pause filled the room.

Then Scy's voice cut through the silence, sharp as a blade. "He's dead. And the gods didn't lift a damn finger to stop it." Sol's stomach clenched, twisting cold and tight.

"Cut down like a dog, left to bleed in the dirt. And for what? A half-empty coin purse? A crust of bread? No, just because they could. Because the world is full of bastards who take what they want and leave the rest of us to bury the dead."

"And now Old Magpie's got him. Guess that's fitting, Orin never got a chance to run the game. Maybe now he'll get to play for real. Maybe he'll slip into some god's pocket, turn their own luck against them. Snag something better than the piss-poor hand he was dealt here."

"Or maybe—"

Scy exhaled sharply, bitter.

Sol barely breathed. The room hung heavy with silence, as if the world itself was holding its breath, waiting, holding something back.

"Maybe the gods are just watching. Sitting back while boys like us, like him, bleed out for nothing."

Scy shook his head, voice low and dangerous, like a storm barely contained.

"If that's what they are, maybe it's time we stop pretending we owe them a damn thing."

The words hung in the air, sharp as a blade just unsheathed.

No one spoke.

Sol's breath came slow and uneven. He tried to swallow, but his throat clenched shut. The inn seemed to shrink around them, candlelight flickering weakly, shadows creeping closer.

Wyatt's fingers tightened around his mug, knuckles pale and rigid. Ysella's lips pressed into a thin, unreadable line, an unspoken barrier.

Silence settled like a weight between them.

Sol's breath caught and shuddered, breaking the stillness.

Orin.

Orin Marsh, only a few months older than Sol. The boy who once caught fish from the pond with him, who once laughed beneath the same sun.

They had grown apart over time, but that didn't change what Orin had been.

He was a person.

And now, he was gone.

Sol stared at the table, his hands curling into fists.

Scy exhaled through his nose — soft, bitter.

"Sorry," he muttered, dragging a hand over his face. "I just… hate how easy it is to get used to this. Like we're supposed to just carry on."

Scy rubbed the back of his

neck. "Didn't mean to run

my mouth."

A weak, hollow chuckle.

The conversation shifted, just barely. They grasped at smaller topics, trying to fill the heavy silence, but the weight in the room refused to lift.

Sol's gaze drifted to the window.

The first fat raindrops splattered against the glass.

Then, as if time itself stuttered, the world seemed to freeze.

The rain hung suspended in the air, still, fragile, like a held breath between heartbeats.

A stillness pressed in, too complete to be natural.

Sol's breath caught.

He knew this feeling.

Like something just beyond the veil had opened its eyes.

He had to go home. Now.

Sol stood so abruptly that his chair scraped across the floor with a sharp screech.

"I have to go," he said, though his voice sounded far away, like it didn't quite belong to him.

Wyatt rose instantly. "I'll come with you." His voice was steady, with no hesitation.

Sol grabbed his shoulders, pulling him into a tight, desperate hug. He held on.

Then he kissed him—soft, fleeting, full of quiet fear.

"No, love."

Sol swallowed hard. "You stay — I have to go. Now." Wyatt's fingers curled into the fabric of Sol's tunic. "Sol—"

But Sol tore away before the word had fully landed.

He turned, and ran.

Rain struck him like needles, cold and unrelenting.

The mud clung to his boots, pulling at him with every step. He slipped, stumbled, and crashed through puddles that slapped up against his legs, but he didn't stop.

Didn't slow.

Didn't look back.

As he made the last curve in the road, his house came into view—

And his breath caught.

The windows glowed too brightly.

Too many candles.

A carriage stood in front.

The horses stomped the wet ground, restless.

Sol's heart slammed against his ribs.

His lungs burned.

He forced himself to walk the last few meters, catching his breath, swallowing his fear.

The door loomed before him.

Sol pushed the door open slowly, carefully, his fingers trembling on the handle.

Candlelight danced along the walls, casting long,

hollow shadows that swayed like phantoms.

At the center of the room, seated with unnatural stillness, like a king upon his throne…

High Priest Drevan waited.

"Soltic."

The name slipped from his lips like a blade, low, sharp, and coiling through the air like smoke.

High Priest Drevan sat motionless in the glow of the candlelight, his gaunt face carved in shadow and bone. Eyes unreadable.

His long, skeletal fingers were laced together in his lap, a portrait of ritual patience.

And then, he smiled.

Slow. Cold. Certain.

"Sit."

Chapter Eleven

———

Correction

Golden light soaked the room, casting twitching shadows that danced along the walls like restless spirits. The air hung heavy with heat, thick and unmoving, as if time itself had paused. The scent of clove and resin incense curled through the space, serpentine and alive.

His father stood solemn and unmoving to one side of the Hand, while his mother and siblings gathered on the other. The twins clung to Petra's hem, their small bodies trembling, tiny fists buried in the folds of her skirt. Petra stood rigid, her spine straight as a blade, eyes wide yet unreadable, frozen somewhere between fear and defiance.

"Do you deny it, boy?" High Priest Drevan hissed.

Sol's mind reeled, spiraling with confusion and dread. He didn't even know what it was, not really. But there was something in the man's voice—something cold and coiled with venom, that made his skin crawl and the hair rise on the back of his neck.

"What am I being accused of?" he asked, forcing his voice to stay even.

Drevan's eyes gleamed, sharp with accusation. "Do you deny the filth in your heart?"

Sol's jaw tightened. "There is no filth in my heart, High Priest."

"LIES!" Drevan's voice cracked like a whip through the chamber. "Do not pretend innocence. You are engaged in an unnatural relationship with Wyatt Thornbrook. We have evidence. Witnesses. You cannot hide, boy."

He turned slightly, not taking his eyes off Sol.

"Petra."

She stiffened, then stepped forward, clutching a bundle of parchment with trembling hands.

Drevan took it without so much as a glance in her direction, raising the pages aloft as though they were a holy relic.

"The proof of your corruption," he declared, voice low but ringing with finality. "Your words. His."

Sol's stomach dropped, a cold weight sinking through him.

His gaze fell on the top page, Wyatt's handwriting. The letters wavered, smudged by the sudden sting in his eyes, but one phrase burned through the blur: *I think of you when the sun turns the wheat fields gold.…*

"No!"

A cry tore from his throat as he lurched forward, but Drevan was faster. With a flick of his wrist, he tossed the bundle into the hearth.

The fire took them greedily. Pages curled and shriveled, edges blackening, his words devoured one by one in a slow, crackling feast.

Sol stared, breath heaving. He didn't move. Didn't dare.

Drevan's smile was all teeth, glinting in the firelight.

Sol's heart pounded. He could feel every eye on him.

Drevan's smile was all teeth. "Do not lie to me, boy."

Sol could have lied. Could have forced it down and let the moment pass.

But something inside him, ancient, trembling, burning, rose like smoke to the surface.

He lifted his head, spine stiffening. Met Drevan's gaze.

And then his father's.

"The love we share is not filth," he said, the words breaking free like a flood. "It is not unnatural. I could no more stop loving Wyatt than I could stop breathing."

A sudden crack of flesh against flesh.

Kellan's hand struck across Sol's cheek with brutal force.

The world went white.

A gasp tore the silence. Petra's breath caught sharply, barely stifled behind her hand.

Sol staggered back, a high, relentless ringing flooding his ears. His vision blurred, the edges of the room swimming as he fought to steady himself.

"You will show High Priest Drevan respect," Kellan spat.

Sol turned slowly, meeting his father's eyes. Searching for what, he wasn't sure. *Remorse? Regret? The father he used to know?*

But there was nothing. No flicker of conflict. Only cold, unyielding resolve.

"Papa, you liked Wyatt," Sol said, his voice hoarse, thick with disbelief.

That broke something. Kellan's anger surged to the surface. He began to pace, a storm barely contained, his movements restless and jagged. His voice, when it came, was raw with fury.

"You want to lie with him like a wife?" he seethed, voice shaking with rage. "Do you imagine bearing his children? Or is it just lust? Do you crave the feeling of him inside you?"

The Hand smiled, watching the scene unfold.

"I raised you better than this," Kellan spat. "I gave you the Keeper's truth, and you threw it away, for what? That boy? That craving?"

His voice dripped with disgust. "You shame this family."

Then came the final cut.

"I wish you had died as a babe."

The words didn't just land; they buried themselves in Sol's chest like a blade, cold and final.

His breath shuddered. His vision blurred with tears he refused to shed. But his voice did not waver.

"Real love is never wrong."

Silence followed, thick, charged, absolute.

Sol's heart pounded against his ribs like a war drum. He held his father's gaze, defiance flickering in his eyes, the fire behind them steady and unflinching.

For a long, breathless moment, Drevan simply stared. Then his lips curled into a slow, knowing smile.

"Love, boy?" His voice was soft now. Mocking. Dangerous. The kind of quiet that made people lean in to listen.

"You are young. You are foolish. But I will not let you be lost."

He turned slightly, casting his shadow over Sol like a looming specter.

"This is not punishment, Soltic Arden." His smile deepened, cruel and deliberate. "This is a correction."

The room fell still, the air tightening around them.

"Take off your shirt."

Drevan's voice sliced through the silence.

"Let your flesh learn what your soul refuses to see."

Sol froze.

Just for a breath — he hoped. Prayed.

He waited for his father to speak. To say no. To see

him.

But Kellan said nothing.

The silence stretched, long and heavy, loud enough to answer everything.

Sol's hands trembled as he pulled his shirt over his head. The air hit his skin like ice, and he flinched. He felt small. Exposed.

Alone.

"Now sit," Drevan said.

Sol obeyed. Numb.

Drevan lifted a hand, fingers steady with purpose.

"Brother Kellan. Bring me the whip."

Kellan moved at once. His steps were stiff, mechanical, like a man sleepwalking through a nightmare he no longer questioned. He silently crossed the room and returned with the braided leather, reverently placing it in Drevan's outstretched hand.

Drevan turned to Sol. The whip hung loosely from his fingers, its coils swaying with quiet threat.

The weight of what was coming pressed into the room, thick and inescapable.

"Hold your son's arms."

Kellan obeyed.

Without pause. Without resistance. Without a single word.

Like the choice had been made long ago.

Like it had always been this way.

The twins screamed.

Their cries shattered the stillness as they bolted toward him, sobbing, small hands reaching, grabbing, trying to tear him free.

Their voices were desperate, their grief wild and unfiltered.

But no one stopped them.

And no one helped.

"Papa, don't!" Mira sobbed.

"Sol, Sol, please—" Theo shrieked, hysterical.

Petra caught them both, arms outstretched as they lunged past.

She gripped them tightly, crushing their small, trembling bodies against her chest.

"Go to your rooms," she ordered, her voice low

but firm—too calm for the chaos around her.

But they fought. They thrashed and screamed, their limbs flailing like they could undo the moment with force alone.

For one fleeting second, Sol felt their tiny hands on him— clutching, pleading, desperate.

Refusing to let go.

And then they were gone.

But Petra pried them away.

She held them tight, muffling their sobs against her dress.

Then—

The lash landed, searing across his back like fire. His vision went white as pain erupted through him, his body convulsing in Kellan's grip. Again, it came, snapping across his skin. He arched against the restraint, bit down hard on his tongue, and metal flooded his mouth. Blood. Still, the whip fell. Again.

Breath ragged. Knees buckling.

Again.

Something warm ran down his spine. The drops hit

Kellan's cheek. Red. Sharp. Kellan didn't flinch, didn't even blink. That's when Sol knew. It was blood. His blood.

And that's when he broke.

A sob tore from his chest, raw, sudden, loud. Not from the pain, but from the brutal truth of it all. From knowing it was real from the silence in Kellan's eyes.

But because Kellan's hand was still gripping his arm.

Because Kellan didn't look away.

Because the father who once lifted him onto his shoulders, who taught him to pray, who kissed his scraped knees…

Was now the one holding him down.

And he didn't stop.

Not when Sol sobbed. Not when his blood slicked the floor.

Sol's body trembled, not just from the lash, but from that truth.

From the unbearable fracture between love and loyalty.

The Hand stepped closer, silent as judgment.

His voice dropped to a whisper meant only for Sol.

"You will marry Lady Alina."

"You will bring prosperity to Oswynn."

"You will walk the path, Soltic."

A pause. Then, soft as breath, came the words:

"Or you will suffer more than this."

Sol didn't respond. Not because he agreed. But because there was nothing left inside him to react with. No defiance. No voice. Just a hollow ache, deep and echoing, where the fight used to live.

The Hand turned.

He wiped a smear of blood from Kellan's brow — gentle, almost reverent.

"You are blessed, Brother Kellan."

"Your son will return to the path."

Kellan followed him out. He didn't look back.

The twins rushed to Sol, their small arms flinging around his chest, squeezing too tightly. He didn't flinch. But he didn't hug them back. He couldn't. There was a silence in him now—dense, unreachable.

The twins pulled away, faces streaked with tears,

and vanished up the stairs, still crying, still believing someone might come.

But no one had.

No one ever had.

The house was silent.

Sol didn't move.

His gaze locked on the hearth, on the soft, gray bundle of ashes. One page remained. Curled at the edge, ember-singed, but not taken. His breath hitched, slow, shallow, thin. He wanted to scream. He wanted to crumble. To break apart where he sat. But he didn't. He sat upright, stiff with the remnants of defiance, hollowed by everything else. Cracked. Waiting for something that wasn't coming. Not now. Maybe not ever.

He didn't even register Petra approaching until her shadow passed across the floor.

Not the warm quiet of night, when embers softened into the hearth and the twins whispered their last sleepy thoughts.

This was emptiness.

The front door had shut behind Kellan. The Hand was gone. The incense had burned low, leaving only the acrid sting of smoke and blood.

The twins had been dragged upstairs, still sobbing. Their muffled cries drifted from behind closed doors, the desperate sound of children who still believed that someone would come if they screamed loud enough. That someone would stop this.

No one had.

And now, the silence felt louder than their screams.

Petra moved through it without a word. Not tender. Not cruel.

Just efficient, like someone trained long ago to clean up after things that shouldn't have happened.

She cleaned his wounds the way she kneaded dough, steady, practiced, without flinching. There was no tenderness in it, but no cruelty either. Just hands doing what they had done before. Sol sat motionless. Her touch didn't sting. Nothing did. He felt scraped clean. Hollow. As if pain had passed through him and left only air behind. When she finished, she pressed a sodden, heavy, red cloth into his hands. His blood. Proof he hadn't dreamed any of it.

She still wouldn't look at him.

"You will marry Lady Alina."

A pause.

"You will never see that boy again."

Another pause. Longer.

"Or you will leave Oswynn."

"And you will never see this family again."

Not a question. Not a plea. Just a sentence, cold and final, like a door closing.

Sol opened his mouth to beg, maybe, to ask for a scrap of something he could still hold on to.

But Petra had already turned away.

She wiped her hands on her apron.

And walked out of the room.

Sol sat alone.

The cloth remained clutched in his fists, the dried blood stiffening the fabric like old glue. His back burned. His cheek throbbed. But the emptiness, the vast, echoing hollowness, carved the deepest. He didn't cry. He didn't move. There was no strength left for either.

The last candle sputtered in its holder, flame dancing uncertainly before it gave out with a whisper of smoke.

Darkness fell.

And no one came.

Chapter Twelve

———

The Ashes Settle

The only sound was the soft crackle of nearly spent embers, a fading whisper of warmth pressing into the thick silence that filled the house. Their feeble glow wavered along the walls, shadows stretching and shrinking in tired rhythm, as if the light itself was struggling to hold on.

Sol's thoughts dragged, thick as molasses—slow, sluggish, weighted. His body mirrored his mind, slumping onto the unyielding floor. The wood beneath his palms was cold and splintered. He pressed against it, unsteady, his fingers twitching as if resisting command.

His breath shuddered. Thick air clung to his skin but was devoid of warmth. The embers gave off no true heat, only the memory of it. The scent of burnt wood lingered, receding like everything else.

His mouth was dry, his tongue thick with the metallic tang of blood, bitter and sharp against the raw lining of his throat. *Had he screamed?* He couldn't remember.

He couldn't remember much at all. Just the hands that held him down. The ones that didn't stop it.

His stomach churned. How could his family have watched? Worse, how could his father have taken part?

And Alina…had she known?

No.

She had promised him safety.

Ysella had promised him safety, too. But no one could keep him safe.

His gaze drifted to the hearth, where the memory of burning letters struck like a lash. Wyatt. His stomach twisted, sharper this time, with a gut-deep terror. *If they could do this to him, what would they do to Wyatt?*

The thought ripped through the numbness, jolting his limbs to life. He had to get to Wyatt. *He had to warn him.* Protect him, Sol gritted his teeth and forced himself upright.

Agony.

Fire tore through his back as his muscles seized. The wounds split open, fresh blood soaking through his shirt.

His arms trembled, shoulders locking up. He bit down on a whimper, forcing himself through it.

Again.

He planted a foot beneath him, but the motion sent a hot, sickening wave of pain tearing up his spine. His vision blurred. His stomach twisted.

His knee gave out, and he slammed to the floor, breath knocked clean from his lungs.

Too much. Too soon.

His fingers curled against the wood, trembling. He was still bleeding. He needed time.

But time meant nothing if Wyatt was in danger.

He clenched his jaw and forced himself onto his knees. Slow. Steady. Through the pain.

The embers blurred in his vision, their dim glow the only light in the suffocating dark. He went still. Breathe in. Hold. Breathe out.
Again. The embers flickered—then, suddenly, they didn't.

The crackling faded. The shifting glow motionless.

Not gone. Not extinguished. Just... suspended. A silence so deep it pressed against his skin, stretching outward, reaching through him, settling in his bones. And then came the knowing.

It was not a vision. Not a dream. There was no

whispered prophecy, no voice of a god. But something ancient and unseen opened inside him.

He didn't see the futures laid before him; he felt them. Both paths existed in his body at once, pressing against his ribs, flooding his lungs, his mind, his marrow. The weight of them was unbearable. The first: a life of quiet deception.

A lie that would bind them all, himself, Alina, and Wyatt. They would survive, but never truly live. His family would be content, but never happy. And he? He would exist but never breathe.

The second. Fear. Loss. Loneliness.

His family's pain, sharp at first, then dulling with time. Struggles he couldn't yet name, hardships still unmeasured. But at the end of it all? Freedom. Strength. Alina, with children of her own, was smiling in truth. Wyatt, with a husband who could love him without hiding.

And himself, whole. It hadn't been a choice. It had already been made. His breath shuddered as the silence released him. The embers still smoldered low, untouched. The fire had not returned.

Only time. He had to leave.

Wyatt deserved happiness.

Alina deserved happiness.

And so did he.

Slowly, carefully, Sol rose to his feet. He drew a deep, steady breath, gritting his teeth as the muscles in his back flared in protest. Every movement tugged at torn flesh, a sharp, unforgiving reminder of what had been done to him. He paused beside the hearth.

The ashes had settled, but the memory of heat still clung to the stone. Something flickered in the shadows, half-hidden.

He knelt, fingers sifting gently through the soot.

It was still there.

The one letter that hadn't burned.

Curled at the edge, ember-singed, but not gone.

The words met his gaze like a whisper:

"…almost as deep as your eyes."

He exhaled slowly.

Drevan had tried to destroy everything. Kellan had held him down. But some things refused to be taken. Sol folded the fragment with care, as if the act itself could preserve its meaning. It wasn't a keepsake; it was a truth that had survived the fire. A thread he would carry forward. He had to warn Wyatt and Ysella.

Then, he would leave. Tonight.

He moved quietly down the hall to his room. It was plain:

peeling whitewash, a simple bed with dingy sheets, and the old writing table where he had spent so many hours.

Kneeling, he pulled his worn traveling pack from beneath the bed and began packing quickly. There wasn't much to take. When his hand reached for the loose floorboard, his pulse quickened. He pried it open and reached inside.

Mira's ribbon…faded, frayed, familiar.

A few small treasures wrapped in a faded, stained green handkerchief.

He lingered on the fabric, fingers ghosting over it, his father's. His throat tightened. He'd been twelve when he sliced his hand on a fence post, deep enough for blood to pool in his palm. Kellan had taken this very handkerchief, his favorite, and pressed it to the wound without hesitation.

The memory blurred at the edges. His vision swam.

Slowly, he unfolded the handkerchief. Then, with quiet reverence, he placed the burned letter inside. Not hidden. Not buried.

But carried.

He folded the cloth again and tucked it away.

He moved to the twins' room, pausing at the door. Listening. Faint snoring.

They were safe.

He stepped inside, swallowing against the ache rising in his throat. They lay tangled in the sheets, arms wrapped around each other, the way they had since they were small.

And something in him broke.

He knelt beside them, brushing Mira's hair back, resting a gentle hand on Theo's shoulder.

"I will never stop loving you." His voice was barely a breath. "Be strong. And if the gods will it, we'll be together again someday."

He pressed a trembling kiss to each of their foreheads, then wiped his cheeks, erasing all trace of his tears.

At the door, he paused, fingers hovering over the

handle.

Then, without a sound, he closed it behind him.

Back down the hall, his eyes caught on the small traveling bag sitting on the table.

That wasn't there when he left.

He approached carefully, hesitating before pulling it open.

Inside—simple survival gear. A coin purse.

This was for him.

His breath hitched. *Mama?*

He looked up, but the room was empty.

A lump rose in his throat. He swallowed it down, shifting his pack and stuffing the smaller bag inside.

He tried to sling it over his back, but pain exploded through him, white-hot and blinding.

His knees gave out, and he barely caught himself against the table as the room tilted. His breath came in fast, short, shallow gasps.

Slowly, his vision cleared. He adjusted the pack, pulling it over his chest instead. His back still stung with every breath, every shift of movement. But he would endure.

He had no other choice.

The night air was cool and crisp, a welcome contrast to the fire still burning in his back.

The scent of earth and damp hay mingled with the faintest trace of rot, the familiar musk of the barns. Not unpleasant. Just... home.

The night was quiet. Crickets chirped. An owl called in the distance. Each step on the gravel path sent a soft crunch into the hush of the evening.

At the last fence post, he stopped.

He turned, one final time.

This was it.

He drew in the cool night air and let it settle deep in his lungs.

He should have been devastated. But he wasn't. The weight of this night should have broken him completely, but it hadn't.

Stripped bare, somewhere beneath the rawness, beneath the pain, there was calm, a certainty.

He couldn't stay.

He would miss the twins' laughter—the way they always pulled him from his thoughts before he could drown in them.

Mama, the warmth of her hands cupping his face, the way she whispered love into his bones.

Papa, his quiet strength, his steady, unwavering guidance.

But tonight, had changed everything.

Even if he stayed, the memories he treasured would never be repeated.

They were gone. Frozen in time, untouched by what came next.

Breathe in. Hold. Breathe out.

His fingers curled around the strap of his pack.

He took his first step away from the only home he had ever known.

The walk to the inn stretched endlessly. Sol moved as quickly as he could, too weak to run, too desperate to simply walk. Every step burned. But it didn't matter.

I have to get to Wyatt.

To say goodbye.

He couldn't ask Wyatt to come with him. If Ysella and Scy were here, Wyatt would be safe. He had to be.

The thought of leaving Wyatt destroyed him.

Sol wanted nothing more than to give him the happiness he deserved, but that had never been an option. Sol couldn't even keep himself safe. He had no idea where he was going. No plan. No destination. Only the certainty that the path ahead would be near impossible.

And he couldn't bear the thought of Wyatt suffering alongside him.

The inn was dark, with only a few windows flickering with dim candlelight. Sol circled the building once, scanning the quiet night. Satisfied, he slipped through the back door, set his pack down, and crept toward the far room, Wyatt's room.

He barely made it three steps before a hand clamped over his mouth.

He struggled, but the grip held firm.

This was it.

He was spun and slammed against the wall, a dagger flashing at his throat. Pain flared through his back, a sharp, searing shock that tore a muffled cry from his lips.

Wide eyes. A glint of silver.

Scy.

The knife dropped from his hand in an instant, replaced by a

sharp smack upside Sol's head.

"What in all of Old Magpie's tricks is this?" Scy hissed. "Did you forget how to use the front door?"

Sol swallowed hard, trying to steady his voice. "Scy, I need to talk to Wyatt. It couldn't wait."

Scy narrowed his eyes, suspicion flickering across his face.
"And Ysella? Will you be tellin' her this urgent news too?"

Sol hesitated. He was already caught.

"Yes," he said. "I just… didn't want to wake her at this hour."

Scy exhaled, dragging a hand down his face. "I'll fetch her. But you'd best knock before goin' in, Wyatt may not recognize you in the dark."

Then he was gone, vanishing down the hall.

Sol drew a breath and knocked softly, twice.

"Wyatt, it's me."

The door creaked as Sol stepped inside.

Wyatt was already sitting up, the lamp still unlit. His silhouette tensed in the dark.

"Sol?" His voice was quiet, strained. "Are you okay?"

He struck a match with shaking fingers and lit the lamp beside the bed. The moment the flame caught, he was already on his feet.

He crossed the room in a heartbeat, reaching out, and Sol stepped back.

"Please. Don't."

"What?" His voice cracked with hurt.

"I—" Sol started, but the door swung open.

"What in the names of the gods—?" Ysella gasped.

Scy entered behind her, his expression dark. "My boy. What happened?"

But Wyatt moved before Sol could answer. He grabbed Sol's shoulder and turned him around, lifting his blood-stained shirt without hesitation.

The room fell into stunned silence.

"Ysella." Wyatt's voice shook, "We need bandages

and poultices now."

Ysella stepped closer, her gaze sweeping over the torn flesh of Sol's back. She didn't speak. She only nodded once.

Scy, for once, had no jokes. He slipped out the door, moving fast.

Wyatt gritted his teeth and turned Sol back around. His hands were on Sol's face before he could protest, and then…A kiss.

Fierce. Desperate. A plea spoken in the only language Wyatt had left.

Sol didn't move, didn't respond. He simply let himself feel it, one last time.

When Wyatt pulled back, something dangerous flickered in his eyes. "Who did this to you?" His voice was deadly quiet.

Sol exhaled slowly, letting calm settle over him.

He turned to Ysella first. She met his gaze and gave a single nod.

Then, locking eyes with Wyatt, he spoke.

"High Priest Drevan."

Wyatt's body went rigid. His jaw clenched, his fists curling at his sides.

"I'll kill him myself," he growled.

Sol placed a hand on Wyatt's shoulder.

"And my father."

Silence.

Wyatt stared at him. Ysella did too.

Neither could find the words.

The only sound was the soft creak of the floorboards as Scy returned.

Wordlessly, they guided Sol into a chair. Ysella got to work, tending his wounds with the practiced hands of someone who had done this before.

Wyatt sat on the floor, his fingers wrapped tightly around Sol's hand.

And Sol told them everything.

The lamp flickered. The air grew thick with tension.

Sol drew a breath and said, steady, defiant, "I'm leaving Oswynn. Tonight."

The words had barely settled before Wyatt moved. "I need to pack," he said, already getting to his feet.

Sol yanked him back, gripping his wrist tightly.

"No." His voice was barely above a whisper, but it carried every ounce of finality he could summon.

Wyatt froze, eyes narrowing.

"Like hell—"

Ysella cut him off before he could say more, her voice sharp and steady, laced with a weight Wyatt knew all too well.

"Hush now."

Wyatt fell silent under her stare, one filled with unspoken promises.

Scy leaned against the doorway, arms crossed, watching. His usual smirk was gone. He didn't interrupt, just listened.

Ysella turned back to Sol. "You're exhausted. You're hurt. You cannot leave tonight."

"I have to," Sol said, his jaw clenched.

Ysella took his free hand in hers, brushing her fingers gently through his hair as she searched his face.

"My darling boy," she murmured, "you don't have to leave. We won't let any harm come to you. You have friends here, Hettie, Rein,

Thom, Maris—people who care for you."

"If I go, Wyatt will be safe," Sol said, his voice tight.

He hesitated. Then, softer, "I couldn't bear to see Mira and Theo and not be able to go to them."

Ysella's grip tightened. "We can figure this out. We can protect you."

There was uncertainty in her voice, soft but sharp enough for him to hear it.

Sol felt it. Heard it. Knew it was true.

Drevan's power was growing. The Baron was burning the shrines of the old gods. Nothing was safe.

"No," Sol said, quiet but confident. "You couldn't protect me from this. No one can. Not now."

He swallowed hard.

"The Baron is tearing down anything that stands in their way. If I stay, it will only get worse."

A pause.

"But if I go… they won't look to Wyatt. My leaving will be a distraction."

Silence.

Then, "Then I'm coming with you," Wyatt said, firm and unshaken.

Sol's grip tightened. "You are not."

Wyatt lifted his chin. "Try and stop me."

"This isn't a game, Wyatt!"

"You think I don't know that?" His voice cracked. "I saw what they did to you."

Sol's stomach twisted. He couldn't do this.

"You still have a life here. A home. A future—with Ysella.

Don't throw that away."

"I belong with you."

Sol shook his head, sharp and quick. "No. No, Wyatt, you don't understand what this will be."

He drew a shaky breath, forcing the words out through the panic rising in his throat.

"I don't know where I'm going. I don't know if I'll survive. There will be nights when I go hungry. Days I'll be hunted. And if you're with me—"

His voice broke. He couldn't finish.

Wyatt stepped forward, taking both of Sol's hands

in his.

"Then let me come with you. Because if you go without me… every moment you're gone, I'll be wondering if you're still alive."

Sol exhaled, his hands trembling in Wyatt's.

He opened his mouth to argue, to beg, to protect him.

But the words didn't come.

The fight had already left him.

"You stubborn idiot."

Wyatt grinned, soft, unwavering.

"And you love me anyway."

Sol let out a breathy, broken laugh, shaking his head.

"Yeah," he admitted, voice raw. "I do."

Ysella sighed deeply, rubbing her temples. "Goddesses help me. Both of you are fools."

Scy, still leaning in the doorway, gave a small shake of his head. "That makes three of us, then."

Scy exhaled through his nose and pushed off the doorframe, stretching his arms with lazy ease.

"I suppose I'll be gettin' the supplies ready."

He left without another word.

Ysella's gaze lingered on Sol as she tied the last bandage. Her hands were steady, but there was weight in her silence, a heaviness that hung between them, unspoken and unmoving.

She let out a quiet sigh and squeezed Sol's shoulder. "Get some rest. You'll need it."

Sol nodded, though he wasn't sure if sleep would find him.

Ysella turned to Wyatt. "Watch him. If he so much as twitches wrong, wake me."

"I will," Wyatt said, firm, without hesitation.

She studied them both for a long moment, then leaned in and pressed a kiss to Wyatt's forehead, quick, familiar, maternal.

Then she was gone, closing the door softly behind her.

The room was quiet.

Wyatt didn't move at first. He just sat there, watching him, as if trying to commit every detail of this moment to memory.

Then, slowly, he shifted closer.

Sol wasn't sure when he lay down.

Maybe it happened when the tension finally broke. Maybe Wyatt guided him gently, without protest.

All Sol knew was the weight leaving his legs, the ache in his spine, and the warmth that met him like mercy.

The mattress dipped as Wyatt shifted beside him, careful, deliberate—a steady presence in a world that had been anything but.

The inn was quiet. No more fighting. No more choices left to make.

Wyatt didn't speak right away. He pulled the blanket over both of them, his touch light but certain. Sol felt him hesitate, then a warm hand settled over his wrist, a silent question.

Sol answered by turning toward him.

They lay facing each other in the dark, close but not tangled, breathing the same air.

Wyatt's fingers found his, tracing over his knuckles, grounding him.

"We'll be okay." His voice was soft, steady, like a promise.

Sol exhaled, something loosening inside him. "I know."

Wyatt shifted closer, pressing his forehead to Sol's, a touch so careful, so achingly familiar, that it nearly undid him.

"You don't have to be strong tonight."

Sol's throat tightened. He let his eyes slip shut.

Wyatt's arm curled around his waist, pulling him gently against his chest, not demanding, not asking for anything. Just offering warmth. A stillness Sol could hold onto.

For the first time all night, he let himself lean into it—and believe it.

Chapter Thirteen

———

Between Hearth and Horizon

The inn was steeped in the rich, savory scent of sausage crackling in the pan, the aroma curling through the air like a promise. Flames danced in the hearth, their light flickering over the worn wooden floorboards, casting shifting shadows that moved like ghosts.

Sol and Wyatt sat near the fire, checking their packs for the third time. Wyatt moved with his usual quiet certainty, every motion deliberate, unbothered. His steady presence anchored the room, a quiet bulwark against the storm of nerves coiled tight in Sol's chest.

Scy leaned against the table, hands clasped behind his back, that ever-present sly grin tugging at the edge of his angular face.

"My boys," he drawled, his voice as smooth and lazy as a cat stretching in a sunbeam, "it's going to be rough out there. Dangerous.

And I can't have you dying on me, now, can I? What would Old Magpie say?"

He placed two short swords on the table, their plain sheaths unassuming, but the edges of the blades whispering a deadly promise.

Beside them, he arranged daggers, their cords coiled neatly.

"They ain't much, but they'll do," Scy said with false modesty.

Sol hesitated, fingers suspended just above the hilt. Even without touching it, the weight of the blade pressed into him— unfamiliar, unwelcome. It didn't belong in his hands. It didn't belong to him. And yet, there it was, cold and waiting beneath his fingertips, a silent promise of what was coming.

Beside him, Wyatt reached for one of the short swords and turned it with a practiced ease, testing the edge against his thumb. "Good balance," he murmured, unfazed.

"I've never used a sword," Sol admitted, his voice quieter than he meant.

Scy snorted. "Well, Wyatt'll have to teach you the basics on the road. But first, stand up. I'll show you how to wear the daggers without skewering yourself like a storybook idiot."

Sol stood, stiff-limbed, as Scy crouched in front of him and yanked up his trouser leg. The first dagger was lashed tight against the inside of his boot, the leather cords biting into his skin. It would press with every step, a reminder of its presence, its purpose.

"Easy reach," Scy muttered. "Try not to lose it. Knives like to slip out when you're running."

The second dagger was strapped to his wrist, the leather grip chafing against his pulse like a quiet threat. The last slid into place at his belt, nestled against the small of his back—light, but insistent, like it was already whispering its purpose.

Sol flexed his fingers and rolled his wrist. "This is uncomfortable," he muttered.

Scy cinched the belt sheath with a sharp, practiced tug. "Comfort's a luxury you won't find on the road."

Sol sighed. This was his life now. He had to be ready. He had to be better than his nerves. "Aye, you're right."

Sol reached for the short sword and gave it a tug, but the blade snagged awkwardly in the sheath, refusing to budge with any grace.

Wyatt stifled a crooked grin. "It's a start. You'll get

there."

Sol shot him a look. "Since when do you know anything about swords?"

Wyatt just smirked and drew his blade in one fluid motion, the metal whispering free before sliding back with a soft shk.

"Scy made me learn," he said. "Told me even shepherds need sharp teeth."

Sol blinked. *How had he missed that?*

Scy stepped in, hand firm on Sol's shoulder. The usual glint in his eye had dulled, replaced with something flint-hard.

"If it comes to it," Scy said, voice low and flat, "don't think. Just swing, like you're splitting wood. And keep swinging 'til they stop moving."

Sol swallowed hard and gave a tight nod.

Behind them, the kitchen door creaked open, and the warm, greasy scent of sausage and hotcakes drifted in like a memory from another life.

Ysella entered with heaping plates balanced in her hands, setting them down with a thud that spoke louder than words. She smoothed her apron once, twice, the gesture sharp with unspoken frustration.

"You boys need a proper meal before you go," she said, her smile too tight, too practiced. It didn't reach her eyes. "You don't know when the next hot meal will come."

Without thinking, Sol reached for her hand. Ysella paused, just for a beat, then gave his fingers a quick, steady squeeze—brief, but sure.

"Be careful," she said softly, not quite meeting his eyes.

Sol nodded, the weight of her touch lingering longer than the moment allowed.

They sat at the table, the weight of steel pressing against their skin, the taste of hot food on their tongues, and the knowledge that this was the last time they'd eat here as just boys.

They ate in silence.

From the back of the inn, Ysella and Scy spoke in hushed, urgent tones, their words barely audible over the hush of the fire. But Sol and Wyatt didn't hear them. Their world had narrowed to the silence between heartbeats.

"There's still time," Sol said, voice low, almost careful. "You could stay. You'd be safe."

Wyatt exhaled, a sound close to a laugh but quieter, heavier. "I already told you. There's nothing for me here without you."

He reached across the table, threading his fingers through Sol's, gripping tight. "I love you. That hasn't changed."

Sol met his gaze, the weight of it settling in his chest like something sacred. "I love you too."

"Then don't even think about ditching me again," Wyatt said—firmer now, an uncharacteristic edge cutting through his voice.

Sol faltered, his words catching. "I'm just… scared for you."

Wyatt's thumb moved slowly over the back of his hand, steady and grounding. "I know. I'm scared for you too. But if I'm with you,

I've got a chance to help. To protect you."

He hesitated, then added, voice dropping lower, rougher, "And let's be honest, did you really think The Hand would just let me walk away once you're gone?"

Sol's jaw tightened. He wanted to argue. To tell Wyatt he was wrong. That he'd be safe here.

But that was a lie—and they both knew it.

"I guess…" Sol said, voice soft, "I was hoping if I believed it hard enough, it might be true."

His thoughts slipped, unbidden, back to the hearth—to that strange, quiet certainty that had settled in his chest like ash after fire.

At the time, he hadn't believed it could be him. Not really.

Now, he held that hope like a flame cupped in trembling hands, fragile, flickering, but still burning.

As they finished their meal, Ysella and Scy emerged from the back of the inn, arms laden with fresh bandages and poultices sharp with the scent of bitter herbs.

Sol realized his back was only mildly sore now—the pain dulled to a whisper, nothing like the raw fire of the night before.

"Take off your shirt," Ysella said gently. "I want to take another look."

He hesitated, then pulled the fabric over his head with a wince. Ysella's hands were warm as they moved across his shoulder blades, her touch careful, fingers pressing over the fading bruises like reading a map.

It should have hurt.

It didn't.

The poultice tingled against his skin, its sharp scent filling his nose. Relief came fast, sudden and almost unreal.

"What is this made of?" Sol asked, blinking in disbelief. "Feels like last night was just a dream."

Ysella smiled faintly as she tied off the last bandage. "Strong stuff. A hedgewitch passing through gave it to me."

"Hedgewitch?" Sol's brow creased.

"You'll still have scars," Ysella continued, ignoring his question for now. "But this will have you feeling better in no time."

Sol flexed his shoulders, rolling them with cautious curiosity.

"It's only been a few hours, and I already feel better."

Ysella watched him for a long moment, her gaze steady and unreadable.

"Sol... you've been sheltered here in Oswynn." Her voice was soft but unwavering. "There's magic in this world, not just the kind wrapped in temple stories. Real magic. The kind of Elion's faith has spent generations trying to erase."

Sol stilled.

Magic. Not the kind murmured in temple sermons or dressed up as parables. Not a metaphor for faith.

Real magic.

Something hidden. Forbidden.

Something that might've always been there, just beyond reach, waiting.

Ysella sighed, running a hand through her hair. "I should have told you more. I wanted to. But I was trying to respect your parents' wishes." She exhaled heavily, shaking her head. "And now… now, there's hardly time."

Sol swallowed, suddenly unsure what to say.

Ysella laid a hand on his shoulder, her touch warm and steady.

"Just promise me one thing, Sol."

He looked up, meeting her eyes.

"Keep an open mind," she said. "There's magic all around you.

You only have to be willing to see it."

"I will, Mum," Sol murmured. "Thank you."

The first rays of sun crept through the window, warming the inn's corners like a slow breath, lifting the hush of night from Sol's skin.

Scy crossed his arms, his expression sharpened by a rare seriousness. "You two will write when you can. Use the Rouge to send them, they'll make sure they reach us, and no one else gets eyes on them."

"Yes, sir," Sol said, straightening with quiet resolve.

Scy's lips quirked. "Now, don't go confusing me for an honest man."

Sol smirked and raised his hand, fingers flicking in a quick sign against evil. "I would never."

Scy chuckled, a low, fond sound, then stepped forward and pulled him into a firm embrace. The usual mischief in his eyes had softened, replaced by something steadier. Quieter.

"You two'll be alright," he murmured. "I'm not the rescuing type, so don't go needing rescuing."

Sol didn't speak. He couldn't. He just held on.

Then Ysella swept in, arms fierce and fast, pulling him into a crushing hug. She pressed quick, frantic kisses to his cheeks, his brow, her breath hitching with each one. Her fingers threaded through his unruly hair, trying in vain to smooth it, as if taming it might somehow make him stay. As if holding on tightly could make time stand still.

"I love you both so much," she whispered, her voice thick with unshed tears. "We will see each other again—do not doubt this."

Sol nodded, squeezing her hand one last time before stepping back.

He and Wyatt shouldered their packs. Sol moved with care, conscious of the dull ache in his back. It tugged at him with every step, an uncomfortable yet manageable sensation. They'd have to pace themselves.

The morning air was cool and clean as they stepped outside, wrapping around them like a second skin. The village lay hushed in the soft hush of dawn, smoke curling slowly and silver from chimneys, the world beginning to stir, but not yet awake.

Sol hesitated. "Ysella?"

She turned, her hands still gripping her apron, eyes full of unspoken things.

"Can you tell my friends that I'm okay?" Sol asked

quietly.

Ysella's smile was sad, but steady. "Of course. I'll tell them what happened and why you had to leave so quickly."

Sol nodded, the weight of it catching behind his ribs, sharp and hollow. It wasn't everything. But it was enough.

He raised a hand in a quiet farewell. Ysella pressed hers to her heart, holding it there like a promise.

Then they turned toward the road.

The sheep pen waited on the outskirts of town, Wyatt's usual starting point. It made for a fitting cover. The flock would slow their pace, which was just as well; Sol's body couldn't handle more than a steady walk, not yet.

When they reached the pen, Wyatt moved instinctively among the sheep, coaxing them into motion.

But something tugged at Sol's senses.

Sol paused. Something felt off. He counted quickly—only fifteen. Half the flock.

"Wyatt," he said, voice low. "Why aren't you taking the rest?"

Wyatt, busy securing the gate, didn't look back right

away. "I gave the other half to Ysella."

Sol blinked. "You, what?"

"Call it a thank-you," Wyatt said, resting his weight on his staff. "For everything she and Scy did for us. The packs. The quiet generosity. The years of kindness."

Sol's throat tightened. "I'm sorry," he said, barely more than a whisper.

Wyatt turned to him, head tilted slightly. "Don't be." His voice was calm, even. "I'd meant to give her something, even before all this.
She'll see they're looked after."

Sol nodded, the quiet conviction in Wyatt's eyes settling something in his chest.

Wyatt exhaled, adjusting his grip on his staff. "Well, we should get moving. Which way?"

Sol glanced toward the open road. He didn't know if it was the right path, but it was a path, and he needed to take it.

"That way looks good," he said.

Wyatt nodded. "Nasareth's that way. We can restock there."

Then he stepped in close, brushing Sol's hair back

with gentle fingers before pressing a soft kiss to his cheek.

Then, without another word, Wyatt turned and took the lead, the sheep moving with him.

Sol followed, casting a single glance, just once, over his shoulder at the village dissolving into the pale hush of morning.

Then he turned.

Faced forward.

And didn't look back.

They had been walking for hours. The sun hung high overhead, beating down on their backs, while birdsong filled the quiet between them.

Sol's stomach growled, loud and unignorable.

Wyatt smirked, casting him a sideways glance. "Well, I guess that settles it. Time for lunch."

Sol blinked, yanked out of his thoughts. "What?"

Wyatt laughed. "Don't even pretend your stomach didn't just announce a full rebellion."

Sol let out a breathy laugh. "Yeah… I guess a break wouldn't hurt."

Wyatt grinned. "Come on, let's find some shade. Can't have you wasting away before we even get away from Oswynn."

They stepped off the road and settled beneath the arching limbs of a tall tree, grateful for the patchwork shade that flickered across the grass. Sol dropped his pack with a quiet groan, shoulders sore from the weight. The cool breeze pressing through his sweatdamp shirt was a small, perfect relief.

Wyatt rummaged through their supplies and unwrapped a bundle of dried meat. He tore off a few strips, passing the rest to Sol. Their fingers brushed, just for a second. But it was enough to anchor something in him, quiet the drift beneath his ribs.

Wyatt took a slow sip from his waterskin, then leaned back against the tree's rough bark, exhaling like he could finally lower his guard, if only a little.

Sol followed suit, sinking down beside him. Grateful for the pause. Grateful for Wyatt.

For a few quiet minutes, they sat in companionable silence. The soft crunch of dried rations filled the air, mingling with the distant trill of birdsong and the rustle of leaves overhead.

Sol broke the quiet. "Ysella said there's magic everywhere."

Wyatt hummed low in his throat. "She's said things like that to me before. I always figured it was just... her way. Like bedtime stories, only for grown-ups."

He chewed slowly, eyes fixed beyond the treeline. "I've seen a healer snap a bone back into place so quick it felt like sleight of hand. But real magic? Big magic?" He shook his head. "It's not just rare. It's wild. Untamed."

Sol glanced over, catching the edge in his voice. "You sound like you're afraid of it."

Wyatt didn't answer right away. His jaw tensed, his gaze turning inward, haunted. Something flickered there, low and dark.

"I am," he said quietly. "It's not like a sword, you can see a sword coming. Magic... you never know when it'll hit, or who it'll hurt. Doesn't matter if it's meant well or not. One moment of carelessness, and the wrong person dies."

His fingers tightened around the waterskin. "Folk like us? We don't get shields. We don't get second chances."

Sol chewed his last bite in silence, then swallowed.

"I know," he said quietly. "But still… part of me wants it to be real. Something bigger than us. Something that says we're not just dust on a road someone else paved."

Wyatt's lips twitched, half amusement, half something softer.

"You just want to throw fireballs."

Sol grinned. "Wouldn't say no."

Once they finished eating, Wyatt stood and stretched, then extended a hand toward Sol. "Alright. Let's start with the basics."

Sol took it, hauling himself up with a skeptical look. "What if I hurt you?"

Wyatt chuckled, thumb brushing over Sol's knuckles in a quiet reassurance. "We'll save knocking me flat for later. First, let's make sure you can draw your sword without opening up an artery."

He took a few steps back and, in one smooth motion, drew his blade. It gleamed in the light, steady and sure in his hand.

"Your turn."

Sol reached for his hilt, trying to mimic the motion, but the blade snagged halfway, nearly twisting his wrist.

Wyatt slid his sword back into its sheath, a flicker of amusement in his eyes. "Not quite."

He stepped in behind Sol, slipping an arm around his waist. His hands found Sol's warm, steady, adjusting his grip with practiced ease.

"Relax your shoulder," he murmured near his ear. "Draw in one smooth motion. Pull and turn."

Sol nodded, jaw set with concentration. He tried again.

This time, the blade came free with a cleaner motion—not perfect, but better.

"Better," Wyatt murmured, his voice low and steady. He adjusted Sol's grip, fingertips firm but careful. "Now, straighten your arm. Keep your wrist loose."

Sol repeated the movement. Then again. And again. Muscle learning. Breath of evening. Slowly, it began to feel like his.

The repetition built a rhythm. A sense of familiarity. Until the sword's weight began to drag on him, slow and relentless. His arm trembled.

Still, he didn't stop.

Wyatt gently caught his wrist, guiding the blade

down. "Easy," he murmured. "Didn't mean to wear you out so fast, love."

"I'm fine," Sol managed, breath hitching. "Just… tired."

Wyatt touched his cheek, fingers light. "Your muscles will catch up. You're stronger than you think."

Before Sol could argue, Wyatt leaned in and kissed him—soft, teasing, a brush of warmth that stole the breath from his lungs.

Sol blinked, startled—but the ache in his arms vanished beneath the heat blooming in his chest. For a heartbeat, there was nothing else. Just that kiss.

When Wyatt pulled back, he was already grinning. "I'm no master swordsman," he said, "but you've got promise."

Sol laughed, breathless. "Liar."

Wyatt kissed him again, slower this time, deliberate, before turning toward the sheep, already easing back into stride like nothing had happened.

Sol stood there for a moment longer, his lips tingling, the echo of Wyatt's hands still wrapped around his own.

The day's heat clung to their backs, heavy as a second skin. Each step pulled at Sol's breath, his wounds tightening, the dull ache creeping steadily into focus.

Ahead, trees rose like watchful sentinels, their branches locked in a silent struggle for light. The sight stirred a flicker of relief—shade, shelter, a place to stop.

Sol lifted a weary arm and pointed. "Is that where we'll camp?" he asked, voice thin with hope.

Wyatt followed his gaze, then nodded. "Yes. We're almost there."

Sol pushed himself forward at those words, forcing his legs to match Wyatt's steady, purposeful stride. His pack bounced with each step, the weight grinding into his shoulders, but he clenched his jaw and pressed on.

Almost there.

Out of the corner of his eye, a flicker—movement. A figure?

He blinked, tried to focus. *Nothing. Just trees and heat haze. Paranoia,* he told himself.

At the tree line, Wyatt veered north, guiding them deeper into the woods. "We'll camp higher up than usual," he murmured. "Just in case someone's watching."

Sol only nodded, too focused on keeping up, on the burning in his muscles, on the way his pack seemed to dig into every sore spot.

As they moved deeper into the forest, the trees pressed closer, and the air turned cool and damp with moss and pine. The golden light of the setting sun splintered through the canopy in fractured beams, shrinking with every step.

Night was falling fast.

Wyatt finally halted beneath a massive old pine, its wide boughs heavy with needles, thick enough to offer shelter from both sight and storm.

The sheep drifted lazily nearby, already settling into their soft, familiar rhythm.

Wyatt dropped his pack and stretched, joints popping. "If you lay out our bedrolls and see to supper," he said, brushing pine needles from his shoulder, "I'll gather wood and start the fire."

Sol huffed, shaking his head. "I never knew you to be so commanding."

Wyatt smirked as he adjusted his staff. "You like it.

Don't pretend you don't."

Sol grinned, the warmth in his chest giving him away. "I do find it rather charming."

Wyatt chuckled, his gaze flicking toward the woods, the edges of his expression softening. "Good. Then you won't mind letting me lead, for a little while."

Sol rolled his eyes, but his heart felt light as he knelt to clear a patch of ground for their bedrolls, the moment settling around them like a quiet promise.

This moment, this quiet rhythm of camp and company, felt almost surreal. He had imagined something like it before, in dreams.

A life with Wyatt. Not like this, not beneath a tree with the world at their heels. It wasn't the life Sol had imagined, but it was real. It was theirs.

The bedrolls were spread out, and a thin stew simmered in a dented travel pot above the fire. Sol watched as Wyatt leaned in to stoke the flames, the light catching the angles of his face, soft and golden, like something out of a memory he hadn't lived yet.

"This would be a lot easier if I could shoot fireballs," Sol muttered, stretching his sore arms with a groan.

Wyatt smirked as he tossed another log into the fire. "We just need a spark, love. You'd probably scorch half the forest—and your eyebrows."

Sol laughed, but the sound cut short as he leaned back too far.

Pain tore through him, sharp and sudden, like fire cracking down his spine.

He jerked upright, breath catching in his throat before he could swallow it.

Wyatt's smile vanished. "Sol?"

"It's fine," Sol lied, eyes darting to the fire.

Wyatt didn't answer right away. He just watched him—steady, unreadable, until Sol shifted beneath the weight of his gaze.

With a quiet exhale, Sol rubbed his knee. "Okay… it started bothering me a few hours ago."

Wyatt ran a hand through his hair, sighing. "Ysella gave me a salve for your back. Said I need to change the bandages every night until it closes up. This'll help it along."

He stirred the soup once before ladling it into their mugs, then set a second pot of water to boil.

Sol took a sip and blinked in surprise. "This is actually… really good."

Wyatt grinned. "She's been stocking our packs for ages.

Probably got tired of us stumbling home half-starved."

They ate in easy silence, the fire's glow chasing the chill from Sol's limbs, the knot in his chest slowly unwinding under the weight of Wyatt's calm presence.

After a while, Wyatt set down his mug and turned to him, his voice gentle. "Love, let me take care of your back."

Sol hesitated only a moment before nodding. He eased his shirt over his head, surprised to find just a few dried patches of blood—far less than he'd braced for.

Wyatt unwrapped the bandages with practiced care, his hands steady, deliberate. But the moment the last layer came free, he drew in a sharp breath.

"Sol… I saw your back last night. It was bad."

He dipped a clean rag into the warm water, letting it cool before carefully wiping away the remnants of dried blood. His fingers traced the wounds with practiced care.

"This is remarkable," Wyatt murmured. "It looks like days have passed, not just one night."

Sol turned, trying to catch a glimpse over his shoulder. "I want to believe it, but it still doesn't feel real."

Wyatt let out a quiet huff, then rummaged through their pack and pulled out a small, polished metal mirror. "Here. See for yourself." Sol angled it behind him, fingers fumbling slightly. When he finally caught the reflection, his breath caught.

The wounds were still red, the skin raised and tender, but not raw. No heat, no bleeding. Just healing. Fast. Unearthly.

A strange pressure built behind his eyes. It should have been a relief, but instead it brought back the sting of firelight, stone, and his father's hand.

He didn't notice the tear until Wyatt's thumb brushed it away.

"I know," Wyatt said quietly. "But they mean you survived." Sol nodded, his throat too tight for words.

Wyatt kissed his temple, voice no louder than a breath. "And you're still mine."

Sol didn't reply. He let the words settle in the quiet

space between them, grounding him more than he expected.

"How's that feel?" Wyatt murmured.

Sol exhaled slowly, the medicine's warmth sinking into his skin, easing the last of the ache. "Better," he said softly. "Thank you."

Wyatt pressed a quick kiss to his forehead. "I'm going to rinse this out," he said, taking Sol's soiled shirt, "and hang it to dry. We don't need an infection setting in."

Sol nodded, eyes following him as he moved, sure-footed, capable, already halfway to the water pot. There was something in the effortless way Wyatt cared for him that tugged at his chest—not pain, but a quiet ache. The kind that came when something broken was beginning to mend.

They finished tidying the campsite, packing away what they could before night fully settled over the forest. The fire crackled low beside them, casting soft, shifting light over the ground.

By the time they settled into their bedrolls, the air had cooled to a gentle bite, thick with the scent of pine and damp earth.

Wyatt curled around Sol from behind, his arms

threading around him, warmth pressing along his spine.

Sol exhaled slowly, melting into the steady rhythm of Wyatt's breath.

"Tomorrow's a new day," Wyatt whispered, hope and fear braided into every word. "There's a whole world ahead of us. And whatever comes… we face it together."

His voice was low, steady, but full of quiet excitement.

"I know it'll be hard," he continued, his breath warm against Sol's skin. "But… I'm excited. The whole world is in front of us."

Sol swallowed hard. The words wrapped around him, warmer than any blanket, steadier than fear. Maybe they weren't ready. Maybe the road ahead was still sharp with shadows and unknowns.

But for the first time in a long time, he didn't feel alone in it.

He reached back, slow but sure, until his hand found Wyatt's.

Their fingers wove together, firm and familiar.

"I'm glad it's with you," he whispered.

Then he let his eyes drift shut, letting the warmth

of Wyatt's arms and the steady rhythm of his breathing pull him under.

The last thing he felt was the soft brush of Wyatt's lips against his shoulder, light as breath, grounding as stone. A silent promise in the dark.

Then sleep came, slow and certain, and carried them both into quiet.

Chapter Fourteen

The Devil We Know

The morning was cool and damp, a hushed stillness hanging in the air like mist. It clung to the skin, soft but unshakable. The scent of wet earth saturated everything, rich, raw, and almost metallic. Even the trees seemed subdued, their branches holding a breath, listening. Sol ate quickly from the cookpot, spooning up thin porridge that steamed in the chill. It was warm but insubstantial, sliding down too easily and settling in his gut like a stone. Hunger remained, dull and persistent, a hollow reminder that the day had only just begun.

Neither of them spoke as they packed, the silence broken only by the crackle of dying embers as Wyatt stamped out the last of the fire. He moved with the ease of habit, every motion efficient, unthinking. Sol trailed behind, his fingers clumsy from the cold, his shoulders aching from sleep. He hadn't yet learned the rhythm of the road. His mind wandered ahead, darting from worry to wonder, already restless for things he couldn't name.

As they set off, the sheep followed without complaint, their wool damp with morning mist. The rhythm of their footsteps was the only sound—boots against soft earth, hooves padding lightly behind.

"We'll need to follow the road for a few hours before we can cut to the trail," Wyatt said, tugging the strap of his pack tighter across his shoulder.

Sol looked up, a faint crease between his brows. "The road?"

Wyatt gave a short nod. "It's quicker. And that trail isn't marked. If you don't know where to look, you'll walk right past it."

Sol hesitated, glancing toward the thin line of packed dirt ahead, cutting through the land like an old scar. Roads meant people.

Meant to be seen.

"It'll be fine," Wyatt said. "We'll keep our heads down."

Sol exhaled and nodded, though unease curled low in his gut— a slow, familiar tension that had settled in his bones more than once before things went wrong.

Maybe it was just exhaustion. The past few days had blurred together: too much change, too many questions, not enough sleep.

Or maybe it was the morning itself, too still, too

quiet, as if the world were holding its breath.

He tried not to dwell on it, that quiet, crawling unease at the base of his spine.

Sol drew in a long breath, the damp morning air filling his lungs like weight.

You're overthinking again.

The road was just a road.

And yet…

As they stepped onto it, the sun climbed higher, peeling back the mist in thin, silvery veils. The fields opened up around them, wide and bare, stretching to the horizon. Too open. Too exposed.

Sol felt it then—not fear, exactly, but the sharp awareness of being seen. The world had shed its cover, and there was nowhere left to hide.

Wyatt kept walking, easy, confident, like he'd done a hundred times before. The sheep trailed behind him, unbothered.

Sol forced himself to keep pace.

Ahead, the road stretched out, long, silent, and empty. But the quiet didn't sit right.

He couldn't shake the sense that they weren't as alone as they looked.

The path was broader than he expected, worn smooth by years of carts and hooves. Deep grooves cut into the damp earth along its edges, as if the land itself had been dragged into motion. Here and there, old stones jutted from the dirt, milestones, maybe, their faces weathered blank by time and rain, like memories rubbed away.

Sol kept his gaze moving, studying the land around them—low hills to their left, a stretch of dense trees to their right. The openness made his skin itch.

Sol had always admired the way Wyatt moved, the quiet confidence in his steps. He had traveled this road before, had spent his life on trails and fields, knowing the weight of distance in a way Sol never had to.

Sol shifted the strap of his bag, already feeling the weight of the morning settle into his body. The sun had climbed high behind them, warming the back of his neck, but sweat still clung under his shirt, damp, stubborn, and clinging like a second skin. The road's slow toll was beginning to seep into his bones.

"Doing okay?" Wyatt called, glancing back over his

shoulder.

Sol gave a shrug, tightening his grip on the strap. "I just don't like roads."

Wyatt gave a knowing hum. "They're meant to make things easier."

"Easier to be seen," Sol muttered.

Wyatt glanced back again. "That's why we don't stop for long."

Sol exhaled slowly and sank beneath the oak's twisted branches. The shade offered little relief, but he welcomed the stillness.

Wyatt passed the waterskin to him without a word.

Then, stillness sharpened.

Something moved in the trees. A flicker. A shift.

Sol's breath caught. The air had gone too quiet, like the hush before a storm.

And then, a figure stepped into the clearing.

Sol felt it before he saw it. The prickle down his neck. The kind of silence that meant you weren't alone.

"Well, well," the man drawled, his voice soaked in mockery. "What've we got here? A pair of soft lads playin' at shepherd?"

His eyes swept over the sheep, then slid back to them. The smile that followed was all teeth—yellow, crooked, and far from friendly.

Wyatt answered without flinching, his tone flat and calm. "We're headin' north. The sheep come with us."

The man scratched at his chin, like he was giving it real thought. "Ain't lookin' like you need all of 'em. We'll just take a few— call it a toll."

The underbrush rustled. Five more stepped into view.

Sol's pulse thundered in his ears.

"We don't want trouble," he said, voice tight. "Let us pass, and we'll be on our way."

"'Course you don't," the leader said, grinning like a dog that's cornered its rabbit. "But we ain't askin'."

One of the younger ones, thin as wire, all bones and greasy hair, slid a knife free with a soft, deliberate hiss.

"Could just gut ya both. Quicker that way."

Wyatt and Sol rose in unison, hands already on their blades, half-drawn steel catching the light.

"We're leavin'," Wyatt said, steel in his tone. "With the flock."

The leader's grin stretched wider. "You sure about that, boy? One twitch from me, and your little friend's bleedin' like a stuck pig."

Wyatt stepped forward, placing himself squarely between them and Sol. His hand tightened on the hilt, knuckles pale.

"Come any closer," he said, voice low and steady, "and you'll be pickin' your teeth outta your guts."

That drew a laugh, rough and mean. The leader looked him up and down, amused. "Go on, then. Make it fun. I ain't had a proper laugh in days."

Wyatt spat into the dirt. His voice was quiet, sharp as broken glass. "We don't need to win — just make sure you crawl home wishing you'd never tried."

The scrawny one lunged.

Wyatt moved faster than Sol had ever seen.

His blade sang through the air, a flash of steel before it struck home. The sword slammed into the bandit's ribs with a wet crunch.

Bone gave way. Blood sprayed in a sudden arc,

spattering the earth. The man screamed, stumbling back, both hands pressed to the gash blooming red at his side.

Sol yanked his sword free, breath tearing ragged from his throat. The stench hit him, a mix of iron, heat, and something foul beneath it. Blood. It coated the air, thick and choking. His stomach turned, bile rising, but he didn't move. Didn't let himself.

Then, Thwack.

A heartbeat.

Thwack.

Sol flinched, the sound sharp as a hammer behind his eyes.

One of the bandits jerked backward, an arrow lodged deep in his throat. He gasped—a wet, gurgling choke, then a second arrow slammed into his chest. He crumpled with a thud, blood spilling from his mouth in thick, pulsing rivulets.

A figure surged from the trees, bow in one hand, already nocking another arrow.

Wyatt moved. No hesitation. No question.

He turned and drove his sword into the next attacker's gut. Flesh gave way with a wet rip. The bandit shrieked, a strangled, highpitched sound, as Wyatt shoved the blade deeper, twisting hard. Blood gushed, hot and fast, slicking Wyatt's hands. The man convulsed, his limbs jerking as steel carved through muscle and spine. Then, one brutal wrench. A sickening squelch. Wyatt yanked the blade free. The bandit collapsed, twitching once before falling still.

The scrawny one dropped to his knees, gasping, his hands slick with blood as he tried to hold his insides in.

The leader locked eyes with Sol.

There was nothing human in his eyes—only hunger. Frenzy.

He lunged.

Sol barely raised his sword in time.

Thump. Thump.

The bandit staggered mid-charge, his body jolting as two arrows thudded into his back. He choked, tried to speak, but blood spilled from his lips in thick pulses. Then he dropped, hard, final, dead.

"Don't let the others run!" a familiar voice shouted—sharp, commanding.

The figure was still moving—fast, relentless.

Wyatt broke into a sprint. One of the bandits had turned to flee, legs pumping, breath ragged. He didn't make it far.

He tripped and screamed.

Wyatt was already there. His blade dropped like a hammer, driving deep into the man's back.

Crunch. The sound was sickening. Final.

The body jerked once, then lay still.

Another bandit stumbled sideways, an arrow buried deep in his thigh. He howled, clawing his way toward the trees, blood streaking behind him.

The stranger closed in, bow lowered now. A long blade flashed in his hand.

The man collapsed, sobbing, blood trailing in streaks behind him. He raised his hands, shaking.

"Please," he begged, voice cracking. "Please, I didn't mean— just, please—"

The stranger didn't slow.

One clean swing, the man's head struck the ground with a sickening thud.

Silence fell, thick and deafening.

The stranger exhaled slowly, then wiped his blade clean on the corpse's tunic. His shoulders rose with a breath, then dropped.

He turned.

Dark eyes met Sol's.

Familiar. No longer wild.

Sharp. Steady. Focused.

A flicker of something unreadable passed through them.

Then, softly, like it was the simplest thing in the world:

"Are you alright?"

Sol's lips parted, but no sound came.

His pulse thundered in his ears.

He swallowed. Once. Hard.

"...Scy?"

Chapter Fifteen

—

Wild Eyes

The metallic stench of blood clung to the air, thick and suffocating. Sol stumbled to the edge of the log and dropped to his knees, heaving. His stomach convulsed, a raw, wrenching force that left him shaking as he emptied what little was left inside him.

A hand clapped gently against his back.

"It's alright, lad. Let it out," Scy murmured, voice low and steady.

But Sol barely registered the words. His fingers clawed at the dirt, grasping for something solid as his body shook uncontrollably.

Dead. They were all dead.

He had never watched a life snuffed out before.

His breath caught, shallow, rapid, spiraling.

Scy pressed a waterskin into his hands. "Rinse your mouth. Drink."

Sol snatched the waterskin, throat tight as he swallowed hard. He tilted his head back and drank deeply.

The water was cool, crisp, even—but it did nothing to erase the bitter tang of bile or the sharp metallic sting clinging to the air.

When he finally pulled away, his breath came slower, steadier.

The trembling eased.

But the anger… that only burned hotter.

Sol's eyes snapped to Scy, his voice cutting through the air like a blade.

"Scy? What the hell are you doing here? Have you been following us this whole time?"

Scy blinked, momentarily caught off guard by the sudden edge in his tone.

"I gave you boys half a day's head start," he said, calm but firm. "But word got out—The Hand's looking to have you found and killed.

Figured it was better me than him, aye?"

Found and killed.

The words lodged in Sol's chest like a stone.

Sol's breath caught. That wasn't a warning. That was a hunt.

The burn in his chest spread like wildfire, blinding, breathless.

Anger surged through him, sudden and electric, and he was on his feet before thought could catch up.

"You told him to kill them?" he shouted. "They were running, gods, they were running."

His voice cracked, raw and trembling. He didn't care.

He turned to Wyatt, chest heaving, breath sharp and fast.

"How could you do it? They weren't even fighting."

Wyatt stiffened beside him, fists curling tight at his sides. But he said nothing.

Sol wasn't finished. He turned sharply, pacing a tight line across the blood-soaked ground.

"I'm not saying they were innocent," he snapped. "But they were running. They were done. They weren't a threat anymore."

Scy watched him quietly, arms crossed. He let Sol burn himself out.

Sol's gaze darted between them, wild and demanding. "Well?

Do either of you have anything to say?"

Scy exhaled through his nose, adjusting the strap across his belt.

"They'd come back. And they wouldn't come alone."

"You don't know that," Sol snapped, though even he wasn't sure he believed it.

Scy's eyes narrowed.

"I joined the Rouge before your voice even cracked," he said, calm but cutting. "I know what mercy gets you out here."

He took a step forward, gaze fixed.

"Don't talk to me about the world, lad, you haven't seen it."

He paused. Then, quieter: "I know you're scared. However, attacking us won't change what has been done. You've got enough enemies without making more."

Sol wanted to hold on to the anger—it was easier than guilt— but Scy was right. Without him, they'd be dead. And the bandits wouldn't have hesitated.

He let out a slow, measured breath, willing the fury to loosen its grip. His fists relaxed by inches, trembling as they opened.

There was no one left to fight but himself.

His gaze dropped to the floor.

"I'm sorry. You didn't deserve that. And… thank you. For pulling us out."

Scy gave a small nod, as if he'd expected nothing more.

After a long breath, Wyatt spoke. "But stay calm," he said gently, then turned to Scy. "We'll burn the bodies. Drag them into the woods and light them there."

Sol parted his lips to object, but the words faltered. He didn't want to take part in this. Every bone in his body screamed no. But leaving them to rot wasn't an option.

He swallowed, the taste of ash still in his throat, and gave a single, reluctant nod.

"Fair enough," Scy muttered. "Let's deal with it before the crows start asking questions."

They worked in silence. The weight of the bodies slowed them down, and though they tried to disguise the scene, blood still soaked the dirt. Sol's hands shook as he wiped them against his tunic, but the stains wouldn't fade.

"Search their belongings," Scy said, his voice brisk.

Then he glanced at Sol and softened. "They won't be needing anything where they're going."

Sol drew in a breath, then gave a tight nod. He crouched beside the bandit leader's body, the man's eyes still wide, frozen in that last, stunned moment of death.

For a heartbeat, Sol didn't move.

Then, quietly, he reached forward and closed the eyes with a careful touch.

"Eli…" he began.

No.

"Beryth, Keeper of the Hunt… walk him home,"

Then he made himself move.

His fingers worked through torn pockets and damp fabric, finally tugging loose a coin purse. He cut the strap at the man's waist and slipped it into his own. Guilt rose in his throat like bile, but he swallowed it.

Then, something else.

A folded writ, edges damp and curling. The wax seal was cracked but still clear: Baron Greywell's crest, stamped deep in bloodred wax.

Sol's breath hitched. His fingers trembled as he

unfolded the damp parchment.

Then the words sank in, his blood iced.

A warrant.

For his life.

Dead or alive.

He rose to his feet, slow and unsteady, the writ hanging limp in his hands. Without a word, he held it out to Scy, the color drained from his face.

Scy scanned the words. Then, under his breath, he swore.

"Knew he was in bed with the bandits," Scy muttered. "Could never pin it, though."

He clenched his jaw, then let out a sharp breath.

"Well, lads. Briarstead's off the table."

Wyatt stepped forward, his expression unreadable. But the way his knuckles whitened around the parchment betrayed more than words could. He read it in silence, eyes darting across the ink with sharp precision. When he finally handed it back, his fingers hovered, just a breath too long, before letting go.

"We'll have to avoid the main roads too," Wyatt

said at last, his voice too even. "A month before we're out of the Baron's lands."

Scy hummed thoughtfully. "We'll make better time cutting through the Blackbriar Wilds. A day's ride to Hallow's Rest from there."

Wyatt's head whipped around. "The Blackbriar Wilds? Are you out of your damn mind?"

But Scy just smirked, unfazed, his fingers tightening the strap on his belt. "Relax. Someone there owes me a favor. We'll pass through untouched."

Wyatt let out a sharp breath, rubbing his temples. "If you're wrong, we'll be dead before we hit the tree line."

Scy smirked. "Then it's a good thing I'm never wrong."

Sol raised a brow. "The Blackbriar Wilds?"

Wyatt let out a slow breath, rubbing his hands together for warmth, or nerves. "It's an old forest, just north of here. Locals say the deeper you go, the more the paths twist, like the woods don't want you to leave." He paused. "The trees... they say they're alive. And the thorns—drink blood, if you believe the stories. Folks who enter without permission don't usually make it back."

Sol let out a short, breathy laugh. "That sounds like superstition to me."

Wyatt didn't smile. "Maybe," he murmured. "But I've never met anyone who lived to tell the tale."

A thick silence fell. Behind them, the fire crackled, flames licking at the dirt where blood had begun to dry.

Then Scy chuckled, cutting through the stillness. "Well, you have now, lad."

He adjusted his belt with a slow, practiced ease—his smirk lazy, but his eyes sharp. "Blackbriar ain't all it seems. We'll keep our eyes open."

He tilted his head, watching them both. "Good thing I've got a trick or two up my sleeve."

The fire burned low and steadily. Flesh sizzled as it blackened, the stench thick and greasy, clinging to Sol's tongue with every breath.

He turned away, jaw clenched, chest tight, swallowing against the urge to gag.

Smoke curled through the trees—thin, white, ghostly, like fingers reaching skyward.

His stomach twisted. The heat, the stink—it clung to him like oil. He stumbled back a few steps, dragging in sharp lungfuls of pine and damp earth, desperate for something clean.

"We should go," Wyatt said quietly. "It's done."

Sol turned. Scy stood watching the fire, his face carved from stone. He dusted his hands, then stepped forward and clapped a hand on Sol's shoulder—firm, steady, grounding.

"Come on," he said. "Still a stretch to camp, and dark's chasing our heels."

Sol swallowed hard and gave a tight nod.

They walked in silence for hours.

The sun was sinking behind the trees when Scy finally stopped, surveying the clearing ahead.

"This'll do," Scy muttered, rolling his shoulders with a grunt.

Wyatt dropped his pack. "Sol, gather some wood. I'll get the bedrolls."

Scy flashed a grin. "Guess that makes me the chef tonight."

Sol gave a sluggish nod. His limbs felt heavy, his

vision smudged at the edges, exhaustion dragging him down like wet cloth.

As he walked toward the tree line, his steps dragged slightly, uneven. He rubbed a hand across his face, smearing dirt into the curve beneath his eye.

When he stooped to gather more wood, his fingers trembled with fatigue. Each branch felt heavier than it should, the bark biting into his calloused palms.

Then, something skittered past. Quick. Low. Just at the edge of his vision.

He startled, the wood slipping from his grasp, hitting the ground with a dull thud. His breath hitched, and for a moment, he just sat heavily on a fallen log. His shoulders slumped forward as he rubbed his temples, the world too quiet, too heavy.

He blinked hard. *Keep moving.*

Dragging himself upright, Sol pushed through the heaviness in his limbs. His movements were slow, deliberate, like every part of him was wading through mud.

Branches cradled in his arms, he trudged back toward the fire—the glow flickering faintly between the trees like a dying heartbeat.

His muscles burned, but it was the hollowness in

his chest that weighed the most.

Wyatt rolled a fallen log closer and patted the seat beside him.

Sol hesitated, then sank down, his body surrendering to exhaustion before his mind could catch up. The moment he hit the ground, it washed over him, like a stone dropped into still water, ripples spreading slowly and deep.

Scy handed him a steaming mug of soup without a word, then ladled his own.

Wyatt passed around strips of dried meat. "We skipped lunch," he said, offering a faint smile. "Figured we could use a little extra tonight."

"Good idea, lad," Scy said between bites. "Besides, now that I'm here, I'll get us some hare."

At the mention of fresh meat, Sol's stomach growled. The thought of hot, glistening roasted hare made the dry strip in his hand feel like leather. He bit into it anyway, dragging himself out of the daydream.

The fire crackled, casting long shadows that danced across their weary faces. They ate in uneasy silence, each lost in the weight of the day and in the looming path ahead through the Blackbriar Wilds. A log split with a sharp crack, sending a spray of sparks spiraling into the dark.

Wyatt broke the silence first. "Are you sure there's no better way out of Baron Greywell's land?"

Scy paused, then shook his head. "No, lad. Not if we want to make it through in one piece."

Wyatt gave a dry snort. "Safer? Sounds more like swapping one blade for another."

Scy chuckled. "My boy, I told you, I'm owed a few favors."

Sol arched a brow. "And what kind of favor gets us through a cursed forest?" His tone dripped with disbelief.

Scy leaned in, voice dropping low, calm, certain, almost reverent. "The kind you only call in once."

"There are forces in this world that defy reason," Scy said, his voice calm but heavy with memory. "Long before Itharen and Othrevia ever clashed—before Tavreyan was even whispered into legend, the gods walked among mortals. They shaped beasts born of dreams and nightmares, and gifted their faithful with magic that could shatter mountains."

Sol leaned back with a bark of laughter. "Alright, alright—keep your secrets, Rouge."

Scy didn't flinch. Instead, he raised two fingers in a Rogue's salute, eyes gleaming with mischief.

"May Old Magpie pluck my tongue if I'm lying."

Sol's smile faltered. He blinked, searching Scy's face for a trace of jest—but the man's eyes held nothing but solemn fire.

The humor drained from Sol's posture. Slowly, he gave a single nod. "Alright. I'm listening."

Scy reached for another log and tossed it into the fire. Embers burst skyward, flickering gold against the dark canopy above.

"The old gods created watchers for their sacred lands," Scy murmured. "Blackbriar Wilds is one of them."

The fire cracked sharply, momentarily filling the hush that followed Scy's words.

"Valkirith, the Worldforger—one of the first gods—created the Veyrnstag to guard it."

Wyatt's brow furrowed. "That ghost-stag from the old tales?

With silver eyes and antlers tangled in vines?"

Scy nodded, his voice low with reverence. "A sacred beast. Nothing like the stags you'd find in a forest.

Its coat's white as snowmelt, antlers draped in living vines, and its eyes—silver, dull as moons behind mist. Some say it leaves no tracks at all. Others swear it slips between worlds, like a breath disappearing in winter air."

A warm breeze stirred the leaves overhead, rustling like a whisper.

Scy's voice dropped—low and steady, heavy with something Sol wasn't used to hearing from him.

"I've seen it."

Wyatt stilled. Sol leaned in, firelight flickering across his cheek. "You're not joking."

Scy smiled — crooked, joyless. "Not this time."

He stretched his legs toward the flames and exhaled—slow, deliberate, his gaze fixed on the fire, as if watching memories take shape in the rising embers.

"I'd just turned sixteen—brash, stupid, convinced I had something to prove. I'd grown up on the old legends and figured it was my turn to chase one."

"The sun had barely cleared the treetops when I slipped into the woods. I hadn't gone far before I heard it, a crash, low and heavy, like the earth itself shifting. Something big was moving through the brush."

"And then I saw it."

"The Veyrnstag. Kneeling at a creek, its antlers tangled in vines and catching the light like threads of silver. It was... breathtaking."

He paused. The fire crackled.

"But I wasn't the only one watching."

"Across the clearing, half-shrouded in shadow, a man raised his bow."

"I didn't know the full stories back then. Didn't even know what it was, not really. Just knew I couldn't let it die. So, I did the first thing that came to mind."

Scy grinned. "I threw a rock."

Sol blinked. "You threw a rock?"

"Square between his damn eyes," Scy said with a dry laugh. "His arrow went wide."

He leaned forward, eyes reflecting the firelight. "The Veyrnstag looked up, and for a heartbeat, I swear, it saw me."

"Did it run?" Wyatt asked, his voice low.

Scy shook his head slowly. "No. The hunter did. Took one look at it and ran like the gods themselves were chasing him."

He paused, exhaling slowly.

"And then… the Veyrnstag turned to me. Lowered its great antlers."

"I thought maybe it would charge, but instead, it just... waited."

"So, I stepped forward, slowly. I raised my hand, and it let me touch its snout."

"And then—a voice. Not one I could place, but one I could never forget, spoke inside my head."

Scy's fingers drifted to the leather cord around his neck. He pulled it out from beneath his shirt, revealing a small, broken antler tip.

Sol's breath caught. This wasn't just a story anymore. It felt like a secret being entrusted to them.

"It said, 'Kindness echoes. This will guide you through the Wilds. When the need is great, bury it in the earth, and I will return." The fire flickered against the carved antler in Scy's hand, its surface polished smooth from years of handling. The cord wrapped around his fingers, a tether to a moment that didn't feel real.

Sol stared at the antlers, thoughts spiraling. He

couldn't tell what unsettled him more—the legend itself, or the fact that Scy wasn't embellishing a word of it.

The silence stretched, thick with something unspoken, until Wyatt finally broke it. His voice came low, more careful than usual.

"And you still have it."

Scy rolled the cord between his fingers, a crooked smirk tugging at his mouth. "Of course, I do. I'm not dull."

Wyatt let out a slow breath and rubbed his jaw, eyes flicking to the fire. "And you think this thing's actually going to help us?"

Scy's grin widened. "Lad, if the Veyrnstag didn't want me in Blackbriar, I'd have never walked out the first time."

That did nothing to ease the tension.

Sol wasn't sure if it was the weight of Scy's words or the way the firelight twisted just slightly wrong, but suddenly, the forest felt too quiet, as if it were listening.

He swallowed hard, then forced a crooked smirk. "So… bury the antler, and the stag comes charging to the rescue? That's some magic."

Scy's brow lifted, his voice dry. "Something like

that."

Wyatt shook his head, staring into the fire. He wasn't laughing.

"I just hope we don't have to find out."

The wind stirred the trees, sending a whisper through the leaves.

Sol pulled his cloak tighter around himself. He realized he wasn't cold, but something deep inside him yearned for the warmth.

A heavy silence had settled, the kind that made the crackle of the fire sound too loud. Sol stared into the flames, thoughts drifting somewhere far from the clearing.

Wyatt's voice brought him back. "Sol, I need to clean your back."

"If you want to see him shirtless that badly, I'll go take a walk," Scy smirked, winking.

Wyatt lobbed a pebble at him without looking. "Careful, or I'll land one right between your eyes."

Sol chuckled, peeling off his shirt and striking an exaggerated pose. "Come hither, my dearest."

Wyatt rolled his eyes and chucked a stick at him instead. "I'm a good aim if either of you wants to test me."

Scy smirked as he helped unwrap the old bandages. "That hedgewitch sure makes a good salve, doesn't she?"

Sol shook his head slowly. "It's still hard to wrap my head around."

Wyatt returned with fresh bandages, a small jar of salve, and something else.

A familiar book.

He paused, eyes downcast, before offering it to Sol. "I meant to give this to you sooner. I'm sorry. Everything that happened… I forgot."

His thumb traced the spine like it held weight beyond the leather and pages.

Sol's breath caught.

He took it, his fingers brushing against the leather cover, the edges softened from wear.

The Longing Letters.

The title shimmered faintly in the firelight, its gold lettering cracked and worn with time. Sol ran his thumb over the cover, feeling the raised imprint press against his skin, following the curves like a memory he'd never quite let go of.

"How did you get this?" His voice was barely more

than a whisper.

Wyatt exhaled, his expression softening. "A servant came to the inn a few hours after you left. She said Alina didn't know what was coming, but she wanted you to have it. Thought it might bring you comfort… when you'd need it most."

He hesitated, then added, "She left you a note. I figured… if you want me to know what it says, you'll tell me."

Wyatt's hands were steady as he began cleaning Sol's back, but Sol barely noticed.

His fingers trembled as he opened the well-worn cover. The familiar scent of parchment and ink rose to meet him.

A single folded letter lay tucked between the pages.

Slowly, carefully, he unfolded it.

Sol,

I know that you never asked for any of this. But I'm grateful our paths crossed.

When I miss my uncle, I read these stories. For a little while, it feels like he's still with me.

I hope they bring you the same comfort. Keep them safe.

With love,

- A

For a long moment, Sol simply stared at the ink, each stroke of Alina's handwriting precise, delicate, aching with intention.

His chest tightened, breath caught between ribs, the words settling into a space he hadn't known was empty.

He swallowed hard. The firelight shimmered at the edges of his vision, soft and unfocused.

At some point, Wyatt had finished rebandaging him, but Sol hadn't noticed.

"Sol? You okay?" Scy's voice sliced through the haze.

He gave a stiff nod.

Scy watched him, but didn't press. "Well then, my lads—since we're being hunted, we'll have to take turns keeping watch. I—"

"I'll take first," Sol cut in, voice low but steady.

Wyatt immediately frowned. "Sol, you're still hurt. Even with the salve, you need your rest."

Scy placed a hand on Wyatt's shoulder and gave a

small shake of his head. "Let him be."

Then he turned to Sol. "Alright, lad. Wake us if there's any sign of trouble. I'll take second."

He stretched with a dramatic groan. "Which means I'm off to dream of rivers and roasted pheasants." With a grunt, he slipped into his bedroll, already wriggling into comfort.

Wyatt stood still for a moment, blinking slowly. His shoulders dropped, but he didn't move toward his own bedroll.

He hesitated, then sat beside Sol. "Are you mad I didn't give this to you sooner?"

Sol shook his head. "No… I get it. It's just—" he drew in a breath, slow and heavy. "It's a lot."

His voice cracked, barely above a whisper. "I didn't even get to say goodbye."

Wyatt was silent for a beat. Then, gently: "She knew you would have, if you could."

Sol didn't reply.

Wyatt sighed. "I can sit with you a little longer if you want. I'm not that tired." But his voice was heavy with exhaustion.

Sol leaned in and pressed a soft kiss to Wyatt's cheek. "Get some sleep," he murmured. "I've got a lot on my mind."

Wyatt turned, catching Sol's lips in a firmer kiss before rising to his feet. "I know," he said, his gaze lingering. Then, with a half-smile: "Just… don't spiral, alright? You know how your mind gets."

A faint smile tugged at Sol's lips as Wyatt finally slid into his bedroll beside Scy, who was already snoring softly.

And then, Sol was alone, with nothing but the firelight and the weight of his thoughts.

The fire crackled, the warm glow flickering across his hands as he held the book tight to his chest. His breath felt too heavy, his mind too loud.

He thought about everything they had lost.

The twins, he could still hear their mischievous laughter, feel the chaos of their boundless energy trailing behind them like sparks. *How would they cope without him?*

His mother. His father. Did they lie awake wondering where he'd gone? Did they know there was a price on his head, or worse, had they put it there?

Alina. Would she grieve his absence or curse him for leaving without a word?

And Oswynn, how much longer until the shrines crumbled into dust, until the old gods were nothing more than forgotten names?

His hands curled into fists, tight with guilt, fury, and something he dared not name.

Wyatt was right. The whole world was theirs now.

Then, in the quiet echo of his memory, Ysella's voice came to him.

Real magic. Just promise me one thing, keep an open mind.

Sol let out a breath he hadn't realized he'd been holding. The tension in his chest eased, just a little.

The fire cracked and shifted, sending golden sparks spiraling upward like fleeting stars vanishing into the dark.

You just have to be willing to see...

Chapter Sixteen

———

Through Mud and Misery

The afternoon sagged beneath a heavy, humid sky, the air thick as a soaked woolen cloak draped across their backs. Rain had fallen for days without pause, saturating the trails until they dissolved into trenches of sucking mud, each step a slow wrestle against the earth. The relentless plod of boots, the wet squelch with every pull, the constant drumming of rain, it all gnawed at Sol's nerves, a steady erosion of patience.

He wasn't the only one carrying the weight of the journey, though he doubted anyone else had let it seep so deeply into their bones. Wyatt, ever the anchor, adjusted his pack with a quiet sigh, his silence speaking volumes. His quiet endurance stood in sharp contrast to the irritation prickling just beneath Sol's skin. Scy, by contrast, moved as if untouched by the misery, whistling under his breath, dancing across the worst of the muck with a light-footed ease that felt almost mocking.

When they finally stopped for their afternoon rest, Sol dropped his pack with more force than necessary, exhaling sharply. Wyatt cast him a glance, not quite chastising but knowing. Scy just grinned, flicking water from his sleeve as if the wet didn't matter.

"Lovely weather, isn't it?" Scy drawled, tilting his head toward the sky, where bloated clouds threatened another downpour.

Sol dragged a hand down his face, smearing rain and sweat from his brow. "I swear to every god still listening, if you actually find this charming..."

"What's not to love?" Scy stretched with feline ease, utterly unfazed by the mud caked to his boots. "Good company, a road full of chaos, and you," he flashed a grin at Sol. "You're downright delightful when you're miserable."

"You take too much joy in being impossible, you know that?" Wyatt laughed

"That's what keeps life interesting," Scy said with an exaggerated sigh, arms outstretched like a man performing for an invisible audience. "Now, are we eating, or just marinating in our collective misery?"

Sol huffed and rolled his shoulders, trying, unsuccessfully, to shake some of the damp from his tunic. The day loomed ahead, long and unforgiving, and he already knew the road would only feel heavier once they set off again.

"Let's eat something," Wyatt said, sliding his pack off with a relieved sigh. "I could use the break."

Sol rummaged through his satchel and pulled out rations that had clearly lost the battle against the rain. The dried meat was damp, the bread soft and spongy at the edges, but it would have to do. Wordlessly, he handed portions to the others.

"We could stay in Nasareth tonight," Scy suggested, chewing on a strip of jerky. "If we stick to the main road, we'll make it before nightfall."

Sol's reply came fast and flint-edged. "We're still in Baron Greywell's lands. Nasareth will be just as dangerous. In case you forgot,

I'm being hunted. I'd rather not walk into a trap with a welcome sign."

Scy barely blinked at Sol's tone. "In this weather? We'll be safe. We just need to pull our hoods up and blend in with the next group on the road." His voice was maddeningly matter-of-fact, as if the risk was barely worth acknowledging.

Wyatt frowned. "And what about the sheep? People know I'm a shepherd."

Scy drummed his fingers against his knee, thoughtful. "We'll pasture them just outside town. I know a farmer near the ridge who can keep an eye on them for a night or two. That way, when we enter Nasareth, it's just three weary travelers, nothing more."

Sol exhaled through his nose, the fatigue in his eyes giving way to mounting irritation. "It still feels like a needless risk."

"Our gear needs to dry before it starts growing moss," Scy said, wringing out a soaked glove with a grimace. "And come on—a night indoors won't kill us."

Sol hesitated. The thought of a roof, a real bed, and a hot meal gnawed at his resistance. His shoulders throbbed, his patience was fraying, and, despite everything, he wanted that comfort more than he cared to admit.

"Fine," he muttered, dragging a hand down his face. "But I'm not happy about it."

Scy's grin was instant. "We could always continue through the woods. Should only take another month or two to reach Hallow's Rest."

Sol exhaled sharply, shooting Scy a withering look. "Could you at least pretend you're not enjoying this?"

Scy's laugh cracked through the damp morning like

kindling catching flame. "Not a chance."

Silence fell between them again, broken only by the occasional squelch of wet gear and the chew of stubborn rations.

When they'd scraped the last bites from their meager meal, Sol stood with a grunt, joints protesting. He stretched, rolling his neck until it popped. "No sense in lingering. The weather's not changing, and we've still got miles ahead."

Scy and Wyatt quickly arranged their gear, securing their damp packs before setting off again. They tried to pick up the pace, but the effort was fruitless. The mud sucked at their boots, dragging them down with every step.

"This weather reminds me of the year High Priest Drevan first came to Oswynn," Scy said, his voice casual as he broke the lingering silence.

Wyatt kept his gaze fixed on the trail ahead. "He wasn't born there?"

Scy shook his head. "No. Arrived fifteen years back, middle of the rainy season. I remember it clear as day. Flooded streets, skies that wouldn't shut for weeks. Not unlike this summer."

Sol let out a dry scoff. "Figures."

"He showed up alone, dragging a massive cart," Scy went on. "Never gave a straight answer about where he came from. Just said he was 'drawn' to Oswynn, to enlighten us."

Scy snorted. "And wouldn't you know it? A bit of bad weather, a few weak harvests, and suddenly it was all divine punishment for our sins."

Wyatt frowned but said nothing, eyes fixed on the trail ahead.

"At first, only a handful of villagers gave him any real attention," Scy continued. "But Oswynn's always been the sort of place that welcomes strangers. Quietly, his influence grew, just a word here, a prayer there."

He paused, thoughtful. "Then the rains eased. Crops came in stronger. Folks started saying the gods were listening to him."

His voice darkened. "And before long, anything outside

'Elion's Path' was suspect. People who disagreed either left quietly… or vanished." Sol glanced over, brows furrowed.

"Disappeared?"

Scy hesitated before nodding. "One by one. Some vanished in the night. Others right after private meetings with Drevan." His gaze turned grim. "By the time, the mage, Master Mirrowind was gone, it was already too late, we just didn't see it yet."

"Master Mirrowind?" Sol slowed his pace. "Never heard of him. I thought mages were just old tavern stories."

"He was real," Scy said, voice low. "A quiet old mage, wellrespected, though he kept mostly to himself. He helped the town in small ways, healing charms, calming fevers, easing births. Never asked for much, just wanted to be left in peace."

Wyatt glanced up. "And he just… left?"

Scy shook his head. "Not quietly. Before he left, he warned us—said a dark shadow was swallowing the village, and when the sun finally rose again, there would be a reckoning."

Sol exhaled sharply, shaking his head. "Strange. I've never heard a single word about him."

"Because the ones who remember have learned not to speak," Scy murmured. "Those who still follow the old gods, they're afraid. Afraid of what The Hand might still be capable of."

He paused, eyes narrowing slightly. "Maybe more will walk away when the shrines fall. But some of us…"

His gaze slid toward Sol. "Some of us aren't ready to forget."

The rain whispered against the leaves, steady and soft, filling the silence that followed, one heavy with things left unsaid.

Sol recognized the road the moment they broke through the tree line. Nasareth was close now, just a few more hours if they kept a steady pace. Maybe, if the weather held, they'd reach it before nightfall.

The rain had worsened, pounding in thick sheets that blurred the distance. Water coursed through the rutted road, turning it into a maze of slick channels and sucking mud. They drew their cloaks tighter against the downpour as the sheep began to cry out, their bleats sharp and anxious beneath the weight of the sky.

Up ahead, a lone figure wrestled with a cart mired deep in the mud. The horse remained hitched, snorting and tossing its head, hooves stamping in frustration as the wheels sank further.

"Looks like he could use a hand," Scy said with a crooked grin.

"We could use one ourselves," Sol muttered. "Let's keep moving. He'll figure it out."

Scy's grin faded. "No. We're not the kind who turn away."

Without waiting for a reply, he broke into a trot toward the man.

Wyatt hesitated, then shrugged. "Come on." He followed.

Sol exhaled sharply, frustration knotting beneath his ribs. He hated this, hated how easily guilt could drag him back. Damn it. He stomped after them, each step heavier with reluctance.

By the time he reached the cart, the old man was at the horse's head, murmuring soothing words as he stroked the animal's muzzle. Scy crouched near one of the wheels, inspecting the damage, while Wyatt was already bracing himself at the rear.

"We'll push from the back and side," Scy said, voice clipped but focused. "You—keep the horse steady and guide it toward the center. The ground's firmer there."

The old man nodded. "Aye, just let me know when you're ready."

Sol dropped his pack into the soaked grass with a wet splatter, then took his place beside Wyatt, shoulders squared against the weight of the cart.

"One, two, three—go!" Scy shouted.

They pushed. The horse strained.

Boots slid in the muck, scraping for traction as the wheels groaned in protest. Rain hammered down, relentless, churning the road into a river of sludge. Sol clenched his jaw, muscles burning, and shoved harder, as if sheer force of will could move the earth itself.

With one final heave, the heavy cart lurched forward—just as Sol's foot slipped.

He hit the ground face-first.

Mud filled Sol's mouth and nose, cold, choking, and thick as paste. He cursed, spitting grit as he wiped at his face, but the muck clung stubbornly to his hair, his cheeks, his cloak.

By the time he staggered upright, slick with grime, the cart had been dragged back onto the firmer middle stretch of road. The old man stood beside his horse, murmuring quiet thanks as he ran a weathered hand along its neck.

"Appreciate the help, lads," the man said, extending a mudcaked hand toward Scy. "Name's Harlan. I've a home just north of Nasareth. Not much to offer, but you've got my thanks."

Scy clasped the man's hand without hesitation. "Scy. And this is Ren and Jonas," he said, introducing Sol and Wyatt without missing a beat. "We're just glad we could help. We're headed to Nasareth ourselves. Mind if we travel with you?"

Harlan smiled, the lines on his weathered face deepening with genuine warmth. "Course. Road's a mess—I'll be crawling along anyhow. Your sheep'll keep up just fine."

Sol wiped a cold clump of mud from his cheek, exhaling through his nose as they hauled their packs into the cart. Maybe this wasn't the worst outcome. At least he didn't have to walk the whole damned way.

Even if every squelching step in his boots reminded him he'd already been through it.

As they settled into a slow, steady rhythm beside the cart, Sol kept wiping at his clothes, smearing mud more than removing it. The rain had let up slightly, but his mood had not.

"I still think this was a risk for nothing," Sol muttered. "The man would have figured it out eventually."

Scy, walking a few steps ahead, shot him a glance over his shoulder. "You think so?"

He slowed until he was shoulder to shoulder with Sol, the usual glint in his eyes dimmed. "Let me tell you something, Ren," he said, drawing out the name with pointed weight. "Back before I became the dashing, quick-witted scoundrel you see now, there was a time I was half-dead on the side of a road, starving in the middle of nowhere."

Sol glanced at him, waiting.

"A man passed by. A stranger. He could've kept walking—had nothing to gain, but he stopped. Shared his meager rations. Pointed me down the right road, said it'd lead to the next village."

Scy's tone stayed light, almost careless, but something raw flickered underneath.

Sol frowned. "Did you ever see him again?"

He didn't know why he asked. Maybe part of him just wanted to believe people like that were still out there.

Scy shook his head. "No. I never saw him again.

Don't know

his name. Don't know where he came from or why he stopped. But I know this, if he hadn't, I wouldn't be standing here."

He glanced down the muddy road ahead, then back at Sol.

"You never really know who you're helping. Maybe it's nothing. Maybe Harlan's just a tired old farmer. Or maybe one day we'll be stranded in Nasareth, and he'll remember our faces."

Sol glanced at him, brow knitting. "You really think that old man's gonna show up someday and pull us out of a ditch?"

Scy let out a quiet snort. "Maybe. But that's not the point."

He looked ahead, voice softer now. "You help because it's right. Because if it were you lying in the mud, you'd hope someone would stop."

Sol exhaled through his nose, dragging a hand down the back of his neck. "You always gotta be right, don't you?"

Scy smirked. "I prefer 'occasionally wise.'"

Wyatt, Scy, and Sol took turns riding in the cart, careful not to throw off its balance with too much weight. Conversation with Harlan stayed easy, even playful at times, and despite himself, Sol found he didn't mind the old man's company.

Now and then, one of them would hop off to steady the load or put their shoulder to the back when the road turned to muck. The going was slow, grinding, back-aching work.

By late afternoon, a squat, weathered farmhouse appeared on the horizon, its tilled fields rolling out in every direction. Scy lifted a hand and called for a stop.

"Harlan, my friend, thank you for letting us travel with you."

Harlan chuckled, shaking his head. "I'd still be stuck in that mud if it weren't for you boys. The gods smiled on me today."

His tone shifted, growing more reflective as he adjusted the reins. "If you're ever in need, my place is just north of Nasareth, two miles out. It's nothing fancy, but the door's always open."

Then, with a glance over his shoulder and a quieter edge to his voice, he added, "Just watch yourself in town.

Elion's got a firm grip on this place."

With a final snap of the reins, Harlan rumbled down the road and out of sight.

Sol watched him go, unease knotting in his stomach. Of course, Elion's grip would be strong here. He just hadn't let himself face it, until now.

Scy stepped ahead, already moving toward the farmhouse. "Wyatt," he said, pointing toward a fenced pasture, "take the sheep over there. I'll go speak with Widow Brackett, let her know we've arrived."

Wyatt guided the sheep through the gate, their restless bleats softening as they settled under the weathered wooden overhang.

Sol lingered behind, his gaze catching on something etched into the main fence post, a feather, crudely carved and slightly tilted to the left.

"Wyatt, did you see this?" Sol asked, voice low.

Wyatt brushed his fingers over the marking. "It's a sign for the Rouge. Let's them know this place is safe."

Sol ran his fingertips along the carved feather, a flicker of recognition lighting in his eyes. "Ysella has the same mark on her back door."

Wyatt offered a half-smile, something knowing in his gaze. "She's a woman of many secrets." He paused, then added in a lower voice, "Let's just say... there's an arrangement. Of sorts."

Sol didn't press. He only nodded, letting the thought settle. The inn had always drawn its share of travelers, some rough around the edges, but come to think of it, Ysella never had trouble. No theft. No broken chairs. No brawls.

Scy emerged from the farmhouse, walking back toward them with a lazy wave. Widow Brackett stood in the doorway, waving a black handkerchief as if dismissing them.

"Well, my lads," Scy said smoothly, "Tilda's kindly agreed to keep an eye on the sheep while we head into town."

Before setting out, they scrubbed off what mud they could at the trough. It wasn't much help; the rain had soaked them to the bone, and their clothes hung damp and heavy against their skin. By the time they reached the edge of Nasareth, they were a sorry-looking lot. But the air held the rich scent of roasting meat, and the old inn's smokecurling chimney felt like a beacon.

The inn stood at the town's center, squat and sturdy, its windows glowing with lanternlight. Inside, warmth and supper waited.

Inside, the heat from the great hearth wrapped around them,

the scent of spiced pork and ale filling the air. Scy took the lead, striding up to the innkeeper. In short order, he arranged two rooms, side by side.

They climbed the narrow stairs, peeling off soaked layers and wringing water from their sleeves. Changing into the driest clothes they had, threadbare but clean, they felt a little more human.

Back in the main hall, they settled into a table tucked against the wall, half-shadowed by a crooked beam. They kept their heads down, hoping to pass unnoticed.

A serving woman approached, her steps slow but steady. Weariness lined her face, but there was a quiet kindness in her eyes. She glanced at their damp cloaks but said nothing.

"Roast mutton or pork stew tonight," she said, her voice dull with routine but not entirely without warmth.

Scy leaned forward, his grin wide and easy. "Evenin', darlin'. You're a welcome sight for road-weary eyes."

The woman gave a soft laugh, shaking her head as she balanced her tray. "Flattery like that'll cost you extra."

"Worth every coin," Scy replied smoothly. "We'll take two bowls of stew, a plate of mutton, and a tankard of your strongest ale."

As she turned and moved off, Wyatt tipped his tankard toward Scy with a crooked smile. "You always that smooth, or just when you're hungry?"

Scy stretched, smug and unbothered. "Only when it's worth the trouble."

No one asked questions. No one stared for too long. And somehow, in that quiet anonymity, Sol found a sliver of safety.

He'd only just begun to thaw beside the hearth when a voice, sharp and unmistakable, cut through the tavern's low hum.

"Gods, you three look like a heap of drowned rats."

Sol turned even before his eyes caught him, recognition already curling at the edge of his smile.

Luthen Carron stood a few paces off, shaking rain from his dark curls as his sharp brown eyes scanned the trio with an easy, crooked grin. He was younger than Petra and Kellan, more the age of a roguish uncle or an older brother than a father figure, but there was a quiet authority in the way he carried himself, like someone who had stared down storms and come out smirking.

Sol's expression broke open with relief. "Luthen."

Luthen snorted and folded his arms. "Didn't expect to find you lot in town looking half-drowned and twice as lost. But then again, when have you ever made things easy?"

Scy, ever the opportunist, raised his tankard in greeting. "A pleasure, my good man. You know our dear shepherd and scribe, I take it?"

Luthen gave Scy a once-over, then snorted. "Something like that."

Luthen's grin faded into something softer as he looked back at Sol and Wyatt. "You'll stay here tonight, sure. But tomorrow—you're eating at our place. Thyra'll have my head if I don't drag you back for a real meal."

Sol blinked, caught between warmth and the old, stubborn ache of not knowing how to belong. The Carrons had always been kind, always opened their doors without question, but that kind of welcome still felt like something fragile, something he hadn't yet earned.

Wyatt gave a quiet nod. "We'd be honored."

Luthen nodded, clapping Wyatt on the shoulder before stepping back. "I'll let you lot enjoy your ale. Come by after midday – I'll see you then."

And just like that, he was gone, slipping back into the crowd with the kind of ease that came from knowing he belonged anywhere he chose to be.

Sol let out a breath he hadn't realized he'd been holding.

Scy leaned back with a crooked grin. "Well," he said, drawing out the word, "looks like we've got plans."

Wyatt didn't answer. He just sat there, one hand wrapped around his tankard, the other resting loosely in his lap, eyes fixed on the fire like it might answer something he couldn't yet name.

The hearth's steady glow, the low murmur of conversation, and the comfort of not being under anyone's gaze settled something quiet and deep in Sol's chest.

The road had been long. The days, unforgiving.

But for tonight, they weren't hunted. They weren't hiding.

And for now, that was enough.

Chapter Seventeen

———

Still Ours

The Carrons' home wrapped around Sol like a well-worn quilt, cozy, lived-in, and full of gentle noise. The scent of hay, animals, and simmering herbs clung to the air, tugging something tight and aching in his chest, an old echo of home.

Thyra—Petra's younger sister, moved effortlessly through the kitchen, balancing baby Havron on one hip while stirring the pot with the other.

On Sol's lap, Calla shrieked with laughter each time he dipped her toward the floor, her golden curls sweeping the wood like a little mop of sunlight.

"Sol, we weren't expecting you," Luthen said as he stepped in from the doorway, brushing the last of the wind from his coat. "Petra mentioned the trouble with the fields. How are things shaping up? She said Elion blessed you, but we haven't heard much since."

Sol's fingers curled against the fabric of his trousers. He kept his gaze low.

The Carrons still honored the old gods, Zayren

above all, with their belief that fate was forged through grit and choice, not divine favor.

He was safe here, yes. But speaking too freely might feel like spitting on the very soil his family came from.

Thyra caught his expression and gave him a soft smile. "Sol? Are you alright?"

Wyatt placed a steady hand on Sol's leg, anchoring him.

Sol exhaled through his nose, then lifted Calla from his lap and passed her to Luthen, who caught her with practiced ease.

"You look like you've seen a ghost," Thyra said softly, eyes narrowing with quiet concern.

Sol hesitated. "It's a long story," he murmured. "And I didn't come here to speak poorly of my family."

Luthen lowered himself into his chair with a grunt. "Lad," he said, his voice gentler now, "you three looked half-dead when you arrived. Start at the beginning. We'll listen, with open minds."

Sol took a breath and began. He told them everything, starting with the night the Greywells were introduced at temple. Wyatt and Scy stepped in to fill the gaps, each voice layering over the next.

When Sol finished speaking, a long silence settled over the room.

Thyra and Luthen sat motionless, their expressions unreadable, carved from stone.

At last, Thyra stirred.

"It's a lot to take in, Sol," she said, her voice barely above a whisper. "And I believe you. I do. But what you've described... It's hard to wrap my head around."

She paused, her eyes locking with his, searching for something, confirmation, perhaps, or clarity.

"Just to put my heart at ease... may I see your back?"

Scy shot to his feet, his chair scraping across the floor.

"Are ye sayin' you don't trust him?"

Thyra met his anger calmly but firmly. "No. It's not about trust. It's about peace of mind. For all of us."

She looked down, then back up. "She's my sister. I grew up with her hands in my hair. And now you're saying she stood there and let it happen."

Sol placed a hand on Scy's arm. "It's alright. I understand." It was hard for him to believe, too.

He rose to his feet and peeled off his shirt, the fabric catching slightly against his shoulder.

Thyra stepped forward. Her fingers grazed the healing scars along his back, and Sol winced at the contact, less from pain than from the memory it stirred.

"Oh, my dear heart," she breathed.

She gently turned him to face her. Her eyes, dark and rimmed with sorrow, searched his. Then, without hesitation, she pulled him into a fierce embrace.

"This is not right," she murmured against his shoulder.

"That is one hell of a salve," Luthen said quietly, his voice rough.

Thyra wiped her eyes, then gave a shaky smile. "Well, let's not let the stew burn."

Thyra turned back to the hearth, ladling generous portions of stew into bowls, the rising steam curling in the firelight. She set them down gently in front of each of them, one by one.

The silence lingered until Luthen spoke, his voice

low but

certain.

"Sol… where are you planning to go?"

Sol exhaled and gave a half-shrug. "First, we need to get clear of the Greywells' territory. We're aiming for Hallow's Rest. After that…" He paused, staring into the flickering fire. "I'm not sure."

Luthen leaned back, stroking his beard thoughtfully. "It's another three weeks if you follow the main trading roads."

"That's why we're going through the Blackbriar Wilds," Scy added, far too calm.

Luthen choked on a mouthful of stew, coughing into his sleeve. "The Wilds? Gods, Sol, you can't be serious. You might save a few days, but it's vast and deadly."

Scy let out a low chuckle. "It's a long tale, but I've crossed the Wilds before. I know how to move when the trees stop following the rules."

Thyra's voice slipped in, quiet and careful. "Why not stay? Here, in Nasareth." She glanced between them, eyes hopeful yet afraid to hope too much. "We've been saving to buy land. Start a farm of our own. We're nearly there."

She hesitated, then added, more softly now, "If you worked with Luthen… you could live here. With us. Both of you."

Sol's breath caught.

Across the table, Wyatt met his eyes, steady, warm, unspoken understanding flickering between them.

He didn't say a word. Just reached under the table and gave Sol's thigh a gentle squeeze.

A quiet question.

A silent offer.

He was waiting.

Letting Sol decide.

It would be so easy.

Luthen and Thyra had always been kind. And Nasareth… it felt like Oswynn before the ruin, soft skies, gentle voices, the scent of rain sinking into tilled earth.

A life with Wyatt. With family.

But that was the problem.

It was too close to the dream he'd already lost.

Sol drew a breath. "No. Thank you… but no."

Sol looked down, then back up, his gaze clear and unwavering.

"The Keeper's Path is spreading here, too. The Baron still holds this land. Maybe not today, maybe not tomorrow, but how long until trouble knocks again?"

Thyra and Luthen exchanged a glance.

Luthen exhaled, voice low and heavy. "We understand. You're not wrong."

He gave a small shake of his head. "Wishing something were true doesn't make it so."

Silence settled over the table like dust.

Not cold.

Just the quiet that comes after a truth too heavy to argue with.

The hush stretched long enough that the crackle of the hearth filled the space between them. Sol stared at his bowl, appetite gone, the weight of the road already settling on his shoulders again.

Then—soft footsteps.

Calla padded over from the corner, where she'd

been quietly playing with a worn cloth doll. She reached up and tugged at Sol's sleeve.

"Are you leaving again?" Her voice was small, but steady.

Sol turned, surprised. "Not tonight," he said, offering a faint smile. "But soon."

Calla stared at him for a long moment. Then, without a word, she held something out, a small, lopsided daisy crown, its petals bruised and tangled, woven by fingers too young to know the pattern but determined to try.

"It's for your head," she said solemnly. "So, you don't forget how to be happy."

Sol blinked, the words catching somewhere deep in his chest.

He took the crown, delicate and uneven, and gently set it on his head. It tilted slightly.

Calla giggled.

"There," she declared. "You're Sir Sol, protector of sheep and fixer of bad days."

Wyatt snorted, trying to stifle his laugh. Scy cackled without restraint, and even Thyra's laughter broke through the tension, rich, warm, and unguarded.

Sol let out a soft breath and pulled Calla into his lap, burying his face in her tangled hair.

"Thank you, Calla," he murmured, his voice barely above a hush.

"You're welcome," she replied, puffing up with pride. Then, leaning closer, she added in a whisper, "You can give it back when you're done saving the world."

The room eased into a gentler rhythm. The conversation wandered back toward familiar ground, village gossip, old neighbors, harmless rumors.

They laughed. And for a little while, the world felt simple again.

But Sol was reluctant to leave. The sun had dipped low, and though the rain had slowed, it hadn't stopped. The walk back to the inn would be long and wet.

He stood slowly. "We should get going. It's getting late."

Thyra rose with him. Without hesitation, she wrapped Wyatt in a hug, then turned to Sol.

As she held him tight, she murmured, "If you need anything, you send word. You hear me? You are family.

And to us, that still means something."

Sol gave a small nod, unable to speak past the tightness in his throat.

Then came Luthen, pulling him into a rough, steady embrace. "Stay strong. And don't even think about leaving town without saying goodbye, you hear?"

Sol nodded again, eyes stinging.

The three of them set off into the dusk. Rain whispered against the rooftops, soft and cold. The world around them gleamed wet and hushed, as if holding its breath.

"Well, my lads," Scy said with a sly smile, "I'm off to visit Widow Brackett. No need to wait up."

Sol and Wyatt exchanged a quiet glance. Everyone knew about Scy and Ysella, how they shared a bed now and then. It wasn't a secret, and it wasn't complicated. They simply understood each other.

At the next corner, Scy peeled away with a low whistle, vanishing into the mist.

Sol and Wyatt stayed on the main road, the path ahead long and empty.

After a moment, Wyatt reached over and laced his

fingers through Sol's, giving a small, steady squeeze.

"You know I'll follow you wherever you want to go," Wyatt said. "If you want to stay here… or cross the Bleeding Reach and start over in Tavreyan."

Sol glanced at Wyatt. "Where do you think we should go?"

Wyatt hesitated. "I don't know. But once we reach Hallow's Rest, maybe things will make more sense."

Sol gave a slow nod. "Yeah. Maybe they will."

When they stepped into the inn, the mood hit them like a wall, low murmurs, stolen glances, tension coiled in the air like a held breath. The place felt heavier, watchful.

They exchanged no words and headed straight upstairs, boots thudding softly against worn wood.

Their room was small, every nail and hook claimed by some part of their gear. Damp cloaks hung from the wall, and a half-packed satchel leaned against the door. It looked like they lived there, just barely.

Sol lit the lamp on the table between the two narrow beds, its amber glow spilling softly across the room. Outside, rain tapped gently against the windowpanes, a steady, soothing rhythm.

Wyatt sat on the bed closest to the window, his gaze distant as he watched the darkened street below.

Without a word, Sol crossed the room and sat beside him. He leaned in, pressing a kiss to Wyatt's cheek.

Wyatt turned to him with a small, tired smile. "There's still a little salve left," he murmured, rising to his feet. "Let me clean your back."

Sol exhaled, the sound low and grateful, and pulled his shirt over his head. "Thank you," he said quietly.

Wyatt returned with the small tin in hand, his smile quiet and tender.

Sol turned away, his back taut with tension, skin still marred by healing lines.

The salve was cool against his scars, its earthy scent rising in soft waves, lavender, yarrow, and something bittersweet. It wrapped around him like memory, like breath. He closed his eyes, surrendering to the press of Wyatt's callused fingers, warm and steady.

Wyatt worked slowly, delicately tracing over the last stubborn scabs before kneading deeper into the knots along Sol's shoulders.

A breath escaped Sol as Wyatt found the tight

muscle near his spine.

"Just breathe, love," Wyatt whispered, voice low and close.

Sol inhaled, then let it out slowly. The tension eased, inch by inch, breath by breath.

"Lie down," Wyatt murmured.

Sol lay on his stomach, cheek resting against his folded arms, his gaze drifting toward the window. The rain had quieted to a whisper.

Beyond the glass, the moon slipped free of thinning clouds, and behind it, stars waited, soft, insistent, almost shy.

Wyatt's hands moved with quiet reverence, slow circles smoothing over tired muscles, easing pain with touch and presence. He bent low, pressing a gentle line of kisses up the length of Sol's spine, slow, warm, unhurried.

Then he lay beside him, tucking close, one hand curving around Sol's waist as if to gather him whole.

The room was dim but warm, lit only by the lamp's flicker and the moon's silver hush. Wyatt brushed a strand of hair from Sol's forehead and pressed a gentle kiss there.

They looked at each other, calm, steady, nothing

between them but breath and belief.

Sol's eyes, deep and blue as a storm held still, shimmered with devotion. "I love you, Wyatt Thornbrook," he whispered.

Wyatt's smile was quiet and sure. "And I love you." He leaned in and kissed the tip of Sol's nose, soft as a vow.

Sol shifted, straddling him with care, then bent to kiss him, slow, deep, and searching. Wyatt met him fully, hands strong on Sol's hips, holding him like something sacred.

Sol's mouth found the curve of Wyatt's neck, then wandered lower, tracing a slow path across his collarbone. He bit down, just enough to draw a gasp, then soothed the mark with his tongue. A low, amused laugh hummed in his throat as Wyatt shivered beneath him.

He moved lower, his mouth exploring every inch of skin it could find, slow, unhurried, reverent. Wyatt's breath hitched, coming faster now, the tension in his body coiling tighter with each kiss. Every soft gasp, every restless shift only stoked the heat smoldering between them.

When Sol reached his waist, his fingers brushed the edge of Wyatt's trousers. He paused, gaze rising, the question unspoken but unmistakable.

Wyatt caught his hand, not to stop him, but to hold him there. Their fingers threaded together, steady and sure.

He pulled Sol up and kissed him hard, mouths crashing together in a breathless tangle of need.

Wyatt's voice was rough in his ear. "We don't have to."

Sol pulled back just enough to look into his eyes. "I love you. Do you want to?"

Wyatt nodded slowly, like the weight of it had just settled across his shoulders. "Of course, I do. I want you. I just…"

His fingertips sketching trails of heat along his spine. "I want this to be ours. Not something stolen by fear. Not something the road takes away."

Sol's breath caught, voice dropping to a hush. "Then let's make it ours."

The next kiss burned, full of fire and surrender. Clothes fell away beneath eager hands. Skin met skin in sparks and gasps, laughter breaking between kisses, breathless groans rising between touches that knew and needed.

Wyatt growled and rolled Sol beneath him, breath

hot against his throat. Sol laughed, his fingers already tugging at Wyatt's belt, slipping beneath the waistband of his trousers…

The door slammed open.

They jolted apart as Scy stumbled in, gasping for breath.

He kicked the door shut behind him. "Well, don't stop on my account," he wheezed, utterly unfazed.

"OH MY GODS—SCY!"

"GET OUT!"

"I knocked!"

"NO, YOU BLOODY DIDN'T!"

Scy, entirely unfazed, raised a hand. "Relax. I don't care who was on top. We've got a bigger problem."

Sol and Wyatt were already scrambling into their shirts, faces flushed with heat.

Scy's tone shifted, the humor draining from his face. "Tilda told me, at Temple tonight, High Priest Maevan delivered word to the flock of Elion." He glanced at Wyatt. "No offense to your actual sheep."

He stepped fully into the room, voice dropping.

"They've called for your death, Sol. It's out."

Sol went still.

Scy continued, "The High Priest called you Spillborn. Said you twisted the shepherd. Said the storms, the blight, the wood eaters, it's all on you. Your punishment."

Wyatt sat down hard on the edge of the bed, pale.

Scy's jaw tightened. "He said Elion would reward anyone brave enough to bring 'immediate divine justice.'"

Sol didn't speak.

His shirt clung to damp skin, half-buttoned, hands trembling at the hem. He lowered himself onto the edge of the bed, eyes fixed on the flickering lamp between them, not on Scy, not on Wyatt.

Spillborn. Twisted the shepherd. Punishment.

The words roared louder than the rain ever had.

Wyatt rose sharply. "We need to leave. Now."

Scy didn't move. He shook his head once. "And do what? Run blind into the dark? You think the streets aren't already crawling with eyes?"

"Then we go through the fields—"

"And catch a blade in the dark?" Scy cut in, sharp as flint. "No. We wait for the right moment. I've already made arrangements."

Wyatt went still. "What arrangements?"

Scy let out a short, frustrated breath, like it should've been obvious. "Tilda's meeting us just past midnight. Southern edge of town. Carriage. Covered. We slip out clean."

Wyatt was already pulling their packs down from the wall. "You saw the crowd. If he's stirred them up, they'll be foaming by morning."

"Which is why we don't run like fugitives," Scy said, his voice dropping. "We walk out quiet. Invisible. Leave too soon, and we lose the only clean exit we've got."

Wyatt turned to Sol, breath catching. "Sol, what do you want to do?"

But Sol had no words.

His fingers curled hard against his thighs, nails digging into fabric he barely felt.

The silence settled between them like ash.

Plans were accepted. Packs readied. No light, no noise. They would slip out through the back stairs and into whatever came next.

Scy's plan looped in Sol's mind like a memory that didn't belong to him: Tilda waiting by the old dry well, a borrowed cart, the winding road through the hills leading somewhere quieter. Safer.

A few hours. Maybe more.

Just enough distance to almost feel free.

They waited until the inn fell still, until midnight pressed down on the town like a held breath.

Scy moved first, slipping through the door and scanning the alley beyond.

No torches. No guards.

Just mist and the scent of wet earth.

They moved quickly, cloaked and hooded, packs slung tight to their backs. Sol didn't speak. Wyatt stayed close, one hand brushing his shoulder every few steps, as if reminding him he was still there.

The old dry well loomed in the dark, silent and skeletal—more monument than ruin.

And beside it, waiting, Tilda.

She stood at the reins of a plain wooden cart

hitched to a broad-shouldered mare. A shawl draped over her braid, casting her in the likeness of any road-weary traveler, but her eyes, sharp and scanning, missed nothing when they landed on Scy.

"Took you long enough," she murmured. "We've only got a few hours before the roads remember how to breathe."

They climbed into the back without ceremony.

Wyatt lingered a moment.

"Tilda," he said quietly. "The sheep."

Tilda raised an eyebrow. "You planning to herd them behind the wagon?"

Wyatt shook his head. "Can you sell them? Or find someone kind enough to keep them safe?"

She studied him for a long beat. "You sure?"

His eyes drifted toward the carriage, where Sol waited, half in shadow, watching.

"I'm sure," Wyatt said quietly.

Tilda gave a short nod. "I'll see to it."

Wyatt climbed in beside Sol, their shoulders brushing. He reached for Sol's hand, and this time, Sol didn't pull away.

As the wheels began to roll, the only sound was the hush of hooves on wet stone, and the quiet, final severing of a life left behind.

The road stretched ahead, quiet, but uneasy, the cart wheels thudding gently against stone and packed earth. Trees slipped past in a blur of silvered shadow, moonlight dripping between branches like whispered secrets.

Sol sat stiffly, the words still echoing in his head: Spillborn.

Justice. Divine reward.

He hadn't wanted to ask. But silence was no longer enough.

"What does it mean?" he said softly.

Wyatt turned toward him, brow furrowed. "What?"

"Spillborn," Sol said, barely above a whisper. "What does it mean?"

Wyatt hesitated. "I've… heard it before. Once or twice. But I don't really know. Just, whatever it is, it's not good."

Scy didn't look up. The silence stretched, taut and

heavy.

Then, flatly: "It means you were born wrong."

Sol blinked.

Scy finally lifted his eyes. "To them, anyway. Spillborn's what they call men who love other men. Or anyone who doesn't fit where they're told to." He paused. "It's not just about who you love. It's about what you are. What you refuse to be."

Wyatt's jaw clenched. His hand found Sol's under the cloak, warm and steady.

Scy continued, his voice even. "The name says it all. Wasteful. Wrong. Something that spills instead of takes root. That's how they see you."

"And the punishment?" Sol's voice was tight.

Scy glanced away. "They call it justice. But it's not. It's permission to hurt you and feel holy doing it. A rope. A blade. A fire, if they want to feel righteous."

He paused. "Some call it cleansing. Others call it mercy."

A beat.

"It all ends the same."

The wagon rocked gently.

Sol stared into the dark, but his eyes didn't catch on anything.

His stomach churned, shame, confusion, anger—knotted together so tightly they felt familiar.

Not a surprise.

Not anymore.

"You're not wrong," Wyatt said softly. "You're not wasted. You're not anything they call you."

Scy's voice followed, gentler than before. "And even if you were… you'd still be ours."

Sol didn't answer. He couldn't.

The wheels kept turning, steady as breath.

Chapter Eighteen

———

Blood Beneath the Boughs

Morning light streamed through the cart's slats, laying shifting bars of gold across the worn wooden floor. The world outside was hushed, broken only by the soft rattle of wheels and the muted splash of puddles as they trundled up the slick, muddy road. A faint breeze carried the damp scent of rain and earth inside.

Sol stretched, his muscles stiff from the long night, just as the cart creaked to a halt.

He pushed himself up and peeked out the back. The road ahead forked into two narrow paths, both deserted, the morning mist curling low across the ground. Trees flanked either side, their long shadows stretching like fingers across the damp earth.

"This is our stop," Scy called from the front, seated beside Tilda with his boots braced against the wagon's edge.

Wyatt caught Sol's pack with a practiced toss and adjusted the strap of his own, readying himself for whatever came next.

They stood at the fork where the road split in two.

To the left stretched the open road, washed in pale morning sunlight, a ribbon of dust and promise.

To the right, a narrow path disappeared into the trees, where moss clung to twisted roots and cool shadows swallowed the light.

Tilda hopped down from the wagon and pulled Scy into a fierce hug, holding him for a beat longer than words allowed. Then her gaze shifted to Sol and Wyatt. She offered a warm, knowing nod.

"If you take the woodland path," she said softly, "the road bends north and skirts the Wilds. It's quieter there, but watch where you step."

She kissed Scy hard. He stumbled back, grinning like a fool.

"If I come back injured, promise you'll nurse me back to health?"

Tilda chuckled as she hauled herself back into the driver's seat. "Try not to get yourselves killed," she called, her tone light but edged with worry.

With a final wave, she snapped the reins, and the

cart rolled away, hooves splashing through shallow puddles until it vanished down the bright, sunlit road.

Sol hitched his pack higher on his shoulders and fell in step behind Scy, their boots sinking softly into damp earth as they turned toward the shadowed, tree-covered path.

Without the sheep, he hoped, they'd draw less attention.

They walked in silence, stepping around the worst of the standing water.

But something tugged at Sol—a taut, invisible thread pulling in his chest.

His pace faltered. He glanced over his shoulder. The road lay empty, stretching silent and bright behind them. Ahead, Scy and Wyatt walked on, unaware.

The feeling sharpened, coiling low in his ribs. He let his eyes lose focus on the muddy path, hoping it would fade, but when his gaze snapped back, the world felt… wrong.

Still. Too still.

Wyatt and Scy had paused mid-step, breath suspended.

The wind in the trees stopped. The leaves above didn't move.

The world seemed to hold its breath, every rustle of wind swallowed by a heavy, unnatural silence.

Sol felt it in his bones.

They weren't alone. Eyes moved somewhere in the trees, watching, waiting.

And there was nowhere to run.

"Steel in hand," Sol said, his voice low but sharp enough to cut through the stillness.

Scy slowed, frowning over his shoulder. "Sol, we're in the middle of nowhere. Nobody comes this—"

"Trust me," Sol hissed, hand already inching toward his blade.

Wyatt looked over, searching Sol's face. "Scy… we better listen to him. He's got that unnerving way of being right."

Scy let out a resigned breath and slipped his bow from his shoulder. "What kind of trouble are we talking about?"

"I don't know," Sol admitted, jaw tightening. "But it's close."

He nudged a loose stone with his boot, sending it skittering across the damp road.

Wyatt moved closer, his voice steady. "It's alright. We'll stay sharp. That's all we can do."

They pressed on, weapons loose in their hands but not yet drawn.

Every rustle of leaves made Sol's muscles tense, every distant crack of a branch a silent threat carried on the damp air.

Then—hooves.

Slow, deliberate. Drawing nearer.

Four riders emerged from the trees.

Too late to run. Too late to hide.

The lead rider's horse bore Barron Greywell's sigil.

Sol's breath hitched, tight and shallow.

"Stay calm," Scy murmured without moving his lips. "Let me handle this."

The riders emerged fully now, hooves squelching in the mud, their cloaks dark with rain. The lead rider, broad-shouldered and grim, eyed them like men already condemned.

"Where are you three-headed?" he demanded, voice low and edged.

Scy flashed an easy grin that didn't reach his eyes. "Just on our way to see my dear old mother. Storm knocked a tree onto her roof, and she's not as spry as she used to be. Needs a few strong backs to help."

The rider's gaze slid to Wyatt and Sol, assessing, distrust sharpening his features. "And these two?"

The largest rider leaned forward. "These two look like spillborns."

"They're my sons," Scy replied without missing a beat. "Mama wanted all the help she could get. And being men of Elion… maybe you'd lend a hand to a faithful family?"

The rider swung down from his horse, boots striking the wet earth with a heavy splash. His eyes locked on Sol as he closed the distance, each step deliberate, a predator closing in.

Instinct pulled Sol's hand toward the hidden hilt beneath his cloak.

The man's sneer curled, fingers darting for Sol's shoulder… Thud.

A dagger struck deep between his shoulder blades. His breath hitched, eyes wide with shock.

Wyatt stood a few paces away, chest heaving, another blade already sliding into his palm.

Scy's bowstring hissed through the damp air. Thwack. The leader collapsed soundlessly, an arrow jutting from his chest.

The remaining two riders roared and spurred their mounts, mud flying as they charged like unleashed fury.

"Slash the haunches!" Scy shouted.

Sol twisted, bringing his sword across one horse's side. It screamed, veering off as Wyatt rolled beneath it, barely missing the hooves.

Another arrow whistled through the mist—Scy's shot buried deep in a rider's shoulder, wrenching him sideways in the saddle.

A second horse thundered past. Sol dropped low, mud spraying as he lunged, his blade punching into the rider's thigh. The man shrieked, crashing to the ground in a tangle of limbs and leather.

Scy's next arrow sang, driving clean through the rider's chest before he could rise.

Only one attacker remained, stumbling from the wreck of his mount, clutching a bleeding gash along his ribs.

Sol closed the distance in a blur of motion, no hesitation, no wasted breath. His dagger flashed from its sheath, plunging into the man's side with a brutal, efficient thrust.

Once.

Twice.

Again.

Again.

The man collapsed with a guttural groan.

But Sol didn't stop.

Blood slicked his fist, his dagger slipping as he drove it down again. And again. Each thrust sharper, faster, as if carving out something he couldn't name.

"Sol!"

"Sol, stop!"

Hands seized his shoulders, dragging him back. He twisted violently, teeth bared, scrambling for the dagger like he needed it to breathe.

"Sol!" Wyatt's voice cut through the haze, raw and desperate.

"It's us, it's me!"

A hand closed over his, firm and unshaking.

Wyatt.

Scy.

Sol blinked hard, the red fog ripping apart like torn cloth. Air rushed in sharp and cold as his gaze fell to the man sprawled at his knees, chest shredded, face slack in death.

Scy crouched low, voice quiet but steady as stone. "Sol… it's over. They're gone."

Something in Sol cracked. He stumbled to the roadside, knees buckling as bile surged. Last night's meal hit the mud with a wet splash. His breath came ragged, hitching, his whole body shaking as if it wanted to crawl out of itself.

Behind him, Wyatt and Scy dragged the bodies into the ditch, out of sight.

"There's no covering this up," Scy muttered, voice grim but steady. "We move. Into the trees—now."

Wyatt gave a sharp nod, already shifting Sol's pack

into place. He pressed the waterskin into Sol's hands without a word.

Sol swished the bitter taste of bile from his mouth, swallowed hard, then tipped the skin over his face. The water struck cold as riverstone, dripping down his neck, but it couldn't wash away the feverish burn crawling beneath his skin.

They slipped into the treeline, just far enough that the road disappeared behind veils of green. They walked in silence, following narrow deer paths that curved and wandered without purpose.

Eventually, they stumbled upon a narrow stream cutting through the underbrush, its water glass-clear and bitingly cold. One by one, they crouched along the bank, scrubbing away the worst of the blood and caked mud until the current ran red, then clear again.

"We'll need to change before we hit the Wilds," Scy said, peeling off his tunic with a wry grin. "Can't risk leaving a scent trail behind. Not in there."

Sol stilled, droplets sliding from his fingers into the stream. "That sounds… ominous."

Scy only shrugged, tone casual but edged with warning. "Blood brings predators. Always does."

Wyatt pulled out stale bread and a wedge of hard cheese, passing it between them.

"We've got a few more hours on foot before we reach the Wilds," Scy added between bites. "We'll camp just outside the edge. There's a clearing I know."

"Why not keep moving?" Wyatt asked, scanning the thinning trees. "Nightfall's hours off, and no sane traveler would enter the Wilds. We'd have the road to ourselves."

Scy's grin faltered, replaced by a flicker of something heavier.

"Because we don't just stroll in uninvited," he said quietly.

Wyatt glanced at him, brow furrowed. "Uninvited?"

"Yeah," Scy replied with a low chuckle that didn't quite reach his eyes. "You don't cross into sacred ground without asking first."

Sol tilted his head, a smirk tugging at his mouth. "And who exactly are we asking? The trees? Wandering spirits?" The grin stayed, but doubt edged his voice now.

Scy didn't rise to the bait. "We make an offering to

Valkirith," he said plainly.

Wyatt glanced at their packs. "We don't have much left to offer."

Scy gave a knowing, cryptic smile. "Leave that to me."

They packed up and set off again, the shadows deepening as the canopy thickened above them.

The fire popped and hissed, throwing restless shadows across Wyatt's face.

Sol sat cross-legged on the cold earth, knees drawn tight to his chest, damp from the stream and unwilling to dry in the night air.

Scy had vanished into the treeline a while ago, muttering about snares, old shadows, and "giving the gods their teeth." His absence made the woods feel wider, less forgiving.

"You holding up?" Wyatt asked softly, his voice nearly swallowed by the fire's whisper and the distant rustle of unseen things. "I'm sorry," Sol murmured, not lifting his gaze.

Wyatt wrapped an arm around him, gentle and

steady. "You don't need to be sorry."

"I really lost it back there."

"Aye. That's one way to put it," Wyatt said, with a small laugh. "But it's over."

"It's not over," Sol burst out, voice raw and unsteady. "It may never be. We don't even know where safety is anymore. I dragged you and Scy into this, and when I saw them coming for you—"

Wyatt caught his face in gentle but unyielding hands, forcing Sol to meet his gaze. Firelight flickered in those steady green eyes, warm and unwavering.

"We chose this," Wyatt said, his voice low but certain. "We chose you. At any point, we could've walked away. None of this—" his thumb brushed Sol's cheek, "—is your fault."

Sol's breath shook. "I killed a man."

"And you saved my life." Wyatt didn't flinch. "They would've killed us both. You did what you had to do."

Sol crumpled forward.

Wyatt folded Sol into his chest, holding him like a shield against the world.

And Sol broke—shaking, breath hitching, tears spilling hot and helpless.

Wyatt kissed his temple, voice low and steady.

"You've always had the biggest heart," he murmured. "When Maris vanished in the marshes, you searched until dawn and carried her home yourself. When the twins were burning with fever, you stayed up all night just to see them smile again. You've given everything you have, Sol. Let someone, just once, give it back to you."

Sol's voice fractured into a whisper. "My family… they cast me out."

Wyatt's arms tightened, a fierce, protective hold. "Then they're fools. Blind. Poisoned by fear. If The Hand hadn't sunk its claws into their minds, none of this would've ever happened."

He pulled back just enough to look Sol in the eye.

"You're allowed to be angry. Be mad at Kellan. At Petra. Be mad at The Hand. At Elion. Hell, rage at the stars if you have to. But not at yourself."

A pause.

"You're still you. And that's why I love you." Sol looked up, eyes shining, breath shaking.

And then, Wyatt kissed him.

Desperate. Starved. Real.

They lingered there, breath mingling, before parting slowly. The fire popped softly between them, casting long, wavering shadows. Sol rested his forehead against Wyatt's, drawing a shaky breath as the world steadied, inch by inch.

A soft crunch of leaves broke the moment. Sol turned just as Scy emerged from the treeline, a bundle of slender branches balanced on his shoulder. A knowing smirk played at the corner of his mouth.

He didn't speak right away. Just tossed the sticks onto the fire's edge, brushed his hands clean on his trousers, and dropped onto a nearby stone with a grunt. The silence stretched for a beat before Scy finally cleared his throat.

"Well," he said, eyes firmly elsewhere, "if that's stargazing, I've been doing it wrong."

Sol groaned and hid his face in his hands. Wyatt snorted.

"Easy, Scy," Wyatt said with a quiet laugh. "We're allowed a moment."

"I never said it wasn't deserved," Scy drawled, leaning back with his hands laced behind his head. "Honestly, if anyone's earned a little fireside comfort, it's Sol. Just… try not to make me wallow in a puddle of leftover tension when we're all trying to sleep."

Sol peeked at him through his fingers. "You're an ass."

Scy pressed a hand to his chest in mock offense. "A charming ass, thank you very much. Frankly, I'm wounded that neither of you ever thought to invite me to the party."

He popped to his feet, swung his cloak dramatically, and gave his backside a theatrical little shake before collapsing back onto the stone with a grin.

Wyatt threw a rock at him. "You're just so old, Scy."

"I'm like old mead, stronger and sweeter with time." "You mean sour and full of bees," Wyatt said with a grin.

They all laughed.

Scy rose with a dramatic stretch. "Since my genius goes unappreciated, I'll take my talents elsewhere— namely, checking the traps." With a lazy salute, he disappeared into the trees.

Sol shifted to the fire, stirring the stew with grim determination. The pot hissed and spat, a pungent mix of scorched herbs and overzealous spice curling into the air.

"Burn it again?" Wyatt asked dryly.

Sol winced. "It's… caramelized."

Wyatt lifted the pot off the fire, wrinkling his nose as the thick, blackened mess clung stubbornly to the sides. "I love you," he said, "but I'm fairly certain this could be classified as a weapon."

Sol dragged a hand through his hair with a groan. "I don't know why I'm cursed in the kitchen."

"I'll toss this disaster," Wyatt said, hoisting the pot and heading toward the trees. "Grab another spice pack before Scy comes back and mocks us both."

Sol dug through their packs with a resigned sigh. "Gods have mercy… only three spice satchels left." He shook his head, muttering, "Fine. From now on, I'm strictly on dish duty."

By the time Wyatt returned, the ruined stew was gone. He spread the embers with practiced hands and set the pot over the low flame again.

Sol eased back onto his elbows, gaze drifting skyward. Above the treetops, Flitcher's constellation gleamed, five sharp stars arcing like a hunter's bow. He traced the shape with his finger, pausing on one particularly bright star that seemed to pulse a little more complicated than the rest, like it wanted to be noticed.

"Looks like the gods are watching," he laughed, pointing.

"They always are," Wyatt murmured as he stirred the new stew. "For better or worse."

Sol slipped in behind Wyatt, fingertips ghosting over the muscles of his back. "Do you think they're always watching?" he murmured, voice low as his hands slid beneath Wyatt's shirt.

Wyatt turned in one smooth motion, sweeping Sol into his arms and stealing a slow, heated kiss. "Careful," he warned against Sol's lips, breath warm. "Don't start something we can't finish out here."

Sol's grin turned wicked as his hands wandered lower…

From the treeline, Scy's voice cut through like a thrown stone. "If you two are about to rut like springbucks, at least give a man some warning."

Sol flushed crimson. "Gods, you're a wet blanket."

Wyatt chuckled, pulling Sol closer. "An ancient, fraying wet blanket," he added, laughter spilling easy between them.

Scy strolled into the firelight holding two snares. The hares still twitched faintly, barely alive.

Sol lifted a brow. "Don't most people… kill the hares when they set a trap?"

"Well, yes," Scy drawled, dangling one of the squirming creatures by its long ears. "But an offering's got to be alive. Valkirith doesn't take kindly to cold meat."

"Alive?" Sol echoed, the word heavy on his tongue. He'd heard the old stories of blood rites whispered around winter fires, but seeing it here, in the quiet glow of their camp, felt different.

Scy's grin faded, his tone shifting into something quieter, almost reverent. "It has to be pure. Dried meat, a sprig of herbs, that's good enough for small favors. But asking the Wilds to let us through?" He shook his head. "That's no small thing."

He strung one of the hares from a nearby tree, fingers deft and practiced.

"Let's get this done," he said. "We can leave at first light."

Scy turned and walked with purpose into the trees, carrying the second hare and the tools of the old rites.

"Well—Come on?" Scy called over his shoulder without breaking stride. His voice had changed, lower now, carrying weight. "This isn't a spectator sport. We all take part."

Wyatt quietly shifted the pot from the fire, draped it with a cloth, and rose. Without another word, he and Sol followed.

The trees pressed close as they trailed Scy into a narrow clearing beside the stream. Dark water coiled through mossy stones, sliding silently toward the deeper Wilds.

Above them, the moon had vanished behind a thick shroud of clouds, and not a single star pierced the canopy. Sol's eyes strained against the dimness until he caught the subtle shimmer of dew, the restless flicker of shadow and leaf.

But it wasn't just darkness that met them; it was silence. A hush that felt alive. The forest here didn't sound like any they had crossed; it breathed slower, watching.

This wasn't simply a clearing. It felt like a threshold. Like the Wilds themselves were leaning forward, waiting to see who dared step inside.

A path unfolded before them, worn by generations and time.

At its center stood a tall stone, surrounded by a circle of smaller ones.

A cold breath swept through the clearing.

Scy placed the bound hare on the altar stone.

Scy's voice dropped, soft and reverent, carrying like a hush through the clearing.

"Follow," he said, almost a whisper. "And repeat after me."

He moved to the northernmost stone and began a slow, deliberate circle, boots sinking slightly into damp earth. From a small leather pouch, he pinched out a dark, fragrant powder, letting it sift into the soil with every step. His breath shaped the words like an offering:

"Valkirith ena silen,

Threnai vi'morra,

Kai'vren shal thaluen…"

Sol and Wyatt fell in behind him, voices low, stumbling at first over the strange syllables. They paced the circle three full times, their chanting weaving with Scy's until the air felt thick with sound and intent. By the final pass, the words no longer felt foreign, they pulsed like part of the earth itself, drawn into the hush of the Wilds.

With each step, the chant sank deeper into Sol's bones. It wasn't just sound anymore, it felt like he was speaking a memory not his own, words carried on a voice older than his.

By the final repetition, the Wilds had gone utterly still. No rustle of leaves. No whisper of wind. Even the night creatures seemed to crouch in silence, waiting.

They gathered around the altar. The hare lay upon the flat stone, its tiny chest rising calm and steady, as if the forest itself had hushed its breath.

Scy bowed his head, the weight of ritual heavy in the air.

"Valkirith, kai'vren thaluen.

Ena morra silen.

Esar vi'threnai."

Sol and Wyatt echoed the words.

Without hesitation, Scy drew an ornate dagger and slit the hare's throat.

Blood pooled at the base of the stone and spilled over, steaming softly in the cold.

He rolled up his sleeve and drew the blade lightly across his wrist. A thin line of red fell across the offering.

"Esar'kai vren'dai,

Shal morra,

Valkirith, nora'en."

Sol stepped forward without thinking, wrist extended toward the stone.

He whispered the chant again, softer this time, as if the forest itself were listening.

The blade kissed his skin, a shallow sting, nothing more. But the words… the words cut far deeper. They weren't his to claim, yet they felt carved into something older inside him. Something that recognized the truth when it heard it.

Wyatt followed, calm and unflinching, offering his own wrist without a sound.

Scy dipped two fingers into the warm blood and pressed them to each of their brows, leaving crimson marks in deliberate strokes, symbols of binding, recognition, and passage.

"Kai'vren silen.

Ena thaluen shal.

Valkirith, amin'dor."

The moment Scy's bloodstained fingers pressed against his brow, Sol felt it, not warmth, not grace, but something more profound.

An awareness slid beneath his skin, ancient and watchful, curling around his pulse like a quiet claim.

It wasn't a blessing.

It was a bargain.

The Wilds had taken his name and tucked it away, promising nothing… except that they knew him now.

In silence, they resumed the ritual, feet tracing the earthen path in unison.

Three full turns.

Always clockwise.

The forest seemed to lean closer with every step.

Each time, they whispered the invocation:

"Valkirith ena silen,

Threnai vi'morra,

Kai'vren shal thaluen."

They stepped from the circle.

No voice answered.

No light flared.

Only silence.

Sol waited… and waited.

No thunder. No flash of light. Just the weight of unseen eyes, the faint, unsettling certainty that something in the Wilds had learned his name and would not forget it.

Then, like a held breath finally released, the world exhaled.

The hush broke. Leaves rustled again. The stream found its voice, trickling softly through the clearing.

Sol swallowed hard. "How do we know if it worked?" he whispered, the sound barely stirring the quiet.

Scy glanced at him. "You don't. You have to trust. The gods don't measure worth by signs. It's the act that matters."

They walked back to the fire in silence.

The embers had gone dark.

Wyatt crouched by the fire pit, quietly laying fresh tinder. He didn't ask why the flames had snuffed out as though the Wilds themselves had drawn breath and swallowed them whole.

Sol's fingers twitched at his brow, aching to wipe away the drying blood, but he didn't. It felt heavier than it should, no longer his own. Not protection. A promise. One he hadn't spoken, yet somehow had already made… and one he knew couldn't be undone.

"What language was that?" he asked softly.

Scy glanced over, his usual sharpness muted. "Valkiric," he said. "Old as these woods. The words don't have clean edges in

Common, but…" He gestured vaguely toward the circle they'd walked. "Mostly prayers. An offering. A stilling. We ask not to be hunted by shadows. We give in peace… and hope the Wilds see us." Wyatt touched the mark on his brow. "And this?"

"That stays," Scy said, firm. "The blood's part of the rite. It's not just for the gods, it's for the Wilds themselves. As long as we wear it, we're under their watch."

Sol hesitated. "And if we wipe it off early?"

Scy stayed quiet for a long moment, gaze fixed on the treeline.

When he finally spoke, his voice was low, almost wary.

"You risk being unseen," he said. "Or worse… misseen."

His eyes drifted to the dark where the Wilds breathed slow and steady, like some vast sleeping beast. "Keep the mark," he added. "Until we're clear of this place. Then, when it's safe, we'll thank them properly… and let it go."

The blood on their brows had begun to crust, pulling tight against their skin. The fire shivered back to life with a faint crackle.

And somewhere beyond the ring of light, in the thick hush of the trees, something watched.

Chapter Nineteen

———

The Hollow Mile

Morning fog draped the forest in a heavy shroud, damp and close, clinging to Sol's skin like the ghost of another's breath. The air felt charged, alive in a way that made the fine hairs on his arms stand on end, every fingertip buzzing as if brushing unseen threads.

They broke camp without speaking. Not by choice, but by something more profound, an unspoken knowing that even a single whisper might stir the mist and rouse whatever waited, just beyond sight.

The Wilds waited ahead, shrouded and unmoving. The silence around them was unnerving; even Scy looked grim as they approached the clearing where they had offered the hare to Valkirith.

This time, Scy didn't cut straight through. He drifted around the circle's edge, boots sinking softly into damp earth. As they drew closer, Sol spotted it, a narrow break in the trees, a faintly trodden path he could've sworn wasn't there last night.

Maybe it had been too dark.

Or maybe the Wilds only opened doors when they felt like it.

Scy halted just shy of the threshold. From his coat pocket, he pulled a single gold coin, dulled by age and worry-smooth at the edges. He crouched by the roots of an ancient pine, its bark twisted like old scars, and pressed the coin into the moss.

"Old Magpie," he murmured, voice pitched low to the trees, "you greedy feathered bastard… keep our feet light and our luck bent sideways. If something's waiting in the dark, flash this trinket and let it chase you instead of me."

He paused, then added with a smirk, "We walk crooked. We walk clever. Watch our backs, and I'll leave you a shiny for your troubles."

Sol raised an eyebrow. "I thought Valkirith was the god of these woods."

"Never hurts to have another god watching your back," Scy said. "We gave Valkirith a hare. I'm hoping Old Magpie will tip the odds in my favor."

The three lingered at the threshold, suspended in a breathless stillness. Even the forest seemed to hold its inhale. Beyond, the fog thinned into ghostly ribbons of mist that slithered along the ground, veiling a narrow path that vanished into the dim unknown. The wild growth on either side clawed toward what little light there was, tangled vines wrapping the massive tree trunks like pulsing veins beneath taut skin.

Sol felt Wyatt's hand slip into his, a fragile tether, equal parts comfort and plea. Ahead of them, Scy tugged at his pack straps, jaw tight, shoulders braced as though trying to summon courage from the weight he carried.

Sol drew in a slow, unsteady breath. Whatever waited within the Wilds remained hidden, but beyond its shadow lay something he craved more than safety—freedom.

And so, it was Sol who moved first.

Gravel crackled under their boots, the sound unnervingly sharp in a world stripped of life. No birdcalls. No rustle of leaves. Even the air seemed to recoil from them. As they crossed the threshold and set foot on the narrow path, a sudden chill gripped them, not a whispering wind, but a heavy, unseen weight that pressed against their chests and dragged at every step.

The farther they walked, the more the silence wrapped around them. Sol felt as if he were underwater, the world muffled, the air too thick, each breath dragging. Even his hearing dulled, his own heartbeat was louder than their footsteps.

What were they doing in here?

The path ahead cut unnaturally straight through the forest, as though some long-forgotten blade had sliced the earth open and left it raw. Towering trees leaned inward, their branches knitting together high above, forming a vaulted canopy that muted even whispers of wind. Yet the leaves stirred soundlessly, shifting like restless ghosts in a breeze Sol couldn't feel.

He rubbed at his arms, but the cold clung to him like a second skin. It wasn't the sharp bite of wind or the damp chill of shadow; it was deeper, marrow-deep, a creeping cold that made his joints stiffen and his thoughts drag as though weighed down by unseen hands.

Their footsteps were the only sound, yet even that felt wrong, muted, hollow, as though the earth itself resisted carrying their presence. A place like this should have swallowed sound whole, but instead, it lingered unnaturally, bouncing back faintly from nowhere. More than once, Sol glanced over his shoulder, not because he believed someone followed, but because he couldn't be certain they didn't.

At one point, he swore the path ahead dipped into a gentle curve, a promise of change in the unbroken monotony. But when they reached it, nothing had shifted. The road   stretched on, unnervingly flawless, as if some invisible hand kept redrawing it straight beneath their feet.

Wyatt kept his eyes forward, jaw tight. Scy was unusually silent.

Sol shifted his pack higher on his shoulder, trying to shake the heaviness gathering between his ribs. His legs weren't tired, not really, but every step felt slower. Like the ground was resisting him. Like he didn't belong here.

You're slowing them down.

The thought struck without warning, sharp and electric, flaring like a spark behind Sol's eyes. He blinked hard, trying to snuff it out, and fixed his gaze on Wyatt's back just a step ahead.

Mist coiled around his boots, clinging and tugging, cold and deliberate as ghostly fingers. He didn't remember it being this thick moments ago.

Ahead, Scy halted briefly, squinting into the trees as though catching a movement just beyond sight. A beat later, he shook it off and pressed forward.

Time bled strangely here. They walked, and walked,

long enough that Sol's legs ached and his breath grew shallow, but the light never shifted, and the forest never changed. The same warped branches hunched over them, the same moss-matted bark oozed damp green, the same vine dangled too far into the trail before dissolving into nothing.

Finally, without a word, they stopped.

Scy crouched to rummage through his pack, pulling out a hard bit of bread and dried meat. Wyatt stayed standing, staring off into the trees like he was trying to listen for something that wasn't there.

Sol sank down with his back against the trunk of a massive tree, trying not to shudder at the clammy dampness seeping through his shirt.

That's when he heard it, a sound so faint it almost didn't belong here. A baby's cry.

He froze, lungs tight, listening hard against the suffocating hush of the Wilds. The wail was distant, thin as spider silk, yet it wormed its way into his chest and tightened there, impossible to ignore.

Slowly, he pushed to his feet, eyes narrowing as he scanned the dense undergrowth.

Another cry. Louder this time.

Sol edged a step toward the path's border.

"Sol?" Wyatt's voice came softly behind him. "Are—"

"Shhh." Sol's hand lifted sharply, silencing him without turning around.

Sol's grip tightened around the hilt of his sword, knuckles blanching as he prepared to hack his way through the thick brush. One more step and he'd be off the trail completely.

Before he could move, Scy's hand clamped hard on his shoulder. "Lad—don't," he said, voice edged with warning. "It's the Wilds callin' you."

"There's a baby out there," Sol shot back, voice frayed and cracking under the strain. "What kind of parents just… just abandon it? Leave it out here to die?"

Scy's face shadowed, his jaw tightening. "I don't hear what you're hearin'." His gaze slid past Sol toward Wyatt. "You?"

Silence settled heavy between them.

Then the cries came again, sharp, wet, heartbreakingly real— boring into Sol's skull like a needle. He flinched, boot inching forward before instinct could stop him.

Scy's hand clamped down and yanked him back.

"Sol," Wyatt said softly, moving to block his path. His voice carried a fragile calm, like one wrong word might splinter everything. "I don't hear anything either."

Wyatt's hand found his, grounding him. Pulling him back to the center of the path.

Sol clamped his hands over his ears, desperate to shut it out, but the cries only swelled, slicing through his skull, raw and relentless. His breath hitched, chest tightening, eyes stinging until he thought he might scream just to drown it out.

Then—

Silence.

The wail vanished mid-sob, snuffed out as if it had never existed, leaving only a crushing stillness that pressed on his ribs.

When Sol finally looked up, Scy's weary gaze met his. The older man slowly shook his head, a shadow of pity in his eyes, and forced a fragile, almost broken smile.

"The first time I walked these woods," Scy said, "I saved a woman tied to a burning pyre."

Sol blinked.

"Turns out, I was just thrashin' in a bramble bush," Scy said, voice rough as gravel. "Clothes torn, arms bleeding… not a soul in sight." A dry, humorless chuckle escaped him. "The Wilds don't always lie, lad. But they never tell the truth straight, either."

No one spoke after that.

The forest seemed to tighten around them, holding its breath, waiting. Every creak of bark, every faint rustle of unseen things pressed in on the silence. Sol kept his gaze locked on the ribbon of trail ahead, fists clamped hard around his pack straps, jaw set like stone.

Eventually, Scy stood with a grunt and brushed off his coat. "We shouldn't linger too long," he muttered. "The Wilds don't like it when you sit still."

Wyatt offered Sol a hand up. He didn't speak, but his grip was steady. Sol took it without a word.

They moved on, gravel crunching underfoot like brittle bones. The trees pressed closer now, their looming trunks casting long, skeletal shadows that seemed to lean inward as the silence thickened.

This time, Sol didn't dare glance into the woods.

They trudged on in wordless tension, mist coiling around their boots like something alive, the trail tightening until it felt as though the Wilds were trying to squeeze them out.

Scy broke the quiet with a dry, rasping mutter. "Y'know," he said, voice roughened by fatigue and something darker, "if the Wilds eat us, at least it'll save Elion the trouble. Spillborn meat probably tastes like shame and bad decisions."

The words hit like a slap, sharp and stinging in the still air.

Wyatt stopped short. Sol did too, though he didn't turn. His fists were clenched, breath sharp through his nose.

Even Scy looked surprised. His own face tightened, like he was hearing it for the first time.

"Shit," he muttered. "That… wasn't what I meant."

No one spoke.

Scy dragged a hand across the back of his neck, eyes fixed on the ground. "That wasn't me," he muttered, voice rough. "Not really.

The Wilds—" He stopped himself, jaw tightening. "Doesn't matter.

I'm… sorry."

Sol said nothing. He only turned and moved on, boots crunching softly before the mist swallowed the sound whole.

Scy stayed where he was for a beat, shoulders slumped, then followed, lagging a few paces behind as though the weight of his own words held him back.

Fingers brushed the small black feather tucked inside his coat — one he always kept close, though he never said why.

Under his breath:

"Old Magpie, that one was mine. I know better."

A pause.

"Keep me clever. Keep me kind."

Scy finally moved, falling in step behind the others as they pressed deeper into the mist.

Without warning, the path split.

No marker. No sign. Just two spindly trails clawing away into the trees, each swallowed by fog as if they had existed forever, waiting for this moment.

Scy halted first, muttering under his breath, "Perfect. A trap that gives you choices."

Wyatt's gaze shifted to Sol, his tone quiet but heavy with expectation. "Well?" he asked. "You're the one who feels things the rest of us don't. Left… or right?"

The words hit harder than Wyatt likely intended, but he didn't call them back.

Sol blinked, the breath leaving him in a sudden rush as if he'd been struck.

He said nothing. Didn't even twitch.

Scy arched a brow but stayed silent, watching.

Wyatt shifted his weight, jaw clenched tight. "I just mean…" he muttered, voice rough with frustration. "It'd be nice to have something solid. Just once."

Sol's thoughts spun, tangled with all the things left unsaid, the words he couldn't seem to force past his lips.

I didn't ask for any of this.

His voice came out small. "I don't know."

Scy dragged a hand across the back of his neck, voice softening. "It's alright, lad," he said gently. "We'll figure it out." He gave a slight nod toward the left path. "I say we go this way. Old Magpie wouldn't steer us right."

A crooked smile ghosted across his face, just a flicker, but enough to feel like the Scy Sol knew, and he stepped forward.

Sol fell in behind him.

It wasn't until a few paces in that he realized Wyatt's footsteps were missing.

"Wyatt?" Sol spun around, scanning the mist. "Scy—hold up."

He ran back to find Wyatt frozen, eyes fixed on the edge of the path, brow furrowed like he was trying to listen for something far away.

Sol reached for Wyatt, fingers closing around his hand. "It's not real," he murmured, voice steady but soft.

"I know," Wyatt said, though his voice sounded far away, lost.

"It's the sheep… they're being slaughtered. I can smell the blood."

Sol's grip tightened, a silent anchor.

He didn't try to reason with him, just gently, carefully pulled him back toward the trail.

Scy met them halfway, sliding an arm around Wyatt's shoulders with the ease of someone who'd done it a hundred times before. "Come on now, lad," he said, tone rough but kind. "We've gotta keep moving."

Sol let Wyatt's hand slip from his grasp. His pace slowed, boots dragging slightly as he allowed Scy and Wyatt to drift ahead, their shapes dissolving into the thick mist like fading memories. He strained to catch anything, any flicker of life. A birdcall. The crack of a twig.

Even the whisper of wind.

Nothing.

Only the heavy, unnatural stillness pressed against Sol's ears, a weight that dulled every sound but his own breath.

Up ahead, Scy kept an arm looped around Wyatt's shoulders, his voice a low, steady murmur, thin as thread, but strong enough to hold them together.

Scy doesn't even like you.

Wyatt's only here because he doesn't know how to leave.

The thought slithered in, curling like smoke deep in Sol's chest before he could force it away.

That's not true, he told himself. It's not.

But the lie clung stubbornly, refusing to lift.

The road curved again—no sharp bends, no sudden shifts, just a slow, deliberate spiral that felt intentional, like the Wilds were guiding them in circles.

Sol fell back in step with the others, keeping just an arm's length between them, eyes sweeping the misted trail for anything out of place.

That's when he saw it…

A stone was overturned near the edge of the path. Then another a few paces ahead. The pattern tugged at him, something about the angle, the press of dirt disturbed beneath.

He crouched low, leaning closer, breath caught in his throat.

Boot print. Had to be.

"There are boot prints," Sol said, louder than he meant to.

Scy and Wyatt stopped and came back to look.

Wyatt stepped forward first, setting his boot beside the print. Scy followed, matching his own foot to another mark just ahead.

"God bless," Sol hissed, snapping upright. "We've

been walking in circles."

Wyatt's brow furrowed as he stared between the track and the path that stretched endlessly into the fog. "That's…impossible," he muttered. "We never turned back."

Frustration flared hot in Sol's chest. He snatched up the loose stone and flung it hard into the trees.

The sound that came back wasn't right. A dull, meaty thud echoed faintly from the dark, reverberating like a fist striking stretched skin.

Sol froze mid-breath. That… wasn't wood.

Not quite.

It was too soft. Too close.

His chest tightened.

"Now what?" he snapped, throwing up his hands. He began to pace, tension pressing down on him like a second weight.

They were lost. The Wilds had them. Every step twisted the world around them, bending sound, bending sight. Night would fall soon, and the thought of pitching camp in the middle of that cursed road scraped raw against Sol's nerves.

Unless…

He stopped mid-stride, the thought breaking through like a spark. "What if it's the Wilds?" he said suddenly. "Maybe we just keep moving forward. Maybe this—" he gestured to the looping trail, the boot prints "—isn't real. Just another trick."

Scy's hand dragged over the scruff along his jaw, eyes narrowed. "Aye," he muttered. "The Wilds are clever like that. Tricky bastards."

"What other choice do we have?" Wyatt asked, voice tight.

"Alright then," Scy said with an exaggerated salute, trying to lift the mood. "Onward."

He took the lead again.

They continued following the road's twists and turns. It felt like hours. Sol's stomach growled, his pack heavy, every step a labor. His feet ached.

Scy and Wyatt didn't seem to notice. Or maybe the Wilds just didn't sink their claws as deep into them.

Sol kept silent.

You're the weak link.

Always have been.

He paused to breathe, tugging at the straps of his pack as if tightening them might hold him together.

They'd go farther, faster, if they didn't have to drag you along.

He tried to push forward, forcing one heavy step after another… and his boot caught.

The ground rushed up to meet him. Gravel bit into his knees, sharp and unyielding, stealing the breath from his lungs.

When Sol finally looked up, Scy was already there, hand extended. But Sol didn't take it. He stayed on the ground, breath coming in shallow, ragged pulls, eyes blinking against the blur.

He didn't move. Couldn't.

The air had turned heavy, thick as wet cloth draped over his chest. It felt like the trees were watching, like the very earth beneath him had grown hands, gripping his limbs and pinning him in place. His lungs strained, dragging in thin threads of breath that never seemed enough.

It wasn't pain that kept him down.

It was weight. Old, heavy, and everywhere.

"Wyatt?" Scy called. "A little help over here?"

Wyatt stood frozen a few paces away, whispering to himself, palm striking the side of his own head in sharp, frantic taps.

Scy's face changed in an instant, eyes narrowing, jaw tightening. "Stay put," he ordered Sol, voice low but cutting, before striding toward Wyatt in quick, deliberate steps.

Without warning, Scy's hand cracked across Wyatt's cheek, the sound splitting the mist.

Wyatt jerked as if yanked from deep water, eyes wide. "What the hell, Scy?" he barked, clutching his stinging cheek.

"Sorry, lad. The Wilds had you." Scy's voice was calm, steady.

"I need your help with Sol."

Wyatt blinked, still dazed. "Why didn't you slap him?"

Scy let out a sharp breath. "Take his other arm," he muttered. "We're gettin' him up."

Hands gripped Sol beneath the shoulders and hauled him upright, not gently, but not cruelly either. His knees buckled, threatening to give out before he caught himself.

"Sol," Scy said again, this time softer, the edge in his voice dulling. "You with us?"

Sol swallowed hard and nodded faintly. "Yeah… I think so."

Scy's gaze lingered on Sol, a flicker of worry softening his otherwise rough edges. "The Wilds will keep gnawin' at you," he murmured. "I hear it too, whispers, calls. When it gets bad, I dig my nails in, give myself a good pinch… reminds me I'm still flesh and bone."

Wyatt and Sol exchanged a slow, silent nod.

Scy's mouth tugged into a crooked grin. "Hell, I'll start pinchin' you both if it keeps you upright." He gave a quick wink, the levity thin but welcome.

They moved forward again, each step dragging heavier than the last, exhaustion settling on their shoulders like wet cloaks.

"Wait," Scy said suddenly, calm but firm.

He stepped in front of them and studied the trail ahead.

Sol, still jumpy, pinched him.

Scy let out a sharp yelp. "What in the bloody hell was that for?" he barked, twisting to rub his ribs.

"There's nothing there," Sol said, feigning innocence.

"I know that!" Scy snapped, voice dropping to a hiss. "I'm tryin' to call for shelter, we can't stumble through this cursed place all night."

Heat crept up Sol's neck. "Sorry, Scy…"

Scy huffed but waved it off. "Aye, just give me some space."

He strode a few paces ahead, then glanced back with a lopsided grin. With deliberate exaggeration, he lifted his hand and threw Sol a mock evil eye, sharp, dramatic, and almost playful enough to cut through the fog.

Then he crouched low, drawing into the earth with the edge of his blade:

A circle.

A triangle, nested within.

A single horizontal linecuts through them both.

He didn't look up as he whispered:

"Valkirith ena silen.

Shal'kai thaluen.

V'ren'dai kai.

Ena esar'amin'dor."

Scy drew in a slow, measured breath, steadying himself before kneeling. With deliberate care, he set a flat stone over the mark.

"May the Wilds lie quiet tonight," he murmured, "and sleep beside us."

The three of them stilled, breath held, ears straining for any sign, a whisper of wind, a shifting branch, something that might answer.

Nothing came. Only silence.

Scy rose, brushing dirt from his knees, his expression unreadable. "Come on," he said at last. "We'll walk a little farther. Got a feeling we're close."

Sol glanced at Wyatt. Wyatt only gave a faint, wordless shrug. With no better choice, they fell in step behind Scy, the mist swallowing their sound.

The trail pinched tight, funnelling them single-file, before easing wider again, just enough to stir a quiet unease, like the forest was breathing with them.

Gradually, the trees began to fall away. The mist

receded, too, drawn back like a heavy curtain revealing a stage no one asked to see.

And then, without warning, they stepped into an open clearing.

It spread wide and near-perfectly round, moss-draped stones scattered across a bed of damp, springy earth. Along the far edge, a slender creek snaked through, its waters moving slow and smooth, glimmering faintly as though lit from within.

The air here was cooler, gentler. Still strange, yes, but unlike the rest of the Wilds, it didn't feel cruel. It felt… watchful.

There was no path forward. Only the one they came from.

"This'll do," Scy said at last, voice low, as if speaking too loud might wake the Wilds again. "Nothin' stalkin' us, no teeth hidin' in the trees… aye, could be worse."

They shrugged off their packs without a word, the sound of buckles and canvas hitting the earth louder than their voices.

Camp took shape in weary, automatic motions, hands moving by habit more than thought. No jokes. No idle chatter.

Dinner was the same: a thin, flavorless meal swallowed in silence, settling in their stomachs like cold stones, leaving them heavier and more drained than before.

"I'll take first watch," Scy said eventually. "I know we're all feeling it. But with some rest, I think you'll be able to fight the call on your shift. No one leaves the clearing."

Sol and Wyatt both nodded.

"You lads get some rest," Scy added. "Sooner you sleep, sooner I can."

With nothing left to say, Sol and Wyatt turned to their bedrolls. The silence between them felt heavier than words.

Sol parted his lips once, almost speaking, but whatever thought had risen slipped away before it could take shape. He sighed softly, crawling into his bedroll and pulling it snug around his shoulders as though it could shield him from more than the night's chill.

He curled on his side, back to the others. The creek whispered faintly nearby, a thin, silver murmur. Yet even that sound seemed distant, like it belonged to some other world where the Wilds couldn't reach them.

He watched the soft glow of mist above him shift and blur, slow and steady like breath.

Wyatt's breathing had settled into a faint, steady rhythm. Scy hadn't shifted in what felt like hours, one arm slung over his pack as though anchoring himself to the earth, daring the Wilds to pull him away.

Sol, meanwhile, felt anything but anchored.

His legs throbbed with a deep, restless ache, his chest tight like a coiled spring. Every muscle in his body pleaded for sleep, yet his mind clung stubbornly to wakefulness, circling through unease and exhaustion with no way out.

You're slowing them down.

You're the reason they're still out here.

They'd be better off if you just disappeared.

Died quietly. In your sleep. At least then you wouldn't be in the way.

He pressed his face into the crook of his arm, willing the thoughts to stop.

But they didn't.

You're just a spillborn who made things worse.

It would be easier, wouldn't it?

Just... not waking up. Letting the Wilds take him. Letting the ache go quiet.

And still— He didn't cry.

He didn't pray.

He just closed his eyes and waited for sleep.

Chapter Twenty

———

A Path Not Given

The moon hung far too large in the sky, swollen and unnervingly bright.

It's cold, silvery light spilled across the clearing, bleaching the earth pale. The fire was gone. No glowing embers. No curling smoke.

Only a suffocating stillness pressed against his ears.

Sol sat up sharply, scanning the clearing.

Scy was nowhere. Wyatt too vanished as though they'd never been there at all.

Sol pushed free from his bedroll slowly. The grass was cold beneath his feet. He felt eyes on him.

Did something happen to them?

He wanted to call out, anything, a name, a sound, but instinct clenched his throat. Breaking the silence felt wrong. Dangerous. As if a single word might summon something unseen.

The mist had thickened, glowing faintly beneath the swollen moon, curling and shifting like the whole clearing was drawing breath.

Barefoot, Sol stepped forward, the damp earth cold under his feet. The mist swirled around his ankles, coiling higher as he moved.

He took one cautious step, then another…

And the fog peeled back without warning, revealing a wide, shallow lake stretched before him, its glassy surface perfectly still, reflecting the oversized moon like a silver eye.

Maybe he shouldn't go back to the camp.

Maybe he should just keep walking into the water.

Let the cold sink its teeth in. Let it drag him beneath the silver surface and hold him there.

No more clawing for a way forward. No more stumbling, failing. Wyatt could stop looking over his shoulder, stop carrying his weight. He could grieve, finally, and let go.

Better that than dragging him down too.

Better that than pretending he still knew how to climb out.

But something called to him.

The moon hovered on its surface like it was waiting to be touched.

Flat stones jutted from the water in a deliberate pattern, each spaced just wide enough to make every step a test of nerve and balance.

Sol placed his foot on the first stone. It held steady beneath his weight. He moved to the next. Then the third.

Each step carried him farther from the shore, deeper into the silver glow, as though the lake itself were drawing him in.

The water below was so clear it felt wrong. He couldn't see his reflection. Only the sky.

He leaned closer over the glassy surface. Nothing. No ripple of his outline, no faint suggestion of a shadow where his face should be.

It was as if the world had scrubbed him away entirely, or worse, had never acknowledged he existed at all.

Then a breeze rolled across the lake, not soft, not warm, but sharp and hollow, carrying with it a whisper of something unseen.

It cut across the lake like a blade, sharp enough to raise goosebumps.

Sol straightened instinctively, pulse spiking, like

something had noticed him.

Halfway across, the mist parted again.

On the far shore, the ruins of a temple clawed skyward. Tall, splintered pillars jutted from the earth like the bones of some ancient titan, their surfaces strangled by thick vines. Shattered stones lay scattered like offerings long forgotten. At the heart of it all stood an altar, half-buried yet unbroken.

The gray stone was the same as the temples outside

Aurelthane, but older, worn thin by centuries, as if time itself had tried to erase it and failed.

This place was not merely abandoned. It was sacred, and it remembered.

He climbed the cracked stairs, the stone warm beneath his feet.

Whispers drifted through the air, spoken in a language he didn't know, yet something deep inside told him he was safe here.

Crumbling walls rose on either side, draped in creeping vines. The fractured ceiling gaped open to the night, and pale beams of light spilled through, but as Sol moved deeper into the ruins, a chill realization struck him.

The moon wasn't lighting this hall.

The glow came from within the stone itself, a faint, silvery pulse that seemed to breathe as he walked.

Drawn forward, he stepped into its quiet radiance.

Murals of mighty figures stared back at him.

He walked closer.

The first figure stood tall, robed in the hues of soil and storm, their hood drawn low over their brow. Their face held no features, only a single arc of silver where their eyes should have been — a crescent, or perhaps a hammer's curve.

They stood with one hand resting lightly against the flank of a towering creature, the Veyrnstag. Its massive antlers stretched like living branches, tangled with vines that shimmered faintly in the moonlight. The stag's head was bowed, not in fear, but in solemn reverence, as though listening to a voice carried only on the night air.

Around them, the world unfolded like living art: rivers etched like glimmering veins, mountains rising in shadowed layers behind their flowing cloak, roots spilling from their feet and threading deep into the painted earth. At the figure's feet, offerings had been rendered in delicate, reverent strokes, smooth stones stacked in balance, feathers fanned like rays of light, and a lone, steady flame burning as if the paint itself carried breath.

The name beneath the mural had nearly worn away, but the title remained etched in deeper lines:

Valkirith, the Worldforger.

Sol placed his hand against the mural.

His mouth moved before he could stop it.

"Valkirith etai'ven dorakai. Shal'kai emen veyr."

The words tasted foreign, shaped in an ancient tongue long forgotten by the living, yet when they touched his lips, they felt achingly familiar, like echoes of something he'd spoken in another life.

He couldn't grasp their meaning, not fully.

Only that they belonged to him as much as his own breath.

Drawing in a slow, deliberate inhale, he felt the fog in his mind begin to thin, his thoughts settling like dust after a storm. His feet felt steadier beneath him.

Wyatt's voice echoed in memory:

"We chose this. We chose you."

One mural drew him in, faint with age yet

stubbornly defiant of time's decay.

Three women stood entwined, hewn from dusk-colored stone as if carved from the fading edge of night itself.

The central figure towered over the others. She was robed not in silks but in garments that clung like armor, a single thread coiled tight around one hand, while a flame burned unwavering in the other.

Her face was not soft, not meant to soothe, but carved with a stern majesty, lips slightly parted as though the next breath would release a command that could shake the earth.

To her right stood a younger woman, soft-featured and fair, her gaze lifted toward the sky.

She held a flower Sol didn't recognize, reaching toward something unseen — stars, or maybe nothing at all.

There was a fragile innocence in her carved face, a quiet ache of longing frozen in stone.

The third figure hunched with age, her frail frame wrapped in a thin, tattered veil. Wisps of it slipped through her fingers like smoke, coiling downward as though time itself unraveled in her grasp.

Her eyes, or where eyes should have been, were hollowed out, smooth and vacant, like something had carved the soul clean from her face. The sight made Sol's stomach knot and twist, a primal discomfort he couldn't name, only feel deep in his bones.

Beneath the mural, an inscription in worn Valeiric:

"Ven'tara Maerlynth. Veyrn Shal, veyrn Na."

Sol could barely read it.

He fixed his gaze on the central figure, a weight settling over him, unease without shape or name.

It wasn't fear, nor was it reverence. It felt older than both.

Like stepping into a silent room, you were certain it was empty… only to realize it had been watching you all along.

He didn't know her name, yet something deep inside stirred, as if she had always known his, long before he'd even learned to speak it himself.

A hush fell inside him, deep and sudden like standing in the presence of something sacred.

He knew he couldn't linger. The others would be looking for him, wondering.

He started to turn toward the temple's entrance, but then, from a shadowed corridor to his right, a faint ember pulsed, steady and unblinking.

What was that?

A cold shiver swept across his skin, his chest tightening as though the air itself resisted his breath.

Every instinct told him to turn back. To leave.

Yet his feet stayed rooted to the stone.

The next chamber was smaller than the rest, yet the moment he stepped inside, a crushing weight pressed down on him, making him feel not just small but utterly insignificant, like a speck beneath an endless sky.

On the far wall, darker and more imposing than any figure in the larger hall, a mural loomed. It rose nearly twice the height of the others, its shadow stretching across the stone floor as though it could swallow the entire room whole.

His robe was rendered in angular strokes of deep red edged in black, the lines unnaturally sharp. One hand was raised skyward, fingers splayed like a brand. The other gripped a long rod, or a spear, its tip buried in the mural's base, vanishing into a tangle of indistinct forms.

Behind him, there were no trees. No water. No sky.

Nothing else marked the wall, only fire, stylized and curling upward in jagged waves, and above it, a fractured sun rendered in fading gold leaf.

Yet the eyes… they were different. Unshadowed. Stark and pale, drawn in impossibly thin strokes of gold that still caught the light, shimmering faintly like fresh paint laid moments ago.

Sol narrowed his gaze, unease prickling at the back of his neck.

The color wasn't fading like the rest. It was too bright. Too alive.

Almost watching.

He found himself stepping closer without meaning to.

The edges weren't cracked like the others. No dust. No wear.

The red looked almost wet, like it had only just dried.

At the figure's feet, painted throngs knelt in eerie unison. Their faces were smooth, featureless, their bodies bowed not in devotion, but in absolute, unthinking obedience, as though the very act of worship had been stripped from them, leaving only surrender.

No name was carved beneath the towering figure. Only a jagged sigil remained:

A circle split down the middle, like lightning through a sun.

But Sol didn't need to read a name to know.

Elion. The Keeper of the Path.

The words didn't feel new. They reverberated through his mind like an echo from a memory he couldn't place, something he'd always known.

Not a savior.

Not a guide.

A warden.

Sol's breath caught as he stared up at the colossal figure.

Then, with a sound like stone grinding on bone, the mural shifted. The painted hand tore free of the wall—not soft or living, but dragging itself forward as if the rock itself remembered how to move.

Sol stepped back.

Then stumbled.

He slammed into the ground, the impact rattling through his bones, but adrenaline dragged him upright before the pain could settle. He ran.

Didn't dare look back, until raw instinct twisted his neck against his will.

Elion was gliding across the shattered marble like a shadow unchained, silent and impossibly fast, his movement too smooth to belong to anything human.

And then, in a blink, the world folded, and Sol was no longer running.

He stood again in the vast main chamber, breath ragged, heart hammering against his ribs.

Standing before the altar. Barefoot. Breathless.

The air around him hummed like a held note.

Intricate markings had been carved into the altar's stone surface, not words, not symbols he recognized, but something older, more primal. As moonlight spilled across them, they shimmered faintly, like veins of starlight running beneath the rock.

He couldn't read them. Yet standing there, every nerve in his body thrummed with a single certainty: they knew him.

A chill crawled up his spine. He turned sharply, heart pounding.

From the shadowed hall, he glimpsed the faintest flicker of crimson robes, trailing like a dying ember as Elion slipped soundlessly back into the darkness.

Sol's breath slowed.

The chamber swelled with light, a golden warmth that wrapped around him like a long-forgotten embrace. For a breath, he let himself believe it.

He was safe.

He was held.

But then the light changed.

It didn't just shine, it throbbed, pulsing through the stone like a heartbeat too big for the walls to hold.

Sol stretched, reaching for that warmth, and the walls seemed to close in, pressing tight, as if the chamber itself had decided not to let him go.

Not trapped, but not comfortable either. Like he didn't quite belong to his body yet.

His eyes adjusted to the dim light. Wyatt lay

sleeping beside him, peaceful, undisturbed.

Sol glanced around the clearing. Scy was nowhere to be seen.

A flicker of worry tugged at him, then faded, leaving behind an almost unnatural calm, like the Wilds themselves were pressing a hand to his chest, telling him not to panic.

He slipped free of his bedroll, movements slow and deliberate, and padded toward the fire. Only faint embers remained, glowing like sleepy eyes in the dark, breathing in and out with the night.

His dream still clung to him, trailing threads of moonlight and ash. It had given him so much to think about.

Maybe tomorrow the trek wouldn't be as hard.

He shook his head, forcing away the fragile hope. Just wishful thinking.

But maybe, just maybe, he could fight the Call this time.

The mist still writhed at the edge of the clearing, restless and alive.

Where was Scy?

Sol's gaze drifted toward the creek, half expecting to Scy crouched there, filling his waterskin.

Instead, a shape moved in the pale light.

And then he saw them.

Two pale, silver orbs glimmered in the mist like twin moons suspended in the dark.

And then the shape beneath them emerged, a ghostly white stag, its coat flawless as new snow, its massive antlers snarled with black, living vines that pulsed faintly as if carrying their own heartbeat.

Moonlight clung to its form, painting it in a spectral glow.

Sol's breath hitched, chest tight.

The Veyrnstag.

It didn't move. Didn't even breathe.

It simply watched him.

Unblinking. Eternal.

The stag moved forward, each step measured and soundless, the mist peeling away as though bowing to its passage.

Closer…

Until Sol felt its breath, warm and steady, ghost across his skin, carrying the scent of earth and rain-soaked leaves.

Then, with a grace that felt older than language itself, the Veyrnstag lowered its massive head and pressed its velvet muzzle to his brow, directly over the faint mark where hare's blood had once dried.

The world vanished in a searing wash of white.

Blinding. Searing. Divine.

Something deep within him caught fire, an ember buried in his chest, suddenly roaring to life.

Heat surged outward in a blinding rush, too fast, too wild, flooding his veins like molten iron.

Every muscle locked, every nerve screamed as if his own skin were about to split apart and spill light.

And then…Silence.

Perfect, terrifying stillness.

The unnatural calm devoured him, swallowing everything in its path.

He opened his eyes.

The world was motionless.

And inside him bloomed something vast. Something aching.

A pull.

Lyvareth.

He had to reach it.

He didn't know why, couldn't say where it lay, or even if Lyvareth still belonged to Itharen at all.

But the certainty rooted itself in his bones, unyielding, immovable, as if the world itself would crack if he ignored it.

This wasn't a whisper, not some fragile flicker of instinct. It was pure, blinding clarity, the sharpest truth his soul had ever touched.

It was like being pulled by a tide that had been waiting for him since before he was born.

Like a time, glass had just been turned.

Sol exhaled slowly. The breath shook on the way out.

He looked deep into the Veyrnstag's eyes, and a quiet understanding waited there.

It stepped forward and nuzzled his neck, warm and

steady.

Sol, without thinking, threw his arms around the creature's neck and gave a gentle squeeze.

Stand tall, Orisian Revandor.

You will set the world ablaze in time.

Not by the path they give you, but the one you burn into being.

For you, the breath between steps is the page they could not write.

When the moment comes, you will know what to do.

The fire snapped and roared to life without warning, spilling gold and shadow across the clearing.

Sol flinched, whipping his head toward the blaze.

When he turned back, the Veyrnstag was gone.

No rustle of leaves. No echo of hooves.

Only the soft glow of dying coals and the mist curling like breath at the clearing's edge.

Sol stayed frozen where he knelt, heart hammering against his ribs, heat lingering on his skin as though the creature's touch had branded him.

The name still echoed in him — *Orisian Revandor* —

louder now, like it had always been waiting.

He didn't know what it meant.

But he knew this:

Nothing would be the same.

Sol's gaze drifted back toward the creek, eyes searching the mist for even a whisper of antlers.

Nothing.

Then, a flicker of motion.

Scy stepped out from the treeline, silent as a shadow, a waterskin dangling from one hand, a half-scrubbed root in the other.

He froze mid-step when his eyes found Sol sitting rigid by the fire, its glow painting sharp lines across his face.

"…You alright?" he asked, voice low.

Sol didn't answer at first. He stared into the fire, the echo of the vision still warm behind his ribs.

Finally, he nodded.

"Yeah. I think so."

Scy studied him for a long moment, something unreadable flickering in his weathered face.

Then, without speaking, he lowered himself beside

Sol, the fire crackling softly between them.

In the glow of the flames, Sol's brow caught the light, not from soot or blood, but from a pale, ghostly shimmer.

It glowed faintly, like moonlight trapped beneath his skin, a scar made not of flesh but of radiance.

Scy's breath hitched. His eyes went wide.

"The Veyrnstag visited you?"

Sol only nodded.

They sat in silence, shoulders almost brushing, the fire snapping softly between them.

Beyond its circle of light, the mist still shifted and curled, but it no longer pressed in like before.

For the first time in what felt like weeks, Sol felt tethered.

Not healed.

Not whole.

But steadied, as if unseen hands had finally found him and refused to let him drift away.

Chapter Twenty-One

——

Breath Between Worlds

The embers snapped softly, the fire burning low and casting a warm, flickering glow across their faces. Silence stretched between them, not heavy, not uncomfortable, just waiting. Scy didn't press, only watched Sol, patient as stone.

Finally, Sol's voice slipped into the quiet, rough and hesitant. "I had another dream," he said. "But this one… it wasn't like the others. It felt bigger, deeper, like I wasn't just watching it. I was in it. The Wilds still clung to me, crawling under my skin. And when I found the lake…"

He faltered, the firelight glinting off the faint tremor in his hands. When he finally spoke, his voice was barely more than a rasp. "I thought about… ending it. Thought maybe it'd be easier for Wyatt.

For you."

His gaze dropped to the dirt, shame shadowing his face.

Scy stayed quiet. No questions, no sharp edges, just a single, slow nod. A quiet promise that the moment was safe, that Sol could let the weight settle without fear of it breaking them both.

"But something stopped me. Something ancient. Calling from the water. Stones rose from the water — like a path." Sol said, "I followed them."

His voice steadied, low but charged with a quiet awe. "That's when I saw it, a temple, or what little time hadn't swallowed. Pillars rose like bleached bones against the sky, vines winding through shattered stone. It had the same pale rock as the temples beyond Aurelthane… only this felt older. Ancient. Abandoned, yet still breathing with something sacred."

He took a breath. "The first hall was full of murals — gods I didn't recognize. Twenty of them, maybe more. But I... I knew them."

A breathless laugh escaped him. "That sounds insane, right?"

Scy didn't laugh. He tilted his head. "The Hall of Echoes."

Sol blinked. "The what?"

"That's what it's called," Scy said.

Sol repeated it under his breath. "The Hall of

Echoes."

The name settled heavy in his chest, not like a revelation but like a truth long-buried, clawing its way back.

"I saw Valkirith," he murmured, "and three goddesses I didn't know… not in any way I could name. But I knew them. Like I'd stood in their shadow once, only to forget."

His hand drifted to the back of his neck, fingers digging absently at the skin. "I was on my way out when I saw it, a glow, faint and flickering, like dying embers in a side hall. I followed." His breath caught. "I shouldn't have."

He shivered, the memory clinging like cold mist. "There was another mural. Larger than the others. The paint looked wet. Too red. Too bright. It… it didn't feel old. It felt new."

Scy's voice dropped to a hush, barely threading through the crackle of the fire. "It was Elion… wasn't it?"

Sol's nod was stiff, reluctant. "Yeah." The word rasped out, his throat suddenly parched.

"He wasn't just there, he towered," Sol went on, voice unsteady. "Draped in red and black, one hand lifted like a burning brand, the other clutching a rod sunk deep into this… writhing mass. Shapes, twisted, maybe people. Fire roared behind him. No sky above, no trees around. Just… ruin. Nothing but ruin." He paused. "His eyes—"

He closed his own as if the image was still too near.

"They weren't angry," Sol whispered, his words catching on a breath. "They were… knowing. Like I was just another page in a book he'd already memorized, and he didn't want to burn me, he wanted to wield me."

His gaze lifted to Scy, eyes shining with something raw, voice trembling as it broke. "And the worst part? He was beautiful, terribly, impossibly beautiful. Like judgment sculpted from light. Seductive in a way that made sense and didn't. I almost… stepped closer. Gods, I wanted to hear what he'd say."

Scy's jaw tightened, a flicker of muscle betraying what silence refused to.

"Then the light around him changed. It turned sharply. Hollow. Like it would dig inside me and leave nothing left. I ran."

His words tumbled out faster now, breath hitching. "I made it back to the altar in the main hall. Symbols lit up around me—not letters, not any language I know, but they… recognized me. Like they'd been waiting."

His eyes stayed fixed on the fire, voice thinning to a whisper. "I looked back, and he was already pulling away, dissolving into shadow. Then, just a flash of light. And I was back."

Scy didn't speak at first. He reached for a twig and pressed it into the edge of the coals, watching the end blacken and curl.

"You ran," he said eventually. "That matters."

Sol gave a faint nod. "It didn't feel brave."

"Maybe not." Scy tilted his head. "But it wasn't surrender."

Firelight flickered over Sol's face, throwing his eyes into shifting shadow. He stayed silent, breathing evening out, not the calm of release, but the steady pull of someone carrying a burden and refusing to set it down.

Beside him, Scy leaned back, letting his gaze drift toward the scatter of stars above. When he spoke, his voice carried a quiet certainty. "The Hall doesn't open its doors to just anyone. And that altar…" his eyes narrowed slightly, glinting in the fire's glow, "…it doesn't light for strangers."

He said it casually, but the words landed like something ancient spoken through his mouth.

Sol turned toward him, quiet. "You've seen it."

A pause. Then: "I've heard stories."

The words were gentle. Too gentle to be honest.

But Sol let the quiet linger.

Another silence unfurled between them, no longer weighed down by grief, but woven with a fragile understanding. Something unspoken had passed from one to the other, not yet named, yet undeniably shared.

Sol's breath slowed. He stared into the fire. Then, quieter now:

"That wasn't even the end of it."

Scy waited, head tilted, hands still.

"When I woke from the dream, I came out to the fire. Just needed to breathe. And that's when I saw it."

He paused—not for drama, but just to steady his breath enough to let the words escape.

"Two silver eyes," he said softly, "cutting through the mist. Not human. Just… watching." His voice dropped lower, touched with reverence.

"It was the Veyrnstag." The name slipped out like a prayer, not newly learned, but clawed up from some buried memory.

"Snow-white," he whispered, "its antlers snarled with black vines. The mist peeled away as it stepped toward me, slow, deliberate.

I couldn't move. Didn't even dare to breathe."

Scy's breath hitched — just slightly.

"It came right up to me," Sol said. "And pressed its muzzle to my forehead. Right where the blood had dried."

His fingers touched the spot, as if the heat still lingered.

"And in that moment… I felt it. Something I'd carried all my life — an ember I hadn't even noticed."

He turned to Scy, eyes wide, not frantic, but rooted in something unshakable. "When the Veyrnstag touched me… it ignited," he breathed. "A fire—no, an inferno erupted in my chest. Raging, roaring… like it had been coiled inside me all along, just waiting for that touch to set it free."

Scy didn't stir, yet the silence around him thickened, humming with a quiet, electric weight.

"I saw Lyvareth," Sol continued. "Not with my eyes — with something deeper. Like my bones knew the road, and my breath already belonged to it."

He swallowed. "And I felt like... like a time glass had just been turned."

His voice dropped, barely more than a breath. "The sands haven't started falling yet... but they will. And when they do, there won't be time to stop, won't be room to think. We'll have to move— fast."

Scy's reply came low, almost to himself. "The Veyrnstag never shows without purpose."

"It called me something," Sol said. "Orisian Revandor. I don't know what it means. But it echoed through me like a truth I hadn't caught up to yet."

Scy nodded once, slowly. "You're not becoming something new, Sol."

"You're becoming what you've always been."

Sol let his eyes fall shut for a single, steady breath. When they opened again, his voice carried a fragile softness.

"It saw me... not for what I am now, but for what I could become."

His head dipped, reverent.

"May its path stay protected. May its breath stay

warm."

Scy lowered his head slightly, a gesture not quite a bow, but close, like one instinctively offered to gods or ghosts.

The fire crackled softly as silence draped itself over them once more, not weighty, but full, alive with what had been said and what hadn't. Scy shifted, the corner of his mouth twitching like a word halfborn. Instead, he rose slowly, brushing ash from his coat with deliberate care.

Then, as if tossed casually into the night, but carrying the weight of something far deeper, he said, "I'm glad something stopped you."

He didn't look at Sol when he said it. The words hung there, soft, solid. Enough.

"You're already up," he added quietly. "You've got second watch, then."

Sol only nodded, no argument, no protest, just quiet acceptance.

Scy lingered beside him a breath longer than needed, as if weighing words, he chose not to speak, before finally offering a low,

"Wake him for third."

With that, he eased down into the dark, turning his back to the fire. The flames painted his silhouette for a heartbeat, then let him slip fully into the camp's edge, swallowed by shadow.

The night no longer felt cold, only still, hushed as if holding its breath. Sol remained by the fire long after Scy had turned in, the quiet wrapping around him like a worn, familiar blanket. Beneath his ribs, the warmth the Veyrnstag had kindled hadn't faded. It throbbed softly, not a burn, not a burden, just there, steady and alive, like a second heartbeat whispering of something yet to come.

He didn't bother counting the stars or tracing the hours as they slipped by. The Wilds felt changed around him, not darker, but deeper, as if the night itself had sunk into some hidden current. It was subtle, a shift so slight the world seemed tilted just a breath to the left, and somehow, only he could feel it.

Sol felt the soft warmth of Wyatt's lips on his forehead. His eyes were still adjusting when Wyatt's voice reached him, muffled at first.

"I heard you had quite the night," Wyatt said gently.

"Yeah…" Sol rubbed his eyes. "Did Scy say anything?"

The fog still hadn't lifted. It clung to his skin, cool and close, like a breath ghosting across glass.

Scy was already crouched by the low fire, coaxing breakfast from its fading coals.

Wyatt stepped up without a word, offering his hand and hauling Sol upright. The grip was steady, familiar…but when Sol met his gaze, Wyatt's eyes slid past, not quite landing on him.

"I know you'll tell me. When you're ready."

The fog thinned as they walked, the air sharpening to a crisp, quiet stillness. Sol blinked hard, scrubbing a hand across his eyes. *Had that opening always been there?*

He slowed, gaze fixed on the clearing by the river. "Looks like the Wilds want us heading that way," he murmured, nodding toward the narrow break in the trees.

Then turned, brow furrowing. "There's no going back now."

The place where they'd entered the clearing had vanished, swallowed whole by the forest, as if it had never existed at all.

They ate in near silence, movements brisk but thoughtful, the kind born of travelers with heavy minds. The fire crackled softly between them, its warmth a thin comfort against the unease. At last, with the quiet stretching long, Sol began to tell Wyatt what had unfolded in the night.

"There's more to my knowing than I ever realized," he murmured, voice low but steady. "I can feel it now, that fire burning in me... it wasn't new. It's never been new. It's been there all along, just a flicker, buried beneath everything I mistook for instinct. But it wasn't instinct. It was... something else. Something I've only just started to truly feel."

He shook his head.

"I just don't know what it means."

Scy stirred the coals, eyes on the flame. "Maybe the answers will be in Lyvareth."

"Maybe." Sol was already up, brushing off the last of the ash from his cloak and packing their things.

"Or maybe," Scy said, "the answer already lies in you."

Sol's gaze slid to Scy. There was a flicker in his eyes,

something familiar, but not pity, not comfort. Quieter than that. Older. Sol couldn't shake the feeling that Scy had always known more than he ever said.

He pushed the thought aside.

By the time they finished, the clearing bore no trace of them at all, as if they'd been nothing more than a passing shadow.

Scy knelt and drew the sacred symbol into the earth, a halved triangle within a circle, and whispered:

"Elaran veyr'kai, shal'ven dorathal.

Tey'kai lumen, arin'ven na veyrn."

The words slipped out so softly they were carried away on the breath of the Wilds. They moved without speaking, swallowed by the mist-draped trail ahead.

But this time, something had shifted.

No ancient eyes bore down on Sol's shoulders. No unseen gaze followed his steps. The Wilds felt… lighter.

The trail itself had changed.

Where once thick underbrush had snagged their steps, a mosscarpeted field now opened before them, lush and green, punctuated by dense clusters of towering trees.

The air remained cool, but the silence had changed. It no longer felt empty; it pressed in softly, almost expectant, as if the Wilds themselves were holding their breath.

Like the forest was waiting for them to speak its name.

The mist continued to swirl around their boots.

At first, mushrooms appeared only in small, hesitant clusters, pale caps pushing shyly through the moss. But the farther they walked, the more they multiplied, growing taller, stranger. Their hues shifted from muted browns to washed-out blues and dusky reds. Some gave off a faint, rhythmic glow, as though the forest itself was breathing through them.

A thought crept into Sol's mind, unbidden:

Do you really think you can get them to Lyvareth without getting them hurt?

The instant the thought took shape, his mark stirred with heat. Not a gentle warmth, but resistance.

It flared sharp and bright, like a ward sparking to life, burning away something foreign that dared to settle inside him.

Anchoring. Steadying. Grounding him to himself.

Like something ancient inside him had answered: *Yes.*

Moss thickened over the trail, creeping higher until a fallen tree barred their way. Sol crouched beside it.

In its slow decay, life thrived. Ants streamed in dark rivulets through the furrowed bark. A millipede curled like a tiny, coiled spring beneath a splintered ridge. Overhead, a spider spun deliberate threads, binding a helpless moth in silent precision.

Even in ruin, the Wilds whispered, life endures.

The thought surfaced like a truth he didn't need to question.

He'd never wished to wake with creatures like these so near, crawling through the remnants of fallen wood.

Yet they belonged here, perhaps more than he ever could.

Maybe even decay has its purpose. Maybe even what we call evil.

But then… what is evil, truly? And who among us has the right to decide?

He pushed himself up, brushing soil and moss from his tunic.

They had been walking for nearly an hour when Wyatt froze mid-step.

"Wait."

His whole frame went rigid, eyes widening as if catching something the others couldn't.

He wasn't just hearing, he was listening.

A tremor ran through his hands. Sweat gathered along his brow.

Sol closed the distance quietly, resting a steady hand on Wyatt's shoulder.

Beneath his palm, the mark flared warm again.

Wyatt exhaled sharply, then shrugged Sol's hand off without looking.

Not harsh. Just… reflexive.

Wyatt glanced back at him, voice barely a whisper. "It stopped.

For a moment… I thought bandits were closing in."

Sol didn't answer immediately.

The Wilds had fallen silent again, not with danger, but with gravity.

It felt as though something unseen had been pressing down on Wyatt's chest… and then simply let go.

And when Sol touched him… something had pressed back. A flicker of warmth still lingered in his palm, fading now.

Was that me?

The thought carried no accusation, only quiet curiosity.

Sol couldn't tell if the warmth was a blessing or merely a side effect of something far stranger.

Wyatt gave a weak shake of his head, a laugh catching in his throat but never finding its way out. His voice stayed small. "I feel better now," he murmured. "Weird… but better."

Sol kept walking.

Looking ahead, he saw the mushrooms swelling in size, first to his waist, then farther on, towering nearly as tall as he and Wyatt.

That's when he heard it. Music.

A chorus rose low and layered, underpinned by a slow, steady percussion.

Strings joined in, but not like any instrument he'd

known, each note sounded like bone humming in the wind, like silk stretched thin and trembling.

It grew louder the farther they walked.

Sol's fingers drifted to the mark on his forehead, half-expecting the familiar heat that would tell him this was all in his mind.

But the mark stayed cool.

Around them, the mist thickened, curling low over the mosscarpeted ground until the world ahead shrank to only a few ghostly meters.

The path had almost vanished, marked now only by clusters of glowing mushrooms that cast soft halos of blue and gold along its edges.

Even the trees had changed. No longer the small, tangled growth they'd left behind, these stood vast and towering, their trunks so massive that Sol doubted that even all three of them, hand in hand, could encircle one.

Then, the trees parted.

A clearing unfurled before them, quiet and strange.

At its heart stood a long, dry fountain, its stonework draped in lichen like an old shroud.

Encircling it were shapes that might have been

doors, windows, yet they blended so perfectly with the surrounding trees that they seemed less built than grown, vanishing almost entirely into the bark.

"What in all the gods..." Wyatt whispered.

They slowed. Reverent.

They moved through what could have been a village, yet wasn't.

Not abandoned, merely paused, as if the whole place had taken a breath and never let it go.

Sol's hand drifted toward a handle half-swallowed by the curve of a tree's bark, more grown than carved.

But before his fingers could brush it, Scy's hand settled firmly on his shoulder.

Sol stilled. Scy whispered:

"Shal'kai veyrn, toran elaran.

Lun'kai dorathal, veyr'kai moren.

You walk beyond the branches now — but the forest remembers."

A single tear slid down Scy's cheek.

"Go ahead, lad."

Sol knocked softly, though he knew no reply would

come, and eased the door open.

Inside, the home was elegant, but not with the polished grandeur of noble manors. Not like the cold, gleaming halls of the Greywells'.

Where their wealth shouted, this place breathed.

Every piece of furniture, every curve and corner, felt deliberate, not crafted, but coaxed into existence as if the house had grown itself.

Three plates remained set on the table, their meals untouched, as though waiting for hands that would never return. A cookpot hung over the hearth, its fire long dead, the iron gone cold.

"Looks like they left in a hurry," Sol murmured, his fingers gliding along the mantle's edge, where gilded vines curled in delicate, otherworldly patterns.

Scy stood behind him, unusually quiet.

"Scy?" Wyatt asked gently. "Are you alright?"

"Yeah, lad," Scy replied, voice low. "Just the Wilds creeping in."

They stepped out into the still air once more.

Everywhere they searched, it was the same: meals left halfprepared, doors ajar, hearths reduced to cold ash.

Life hadn't ended here, it had simply… paused.

Sol drifted a few paces ahead, drawn by something unspoken toward the clearing's heart.

The fountain stood waiting, and it was beautiful.

At the fountain's center rose a tree, its limbs spiraling upward in a tangle of roots and branches that seemed to defy order yet belong entirely.

Flanking it on the fountain's rim were two sleek stone cats, small in size yet commanding in presence, their bodies poised and alert, frozen mid-stare as if guarding an unseen secret.

Sol stepped closer, breath slowing. His hand trembled as he reached out.

The instant his fingers brushed the stone, his mark ignited, first a gentle warmth, then a blistering burn, and a surge of golden light swallowed him whole.

He blinked.

Once.

Twice.

Bright spots spun and drifted across his vision like stubborn embers clinging to darkness.

Then—sound.

Water splashing, sharp and real, alive against the silence.

Music followed, no longer distant but enveloping him, rich and lush, filling every corner of the space around him.

And voices, speaking in that strange, ancient tongue he was slowly beginning to recognize.

Valkiric.

The village remained, but now it shimmered with breath and color.

Light softened, draping everything in a golden hum, as though the world itself had begun to sing.

Villagers moved gracefully around him, baskets in hand, laughter lilting, their voices rising and falling in a rhythm closer to music than speech.

But something was different.

They were fair of form, none taller than Sol, most a little shorter. Skin pale yet luminous, never sickly. Bodies lean but corded with quiet strength.

Slender. Graceful.

He turned, instinctively seeking the source of the music, drawn as though by a thread.

No one's gaze met his.

No one saw him.

Except for one.

A child stood a few yards in front of him.

Their eyes met.

The child stopped mid-step, breath catching before a delighted gasp escaped him.

He pressed his small palms together over his chest and dipped into a bow, not stiff with ceremony, but light, buoyant, filled with unguarded joy.

"Sha'rei ven'kai," he said, reverent and bright.

"Kalev'na Ori!"

The child broke into a run, arms flung wide.

Sol dropped to a crouch without thinking, opening his arms in silent welcome.

The child collided softly against him, tiny arms wrapping tight around his neck, and warmth surged through Sol's skin, blooming hot and wild.

His mark flared, then seared, and once again,

golden light swallowed him whole.

The light shattered, breaking apart into mist and breath.

Warmth receded in waves, ebbing like a tide pulling back to sea.

Wind whispered into being, followed by the heavy sound of his own breath. Cool air wrapped around Sol, though sweat still clung to his skin.

Beneath him, the ground was solid and unyielding, anchoring him back to the waking world.

When Sol's eyes fluttered open, Scy and Wyatt loomed over him, their faces drawn tight with concern.

Wyatt's mouth moved rapidly, forming words Sol couldn't catch; only the sharp, relentless ringing in his ears filled the silence.

"Sol, SOL!" Wyatt said again, "Are you ok?"

Sol nodded as the ringing subsided. He tried to sit up, but his head was spinning. Scy put his arm around Sol to steady him.

"I saw the village before they left," Sol said carefully, still breathless. "But it was strange…the people were ancient. They looked like us, but they didn't."

He shook his head. "I know I'm not making sense."

Scy didn't speak. Just watched him quietly, something unreadable in his gaze.

Wyatt slipped an arm under Sol's and helped him to his feet.

"You always have to do things the strange way, huh?" he said, helping Sol up, trying to sound light, but his voice shook.

They led Sol to the fountain's edge, dry once more, where he sank down, breath still ragged.

The air held still.

A hush swept through the village, the quiet before a heartbeat, before life stirs again.

Then, from across the mist-veiled streets, golden beams cut through the fog, silent and certain, as though the Wilds themselves had drawn breath.

Scy rose slowly.

"I think that's our sign to move on."

They moved in silence along the light-streaked path.

At the clearing's edge, Sol slowed, turning to look back.

For the briefest breath, the village shimmered, alive once more. Sunlight spilling across vibrant greens. Music whispering at the edge of hearing.

Then it faded, leaving only stillness.

Waiting.

Sol had already stepped past the threshold when he realized Scy wasn't beside him.

He turned.

Scy lingered at the far edge of the village, just beyond the fountain, his gaze locked on a doorway woven into the living bark of a tree.

He didn't move. Didn't blink. Only watched, as though caught in a spell.

Mist coiled around his boots, tugging faintly, as if urging him to step closer, yet his stance held firm, unmoving.

Sol eased back a half-step, uncertainty prickling his spine.

"Scy?" he called softly.

Scy blinked, just once, as if surfacing from something deeper than sleep. When he turned, it was slower than usual, with a faint stiffness in his movements. He managed a small, tight smile. "Just saying goodbye."

But the words carried no usual bite. No wry humor.

Only a thin fracture in his voice, unguarded, raw beneath the mask he so rarely set aside.

Then he walked forward and didn't look back again.

They walked a few paces down the trail.

When he glanced back again, the mist was curling in, swallowing the clearing behind them. The trees had already shifted, denser than before. Impassable.

He turned back.

The trail widened ahead, spilling into vast, windswept plains that rolled endlessly toward the horizon.

Above, the sun blazed high and unyieldingly in a cloudless sky. Sol blinked, disoriented.

They had been walking for hours, long enough for dusk to be creeping in. Yet somehow, it was still midday.

But time, like the Wilds, had shifted.

He stared out across the open expanse, the wind tugging gently at his hair.

The Wilds were behind them, but something from them remained.

The ember within him still burned, not fierce, not blinding.

Just steady. Quietly alive.

Like a breath that had never left his lungs, only waited. Scy moved to his side, wordless, an arm settling heavy and sure across his shoulders.

On his other side, Wyatt's hand slipped into his without a word, no hesitation, no ceremony.

Only presence.

They stood like that for a long while, breathing in the soft hush of the changed air.

Three figures, poised at the edge of something vast and unknowable.

Sol's gaze stretched toward the horizon, but it offered no answers, only mystery waiting to be met.

Chapter Twenty-Two

———

The Ember Fold

The grass burned vivid beneath their feet, too green, almost unnatural, its brilliance cutting hard against the rich, dark soil.

Above, the sky unfurled without end, a blue so pure it felt like pressure on Sol's skin.

Only a single white cloud wandered the expanse, stark and solitary.

And the sun… it pulsed overhead, alive, spilling both light and quiet warning in the same breath.

The breeze moved through the tall grass in a whisper that felt too sharp, too deliberate.

Birdsong carried from distant branches, weaving with the skittering sounds of unseen creatures darting through the underbrush.

The Wilds pulsed with noise—alive, layered, almost vibrant.

And yet, beneath it all, something felt wrong.

Each step dragged heavier than the last, as if the

earth itself were trying to pull Sol down.

Yes, he was tired, but this felt different. A quiet weight settled deep into his bones, slowing his breath.

Ahead, the trees whispered with color, leaves bleeding into autumn's hues.

He was certain they hadn't looked that way yesterday.

By the third step beyond the Wilds, Sol's head spun violently. The trail wavered, the horizon skewing sideways like the world had lost its balance.

He reached for Scy, fingers grazing fabric before slipping into empty air.

Darkness swallowed him whole.

Behind closed lids, bright spots flared and drifted like embers.

At his forehead, the mark pulsed, not burning, but unmistakably alive.

He found himself sitting, breath shallow, locked in Scy's steady gaze.

Wyatt's arm braced firm against his back, keeping him upright.

The world looked different now—edges too sharp, colors too vivid, as if a new lens had been dropped over his vision.

And beneath it all, something burned low and urgent. He didn't know why, not exactly, but the need to reach Lyvareth had shifted from intention to instinct.

Scy's voice cut through, attempting levity but failing to mask the tension beneath:

"Lad, you planning to keel over the whole way to Lyvareth? That's twice in an hour. At this pace, we'll need a cart just to drag you there."

He reached out, fingers brushing the spot where the Veyrnstag had touched him.

"Hells," he muttered, pulling his hand back. "That's something else."

"What is?" Sol asked.

Scy hesitated, weighing his words before speaking.

"It seems the Wilds have let you go," he said quietly. "Your mark… it's vanished."

Sol's hand shot to his forehead, fingers skimming across bare skin, searching for what was no longer there.

Only a lingering warmth pulsed beneath the

surface, quiet, alive.

"I can still feel it," he murmured, voice thin.

Wyatt caught his chin gently, turning his face toward the light.

His eyes scanned every line, every shadow, before he breathed, almost to himself:

"By the gods… what's happening to you?"

Sol pushed to his feet, slowly, the fatigue still heavy in his limbs — but something steadier held him up now. "We can rest at Hollow's

Rest," he said, "but not for long."

"We can make it before nightfall if we press on," Scy replied. "Let's take a quick meal here, then move."

Sol let himself sink to the ground, the weight of exhaustion pressing him into the earth.

Hunger gnawed deep, raw, and insistent.

He tore into the strip of dried meat with a desperation that startled even him.

Smoke hit first, rich and earthy, then came a faint sweetness, undercut by salt.

The tough fibers resisted before finally yielding,

softening between his teeth as he chewed.

He raised the waterskin and drank greedily.

The water was cold, startlingly so, sharper than memory, crisp as if it had been drawn from a mountain spring moments ago.

He'd had this same meal countless times. It had never tasted like this.

Each swallow seemed to fill something deeper than his stomach, as if his body were trying to answer a hunger it had never known how to name.

In silence, Sol leaned back, letting the ground cradle him, and closed his eyes.

Behind his lids, the sun painted the darkness in molten reds and soft golds.

He listened, first to the whisper of wind threading through distant branches, then to the faint scurry of small creatures in the underbrush.

And deeper still, beneath it all, he caught the quiet cadence of breath: Scy's…steady and low. Wyatt's…lighter, uneven. His own… slowly falling into rhythm with theirs.

Then the heartbeats.

Theirs. His. Louder and louder.

He opened his eyes.

"Does the world feel… different to you?" Sol asked, eyes still fixed on the stretch of sky above.

The question lingered in the air like a wisp of smoke, slow to drift away.

"No," Wyatt said at first. Then, after a beat, "Yes… but I can't name it."

"More alive?" Sol ventured.

"I don't know," Wyatt admitted, his voice softer now, almost uncertain.

Scy's gaze stayed on the horizon, tone measured and low.

"The Wilds touch everyone differently," he said, as if speaking to himself as much as to them.

Sol scanned the horizon. The leaves had turned. "Scy… how long were we in the Wilds?"

"Every time's different," Scy replied. "They keep you as long as needed."

Wyatt followed Sol's gaze to the horizon.

"Maybe it just looks different out here," he offered,

uncertain.

"Or we lost months in there," Sol murmured, the thought heavy as stone.

"Or the Wilds are bleeding into the world," Scy said, his voice flat, unreadable.

A shiver crawled up Sol's spine. None of the possibilities brought comfort, only the quiet weight of something wrong, unseen but near.

They let the silence stretch, thick with questions none of them dared speak aloud.

Then, slowly, Sol shifted, breaking the stillness.

The spell broke, subtle as glass cracking in silence, and Scy and Wyatt fell in step behind him without a word.

Sol hitched his pack higher on his shoulders; the straps bit in deeper than he remembered, and the fabric of his tunic scratched against his skin as if woven with thorns. Gravel shifted and crunched beneath his boots, each step loud in the quiet stretch of land.

He drew in a breath.

In... hold... out.

Again, slower this time.

And then, together, they moved forward into the waiting expanse.

Sol's limbs were still heavy, each step an effort, but he pushed on. They needed to reach Hollow's Rest before nightfall.

They walked in silence, the hush between them stretched thin, like a single thread pulled taut, quivering with the weight of unspoken thoughts.

The road curved lazily ahead, flanked by tall grasses that swayed in a rhythm older than the wind itself, as if moved by something deeper, unseen.

Sol lifted his gaze.

The sky was shifting now, blue surrendering to indigo, clouds edged in molten gold.

He thought of the Hall of Echoes, of the way light had bent there, not with warmth, but with the breath of memory itself, lingering and alive.

He remembered the voices, sounds without faces, names not yet born, yet heavy on his tongue. The silence in that place had pressed against his ribs, ancient and watchful, like the breath of something waiting to be spoken aloud.

And the stag, the Veyrnstag, hadn't been a dream. It was real. Sacred. A living testament that true magic still walked the earth.

When it looked at him, it wasn't seeing Soltic Arden from a forgotten village.

It was seeing something older, something hidden beneath his own name.

What happened in that Wilds-born village had changed him, though the shape of that change was only beginning to surface.

Who were they?

Who was that child? Had he truly been seen?

The questions burned — but the answers stayed just out of reach. Each time he got close, they tangled back on themselves, like thread pulled too tight to unravel.

Sol exhaled slowly, his hand drifting to his forehead where the silver mark had once burned. The skin was smooth beneath his fingers, yet the echo of it lingered— not pain, not heat…presence.

It wasn't something the Wilds had left on him.

It had rooted itself in him.

He stayed silent; language felt too small to hold

what had changed.

But as they walked, the road seemed narrower beneath his boots, and the world around him had sharpened, edges clearer, colors deeper, as if he'd stepped into a reality that had been waiting all along.

Something within him had shifted—subtle but undeniable, like a long-locked door creaking open just wide enough for wind to slip through, carrying whispers he couldn't yet understand.

As twilight thickened, the land seemed to fold in on itself. Hills stretched their shadows long and thin, and the path funneled between ancient, wind-worn trees that leaned as if listening.

Sol blinked, his breath catching. For a moment, he wondered if exhaustion was playing tricks on his eyes.

Then, there it was.

Light.

It wasn't a blaze of brilliance but a hush of light, warm, trembling, scattered like fallen stars across the valley floor.

The city didn't simply appear; it revealed itself in breaths. First, the faint shimmer of rooftops nestled between dark ridgelines. Then terraces rising in graceful layers, climbing the hillsides like ivy reaching for the heavens.

Lanterns winked awake in distant windows, casting pools of molten gold that breathed softly against the settling night. From hidden hearths, slender ribbons of smoke unfurled skyward, catching the last blush of twilight before vanishing into indigo. Far across the valley, a bell tolled, not loud, not urgent, its sound drifting like a memory, weightless yet undeniable.

This wasn't a city that seized attention with grandeur or noise.

It drew you in, quietly, patiently, like an old friend holding out a hand in the dark.

"Well, lads," Scy said, voice low and rough with memory.

"That's her — Hollow's Rest. Oldest of the Rouge strongholds."

He tipped his chin toward the trees. "No noble. No crown. No Keeper's reach."

Scy smirked, already striding ahead. "Come on, then. Don't let her think you've gone shy."

Sol quickened his pace to fall in beside him, eyes narrowing slightly. "Scy…what do you know about that village in the Wilds?"

Scy's answer came slower than usual, measured. "Didn't see it last time I passed through," he said, tone deliberately even.

Sol caught the faint tension in his jaw, the shadow in his voice. "It felt like that goodbye was personal," he pressed, unwilling to let it slip.

Scy was quiet. For a moment, Sol thought he might not answer.

"You saw it," Scy said at last. "Something happened there — something drove them to leave the village like that. The Wilds wanted us to see it. Wanted you to see it."

"When I had the vision," Sol said slowly, "just before I passed out, a child saw me. I don't know if they were a boy or a girl —no older than Theo or Mira."

He hesitated. "They looked at me like they knew me. They said, 'Sha'rei ven'kai, Kalev'na Ori!' And then… they hugged me. And I was pulled back."

"I see your light," Scy murmured. "Uncle Ori."

He looked at Sol. "They saw you?"

"Only the child," Sol said at last, his voice low. "Everyone else… it was like I wasn't even there. I don't know if I truly remembered them — or if I just wanted to."

The words faded into quiet as the looming gates came into view. Massive timbers rose like a fortress wall, seamless and unbroken. No hinges, no handle. Just a barrier meant to keep the world out.

Sol let out a breath, already imagining a night spent curled against the grass. But Scy didn't falter.

Without hesitation, he walked straight to the gate, as if the thought of stopping had never crossed his mind.

From beneath his cloak, Scy drew a silver disk, its surface worn smooth by years of handling. Without a word, he pressed it against the stone flank of the gate.

Moonlight caught on its edges, and faint etchings shimmered to life — a bird mid-flight, wings outstretched, beside the shadowed outline of a hooded figure.

A deep, resonant rumble followed, like the earth itself waking. Dust sifted down in lazy streams as hidden mechanisms groaned.

Slowly, the towering wall split, revealing a narrow

passage, just wide enough for a man to slip through.

From within, an orange glow bled out, pooling around Scy's boots like firelight escaping a long-locked chamber.

"Quickly now," he said.

Sol stepped through first. He looked back just as Scy removed the disk and tucked it back beneath his cloak.

The passage sealed behind them with a slow, grinding groan, followed by a final hiss of settling dust. The sound echoed briefly, then faded into stillness.

Ahead, dim torchlight licked at the narrow space, casting long, uneven shadows that writhed across stone walls shaped more by centuries of erosion than human hands. The air smelled faintly of smoke and old earth.

At the far end, a battered wooden table leaned slightly on uneven legs. Dice lay scattered across its surface, crumbs clinging to the grooves, and a single dagger stood embedded upright in the scarred wood, as if someone had left in the middle of a game and never returned.

And seated beside it, lounging with the easy defiance of someone who'd grown up on secrets and bets. A boy who looked no older than fifteen.

He raised an eyebrow as Scy approached.

Scy didn't speak.

Instead, the boy lifted two fingers — index and middle, and tapped them once against his chest, just over his heart. With a fluid motion, he swept them outward and down, palm open to the air, before curling his hand into a loose fist and pressing it softly against his opposite palm, returning it to his heart.

The gesture was simple, almost casual, yet it carried a quiet weight. Something in its rhythm tugged at Sol — not physically, but deep within, like an invisible thread being drawn tight.

The boy straightened, posture settling into a stillness that felt deliberate, reverent.

Then, without a word, he mirrored the motion.

Tap. Flick. Fold.

The torchlight caught a knowing glint in his eyes.

"Sha'rei veyr'tal," the boy said softly.

"Sha'rei veyr'tal," Scy echoed.

The boy grinned wide, flashing a crooked tooth.

"You've been missed, old friend," he said, voice

still carrying the crackle of youth, but sharp underneath. "Heard whispers you vanished."

Sol blinked, disbelief flickering across his face. "You're the guard?"

The boy only shrugged, his tone dry. "Gatekeeper," he corrected, as if that subtle difference carried weight. "Pulled tunnel duty tonight."

His gaze slid to Scy, assessing, sharp. "Didn't figure you'd be hauling strays," he said, not unkindly, but with the bluntness of someone who didn't waste words. "Guess you've got your reasons."

Scy's smirk was faint but edged with possession as he stepped forward, brushing past Sol. "They're not strays," he said. "They're mine."

The boy's eyes lingered on Sol, then Wyatt, scanning them in a way that felt more like measuring than judging. Whatever he sought in their faces, he found it; a small, satisfied nod followed.

"You're good, then," he said, stepping aside.

With a shove, he swung open a narrow side door, revealing a passage that sloped deeper into the stronghold.

At first, Hollow's Rest felt almost too still, the kind

of silence that held its breath. Then, from somewhere above, the hush fractured: a burst of laughter rolled through the air, followed by the twang of a lute and bawdy voices singing off-key but full of life. The stillness gave way to warmth, unseen yet undeniable.

Scy glanced over his shoulder, his voice low and calm but carrying an undercurrent of warning. "Stay close, lads. Hollow's Rest won't bite… but trouble here never sits far from the fire."

Instinctively, Sol and Wyatt stepped in tighter beside him as they moved forward.

"What was the greeting you used with the guard — the gatekeeper?" Sol asked, trying the words tentatively. "Sha'rah… Sha'rei… veyr't… veyr'tal. Sha'rei veyr'tal?" Sol winced. "Close enough?"

"That?" Scy said with a wink. "Just a bit of old smoke and shadow. Means you're not going to get stabbed. Usually."

It felt like Scy was holding something back, but Sol couldn't quite place what.

They trailed him through a maze of narrow alleyways and tight bends, the stone underfoot worn smooth by decades of passage. At last, they emerged before a tall, three-story inn, its walls whitewashed but weathered, pale yellow shutters dulled by sun and age. Above the door, a wooden sign creaked softly in the evening breeze, a single painted flame glowing faintly at its heart beneath the name: The Pale Hearth.

Fatigue dragged heavy through Sol's limbs, deeper than mere travel-weariness. Yet as he stood there, the inn seemed to hum quietly, not just promising rest but offering a rare, anchored stillness, a shelter carved out of time itself. The sharp, untethered edge the Wilds had left on his senses began, at last, to soften.

Then the scent of herbs and roasted meats hit him — savory and rich — and his stomach growled loud enough to make Wyatt laugh.

"I'll second that," Wyatt said. "Hot food — is there anything better?"

"A hot bath," Scy added with a grin.

"And a warm bed," Sol said. "It's the trinity."

"There's no need for aliases here," Scy said as he reached for the handle. "Just stay close."

Inside, warmth and noise wrapped around them like a cloak.

Scy wove easily through the scattered tables, past knots of patrons leaning close over tankards and half-played games of dice and cards. Murmured conversation tangled with bursts of raucous laughter, and the sharp clatter of mugs striking wood punctuated it all. A minstrel balanced on a chair in the far corner, his lute spilling a tune that curled through the room like smoke, a melody Sol couldn't place, but it stirred something half-forgotten in him.

Scy steered them toward the far end of the long counter, gesturing for Sol and Wyatt to stay put. Then he strode to the barkeep — close enough to speak, but just out of earshot. A low, rolling laugh, unmistakably Scy's, drifted back, drawing Sol's gaze to where the two men leaned in over the bar.

As Scy lingered near the bar, faces lit up at his presence. One man clapped him on the back with a booming laugh; another pulled him into a quick, rough embrace. Even a few women leaned in with knowing smiles, their greetings threaded with warmth and familiarity.

For the first time since Sol had met him, Scy seemed… lighter. At ease.

Yet beneath it all, something taut remained, not

tension exactly, but a readiness, like a bow resting in a skilled archer's hand: relaxed, but only ever a breath away from being drawn.

Scy caught their eyes across the room and gave a small, sharp motion with his fingers, beckoning Sol and Wyatt closer. "Brenn, this is Soltic and Wyatt."

"Masters Soltic and Wyatt," the man behind the bar said, his voice smooth yet edged with authority. Golden eyes caught the lanternlight, glinting like molten metal. "I bid you welcome. Sit by my hearth. May it grant you shelter now… and in whatever hour you may find yourself in need."

The words carried more than courtesy; they felt like a promise, or perhaps a warning draped in warmth.

Sol hesitated, the unexpected weight of the man's gaze pinning him for a breath. He bowed his head in quiet respect, unsure why the moment felt almost ceremonial.

"Master Brenn, we are honored by your generosity. Sha'rei ven'kai."

Brenn paused mid-motion, his golden eyes narrowing, not with surprise, but with a sudden, deliberate focus. He turned toward Scy, voice low and roughened like gravel beneath boots.

"Your palone's got a glint to him," Brenn said, tone almost testing. "But does he know the hidden tread… or is he just tossing shine to see who bites?"

Scy's mouth curved into a half-smile, a flicker of something unreadable in his eyes as he glanced at Sol.

"Not yet," he said softly. "But the thread's starting to twitch."

Brenn held Sol's gaze for a breath longer, like he was weighing invisible scales, then gave a single, deliberate nod. Without another word, he slid two iron keys across the worn wood of the bar — the metal whispering against grain as if sealing some quiet understanding.

"Rooms are at the end of the hall, top of the stairs."

"Thank you, Brenn. After proper baths, we'll be back for food," Scy said, then added with a wink toward Sol:

"Might want to stoke the hearth and tuck a sweet in the larder, starboy turns the wheel tonight."

"Already tucked and twinkling, luv," Brenn said with a shallow bow.

Sol and Wyatt trudged behind Scy.

"The Thieves' Code keeps everyone under its

shadow," Scy said as they reached two narrow doors side by side. His voice carried a quiet certainty, the kind forged by old promises and older debts. "No one here'll touch what's ours. Still…" He rapped lightly on one of the doorframes, a hollow thud in the dim hallway. "…lock up. Habit keeps you breathing."

He stepped back, gesturing toward the rooms. "Drop your packs, shake the road from your boots. Five minutes, meet me out here. Brenn's already having fresh clothes brought up. After the baths, we eat."

Without waiting for an answer, Scy disappeared into his room, the door clicking shut like a whispered secret.

Wyatt eased their own door open, hinges sighing softly. They stepped inside, packs landing with a dull thud against worn floorboards. The room was modest, a narrow bed tucked against one wall, moonlight spilling through a fractured windowpane in pale, shifting bands. The air hung warm and heavy, untouched for hours, carrying the faint scent of woodsmoke and old linen.

Wyatt turned to him slowly, eyes shadowed but certain, and closed the space between them. Their hands found Sol's face, lingering, and then Wyatt kissed him, unhurried, fierce in its quietness, heat curling through the stillness like a spark catching dry grass.

"We made it out of Baron Greywell's lands."

He kissed him again, slower this time. Sol melted into it, the fear finally quiet in his chest.

"We still have to reach Lyvareth," Sol murmured, voice low but steady. "We can't stay."

Wyatt drew him closer, holding him in a quiet stillness where even the muffled laughter and music from below felt a world away.

For the first time in weeks, the noise of the journey didn't reach them.

He pressed a lingering kiss to Sol's forehead before leaning back, a teasing grin breaking through the tenderness.

"But," Wyatt said, eyes glinting, "I think we'll appreciate the moment a lot more once we stop smelling like we've been sleeping in a pigsty."

Sol's laugh came warm and unguarded. He laced his fingers with Wyatt's, and together they stepped into the hall, where Scy was already leaning against the wall, arms folded, waiting with his usual, knowing smirk.

The air was cool outside. They walked to a cave

mouth draped in strips of blue and green fabric, fluttering like offerings on the breeze. Warmth and damp radiated from within.

As they entered, the cave came alive with a ghostly luminescence. Bioluminescent mushrooms clung to the stone walls like fallen stars, their faint blue glow pooling on the damp floor. Steam curled upward in soft ribbons, carrying the fresh scent of mint, lemon balm, and lavender, a strange, soothing blend that made the air feel almost enchanted.

"Is this place… magic?" Sol whispered, his voice barely louder than the drip of water echoing from deeper within.

Scy's low laugh rumbled off the cavern walls. "Not every glowing thing's magic, lad," he said, his boots crunching over loose pebbles. "It's just a hot spring, though, granted, it does a good job of pretending otherwise."

They stepped into a wide cavern where firelight danced across the stone, mingling with the soft bioluminescent glow of the mushrooms. The air shimmered with steam, carrying the mineral tang of heated water. Sol's steps faltered as his gaze caught flashes of pale skin, men and women lounging in the pools, bodies slick with water, laughter echoing off the cavern walls.

Heat rushed to his face. He jerked his eyes to the ground, but it didn't help; the sounds of splashing water and hushed murmurs pressed in from every side. The warmth of the cavern seemed to climb into his blood, too close, too much, until even breathing felt like a trespass.

He wrapped his arms around himself, suddenly aware of every inch of fabric against his body. His clothes felt like a shield. The idea of removing them felt... exposed. Unsafe.

"Scy," he whispered, eyes wide. "They're naked."

"How else do you bathe?" Scy chuckled. "Don't worry, they've seen it all. They won't even notice you."

Scy pointed toward a wicker basket near the cavern wall, steam curling around it.

"Clothes in there," he said casually. "Fresh ones will be waiting when you're done."

Sol froze, his gaze locked on the basket as if it might bite him. Heat crept up his neck. "I can't," he muttered, staring hard at the stone floor. "I can't just... strip down."

Wyatt's laugh slipped out, light, teasing, impossible

to ignore.

Sol's head snapped up, a flush creeping higher. "You're fine with this?" he asked, his voice sharper than he intended, accusation threaded through embarrassment.

Wyatt shrugged. "I'm tired of smelling like a stable. If this means soaking in hot water, I'll suck it up."

"Don't suck up anything in here, or you'll be taking it home," Scy muttered with a grin.

Sol laughed despite himself. His guard slipped, just a little more.

"Fine," he said, resigned.

Once they had undressed, Scy guided them toward the pool's edge.

Sol followed slowly, shoulders hunched, arms wrapped tight across his chest as though bracing against more than just the chill in the cavern air. The cool breath of the cave kissed his bare skin, making every inch of him prickle. It wasn't only his body that felt exposed; it was something deeper, a quiet rawness he couldn't name.

He lowered himself into the steaming water, the heat wrapping around him like a living thing. Muscles that had been locked taut began to ease, yet the flush on his face only deepened.

The heat enfolded him like a living embrace. Sol eased down beside Wyatt, sliding beneath the surface until sound itself seemed to soften, a muted chime, a hush that felt like the cavern was humming to itself. When he rose again, rivulets of warmth traced down his spine, the steam curling against his flushed skin.

"You're not trying to sneak a look at my gems under there, are you?" Scy's voice carried over the water, equal parts mockery and grin.

Sol flicked a handful of water at him, cheeks burning.

"You wish," he grinned.

Then he leaned into Wyatt. Gentle whispers blurred by the water and the soft drip of steam.

They sat in silence.

The noose that had tightened around Sol since Oswynn finally slackened, easing its choke on his chest. Yet his mind wouldn't still; questions about Lyvareth coiled in the corners of his thoughts like restless shadows.

But here, under the drifting steam, beneath a ceiling of pale stars, he let it all slip for a while.

Xander K. Westwood

Just for this night, he allowed himself to breathe.

522

Chapter Twenty-Three

———

Wanderer's Crown

The warmth of the springs still clung to Sol's skin as they stepped into the cool night air. Behind them, the glow of the cavern had faded into shadow, yet something almost sacred lingered, an unseen thread tying the moment to his bones.

For the first time in weeks, he felt almost human again. Clean linen brushed against his skin, boots no longer caked in mud, and for once, comfort wasn't a memory but a presence, soft, fragile, and strangely luxurious after so long on the road.

A small part of him wished they could stay here forever. No more sleeping with one eye open. Just warmth, quiet, and Wyatt beside him in a real bed.

Wyatt walked in step beside him, close enough that their sleeves brushed now and then. In the moonlight, Sol kept catching fleeting glimpses of him, silver glinting in his irises, a soft glow clinging to the curve of his lips when he smiled. It loosened something tight in

Sol's chest, a part of him he hadn't known was still braced for impact.

"So," Scy said, casually booting a loose stone up the path ahead of them, "had a word with Brenn. Turns out we were in the Wilds for a little over two months."

Sol stopped short, frowning. "Two months? That can't be right. It didn't feel like—"

"Time's a fool's compass," Scy muttered with a lopsided grin. "The gods don't count hours. Last time I went in, I thought I was gone a week, turned out to be just hours. This time? Opposite."

Sol shook his head, trying to make the pieces fit. "But how does that even work?"

Scy chuckled, the sound low and rough. "That's the thing about the Wilds, lad — time's never ours to hold onto."

Sol tilted his head back, staring at the sky. The stars felt sharper here, colder, as though someone had scraped new constellations into the heavens while he wasn't looking.

Two months.

The thought landed softly at first, like a feather brushing his ribs, but it cut deeper the longer it stayed. His birthday had come and gone. Forgotten, swallowed whole by the Wilds.

He'd never spent a birthday away from his family before. His father would have taken him boar hunting, not much of a hunter himself, but he always tried. And Kellan… Kellan would've been there, steadying his bow, laughing when he missed the first shot.

His mother baked cheese tarts.

He remembered the twins tugging him into the summer fields, their laughter bright as they chased fireflies that blinked like tiny fallen stars. Later, when the world went quiet and the night wrapped itself around them, he and Wyatt would lie side by side beneath an endless sky, whispering dreams only the dark could hold.

Now, a single tear slipped free, carving a warm path down his cheek as the weight of all he'd missed pressed into his chest. He turned to Wyatt, voice barely more than a breath.

"Can we sit under the stars tonight?" he asked, fingers brushing Wyatt's before curling gently around them. "Just for a little while."

Scy let out an easy chuckle, lacing his fingers behind his head. "Was already fixin' to grab a pint," he said with that careless grin of his.

Sol's lips curved into a faint smile. "We can do that

first," he murmured. He hesitated, the words catching for just a beat before he tilted his gaze toward Scy. "Just… don't wander off too far, alright?"

And he meant it.

He needed something solid to anchor him, and Scy, who had hauled him back from death's edge more than once without a hint of complaint, was as much his family as Wyatt. Different, yes, but no less dear.

Scy must've felt the weight in him because he slung an arm across Sol's shoulders, giving a firm, familiar squeeze. "Come on," he said, voice low and warm. "We'll find some proper food, down a pint or two… then we'll sit under the stars till the night runs out."

Sol nodded, voice thick. "Thank you."

The Pale Hearth emerged through the mist, lanternlight flickering soft and golden, scattered like lazy fireflies against the night. From inside, laughter swelled and broke against the thick timbered walls, muted but warm, carrying the promise of hearth and ale.

Sol kept his gaze on the glow ahead, trying to sound casual.

"Did Brenn say exactly how long we were gone… in the Wilds?" "He didn't say," Scy replied as he stepped into the inn—

Then paused at the door, grinning wide.

"Don't hate me," he said, stepping aside.

A riot of hoots and shouts crashed over Sol like a wave, laughter and clinking mugs rattling the rafters. At the heart of it all stood Brenn, balanced on a wobbling chair, hammering two mugs together in a rowdy rhythm as the room erupted into a bawdy, off-key tune.

He's older now, but none the wiser,

With moonlit luck and bedroom eyes!

So, raise a cheer, then steal his boots—

It's Sol's damn day,

let loose the Magpie King!

Sol's grin stretched until his cheeks ached, heat flooding his face as he fought against the sting of tears. His old life wasn't here…

But he was.

Scy was.

Wyatt was.

And all around, strangers lifted their mugs high, no debts, no demands, just laughter and cheer freely given.

It wasn't perfect. Maybe no moment ever truly was.

Sol swiped at his damp eyes just as Wyatt pulled him into a fierce embrace, anchoring him in the warmth of now.

"Kiss! Kiss! Kiss!" the room chanted.

Sol barely managed a laugh before Wyatt seized him, pulling him close with sudden, reckless certainty. In one smooth motion, Wyatt dipped him low and claimed his mouth in a kiss that stole every breath and thought he had left.

The room exploded, mugs slammed on tables, boots pounded out a rhythm, and cheers rolled like thunder.

When Wyatt finally drew him upright, Sol swayed, laughing through ragged breaths, flushed and utterly undone. He'd never felt so vividly alive… or so undeniably wanted.

"Show-offs," Scy muttered with a grin.

He tapped the serving girl on the shoulder. She turned, winked, and before anyone could blink, Scy dipped her low with theatrical flair and kissed her soundly.

When the room stayed quiet, he pulled back with

an exaggerated pout. "Kas, seems they've gone shy on us, lass. Guess we'll just have to practice harder."

From the far end of the room, a bull of a man emerged, his heavy boots thudding against the floorboards in an unhurried, deliberate rhythm. He moved like a storm contained, broad-shouldered, all muscle and certainty, yet his presence radiated warmth, filling the tavern like a well-fed hearth fire.

Without so much as a word, he wrapped his massive arms around both Wyatt and Sol, hauling them in with effortless strength, as if they were long-lost friends finally come home.

"Aye, lads!" he bellowed, his voice thick with gravel and cheer.

"Welcome to Hollow's Rest."

Sol stumbled a step beneath the man's crushing arm, blinking up at the mountain of muscle beside him. The stranger's beard was a wild, sea-thick thing, shot through with silver and threaded with braids of crimson twine that glinted in the firelight. Weather had carved deep stories into his dark, salt-worn skin, and his eyes, sharp, calculating, hid behind a grin that felt like the start of a swindle and the promise of a drink all at once.

"I ain't interruptin', am I?" the man asked, grinning between them. "Wouldn't wanna come between young love."

Wyatt's laughter spilled out bright and easy, while Sol's face burned hot enough to rival the hearth. The towering man caught his reaction and threw him a conspiratorial wink.

"Name's Garrin," he rumbled, voice rough as old rope. "But 'round here, they call me the Spindle. Scy and I go back a few lies."

Scy barked a laugh and slammed a hand against Garrin's shoulder. "You old bastard! How are you not deposed yet?"

Garrin's grin widened, all teeth and trouble. "How d'you know I haven't?" he shot back, laughing as he steered Sol and Wyatt toward a pair of worn leather chairs near the roaring hearth. Dropping heavily into a third seat, he nodded to his companions, a wiry, scruffy-faced youth with quicksilver eyes, and a woman whose beauty landed like a sharp, sudden blade.

Kas arrived balancing four frothing mugs, foam spilling in soft rivulets down the sides. Scy was already on his feet, helping her distribute them with the ease of old habit.

He passed one to Sol, the cool handle slick in his grasp, then offered another to the woman seated beside him. Her hair was braided tight against her scalp, the plaits glinting like dark rope beneath the firelight. Two green-stoned pins jutted from the knot at the back of her head, sharp as the glint in her eyes.

She didn't sip. Didn't smile. Instead, her gaze flicked over Scy and lingered on Wyatt, measured, cutting clean through pretense like the edge of a honed blade.

Then she nodded once. "I'm Arlen. If you get on my bad side, they call me the Hyena."

She rose from her seat with a deliberate grace, not tall, but built like tempered steel, every line of her frame coiled with muscle and quiet authority. Sol had the immediate, unshakable sense that if it came to a fight, he wouldn't last a breath.

Without a word, she stooped to toss a fresh log onto the hearth. Sparks leapt skyward, embers whirling like fireflies caught in a sudden gale. Heat rushed across the room, painting her silhouette in flickering gold.

Wyatt shifted subtly in his chair, his posture tightening, gaze fixed on her with a mix of wariness and grudging respect.

"Don't let her glare fool you," said the man beside her, flashing a crooked grin around the rim of his ale mug. "Her bark's worse than her bite, most days."

He tipped the mug back for a slow drink, eyes glinting with mischief.

Sol shifted uncomfortably in his chair, uncertain whether to laugh or take cover. Across from him, Arlen leaned back in hers, the faintest smile tugging at her lips, not warm, not soft, but edged like someone who knew exactly how much trouble she could cause.

"Relax, lad. You're in the safest place in all the kingdoms. At least for tonight."

Sol laughed, a little nervously. "Sorry. It's…been a long road getting here."

"Yes, it has," she nodded. "Scy keeps us up to date. Good on ya, lads."

Arlen spat into the crackling hearth, the sound sharp against the fire's hiss. "Wasn't always this," she said, voice rough with old defiance. "Once, they called me lady. A proper noblewoman, stitched up in silks and lies. Tried to sell me off to some dried-up lord old enough to be my grandsire. I was fourteen."

Her jaw tightened. "So, I ran. Had nothing but my fists and the clothes on my back. The Rouge found me before the wolves did."

Sol let out a slow breath, the tension in his shoulders uncoiling just enough. "That took guts," he said softly, meaning it.

"Yeah, it did." Her smile softened into something real. "Remember that when you get in your head. You left. You made the impossible choice. And now you're here. I know what you survived, all the way up to Nasareth."

Arlen leaned in, elbows resting on her knees, gaze fixed on the hearth where sparks spiraled upward like ghosts of memories, she'd never voice. When she finally looked at Sol, her eyes were steady, flint against steel.

"You survived it," she said, low but unwavering. "So, when the next impossible thing stands in your way, don't waste a breath looking back. Look at yourself. At the man you are… and the one you're still becoming."

Sol's throat tightened. He glanced toward Wyatt, who sat with Ruck, laughter spilling warm and bright across flushed cheeks, eyes alight like lanterns in the dark.

Another knot inside him, one wound so tight it had become part of his bones, finally gave way.

A low scrape of wood against stone cut through the fire's crackle. Sol turned to see Garrin muscling a table closer, planting it in front of the hearth with a solid thud. Wyatt slid his chair nearer to Sol's, their knees brushing, no words needed.

The door swung open again. Kas and Scy strode in, arms laden with bounty, platters of roasted meats dripping with glaze, baskets of bread still steaming from the oven, wheels of cheese, and bowls of butter glinting in the firelight. The scent of spice and smoke filled the room, rich and heavy. It wasn't just supper. It was a feast worthy of celebration.

Laughter filled the inn. Dice clacked against wood. Mugs sloshed and stories flowed.

Scy moved through the crowd like smoke curling from a lantern—untouchable yet part of everything it touched. Sol watched him, really saw him, and something shifted. This wasn't just comfort in a familiar place. This was a man whose roots were sunk deep, a man who belonged to these people as surely as they belonged to him.

Sol's gaze drifted to Wyatt. He caught the quiet nod Wyatt gave toward Scy, a smile tugging at his lips, soft, unguarded. It struck Sol like a half-forgotten song. The only other time Wyatt had ever looked that free was in the pastures, beneath a blanket of stars, when the night wrapped around them and the world beyond their little corner didn't exist.

But that had been a lifetime ago.

Sol shifted in his chair, unease crawling beneath his skin. Heat gathered at his hairline, trickling down his temple, and his thoughts began to swim, loose, unfocused. A dull throb built behind his eyes, steady and insistent, like invisible hands pressing inward.

Wyatt appeared at his side, concern carved deep into the furrow of his brow. "You alright?" he asked, his voice low, barely threading through the tavern's laughter and clatter.

"I… just need some air," Sol murmured, pushing himself up. The floor felt treacherous beneath his boots, as if the whole inn had shifted a fraction to the left.

Wyatt didn't wait for an explanation. He slipped an arm around Sol's waist and guided him out into the night. The cool air hit like water, sharp and clean, slowing the whirl in his head but not banishing it.

They stopped against the inn's stone wall. Sol let the silence settle over him, breath evening out, Wyatt's steady warmth at his side anchoring him to the world.

Wyatt pulled him close, resting his forehead lightly against Sol's. Then, in a voice barely above the breeze, he whispered:

For the one who was born tonight,

Under candle, under flame,

May the stars remember your name,

And the night always carry you home.

I'd steal you the sky if you asked me right,

"For now," Wyatt murmured, voice as soft as the night around them, "I'll hold you in starlight."

He pressed a gentle kiss to the crown of Sol's head, reverent and unhurried. They leaned into one another, sharing a silence that felt earned, fragile in the best way.

Beneath it, Sol felt something pulsing, distant yet insistent, like a faraway drum keeping time only he could hear.

"I love you," Sol whispered, the words trembling but certain.

Wyatt shifted, turning to him with care until their eyes met. Moonlight silvered his features. "I love you, too," he said, voice steady but warm. "Tell me… how are you feeling now? Honestly?"

The pressure behind Sol's eyes hadn't gone, but he felt steadier.

"I'm okay. Just tired," he said honestly.

Wyatt pressed a hand to Sol's forehead. "You're a little warm.

Maybe we should call it a night."

"Not yet," Sol said softly. "We deserve a night."

Sol leaned in and kissed Wyatt, slow, deliberate, a quiet promise that whatever came next, they'd face it together.

When they stepped back inside, the room had shifted. The table near the hearth had been cleared away, replaced by a short, broadshouldered woman who sat hunched close to the flames. She wore a shawl of burnt orange linen, its edges embroidered with a garden of tiny green, purple, and blue flowers. A strip of pristine white cloth was tied firmly over her eyes, lending her an air of quiet gravity.

As Sol drew closer, a sharp scent rolled over him, smoky, spicy, threaded with something woody and wild. It filled his lungs, stung his sinuses, and made him sneeze. Once. Twice. A third time before he stumbled, bracing himself against the edge of the table for balance.

And then it struck — a jolt sharp enough to steal his breath.

A gnarled, arthritic hand had clamped around his wrist. The old woman yelped, snatching it back as if burned, but the damage was done, pain spiked through Sol's skull, a throbbing pulse that blurred the edges of his vision.

Warmth spilled from his nose. Before he could react, the woman pressed a handkerchief into his free hand with the swiftness of someone who had done this a hundred times.

"Sit," she commanded, her voice firm and low, carrying an authority that left no room for argument.

Sol blinked down at the cloth. Blood, bright, glistening crimson, smeared the pale fabric, catching the flicker of nearby candlelight. He raised trembling fingers to his upper lip, confirming what his eyes already knew.

She pressed again. "Sit. Pinch the bridge of your nose firmly." He obeyed.

"I'm sorry," Sol said, voice thick. "Thank you. I didn't mean to ruin your—"

"Hush, child," she murmured, her tone suddenly gentle. "All is as it should be."

A long pause. Then, quietly:

"Sha'veri thal'arien, vren'shara kai?"

The words curled through him like a low current. "I'm sorry,"

Sol said softly, "I don't understand the old tongue."

The woman tilted her head, lips pulling into a knowing smile.

"I can't see you."

He blinked, uncertain if it was a jest.

"With all due respect…" Sol hesitated, glancing at the white cloth wrapped neatly over her eyes. "…you're wearing a blindfold."

Her smile deepened, but her voice softened with patience. "I lost my eyes long ago, child. But sight…sight is only one way of seeing." She gestured faintly, fingers trembling yet deliberate. "You must learn to listen with more than your ears, to see with more than your eyes."

She tilted her head slightly, face angled toward him with unerring precision. "I hear the tremor in your voice," she said, her tone even and sure. "So, I know you're standing near. You haven't shifted your weight, haven't stepped away—so I know you're still listening." Her fingers twitched faintly in memory of the touch. "I felt the pulse in your wrist, proof that flesh and spirit both anchor you here. And..." She drew in a slow breath, nostrils flaring ever so slightly. "...the scent of the springs still lingers on your skin. You bathed not long ago."

"And if I still had my eyes... I believe I would see a young man, not very big."

She tilted her head slightly, as though gazing at something far past his shoulder, past the room itself.

"But to the eye that still sees," she murmured, voice low and steady, "you burn... bright. So bright, the shape of your path is lost in the light."

Her fingers tightened on the edge of her shawl. "You'll have to learn why that is... and when you do, you'll know where to find me."

With deliberate care, she reached for a worn leather pouch at her hip. The drawstrings whispered as she loosened them, and from its depths, she poured a tangle of weathered leather into her palm. She extended it toward Sol without hesitation.

He accepted it gingerly, the weight unfamiliar, his fingers tracing the rough grain as he unwound a long, coiled cord.

At the center hung an intricately woven gold circle, no wider than his thumb.

A smooth black stone was set within it, the surface so dark it seemed to drink the candlelight.

At its center, a silver spiral lay etched into the leather, faint, deliberate, like a secret carved by patient hands. Beneath it, a second mark curled through the grain, thin as a thread of smoke caught midturn. When Sol tilted it toward the light, it shimmered softly, as though it still remembered moonlight brushing its surface.

"Take this," the old woman said, her tone carrying the weight of something older than a command.

The leather felt worn smooth by countless palms, yet unbroken, like a truth too stubborn to fade, passed forward through generations, waiting for someone who might finally understand it.

And yet, it felt like it had been waiting for him.

"When your soul stirs… when your mind splits and your heart aches, trace the spiral," she instructed softly. "Start at the center, follow it outward… then return again. Seven times. It will steady you. Not forever, but long enough to stand."

Sol stared down at the pendant resting in his palm.

It didn't feel like a simple gift.

It felt like a promise whispered in silver and leather, a tether meant to hold him when the world tilted too far.

For a fleeting moment, Sol considered handing it back, courtesy murmured that he should.

But his fingers tightened around the spiral instead.

Not from politeness.

From belief. Something in her voice left no room for doubt.

"Thank you, mistress," he said quietly. "I'm Sol… but I don't believe I caught your name."

The old woman's lips curved into a knowing smile.

"I didn't say."

Then softer, almost with fondness:

"I will see you again. When the spiral calls you back."

The words stunned him.

And yet… it almost felt like leaving had been his decision.

Sol rose slowly, the movement deliberate, and made his way back to the hearth. He swiped at his nose without thinking, and the bleeding had already dried.

Garrin's gaze found him before his boots even reached the firelight. "And what wisdom did the Hearth Mother whisper to ye?" His tone was light, but the weight beneath it was impossible to miss.

"She spoke to me in the old tongue," Sol said, lowering himself into his chair. "I couldn't understand a word."

Garrin leaned forward, nodding slowly, as if that answer made far more sense than it should have.

"She said she couldn't see me," Sol added, holding up the talisman, "and gave me this."

Garrin didn't reach for the talisman. His gaze lingered on it instead, not with awe, but with a quiet, knowing recognition that made Sol's chest tighten.

"Keep that close, lad," Garrin said, voice low, threaded with meaning.

Sol slid the cord over his head, the pendant settling against his chest like it had always belonged there. "I will," he promised softly.

"Who is she?"

Garrin's reply came gentle but unshakable:

"She's not of our blood, boy… she's bone. The kind that holds the whole of us upright. The Hearth Mother sees the fractures long before they splinter, and sometimes…sometimes she lets them crack, because that's the only way they'll heal."

"She sees them?" Sol asked.

Garrin nodded slowly, eyes fixed on the fire.

"She sees what we walk on — the threads, the sparks, the weight of what we might become. When the gods speak through storms, she replies through splinters and ember ash."

A man drifted closer, voice lowered to a near-whisper. He had a tangle of short, sun-curled blonde hair and kind eyes that carried a quiet stillness, the sort that made you wonder whether he was guarding secrets or simply too gracious to spill them.

"This ragged soul here is Patch," Garrin said with a broad grin, giving the man a playful shove. "Forgive him, he skipped every class on manners."

The blonde offered a small, unhurried nod. "Tollis," he said simply, his tone warm but reserved, like a man who preferred to be known slowly.

Tollis's gaze drifted over Sol, steady and unhurried,

not unkind, but weighted with quiet curiosity, as if he were assembling puzzle pieces he'd never intended to find. A faint smile touched his lips.

"I swear, you'd like me even less if I'd had a full night's sleep," he said, voice dry and low, carrying the humor of someone who rarely offered it.

"Sol," he replied, blinking.

"I need a word with this one," Tollis said, nodding toward Garrin.

Garrin leaned closer, voice dropping to a conspiratorial whisper. "Pardon me. If I don't give him the stage, he'll sulk for hours."

With a long-suffering sigh, one far too practiced to be genuine, Garrin straightened. The grin on his face lingered, the kind of grin worn by a man who's danced this same playful waltz more times than he can count.

"He's always been this dramatic," he muttered, tossing Sol a wink before stepping aside.

Tollis, meanwhile, felt like a breath held just shy of release, a man who carried too much knowing in his silence and only broke it when the weight demanded words.

The fire crackled in the hearth. Sol winced — the

ache behind his eyes had returned, sharper now, like pressure behind his temples.

When your soul stirs… head and heart ache…

The Hearth Mother's voice still echoed in his mind, soft but unshakable.

Sol's fingers found the pendant, curling around it as though it might steady him.

Within the stone, shadows shifted like whispers of another world, yet his gaze snagged on the faint silver spiral, coiled tight, as if the breath that carved it had never been fully released.

Beneath it, a shimmer caught the light, a thread of smoke suspended mid-turn, poised between movement and stillness.

Sol let out the breath he hadn't realized he was holding.

His gaze traced the spiral slowly, from the center outward. Then back again.

The lines were uneven, imperfect, some curves drawn tight as whispered secrets, others stretched wide like pauses that had forgotten their beat.

His thumb traced the spiral once more.

Then again.

By the seventh pass, the raucous hum of the inn faded to a hush, distant and soft, as though the world itself had leaned back to give him breath.

The spiral didn't just quiet him, it pulled him inward. Not a map, but a rhythm. A way home to himself.

The pressure behind his eyes eased, unspooling like a knot undone.

And for the first time that day, Sol felt… still.

He hadn't realized how heavy the ache had been until it vanished, leaving not just silence in his head, but a rare, startling lightness in his chest.

He waded through the crowd and found Wyatt sitting beside Scy, watching closely as Scy slung dice against the wall. Some people were celebrating, but Ruck glowered.

"Old Magpie, take your luck," Ruck Said, pouting.

"He owes me too many favors," Scy laughed.

Sol stood just behind Wyatt, leaning into the familiar curve of his shoulder. Wyatt's hand found his without thought, fingers lacing briefly before he lifted Sol's palm to his lips, brushing it with a kiss that felt both absentminded and achingly deliberate.

Sol's other hand slid up, fingers threading through the soft hair at Wyatt's nape. Wyatt tilted his head slightly, a quiet surrender to the touch.

Beyond them, Ruck threw the dice. The clatter echoed off stone and wood, the crowd holding its collective breath as the pieces spun and tumbled across the table.

"Ashrot!" Ruck said as he banged the table. "I need to bow out while I still have my shoes." He pushed away from the table and started to walk towards the bar.

"You can bring me another beer," Scy grinned, loving every second of Ruck's misery.

Ruck raised one hand, palm open as though offering a blessing to unseen gods. With the other, he pinched something from the air, nothing visible, yet it carried weight, intention. Slowly, deliberately, he twisted his fingers, like wringing fate itself.

When he spun to leave, his shoulder collided squarely with Arlen.

"Twist the wick one more time and I'll twist you," she said flatly.

Scy was doubled over, laughter shaking his shoulders, tears streaking down his cheeks as he struggled to catch a breath. Sol and Wyatt joined in, their own laughter bubbling up, not because they understood the joke, but because Scy's unrestrained mirth was too contagious to resist.

Wiping his face and finally composing himself, Scy straightened with a crooked grin. "Ruck came up with that one," he said, voice still rough with laughter. "Now every Rogue knows it. Vulgar as sin. Do it in the wrong tavern, and you'll either end up bleeding on the floor…" he smirked "…or in someone's bed. Depends on the crowd."

He started laughing again. Wyatt stood up and clapped his hands on Scy's Shoulders. "I am taking our birthday boy away. Don't wake us. We've earned the morning. We can plan tomorrow, tomorrow."

Scy stood and hugged Sol. "We can go look at the stars before you turn in."

Sol offered a faint smile. "I wouldn't want to pull you away from your winning streak."

Scy barked a laugh, shaking his head. "Winning streak? Lad, I scrubbed these floors tonight. Not a copper left for me to lose."

He pushed open the back door, leading them into a quiet courtyard. The space was small and walled in by ivy-clad stone, but it felt like a pocket of peace carved out of the night. Two weathered benches sat facing a shallow stone tub, its rim lined with tiny Magpie carvings, their wings half-folded as if poised to take flight. The still water mirrored the stars above, a second sky lying silent at their feet.

They all sat on one bench. Scy leaned back, his arm stretched across the backrest behind Sol, while Wyatt's arm slipped around his waist.

They sat in stillness, looking at the twinkling night sky.

"I can't believe ye thought we would let your birthday pass without a little fanfare," Scy said smugly.

"I can't believe it was today," Sol said. "Thank you."

"Aye, don't get sentimental on me, lad. Remember, I like sharp and shiny things," Scy laughed.

Wyatt gave Sol's hand a gentle squeeze. The night air was crisp, carrying the faint scent of damp earth and stone. Wyatt leaned into him, their arms brushing in quiet rhythm.

"See those three stars lined up there? And that faint one just above?" he murmured, tilting his chin skyward.

"That's Whisper's Hook. Supposedly catches secrets before they fall." His voice softened with the weight of the tale.

From behind them, Scy let out a dry snort. "Then it's drowning in ours."

Wyatt chuckled under his breath. "Maybe it likes the taste."

He lifted his hand again, tracing the outline of a crooked triangle low on the horizon, his fingers moving as though stitching the night together.

"And that one there, The Wanderer's Crown. They say it only appears when someone's about to leave home…"

Scy paused mid-step, a grin slowly curling at the corner of his mouth. "…Or when someone's just found a warmer bed to crawl into," he drawled, eyes flicking pointedly toward Sol.

Heat crept up Sol's neck. He huffed out a laugh, shaking his head, trying, and failing, to hide the smile tugging at his own lips.

"You're terrible."

"I know." Wyatt leaned in close. "You keep looking at me like that, and I'll prove it."

Scy muttered something half-caught by the night air — low, rough, and almost certainly obscene, though it carried no edge. Just the sound of a man feeling too much and dressing it in words too small.

He shifted, tugging at his trousers, the faint firelight sketching his silhouette in flickers of gold. With a lazy two-finger salute to Wyatt and a glance toward Sol, not quite a smile, but brushing close enough to count, he leaned back against the bench.

Sol's throat tightened. He tipped his gaze skyward, voice soft but steady.

"They say the Wanderer's Crown only shines when someone's on the verge of leaving… or just about to find their way home."

Scy lingered at the fringe of shadow, his outline caught between firelight and dark. His hand hovered near the doorframe, fingers flexing once, as if debating the weight of touch, but never landing.

"You ought to quit listening to stories," he said at last, quiet, almost tender, as though part of him wished the tale were true.

"They've got a way of making you hope."

Sol stood watching until Scy vanished inside, leaving behind an absence that settled like the hush after a fire's last crackle, just before the cold dares to creep in.

He didn't move, not until Wyatt came up behind him, warm and steady, as familiar as an old memory that refused to fade.

"That flame's not going out," Wyatt murmured, voice low against his ear.

He slipped an arm around Sol's waist, pulling him close, anchoring him against the night.

"Then neither are we."

Wyatt slipped behind Sol and wrapped his arms snugly around his waist, pulling him close until their bodies pressed flush. They stumbled forward a few clumsy steps, laughter spilling between them as Wyatt's lips trailed along Sol's neck, soft kisses turning playful, teeth grazing just enough to spark a shiver.

His breath seared warm against Sol's skin, a heat that curled through him, electric, addictive.

Sol broke into giggles when Wyatt's fingers slid to

his ribs, finding a ticklish spot that made him squirm helplessly. With a breathless laugh, he shoved Wyatt back and darted across the courtyard, heart hammering, Wyatt's chuckle chasing him like a promise.

"Will you stop?" he gasped, half-laughing, half-running.

Sol feinted left, the same classic fake retreat he'd used a hundred times before, but Wyatt read him like an open book. In a blink, Sol crashed into his arms, laughter cut short as their mouths met in a fierce, hungry kiss. Heat surged between them, breath tangling, hearts thundering in sync. When Sol finally tore back for air, his laughter returned in gasping bursts, cheeks flushed, lips tingling.

"If I'd known that's all it would take to stop you," he panted, eyes bright and wild, "I'd never have bothered running."

Wyatt's grin curved slow and dangerous, a promise more than a smile.

"Aye, but I like the chase."

"Is that so?" Sol teased, eyes glittering.

He wriggled free with a triumphant laugh and bolted again, weaving around the bench before darting through the inn's door. Heat and music swallowed him as he slipped through the bustling crowd, boots thudding softly against worn wood as he bounded up the stairs toward their borrowed sanctuary.

Halfway up, Sol glanced back, breath ragged, cheeks flushed, his chest aching with something too vast to name.

Maybe this wasn't home.

But gods, it felt close.

Behind them, laughter chased like fire sparks in the dark, bright, fleeting, carried upward until it vanished into the waiting starlight.

556

Chapter Twenty-Four

———

Burn Bright

The morning sun caught the faded gold lettering of the book's cover: The Longing Letters. Sol sat at a narrow table by the window, where a faint chill threaded its way inside. The warmth of the night before lingered only in memory, dissolving like breath against glass.

His eyes strained against the dim light, the pressure behind them returning in a dull, insistent throb. Sol rubbed at his temple with his left hand, the borrowed quill still pinched between his fingers. Ink pooled where he dipped it absently, a small blot spreading across the page.

There was so much he longed to tell Alina. He trusted her, he had always trusted her—but the thought of his words falling into the wrong hands tightened a knot deep in his stomach.

Alina and Ysella were his last ties to the city. He couldn't risk drawing attention to anyone else.

Something in his gut twisted, a forewarning he could not shake. The shrines of the old gods would not stand much longer; he could feel their fading in his very bones.

Sister of the Path,

Let us speak plain, as Elion guides. iv. vii

I beg your forgiveness for my abrupt departure.

The road here has been long — and I fear the path forward longer still.

The flock rests, though wolves still stir beyond the fence.

Burn bright, Sister of the Path.

Use the Rain, should you find yourself in need.

May the Keeper guide your path.

May we stay steadfast.

Your wayward cousin.

Sol felt the brush of Wyatt's lips against his cheek. He drew in a slow breath, savoring the scent—woodsmoke and forest musk, achingly familiar.

In. Hold. Out.

"My little sparrow is an early bird," Wyatt murmured, stretching before settling across from him.

"I suppose I've grown used to rising with the sun," Sol said with a small shrug, then gestured toward the folded letter on the table.

"I wrote this for Alina. Brenn mentioned a servant

in the

Greywell estate, within the Rouge. Her name is Cloud."

Wyatt's eyes lingered on the letter in silence, his head tilting slightly as he studied it.

"Isn't there a story in The Keeper's Word about sheep?"

Sol nodded.

"Yeah—two brothers, Tharan and Eless," Sol said. "They fight to protect their families, but Eless falls in battle. Tharan is left to carry the burden, care for the widow, piece everything back together." Wyatt's mouth curved faintly. "Sounds familiar."

Sol looked away, out the window.

"There's a passage in Departures—chapter four, verse seven. It's the first time Elion speaks of cutting away a rotten branch to save the tree."

Wyatt let out a low whistle.

"That's brilliant, using the Keeper's own Word against them." His grin spread wide, pride unmistakable.

"Brenn swore no one but Alina would ever see it," Sol murmured. "Still… I'm not sure."

"Makes you wonder how much power Garrin actually has," Wyatt murmured, "and why they were watching Oswynn."

Sol met his gaze again.

"Did Scy ever tell you why he stayed in Oswynn?"

Wyatt huffed a quiet laugh.

"A new reason each time," he said.

Scy flopped into the seat beside Sol.

Sol and Wyatt exchanged a brief glance. Speak of the gods, and they appear, Sol thought.

"I haven't been to bed," Scy grinned. "Had lots catch up on with Kas."

Sol laughed.

"I'm sure you did."

"We'll need to stay one more night," Scy said. "I won't survive the day otherwise."

"I think that's fine. How long until we reach Lyvareth?" Sol asked.

Scy considered for a moment.

"If the weather holds, and we encounter no delays, a fortnight."

"We're out of the Greywells' lands. A single day won't change our chances," Sol said. "Besides… you don't look like you'd survive it."

"How 'bout I get some shut-eye, and we'll take the evening meal together?" Scy suggested. "You'll be safe as long as we stay in Garin's city. Most folk don't even believe Hollow's Rest is a real place." "We're lucky Garrin took a liking to us."

Wyatt nodded.

"Just how far does the Rouge's influence reach?"

"He's got his fingers in every honey pot. I don't know how he gets half his intel," Scy said, rising to his feet. "Secrets from every corner of Itharen—and beyond."

"Good to know," Wyatt said. "I'll wake you for supper."

Scy dramatically pulled his legs together and offered an irreverent salute.

"Aye aye."

He marched straight-legged toward the stairs.

Sol and Wyatt watched him go.

"Well," Wyatt said, "looks like we've got the day to ourselves."

"Yeah. We should get supplies," Sol replied. "We need to be smart, we've got to save at least a gold piece for Lyvareth."

Wyatt hesitated.

"Are you sure we can't stay? I trust them that we're safe here.

Especially with the Rouge on our side."

Sol looked down at the table.

Maybe we could stay.

They had welcomed him as if he'd always belonged.

He did feel safe here. But…

That night in the Wilds, when the Veyrnstag touched him, he had known.

He had to reach Lyvareth. And soon.

Wyatt reached across the table and took Sol's hand, his thumb brushing gently over the knuckles.

"I'm sorry if I upset you."

"It's not that," Sol said softly. "Wyatt, there's something inside me. I think it's been there all along—all those times I knew things I shouldn't…"

"It was small things, and I thought I just had good

instincts. But—how did I know you were coming home that last time? I remember everything falling still. Even the butterfly hung suspended in the air. And beneath that calm, I knew you were near. I knew exactly where to find you."

Sol sighed.

Wyatt didn't speak. He just squeezed Sol's hand gently.

"That night in the Wilds, when the Veyrnstag touched me… I knew I had to go to Lyvareth. I don't know what awaits there, or why it matters, but I can feel it in my bones. If we don't go, something terrible will happen."

Sol stood, beginning to pace, his movements sharp with unease.

"Last night, the Hearth Mother spoke the old tongue. 'Sha… Sha veri tha rien vren shara…' Something. She said she couldn't see me — and that I needed to find out why."

He clutched the token tight in his palm.

"She gave me this. Said it would help with my 'balance,' whatever that means… and damned if it didn't ease the pain in my head."

Sol slammed his fists against the table.

"Burn the gods and their riddles!"

"It's okay, love."

Wyatt stepped closer, cupping Sol's face in his hands.

"There are scholars in Lyvareth, the great academy, Veyndral.

If anyone can interpret the signs of the gods, they can."

He brought Sol's hands to his lips.

"There's no use fighting the gods. All we can do is seek the answers."

Sol drew a slow breath.

In. Hold. Out.

The ache behind his eyes pulsed sharper, but he forced it aside.

He didn't know why, but he wasn't ready to use the godsdamned talisman. Not yet.

"I love you, Wyatt Thornbrook," Sol said, his voice low and solemn.

"I love you too, Soltic Arden."

Wyatt kissed him softly.

"How about we do a little exploring?"

Wyatt smiled, and Sol felt himself begin to steady.

"Thank you."

The bell above the shop door jingled as they stepped into the street, late afternoon light stretching long shadows across the stone.

Sol adjusted the strap of his satchel over his shoulder, wincing as the ache behind his eyes pulsed again.

"Did we get everything?" Wyatt asked, holding up a neatly wrapped bundle of bread and dried meat.

"Close enough," Sol said. "We'll have to stretch it if it rains."

Wyatt linked arms with him, gently steering them down the street. They walked past busy storefronts, admiring the shop windows.

Everyone seemed to carry a sword or dagger at their hip, and most of the women wore trousers. It was nothing like Oswynn.

"I've heard that in Lyvareth there's a River Market," Wyatt said dreamily. "Hundreds of vendors. The finest clothmakers in all of Itharen. Honey sweets still in the comb…"

"Da' used to say Lyvareth was corrupt," Sol murmured. "That Oswynn was a safe haven from its taint."

"He was a fool," Wyatt snapped — then softened. "Sorry. I didn't mean it."

"No," Sol said quietly, eyes lifting to the sky. "He was misguided. Damn the Hand… and curse the day he arrived in

Oswynn."

A young woman brushed against him in the crowd.

The world went still.

The instant her fingers touched his skin, time seemed to hold its breath.

Wyatt froze mid-step.

A blinding white light surged around him, and the world shattered like glass pressed against his ribs.

His soul wrenched as if pulled through a needle's eye.

Despair crashed through him, the woman's grief, raw and endless.

A loss so vast it nearly consumed her.

But she would survive it—after a season or two.

Sol couldn't bear it.

Pain split him wide, and the world went black.

Bright light stabbed at his eyes; his head spun.

He looked up into Wyatt's green gaze as a small crowd gathered around them.

Wyatt's arms held him firm, warm, grounding. Comfort.

Sol's gaze slid to the young woman—late teens, long brown hair tumbling forward.

How could he tell her that something terrible was coming?

What would he even say, something bad is going to happen? That wasn't helpful.

Instead, he whispered, "I'm sorry, miss. I should've watched where I was going."

She looked stunned, concerned.

"Darling, are you alright?"

Sol met Wyatt's eyes and answered weakly,

"Yeah… I'll be okay."

The small crowd was already dispersing as Wyatt helped him to a sitting position.

He was attentive, searching Sol's face, pressing his forehead gently against Sol's, holding him as if he might collapse again.

The young woman straightened and smoothed her plain green dress, regaining her composure.

"I'm sorry, darling. Looks like you're in good hands."

She winked, then disappeared into the crowd.

Wyatt helped Sol to his feet. He was still a little unsteady, but Wyatt held him close, steadying him effortlessly.

He guided Sol to a wooden bench near the nearest shop and eased him down gently.

Sol was exhausted, yet his mind felt unnervingly clear.

"Wyatt," he said, voice flat, "something bad will happen to her."

"What?"

"I saw her future," Sol murmured. "She's going to endure unimaginable pain."

"But I couldn't tell her."

Wyatt's brow furrowed.

He didn't speak right away.

Something in his expression shifted, not fear, exactly, but distance.

As if a door had closed just a little.

Sol couldn't tell whether it was worry… or if he simply didn't want to know.

"What happens to her?"

"I don't know," Sol said, frustration lacing his voice. "She'll come out the other side—but she'll struggle."

Wyatt was silent for a moment, his jaw tightening slightly.

"We all suffer," he said softly.

"But I felt her pain," Sol insisted, more gently now.

He couldn't save her; a shard of that grief would live in him now, quiet, unrelenting.

Wyatt reached over, resting his hand on Sol's knee.

"If you don't know what befalls her," he said slowly, "I think it's better not to say anything.

She'd be afraid of everything—every corner, every

shadow, waiting for something terrible."

Sol thought about it. The weight of it settled, softer now.

"You're right."

Wyatt studied him, concern etched plainly across his face.

"How are you feeling? I think we should head back."

"I'm okay," Sol said, forcing a reassuring tone. "Just tired."

Wyatt didn't look convinced. He scanned Sol carefully, then nodded.

"If we're to be on the road again soon… I'd like a rest, if that's all right."

Sol drew a slow, steadying breath.

"Yeah. We've got a long journey ahead of us. But if we see a sweet shop, let's stop."

Wyatt smiled as he helped Sol to his feet.

"Deal."

They walked down the crowded streets, heading back toward the Pale Hearth.

Sol was lost in thought.

He couldn't shake the sense of inevitable loss; the not knowing what was at stake made it feel worse.

Wyatt had been right: an enemy without a face was almost worse than whatever might come.

His limbs felt heavy. He noticed Wyatt slowing to match his pace.

The pressure behind his eyes had lessened… though not entirely gone.

Sol felt Wyatt's strong hand settle at the back of his neck as he guided him into the bright bakery.

The scent of warm bread and sugar filled the air.

"I think we found your sweets," Wyatt said with a smile.

"Well, good day!"

A short, balding man behind the counter returned the smile, his voice cheerful.

"We don't get many strangers. What you see on the counter is what I've got left from this morning."

"We're just passing through," Sol said brightly, already perking up.

"But I was born rolled in sugar. Got anything sticky, spiced, or spun with sweetness?"

The man grinned and motioned toward the wall.

"I've got the finest sweets in Hollow's Rest, even travel treats."

He came around the counter and held out his hand.

Sol and Wyatt each took a powdered teardrop candy.

It was slightly tart at first, then bloomed into a delicate floral sweetness, like violet.

They exchanged a look.

"Oh, this is really good," Sol said, eyes wide.

The man beamed.

"I know! You won't find anything like it. Gives you a little mood boost, too."

He held up a small pouch.

"Good for the road."

"Can we get three pouches?" Wyatt asked.

"Sure thing," the man replied.

Sol pointed to a row of small golden squares, each drizzled with something dark.

"What's that?"

"Chocolate," the man said reverently. "A rare delicacy. Some folk call it the food of the gods—I call it magic."

"Can we get a dozen?" Sol asked, eyes lighting up.

Wyatt raised an eyebrow, amusement flickering across his face.

"A dozen?"

"Everyone likes sweets," Sol smiled. "And I want to thank Brenn and Garrin and the rest. They didn't have to be kind to us."

"I guess a dozen it is," Wyatt said, already pulling out a coin.

"It's rare, but some people don't like chocolate," the man offered kindly.

"May I suggest six chocolate and six with the sugar frosting?

Saves you two coppers."

"Thank you—that's better," Sol agreed.

"Name's Nollan Thresk," the man said, "but you can call me Noll."

"Thank you, Noll. I'm Soltic, and this is Wyatt."

Sol handed him the last two silver pieces from his pouch.

"Please keep the two coppers as a token of thanks."

Noll smiled, then shook his head.

"I can't do that. I can tell you ain't nobles, so I know you need it as bad as I do. But—"

He disappeared behind the counter. Pots clinked and slid out of sight.

When he returned, he held two brown-covered parcels wrapped in waxed paper.

"Try this."

Sol and Wyatt popped them into their mouths.

The chocolate melted sweetly, but beneath the smooth surface, the bite was crunchy… and faintly savory.

"That was delicious," Wyatt said, licking sugar from his lip.

"What's it called?"

"Chocolate-covered beetles," Noll said casually.

Wyatt turned green.

Sol swallowed hard, forcing a smile.

"Oh… erm," he coughed, "I never would've guessed."

"In my humble opinion," Noll said, grinning widely,

"chocolate makes everything taste better."

"I suppose it does," Sol admitted, chuckling softly.

Sol gathered their sweets.

"Any surprises in the rest of these?"

Noll laughed.

"There's always a surprise in my treats—but nothing unexpected in those, I promise."

"Thank you, Master Noll," Wyatt said weakly.

"Safe journey, lads."

They stepped into the street, taking only a few steps before Wyatt burst out laughing.

"You know, those beetles were good until I realized what they were. But the look on your face! I thought your eyes would pop right out of your head."

Sol smacked his arm, laughing.

"You're one to talk! You looked like you were about to turn into a frog right there on the floor."

They had to stop walking, laughing too hard to move, leaning into each other like drunkards in the snow.

Wyatt took Sol's hand and tugged him forward.

"I'm hungry. Let's get back. I'll put the supplies in our room, you grab us a table?"

Sol tapped his fingers up Wyatt's back like an insect's legs.

"Didn't think you'd be hungry after that beetle."

Sol laughed again, breathless, but a part of him clung to the warmth of it, as if it might vanish when the sun went down.

They broke into another fit of laughter as Wyatt gave a dramatic shudder and tugged him along.

They quickened their pace as the Pale Hearth came into view, the smell of smoked meat drifting through the street—warm, savory, mouthwatering.

Brenn was polishing a glass behind the counter.

"Lads! You found your way back."

"I think we got everything we need," Wyatt grinned, holding up the bulging satchel.

"I'll be right back."

He headed up the stairs.

"A messenger's on their way to Oswynn," Brenn said as Sol approached.

"But no one's daft enough to cut through the Wilds, they'll ride around. It should take just over a month to reach Cloud."

Sol frowned. "That long?"

Brenn nodded. "If the gods are kind."

"Thank you," Sol said with a smile, pulling out a small chocolate square.

"Do you like chocolate?"

Brenn barked a laugh.

"Don't tell me ol' Noll got you to eat his bugs."

Sol made a face.

"I'll take that as a yes."

"They weren't bad," Sol chuckled. "But these don't have any surprises."

He handed over one of the chocolate-covered squares.

"Aye, lad. You've got good taste."

Brenn took a bite and let it melt slowly on his

tongue.

"Don't get to have it much, but... gods, it really is magic." Just then, Sol spotted Scy entering from the courtyard.

He slumped into a chair by the fire without a word—no swagger, no grin.

Sol raised an eyebrow. The cask curse must be strong today.

He sat down in the chair next to Scy. "You look like death warmed twice." Scy didn't look up.

"I've got bad news. And worse news."

"Wyatt's coming down—no need to repeat it," Sol said, steeling himself.

"Lad, I know we thought the worst was behind us..."

"Wow, Scy. Still bitter-backed?" Wyatt called, planting a hand on Scy's shoulder.

He caught Sol's expression—serious, pale.

Wyatt's smile vanished.

"What happened?"

He slid into the seat across from Scy.

Scy glanced toward Brenn, who caught the look and nodded, quietly slipping behind the bar.

Scy leaned in, voice low.

"One of Garin's runners came in, western route. Ashmen. Not priests. Not spies. Ashmen. They were spotted outside Briarstead."

"Ashmen?" Wyatt echoed, frowning.

"Wardens of the Path," Scy said grimly. "That's what they call themselves. But the Rouge just call 'em Ashmen."

He spat near the fire. "Because that's all they leave behind." "That's—" Sol started.

"They're not hunting just anyone," Scy cut in. "They're asking for the Spillborn—the one who vanished from Oswynn after 'inciting doubt in the Path.'"

Sol's stomach dropped.

"How many?"

"A full Lash. Seven in black steel and red sigils, and more behind them. Fast. Quiet. Not looking to question."

Sol's mouth went dry. "They're not trying to convert us anymore, are they?" he said bitterly.

Scy's voice dropped, heavy with warning.

"No. They're trying to clean up."

"Briarstead's over a month from here. And we're out of Greywell lands," Sol said, trying to reason through Scy's fear.

"These aren't the Baron's men," Scy said flatly.

"They're a law unto themselves. The crown doesn't recognize them as knights. Zealots, religious mercenaries."

"They go where they want, claiming divine will," he scoffed.

"But that's the bad news. The worst?"

He exhaled hard, the weight of it pressing the air between them. "Garrin found out that at least ten Lashes are searching the kingdom. The Hand is scouring all Itharen."

Sol went pale.

"What can we do?"

Scy leaned in, voice low.

"The key is getting you to Lyvareth. Fast."

"They're barred from entering, even their High Priests won't risk it."

"You show up at the Council, tell them the Hand's after you. They'll grant you haven and ensure the temple knows it."

He smirked. "That way, if anything happens to you, they've got something to lose."

Then, drier: "And trust me—no one wants to be dragged in front of the city guard. They take real pleasure in watching priests squirm."

Sol nodded slowly. "You said it's a fortnight to Lyvareth?"

"If we get horses and stick to the road, I reckon we could make it in a week."

"Last time we took the road," Wyatt said darkly, "we were ambushed by bandits. They nearly had us."

Scy allowed a faint grin.

"But you didn't know I was trailing you."

Sol sighed.

"I guess it won't matter if we leave tonight or tomorrow."

"Tomorrow night," Scy said. "Travel at night where we can. Keep our heads down."

"But we'll be easier to spot when we camp," Wyatt pointed out.

Scy leaned back, shaking his head.

"You're right. Might be the ale still in me."

Sol inhaled deeply, the weight of their plan settling in.

"Fine. We leave at first light. After supper, we rest."

Wyatt glanced at Sol. "I don't like this."

"Neither do I," Sol said. "But we're out of time."

His heart pounded like a war drum.

They were running again.

And they were close—so close.

Wyatt and Scy continued talking, but Sol couldn't focus.

The pressure behind his eyes was building, sharp and relentless.

Fear gripped him.

They were hunting him like a hare.

Wyatt and Scy were in danger because of him.

"Scy," Sol said suddenly, eyes sharp and steady.

"Can you show me a few drills with my sword?"

Scy looked over, surprised.

Something shifted inside Sol—slow and cold, like iron locking into place.

He didn't raise his voice.

The heat was gone.

In its place, a stillness.

Not fear. Not rage.

Resolve. Sharp enough to cut.

Wyatt was staring at him now, silent.

Sol didn't look away.

"After supper," Scy said, nodding once.

Sol was tired of always being afraid.

He took a deep breath.

In. Hold. Out.

They would make it to Lyvareth.

All of them.

He didn't know what he was becoming, only that he would never be powerless again.

Even if I have to cut down every Ashman myself.

Every last one.

584

Chapter Twenty-Five

—

Held Breath

The morning air was brisk, biting at Sol's skin, and his arms throbbed from last night's sparring. He was certain bruises would bloom by evening. He was no swordsman, yet a quiet pride stirred within him for the few solid hits he had landed. His head throbbed in rhythm with his pulse.

The horses stamped and snorted restlessly in the soft dirt. Sol reached out to soothe a chestnut mare, his fingers brushing her warm coat, and then his eyes roved across the clearing, settling on five saddled horses waiting patiently—or so it seemed.

"I'm not late, am I?" a familiar voice called from behind a sturdy black stallion. Sol glimpsed a mass of dark, curly hair vanish.

He and Wyatt exchanged puzzled glances.

Arlen emerged from behind Scy, a faint grin tugging at his lips.

"A little last-minute, but I think we've got everything."

"Where are you headed, Arlen?" Sol asked, frowning.

"We can't let you have all the fun," Ruck said, stepping carefully around the black stallion, his eyes glinting with mischief.

"There are multiple Lash hunting you," Arlen added dryly.

"You won't make it to Lyvareth on your own."

"Once you set foot in Hallow's Rest, you fall beneath my protection," Garrin said firmly. "Arlen and Ruck are my best. They will see you to Lyvareth."

It wasn't a request.

Sol mustered his resolve. "How can I repay your kindness?"

Garrin smiled warmly. "We ask for no favors in return, Soltic.

It is my duty as Leader of the Rouge — and as Tharan'kai Veyrn'dorath — to ensure you reach Lyvareth safely."

"Tharan'kai Veyrn'dorath?" Sol echoed the phrase, humming in his mind, a whisper of long-forgotten knowledge.

Garrin only offered a half-smile. "We have more in common than you realize. In Lyvareth, should you need, you can call on the Black Coin."

He pressed a burnt copper coin into Sol's palm.

Where the king's portrait should have been, a crooked feather was etched into the metal.

"Thank you, Garrin," Sol said, throat tight. These people had barely met him, yet they were willing to risk their lives for his.

"I would come myself," Garrin said, his voice dropping, "but a storm is brewing — and the Rouge must be ready. Do not delay." Ruck stepped up to the chestnut mare, his hand resting gently on the crescent-shaped mark on her forehead.

"Ginger Snap's a good'un," he said. "Named her that because she can be sweet — but she'll bite or kick to get her way."

"Ginger Snap… what a beauty," Sol murmured, running his hand along her flank. Her tail flicked sharply, lashing against him like a whip.

"Aye. Beautiful and temperamental," Sol muttered under his breath, a small smile tugging at his lips.

Ruck chuckled and helped Sol finish readying the mare.

"The sun'll be up soon," Scy called, adjusting his bracer. "We should get going."

"Let's mount and be on our way," Arlen ordered, swinging gracefully onto her gray mare.

Sol struggled to climb onto Ginger. Strong hands steadied him at the waist, guiding him into the saddle.

"Not much of a rider, are ya?" Ruck teased, a wide grin spreading across his face. "Don't worry, I'll catch you if you fall." He winked, then swung into his own saddle.

Wyatt huffed, muttering something under his breath, and nudged his golden mare up alongside Sol's — just a little too close for comfort.

"Are you ready?" Wyatt asked softly, for Sol's ears only.

"I don't know if I'll ever be ready," Sol said. "But now's as good a time as any."

"We'll walk the horses to the East Gate," Arlen said over her shoulder. "Once we're through, we ride hard until the mounts need rest. Keep up."

She guided her gray mare onto the main street. The

city was just beginning to stir, shutters creaked open, candlelight flickered in cozy homes, and smoke drifted lazily from chimneys.

Arlen led the group, with Scy and Ruck bringing up the rear. They rode in near silence as the massive gates drew closer.

Garrin came trotting up on a white stallion, bareback, and pulled alongside Arlen. The two exchanged words in low and urgent.

"So," Wyatt said quietly, not quite looking at Sol. "Ruck seems to have taken a liking to you."

"He seems to like everyone," Sol replied.

"Open the gates!" Garrin shouted to the guards atop the wall.

The metal portcullis groaned as it rumbled upward. Beyond it, the wooden gates creaked open slowly, revealing the path ahead — long, shadowed, and waiting.

Sol drew a steadying breath.

In. Hold. Out.

"Godspeed, Soltic Arden," Garrin said, thumping his chest three times in solemn rhythm.

"Yah!" Arlen dug in her heels and was off.

The band of misfits tore from the city, swallowed by a rising cloud of dust that hung heavy in the morning light.

A fire crackled softly nearby, its flames flickering against the curve of a well-worn black kettle. Smoke drifted upward into the crisp evening air, disappearing into a canopy of fading stars overhead.

They had made camp just off the main road, sheltered by a sparse ring of trees and a small rise of stone. The horses were tied loosely nearby, heads lowered as they nibbled at the grass. Ginger Snap huffed once and flicked her tail, still not quite finished asserting her attitude toward Sol.

Sol sat cross-legged beside the fire, rubbing his sore thighs. Every muscle in his body ached — and not from exertion done well. He cast a glance at Ruck, who had made a point of unsaddling both their horses, still whistling a carefree tune as he worked.

The warmth of the flames licked at his skin, yet the ache behind his eyes refused to ease. It had started dull and low, then crept deeper with each passing hour. Not sharp, just…insistent. Like something waiting.

"You good?" Ruck asked, settling on a nearby stone. He tossed a twig into the flames. "You've gone quiet."

Sol blinked. "Just tired."

Wyatt sat beside him, close enough for their knees to brush. He hadn't spoken much since they'd stopped, yet every glance he cast at Ruck seemed to carry more weight than the last.

Sol clutched the Hearth Mother's gift tightly in his hand.

When your soul stirs… head and heart ache…

The old woman's voice echoed in his mind.

Firelight danced across the stone's depths. His eyes passed over the faint, twisted feather. The silver spiral glinted softly.

He exhaled.

His gaze followed the spiral slowly, from the center outward — then back again. By the seventh pass, the pressure behind his eyes had eased.

When Sol looked up, Scy averted his eyes. *Had Scy been watching him all along?* He wondered.

Scy leaned back against a log, hands tucked behind

his head, exuding the strange ease of a man who seemed to have nothing and everything to worry about at once.

His voice came lazily:

"We've got a little wager going."

"What kind of wager?" Wyatt asked.

Scy grinned. "How long it will take for Ginger Snap to toss Sol."

"Are you kidding me?" Sol laughed. "I'm in."

Ruck leaned closer, a mischievous glint in his eye. "Oh yeah? And what would you be willing to wager?"

Sol's cheeks heated at the innuendo.

Wyatt snapped, "I'll wager Sol stays on," sliding an arm around Sol's shoulders with a teasing grin.

"I was going to bet the same," Sol said. "I'll cook for the rest of the journey if I fall off."

"We shouldn't be punished if you win," Scy laughed.

"I'm with Scy on this one," Wyatt added with a grin.

Sol gave him a gentle shove.

"If you don't want Wyatt to keep you warm

tonight," Ruck winked, "I will."

"You can keep trying, Ruck," Wyatt said coolly. "But I don't think Ginger's the only one out of your league."

"Will you stop, Ruck?" Arlen asked, amusement lacing her voice. "Watching you strut like a prized cock is… embarrassing."

Wyatt snorted, struggling to keep a grin from spreading across his face.

"Besides," Arlen added, "Sol's not dumb enough to bed someone who flirts like a bored barmaid and smells like saddle oil."

"What was your excuse?" Scy drawled.

"We all make mistakes," Arlen replied evenly.

Wyatt's expression was a little too satisfied.

As the laughter died down, Arlen tossed a piece of kindling into the fire and muttered, almost too low to catch:

"He's not a plaything."

It wasn't clear who she spoke to or if she meant to say it aloud.

Sol looked over at Scy, who simply smiled, his eyes dancing in the firelight.

Ruck stood, brushing ash from his hands. "I don't care what you all think of me. I'll even give you a gift."

He strode toward the edge of the camp, casting a glance over his shoulder.

"You can watch as I walk away." And with that, he vanished into the night.

"Get some sleep while you can," Arlen said. "We ride at first light."

There was a silence then — not uncomfortable, but weighted.

"You're right," Sol murmured. "We'd better turn in. We can take the third watch, if that's alright."

Arlen just nodded.

Sol stood and offered a hand to Wyatt, who took it with a quiet, reassuring smile. Together, they moved toward their bedrolls as the others began to settle, the fire crackling softly behind them.

Sol steadied his breathing and listened. The gentle pop of the flames. A hushed conversation at the edge of the camp. Then, the sharp snap of a twig.

He froze. His heart thudded against his ribs as his hand shot instinctively to the knife strapped at his wrist.

"It's just Ruck coming back," Wyatt said softly. "But I wouldn't mind if you nicked him on the way in."

Sol laughed, the tension draining from his shoulders. He leaned in and kissed Wyatt.

"I've never seen you jealous before. Don't worry, I'm immune to his charm."

"I'm not jealous," Wyatt mumbled. "I just don't like that he's so shameless."

Sol kissed him again, slower this time, then rolled onto his side, tugging Wyatt's arm around his waist.

His heart began to ease, his breath settling into a calmer rhythm.

Arlen raised a hand, signaling them to slow and give the horses a much-needed rest. They had been riding hard all day, stopping only once for a hasty midday break.

Sol's legs were numb. He shifted in the stirrups, rocking his weight from one side to the other, trying to coax some feeling back.

"How are you feeling?" Wyatt asked beside him.

"I'm okay," Sol muttered, miserable. "But my ass fell asleep."

The horses' hooves crunched over dirt and loose stones. Ahead, a dark shape loomed on the horizon, trailing a rising plume of dust.

Arlen's voice was calm. Too calm.

"Looks like we have company." She tightened her grip on the reins. "There's nowhere to run. The horses won't survive a chase."

Scy exchanged uneasy glances with Ruck and Arlen.

The shimmer of dark armor appeared on the horizon, followed by the flash of red cloaks billowing like streaks of blood behind them. Elion's silver eye gleamed from the mounts' barding, a curse stitched in thread.

The Lash was coming.

"Try to knock them off their horses," Arlen said coolly.

Scy and Ruck drew arrows, knocked them, and held their breath. The riders closed in — thirteen men, fast, focused, and merciless.

Arrows flew. They glanced off armor but unnerved

the Ashmen. Horses reared and staggered. Another volley struck, one hitting a mount's shoulder, sending the animal sideways and nearly unseating its rider.

"Turn over the spillborn," the lead rider bellowed, slowing to a gallop, "and we'll show you mercy. We'll forgive your transgression of attacking us unprovoked."

Ruck didn't hesitate. He fired again, the arrow slipped between breastplate and saddle. The rider was thrown, rolling across the dirt beneath pounding hooves.

Wyatt slid from his horse and raised his hands. "We'll give you whatever you want."

One of the Ashmen rode up, grinning widely. "We thought at least one of you would ha—"

Wyatt grabbed the Ashman's cloak and yanked him off his horse, slamming him into the dirt.

Without missing a beat, Arlen let out a war cry and charged. Wyatt drove his blade into the fallen rider and sprinted toward the next.

Pain flared in Sol's ribs before he even hit the ground. The clash of steel, the screams of horses, and the metallic sweetness of blood filled the air.

More riders were unseated than remained

mounted.

Sol rolled just in time — a sword slammed into the dirt where his head had been. He scrambled to his feet. The Ashman before him spat.

"Filthy Spillborn."

Sol gritted his teeth, tightened his grip, and swung. The Ashman parried with effortless precision.

Around them, chaos raged. Men cried out. Steel rang. Blood soaked the earth.

Arlen, still mounted, kicked one man in the throat. He fell choking. Her blade slashed another across the ribs.

Sol caught sight of Ruck fending off a rider on the far side — and another Ashman broke from the fray, charging toward Ruck's blind side.

Wyatt stepped in.

Sol saw it before he could even scream, the blade.

The blood.

Wyatt staggered. A sword protruded from his chest.

Red bloomed across his shirt like ink in water.

Sol screamed.

The world narrowed.

His vision turned red.

He wanted them dead.

Heat erupted where the Veyrnstag had touched him — whitehot, blinding.

Something inside him cracked open, a pulse, sharp and ancient, like the world exhaling through his chest.

His vision blurred.

The man before him vaporized.

No sound. No swing.

Just a sudden, violent absence.

Blood mist.

A scream without a mouth.

Sol dropped.

Darkness swallowed everything.

Scy's hand was gentle against Sol's cheek.

"Sol?" His voice trembled, eyes brimming with unshed tears.

"Wyatt?" Sol fought through the agony coursing

through his mind and body. "No. No, no, no—Wyatt!"

He rolled, crawling through bloodied mud until he could force himself upright.

I got Wyatt killed.

I will never forgive myself.

His breath came in ragged bursts. His heartbeat drowned out everything else.

Ruck sat nearby, eyes closed, lips moving in silent incantation, both hands pressed over the wound in Wyatt's chest. Scy held Sol back, arms wrapped firmly around him.

"Let him be," Scy said softly, his voice thick. "Ruck is a healer."

"He has to save him. Please—" Sol sobbed into Scy's tunic, trembling violently.

"He'll do everything in his power," Scy whispered. "But it's bad."

Sol's knees buckled. Scy braced him, guiding him to the roadside. Sol collapsed, grief swallowing him whole. He cried until his eyes and throat burned.

Arlen rode back into camp, dismounting quickly. She went straight to Ruck, speaking in hushed tones. Ruck was pale, drenched in sweat, yet his eyes still burned with fierce defiance.

"I killed the two who fled," Arlen said flatly. "Ruck's doing everything he can."

"I got Wyatt killed," Sol gasped.

"Wyatt's still alive," Arlen said gently. "Gravely wounded, but alive. You saved his life — and ours. How did you kill those men, Sol?"

"I only killed one with my sword," Sol whispered. "If I'd been better… Wyatt wouldn't be—"

Arlen crouched beside him, calm but firm.

"After Wyatt was stabbed, the men attacking him and Ruck, and the one you were fighting, were unmade. There was nothing left."

"I… I didn't do that," Sol said, voice trembling.

What if he had?

That heat — that snap of something inside him, had felt real.

Final.

Was that him? Was that what had been waiting inside all along?

He shook his head, but the doubt lingered.

"Sol," Ruck's voice was heavy. "He's asking for you."

Sol scrambled to Wyatt's side. He was ashen, skin slick with sweat. Blood crusted at the corners of his cracked lips.

Sol took his hand, voice trembling.

"You don't get to leave me, Wyatt. Not like this."

Wyatt tried to speak but fell into a coughing fit.

"Shhh. Don't talk — rest," Sol said, his voice shaking.

"I... I love you," Wyatt breathed.

Sol froze, heart hammering. That moment, those words…would never leave him.

Then Wyatt's eyes rolled back, and his body convulsed violently.

Sol wailed. Arlen and Scy grabbed him, holding him back as Ruck lunged to Wyatt's side.

"Scy," Ruck snapped. "I need your strength."

Scy dropped to his knees across from him. Their eyes locked, and together they pressed their hands over Wyatt's chest.

Scy spoke first:

"Vareth'an kai'dorel — sha'rei, val'serah, answer me."

The air shifted.

No thunder. No divine voice. Just stillness, as if the world itself had paused to listen.

Wyatt's body stilled. His breathing slowed. Scy trickled water gently into his mouth.

Sol sat frozen beside Arlen, who wrapped an arm around his shoulders, grounding him.

"Take Wyatt back to Hollow's Rest."

"I'll go to Lyvareth alone."

"They're after me."

"If Wyatt still wants me… he can come."

"Once he's healed."

"He'll be safe."

Arlen met his gaze. "And what would he say when he wakes to find you gone?"

"He'd be upset," Sol said quietly.

A beat.

"But he'd be alive."

"Your parents thought the same when they arranged your marriage," Arlen said, not unkindly.

"But he could die," Sol whispered.

The tears returned — hot, helpless.

"I can't—" His voice caught. "I can't have anyone else hurt because of me."

"We'll get him to the city," she said, resolute.

Scy looked pale, his hands trembling.

"He'll make it," Scy said hoarsely. "But gods… just barely."

Arlen rose, her expression hardening with determination.

"We take turns riding with him. No stopping. No slowing."

She looked at Sol — not unkindly, but fierce.

"If another Lash is near, they won't hesitate. And they'll be hungry."

They made camp in silence.

Sol dutifully unrolled Wyatt's bedding, and Scy gently eased him down onto it.

Sol sat beside him, watching every shallow breath.

Scy placed a firm hand on Sol's shoulder.

"Lad… you have to eat something," he said, his voice gentle.

Sol shook his head. "I'm not hungry."

"Wyatt needs us all strong," Arlen said. "If we're attacked again, we'll have to defend him."

She was right. He needed to be strong for Wyatt.

"Fine."

Ruck settled on the ground beside Sol, his voice quiet.

"He saved my life."

Even now, he sounded surprised. "Even though he doesn't like me."

Sol didn't answer.

"Listen…" Ruck glanced away, ashamed. "I'm sorry for teasing you. I didn't mean anything by it. It was just… fun to watch Wyatt ruffle."

"Will he make it to Lyvareth?" Sol asked.

Ruck hesitated. "I… I don't know. We'll have to watch and wait."

Sol stared into the fire.

"I stopped the bleeding," Ruck continued. "This kind of healing can hold for a while, if we're careful. But last time… we were trapped in a temple, and a master healer came to us."

Sol turned slightly. "Why did you call for Scy when Wyatt had the fits?"

"Scy has a deep connection to the old gods," Ruck said. "I needed him to help calm Wyatt."

"How is he connected? I've never seen him use magic."

"His story's not mine to tell," Ruck said simply.

Arlen handed Sol a bowl of soup and sat beside Scy.

"Are you sure you don't know how you saved us?" she asked.

Sol looked up. Her gaze held something that made his stomach twist.

"I didn't do anything, Arlen," he said. "I've never felt anything like that before. How can you be so sure it was me?"

"The Lash wouldn't do that to their own," she said. "I have no powers. He"—she nodded at Ruck—"can heal, but no gift like that."

Scy raised a hand. "Don't look at me. Trust me, I wish I could."

"When a young mage first comes into power, it can… manifest in strange ways," Arlen said.

"I'm not a mage," Sol muttered, shaking his head.

"You've always had knowings you couldn't explain," Scy said quietly.

"That's a far cry from unmaking someone," Sol snapped.

"When the Veyrnstag touched you," Scy reminded him, "you said you felt an ember burst into flame."

Sol hesitated. *This… wasn't the same thing.*

"I've never moved things with my mind," he said. "Never read thoughts. Never levitated. Just… knowing things doesn't mean I killed those men."

"If your power woke in the Wilds," Scy said, "maybe this is just part of it."

Sol took a deep breath. *This isn't happening.*

"Maybe it was the gods," Ruck offered. "Watching over us." A breeze rustled through the trees.

"Whatever it was," Arlen said, "the mages at Veyndral will know more."

"Where is Veyndral?" Sol asked.

"Lyvareth," Arlen replied. "It's a school for those with magical abilities."

"It's more than that," Scy added. "The most powerful mages live there. They lead the Mage's Council."

"It's said no king stays in power without the Council behind him," Ruck murmured.

"Let's get to Lyvareth first," Scy said. "We'll worry about the rest later."

Arlen stood. "Sol, you're on first watch."

Sol nodded, quietly grateful.

"I can stay with you," Scy offered.

Sol shook his head. "No. Rest. If anything changes, I'll wake you, you, and Ruck both."

Scy squeezed Sol's shoulder gently. Ruck did the same as he passed.

Sol sat alone by the fire. Wyatt lay just beyond, pale and still.

He didn't look worse than before, but he didn't look better either.

He has to heal, Sol thought.

The world has no meaning without him.

Sol didn't know what terrified him more, whether he had killed those men… or that he could do it again.

He couldn't stop it. Couldn't control it. And if it happened again… who else might get hurt?

He watched Wyatt breathe, each shallow rise a fragile thread stitching him to the world.

He stayed there, eyes open, heart breaking, because if Wyatt's breath stopped—

Chapter Twenty-Six

———

By Dusk

The sun sagged low in the sky, bleeding what little light remained across the land, while ahead the vast wall of grey stretched higher, swallowing the horizon. Safety was close, so close they could almost taste it, but the horses quivered beneath them, lathered in sweat, their chests heaving as though each breath might be their last. They wouldn't hold this pace much longer.

Wyatt hadn't stirred. His face had lost all color, his skin a sickly shade of ash, his lips dry, his breath thin and faltering. Every rise of his chest felt fragile, as if the world itself was deciding whether to grant him another.

Sol whispered, "You have to hang on."

Arlen lifted her hand, and the riders slowed to a halt.

"I can see the city. We have to keep going. Wyatt—" Sol's voice broke, raw with fear.

"If the horses fall beneath us, he'll be lost all the same," Arlen answered softly. "We'll stop at the river, let them drink. No longer than we must."

Sol swallowed hard and gave a stiff nod, his eyes never leaving Wyatt.

"Here, Sol. I got him," Scy said, helping ease Wyatt to the ground.

"We'll reach the gates before nightfall," Ruck said quietly, though his voice carried the weight of a prayer. "He's going to make it."

Sol lowered himself to the ground and drew Wyatt's head into his lap, holding him as though afraid to let go.

"I have a friend in the city," Arlen said after a pause. "She lives near Veyndral."

"And if she isn't there?" Sol asked, his eyes fixed on Wyatt's pale face.

"She won't be hard to find," Arlen answered, her voice steady but shadowed with doubt.

"Elyshavir was one of the youngest initiates ever to earn the Mantle of Illumination," Arlen said. "Master of the Etherwoven Veil— though you'd never know it to look at her."

"What's the Mantle of Illumination?" Sol asked.

"It's granted only after a mage endures a gauntlet

of trials, each meant to strip them bare and prove their strength," Arlen explained. "Those who succeed receive their Mantle, a mark of mastery and honor. Most wear it proudly." Her eyes darkened. "Elyshavir hides hers."

"I've yet to see her in her formal mage robes," Ruck added. "She skips ceremonies. Says she won't be paraded around to puff up the Council's ego."

"She helped me when I was there," Scy said, brushing a finger along the thin scar beneath his eye. "I asked her to leave it. Makes me look distinguished, don't you think?"

"You never mentioned you'd been to Lyvareth," Sol said, frowning.

Scy froze for a breath, surprised by the question. "Well, lad, I did have a life before I put down roots in Oswynn."

Without waiting for a reply, he pushed to his feet. "I'll check on the horses."

Sol ran his fingers through Wyatt's sweat-soaked hair.

"Arlen, can you hand me a waterskin?"

"Be careful. Only a few drops at a time," she said,

already guessing his intention.

"I know. But thank you."

He trickled water between Wyatt's lips, brushed the excess across his cracked mouth, and pressed a kiss to his fevered brow—the heat still rising.

Gently, Sol lowered Wyatt's head onto the grass.

Then he rose.

The world lurched sideways, a dull thrum beating behind his eyes, not pain, but something stranger.

He braced his hands against his knees, drawing his breath slowly, forcing it into steadiness.

In. Hold. Out.

Ruck appeared beside him and caught his arm, grounding him. "You don't look so good," he said.

"You don't look so good," Sol muttered, then let out a weary sigh. "Sorry."

"No, I get it," Ruck said softly. "But really, Sol. How are you?"

He laid a hand against Sol's forehead, only to snatch it back as if scalded.

"Gods, you're burning."

Sol staggered, his hand rising to his brow. Beneath his fingertips, a faint spark flickered under the skin, a hum pressing too near the surface.

The same pulse from the spiral. The same wrongness that had been waiting for him all along.

But he wasn't afraid.

"I've had worse headaches," he said. "We're all tired. I'll be fine."

Arlen stepped closer, her brows knitting. She laid a cool palm against his forehead, then wordlessly offered him the waterskin.

"Drink."

Sol obeyed, taking two deep swallows. The water cooled his throat, but the low hum beneath his skin remained, stubborn and unshaken.

And still, his thoughts never turned to himself.

Wyatt needed him more. "By the gods... how long have the headaches been like this?"

"I've had them since my twelfth summer, but they've grown worse since the Wilds," Sol admitted. "The charm the Hearth Mother gave me still helps, but I've had to rely on it more and more."

"And the fever?"

"I don't know," Sol muttered, pressing his fingers to his temples.

Scy stumbled back into camp, clothes dripping.

Before anyone could speak, Sol lifted a hand. "Don't."

They all watched as Scy upended his boot, pouring water onto the ground with a scowl.

"The horses will make it to the city. Let's get going."

Sol brought his horse close to Wyatt. "Scy, can you help me get him on?"

"We need to give Ginger a break from carrying two riders," Scy said quietly.

"Let me take him," Ruck offered. "I owe him."

Sol wanted to protest, but he knew better.

He and Scy hauled Wyatt up, and Ruck pulled him carefully into the saddle before him.

Once Sol mounted, Arlen raised her hand, and they spurred forward.

They rode hard for the city, the gates of Lyvareth

climbing against the darkening sky.

Then—everything stilled.

The wind died. The pounding hooves no longer echoed, as if the sound itself had been swallowed.

The very air shifted.

That stillness seized Sol, the same deep calm that always came before. They were close. They were coming.

He dug in his heels and urged his horse alongside Arlen's.

"Something's out there," he said, panic creeping into his voice.

"It'll reach us before the gates."

Arlen's eyes swept the horizon.

"If he feels it, we move," Scy said grimly.

"Ruck, no matter what happens, get Wyatt to Shav," Arlen ordered, her tone sharp as steel. "We ride hard. No stops unless we're forced."

"We try not to engage," she added, gripping the reins.

"Sol," Scy said, drawing close. "If we have to fight, let Ruck take the lead and then, at the first chance you get, break away."

"I won't leave you," Sol snapped. "All that matt—
"

"It's not a choice," Arlen cut in, her tone like a blade.

They can't make me, Sol thought, his jaw locked tight.

"Go!" Arlen shouted, snapping her reins. "Yah!"

The horses lunged forward, pounding toward the gates.

Wyatt's body jolted with every stride, his weight slack, as though the thread binding him to the world was already beginning to fray.

Dust rose in their wake, swallowing the road behind them.

The walls of Lyvareth loomed, stretching wide in both directions, immense, unyielding.

Tiny figures moved along the ramparts, guards, watching, waiting.

At the crossroads ahead, Sol saw them.

Ashmen on horseback, dark shapes against the

road, surging toward them like a black flood.

His heart slammed in his chest.

Still, they did not slow.

The Lash was nearly upon them.

The gates were nearly there.

Scy tore a white cloth from his cloak and thrust it high, the fabric snapping in the wind.

Knights in Itharen gold and cream surged into formation before the gate, a gleaming wedge of steel and banner, silent and unyielding.

The formation split down the center, parting just enough to let Arlen's party through.

She raised her hand, signaling a halt behind the knight's line.

The Lash didn't falter, not until the final heartbeat. Then, with a vicious wrench of reins, their mounts skidded sideways, gravel and dust exploding under hooves as they came to a jarring stop.

A rider moved forward — tall, commanding, draped in crimson and ash-grey.

"I am Isareth Halven, Commander of the 52nd

Lash," the figure barked.

"By authority of Elion, Keeper of the Path, I demand you turn over the spillborn."

A knight answered, his voice cool as stone.

"No god claims dominion in Itharen. By decree of the Mage

Council, Wardens of the Path are forbidden within these walls."

Isareth stood motionless.

Then, his head jerked, a single, violent twitch. A puppet yanked by unseen strings. His spine locked into an unnatural stiffness, and his gaze slid past the knight, straight to Sol.

His eyes drowned in black, the whites vanishing as though midnight itself had been poured into them.

The shift was instant. Wrong.

When he spoke, his voice echoed—layered, as if several mouths moved beneath his skin.

"Give us Soltic Arden."

The name coiled from his tongue like a curse, heavy with venom.

"He is wanted… by Baron Mathren Greywell."

Silence followed, sharp and waiting.

"…and by one who never forgets a face."

Sol's stomach turned.

The knight above did not flinch, but his voice cut the air like a blade drawn slowly.

"No."

He stepped forward, torchlight sliding along the steel in his hand.

"Be gone from these gates… or be broken against them."

Stillness.

Then the voice within Isareth shifted, sharper now, each syllable honed like the edge of a blade:

"Run, if you wish. Hide in your cradle of stone.

I will find you. And when I do… You will not die quickly."

The blackness bled from his eyes in an instant.

He blinked once. Then again.

The voice was gone. But the grin remained, stretched too wide, too certain, too wrong.

With a sharp motion, he turned.

The Lash wheeled their mounts.

And the dust swallowed them whole.

Sol turned to the knight, heart hammering.

"Please, sir, my friend is wounded. He needs a healer."

The knight studied him for a long beat, torchlight catching on the steel of his helm, then gave a single, measured nod.

"I am Sir Cravik of Dorne. You may pass, but you will report to the Vigil's Roost within three days."

"Thank you, Sir Cravik," Scy said with a low bow from his saddle.

Sol felt small as the city swallowed them whole.

The last strands of daylight bled away between the jagged rooftops.

The streets narrowed, pressing them into single file, and even at this hour, the city churned with noise, the grind of wheels, the crush of voices, the restless surge of bodies in motion. No one spared them more than a glance. Faces turned, then slid away again, empty of curiosity, empty of welcome.

In Oswynn, Sol couldn't breathe without someone noticing.

Here, he was invisible.

And for a moment… that was almost a comfort.

Then the stench rose, gutters and unwashed bodies, a tide that threatened to choke him. Even at night, the air lay heavy, rank with rot, smoke, and the sour heat of city sweat. His stomach knotted, but he kept silent. They pressed on, and in the foul blend came a piercing note: the sharp bite of herbed food, pungent and strangely alive.

Above them, a stone castle loomed over the city, its silhouette sharp against the darkening sky.

They veered down an even narrower lane, shadows closing in around them.

At last, they halted before a weatherworn red door.

Arlen swung down and motioned for the others to dismount.

She wrapped her knuckles against the wood, firm, unhesitating, and did not wait for an answer.

From the gloom of the alley, a boy appeared, eyes wide and watchful.

"See to the horses," Arlen said, flipping him a silver

coin.

"Missus, want me to fetch your things too?" he asked.

"Yes, thank you," she replied.

Scy stepped toward Ruck and gently gathered Wyatt into his arms. Without a word, he carried the boy inside, Sol close at his heels.

"It's been a long time, Arlen," came a warm yet raspy voice from within.

"Shav, we need your help," Arlen said quickly. "The boy's been wounded. Ruck did what he could."

Shav clicked her tongue. "If Ruck was the one mending, it must be grave. Bring him to my workroom."

She stepped aside to let Scy pass, her eyes locking on Sol.

She was short, with dark skin and hair that splayed out in every direction, a wild halo around her head. Her skirt looked as though it had been stitched together from strips of bright ribbon, while her loose linen shirt, hanging off her shoulders, was at least two sizes too large.

"And who might this be?" Shav asked, her sharp eyes flicking to Sol.

"Soltic Arden, from Oswynn. Please, you have to save Wyatt," Sol said, his voice trembling but held just shy of breaking.

"I'll do what I can, Soltic."

She turned toward the doorway Scy had vanished through, and Sol moved to follow, but her arm shot out, barring his path.

"You stay. That way." She pointed to a side door. "Your power could interfere with the healing."

"My… power?" Sol blinked. The word sat heavy on his tongue, too vast, too strange to belong to him.

"I see your threads, raw, untamed," Shav said, her gaze narrowing. "We'll deal with that later. For now—go."

With that, she stepped through the door and closed it behind her.

"Wyatt is in the best possible hands," Ruck said gently. "She'll fix him up better than before."

"Ruck, let's go check the horses," Arlen added. "Sol? You can come too."

"No. I need to be here, near Wyatt, when he wakes."

"I thought you would," Arlen said with a gentle

smile. "Still, it might help to keep your mind busy."

Sol shook his head. "Thank you… but I have to stay."

Ruck pulled him into a quick, firm hug. "Hang in there. We'll be back before long."

With a slow breath, Sol turned and stepped through the side door Shav had indicated.

The space opened into a small, welcoming storefront. The air was heavy with the sharp-sweet tang of dried herbs, bundled thick and dangling from the rafters. Shelves climbed the walls from floor to ceiling, crowded with jars in every shape and shade of glass.

Then, a ripple of whispers, broken by a sudden bubble of laughter.

Two figures stood with their backs to him.

Startled, Sol brushed against a table; clay pots wobbled and tumbled, shattering the quiet with their clatter.

The two turned around. A young girl, younger than him, smiled widely as she rushed to help him.

"Be glad nothing broke. Master Dovrekhane is known to be creative when making a point," the young man said.

"Oh, Finn, come off it," the girl said. "Master Dovrekhane's not that scary."

"You weren't the one clucking like a chicken for two days," Finn said flatly.

"Well, you kind of earned it," the girl laughed. "He wouldn't stop flapping his mouth, so she stopped him. Fair's fair."

"You must be new," Finn went on, brushing off the jab with practiced pride. "We're students at Veyndral. I'm Finnian Marek."

"Soltic Arden, from Oswynn in the south," Sol offered, forcing his tone polite.

"I'm Sera Valcrosse," she said, straightening the fallen pots with quick, precise movements.

"Lady Sera Valcrosse," Finn teased.

"Hush, or I'll have Elyshavir fix you again," Sera shot back, grinning.

"Have you had supper?" Finn asked. "We're headed to The Lucky Bastard. Best meat pies in all of Lyvareth."

Sol lowered his gaze. "Thank you, but… my Soven

was hurt on the road. Elyshavir is tending to him."

Soven.

The word lingered, unfamiliar and precious. He had never called Wyatt his partner before, but he was.

If Wyatt had heard it, he would've swept Sol into his arms, grinning like a fool.

Instead, silence pressed in, and Sol's chest tightened.

What if he didn't wake?

What if he never did?

Wyatt lay in the next room, and Sol could do nothing but wait.

A tear slid down his cheek. He wiped it away with his sleeve.

Sera quietly handed him a handkerchief.

"If Master Elyshavir Dovrekhane is healing him, he'll survive," she said, matter-of-factly. "Come."

Without waiting, she seized his hand and tugged him through the door.

On the stoop, Sera dropped down and pulled Sol beside her, while Finn perched on the ledge just above, watching.

"How long will you be in Lyvareth?" she asked.

"I don't know yet," Sol murmured, head sinking into his palms.

"Well, you've got friends here," Finn said with a crooked grin. "Sera's not too bad for a noble."

Sera nudged him with her shoulder, laughing. "And Finn's a pain, but he's tolerable. His family trades in half the city; he'll swindle you into the best deals."

"Aye, that I can," Finn grinned. "Once your Soven's well again, we'll go to the market and get you two set up."

"That would be great," Sol said.

"Does she like jewelry?" Finn asked casually.

"Who?" Sol blinked.

"Your Soven," Finn said, as if it were obvious.

Sol tensed, uncertain how they would take it. But… they seemed kind enough.

"Uh… Wyatt doesn't wear jewelry, not that I've ever seen," he admitted cautiously.

Without missing a beat, Finn smirked. "Wyatt,

huh? I'd wager he wouldn't turn down something sweet."

"We just tried chocolate for the first time," Sol said, a faint smile tugging at his lips. "He liked it."

"Well then," Sera beamed, "tomorrow, while he's resting, we'll take you for a short tour of the market and get him something."

"You're both so kind. Thank you," Sol said.

He still felt as though he were wading through fog, but beneath the numbness, a fragile warmth stirred.

Not joy, but something gentler.

As if simply being seen might be enough, for now.

He drew in a breath.

In. Hold. Out. Again.

Behind them, the door creaked open.

"Soltic, you can come back now," Shav said, her voice softer than before. "And don't let these two drag you into their chaos."

"I resent that," Finn replied, crossing his arms.

"Bawk. B'gawk." Shav smirked.

Finn stuck out his tongue, and Sera doubled over, clutching her sides with laughter.

"Thank you again," Sol said, giving them a small, grateful smile. "We'll come by tomorrow after lessons," Sera promised.

"Welcome to Lyvareth, Soltic," Finn added with a wink. "Until we meet again."

Sol followed Shav into the shop, casting one last glance over his shoulder before turning the corner and stepping into her workshop.

Wyatt was curled on a large pillow in the center of the room.

For the first time since he'd been hurt, he looked calm. Peaceful.

Sol sank to the floor beside him and gently clasped his hand. Scy settled across on the opposite side, quiet and watchful.

Shav returned, carrying a steaming pot and three glasses. She poured the fragrant liquid into each one with careful, measured motions.

"Drink this," she said softly. "It's a tea I blend for strength and calm."

She set one glass aside, placing it near Wyatt. "This one is for him when he wakes."

"Thank you, Master Dovrekhane," Sol said. "Will he... will he pull through?"

"Firstly, call me Shav," she said with a warm smile. "Secondly, when I heal someone, they do more than just pull through."

Sol exhaled slowly. Relief coursed through him, loosening his chest while tightening his throat. His eyes brimmed.

"He'll need rest. A few weeks, at least," Shav continued. "He was lucky. Ruck did well, but if you hadn't arrived when you did... the outcome could've been very different."

"You're a true wonder, Shav," Scy said, admiration lacing his voice.

Shav grinned. "My friend Scy mentioned you'd be staying in Lyvareth. I have a spare room. I rent out the two on the third floor, one just became vacant. You two can stay there."

Sol blinked. Two? He glanced at Scy but said nothing.

"Thank you, but I think we need to find a lodge that can accommodate all three of us," Sol replied.

Shav shot a quick look toward Scy. He gave a faint shake of his head, almost imperceptible to Sol.

"Well… at least until Wyatt's better," she said. "You can stay here."

She turned and left the room.

Sol brushed the hair from Wyatt's face and pressed a gentle kiss to his forehead.

Warmth radiated beneath his lips, faint, but undeniably real.

Wyatt stirred.

His eyes opened slowly, and Sol felt tears slip down his cheeks.

He squeezed Wyatt's hand, gentle but steady, grounding himself in the moment.

"Don't speak," he whispered. "Save your strength."

Scy was wiping his eyes, too. "You gave us quite the scare."

Wyatt tried to sit up. Scy helped him with surprising tenderness.

"Where… where are we?" Wyatt asked, voice dry

and strained.

"We made it to Lyvareth," Scy said gently. "A friend healed you. We're at her home."

"Can you try to drink?" Sol asked.

Wyatt nodded.

Sol blew gently on the tea before lifting the glass to Wyatt's lips.

Wyatt took a tentative sip, then coughed. "That's… awful," he rasped.

Scy chuckled quietly, low, almost off-key.

Wyatt's fingers tightened slightly around Sol's.

"What happened to the ones who… tore apart?" he murmured, barely above a whisper.

Sol hesitated.

"I don't know," he said quietly.

Scy didn't speak.

He simply met Sol's gaze across the room—calm, steady.

After a pause, he cleared his throat.

"I know this isn't the best timing, but… I have to return to Oswynn."

Sol and Wyatt both looked up, surprise flashing across their faces.

"Trouble's brewing," Scy continued. "And I need to make sure Ysella's safe."

The silence between them stretched, heavy and unbroken.

"When will you leave?" Sol asked.

"Tonight," Scy said softly. "Now that I know he'll survive… I can go. If we leave under the cover of darkness, the Lash may let their guard down."

Sol nodded, a quiet ache blooming beneath his ribs. "I… um… thank you for everything, Scy."

He wanted to say more, anything, but no words felt big enough. Scy had saved his life, saved Wyatt's. Held them both together more than once. How do you thank someone for being a tether?

Scy offered a half-smile, small, sincere.

"Lads… if I could stay, I would. But we need to preserve the element of surprise. I'll be back as soon as I can."

"Please send my love to Ysella," Wyatt said. "I want to write her a letter."

"I'll write it," Scy said. "Tell me what you want to

say."

Sol leaned down and kissed Wyatt on the cheek. "I love you," he said softly.

"I love you too, Soltic," Wyatt replied.

"I need some fresh air," Sol murmured, standing.

"Don't go too far," Scy called after him.

Sol paused in the doorway.

He looked back and met Scy's eyes.

And Scy… simply nodded.

A quiet understanding passed between them, not words, not memory, just the kind of look shared by those who've nearly died together.

Scy raised two fingers in a half-salute.

Sol stepped out the back door and into the alley.

He crouched against the wall, letting his back sink into the cool stone. Damp. Rough. Grounding.

He closed his eyes, letting the quiet press in. Let the ache bloom.

The air still carried the scent of blood, sweat, and herbs he couldn't name.

Wyatt was alive. Held his hand. Taken the tea.

But something was different.

Sol hadn't meant to notice, yet he had.

The way Wyatt's fingers had tensed in his. The flicker of unease behind his eyes.

Not fear of death.

Not pain.

Something else.

Could he… be afraid of me?

The thought landed like a stone in his gut. He didn't want it.

Didn't want to believe it.

But the men had torn apart.

And he still didn't know if it was him.

Didn't know how.

Only a part of him, the part that had screamed when Wyatt fell, hadn't regretted it.

Not for a moment.

And that terrified him, too.

His breath caught.

And then… he let go.

His tears came quietly, his body shaking with sobs he couldn't hold back.

Wyatt was alive. He would recover.

But now they had to say goodbye to Scy.

Sol had always known Scy wouldn't stay forever, but he hadn't expected him to leave so soon.

A quiet ache bloomed in his chest. Not panic. Not rage.

Just the weight of a truth too big to face head-on.

He felt a hand settle on his shoulder.

He looked up through blurred eyes.

Shav stood over him, her gaze steady and kind. "How's your head?" she asked softly.

"It's not great," Sol admitted.

"You didn't drink your tea," she said.

"Wyatt woke up. I needed air."

"Scy tells me your headaches have been getting worse," she said. "I'm not surprised. Your aura is twisted in on itself. Tomorrow morning, after breakfast, we'll talk about your symptoms."

Sol nodded, too exhausted to argue.

Arlen and Ruck emerged from the alley's mouth.

"How is he?" Ruck asked, concern clear in his voice.

"He'll heal fully in a few weeks," Shav replied.

"Thank you, Shav."

Arlen reached out and grasped her wrist in a warrior's handshake.

"Scy said he's leaving tonight," Sol said quietly. "I assume... you're going with him."

Ruck and Arlen exchanged a brief glance.

Then Ruck bent down, lifting Sol gently to his feet.

"Aye, Sol," Arlen said softly.

"For now," Ruck added, "Shav will help you get settled."

Shav slipped her arm around Sol's shoulders.

"Well, Soltic," she said with a grin, "looks like you're stuck with me."

Epilogue

———

I Am Here

The room was dark, hushed except for the sound of Wyatt's breathing, deep, steady, almost rhythmic. In the faint starlight, his face took on an angelic glow, softening the hollows beneath his eyes and giving him an otherworldly stillness.

Sol turned onto his other side to face the window, but his mind refused to quiet. The familiar pressure was building again, a slow, relentless swell behind his temples. Sweat beaded on his skin. The fever was worse tonight.

He rose from bed and dressed quietly, careful not to disturb the heavy stillness of the room.

As he slung his travel bag over his shoulder, the small pouch of treasures slipped free. Sol caught it by the drawstring mid-fall, his fingers closing around it with practiced ease. He tucked it into the folds of his cloak without a sound.

On the dressing table in the corner, he left a hastily scribbled note, just a few crooked lines in the dim light.

Then he leaned down and kissed Wyatt gently on

the temple.

"I'll be back soon," he whispered, though Wyatt didn't stir.

He stood there a moment longer, one hand still hovering above the blankets.

In sleep, Wyatt looked peaceful.

But Sol couldn't shake the memory of how his fingers had tensed earlier, the brief flicker behind his closed eyes.

It hadn't been fear. Or pain.

It was something else.

Leaving never stopped being hard, not even for a little while.

With one last glance, Sol crept down the stairs and slipped into the cool hush of night.

His legs trembled more than he expected. The air felt good, but it didn't clear his head.

The alley was still, the silence broken only by the soft echo of Sol's footsteps on uneven cobblestones, quick taps that the stone walls drank in and swallowed.

The air carried a gentle chill, crisp and clean after

days of damp heat and shuttered rooms.

Above, the moon was dark, and the stars glittered like frost scattered across black glass.

He let his feet wander, tracing each turn with quiet intention.

Just in case.

The streets were mostly empty now. A few lingering souls drifted home, humming to themselves or whispering laughter into the dark.

Sol turned off the main road and followed a gravel path that climbed steadily upward, each step lifting him higher above the sleeping city.

At last, he reached a heavy iron gate set into the castle's side wall.

Above it, carved into the stone, were the words: Veyndral Stands.

The gate loomed, closed.

Imposing.

Unmoving.

Sol didn't stop.

He followed the winding path along the outer wall,

where the air shifted — lighter, crisper, laced with salt.

The scent reached him first, then the growing murmur of waves far below.

Shimmering rocks scattered beneath the wall reflected the starlight as the path narrowed, then disappeared entirely.

He stepped into the grass and followed the slope as it slanted gently toward the cliff's edge.

Below, the sea battered the rock face, wild, relentless, and alive.

Above, the stars watched in silence.

Sol closed his eyes and let the wind thread through his hair.

It carried the scent of salt, stone, and something older, something that smelled like promise.

They had made it.

There was no fanfare. No grand welcome.

They had left Oswynn nearly four months ago — broken, hunted, uncertain, and yet here he stood.

He slipped a hand into his cloak and drew out the small pouch from his pocket.

From it, he drew a single metal button.

He held it up to the starlight.

He was nine years old. Petra had just mended her favorite dress.

She'd handed him the spare and said, "You should always have extra buttons."

Such a small moment, but he had never let it go.

Now, Sol clenched the button in his fist until his knuckles turned white.

Back in Oswynn, weeks before they left, that dream had torn him from sleep, gasping.

It hadn't been just a nightmare.

It had been a warning.

Or maybe a promise.

His mother was standing in the sea, ankle-deep.

His father was chasing the twins through the surf.

He remembered the fear, the helplessness, as they grew smaller and smaller in the distance.

No one had come. No one had heard him scream.

I drowned that day — alone, unseen.

But I am alive now.

And tonight, the sea was not the end. He drew his arm back, ready to cast the button, and everything else he carried, into the waves. But his hand froze.

He wanted to let go. To cast it all into the dark and be done with it. But some part of him still wanted to be held by the past.

Still wanted to be seen.

He hadn't forgotten those he'd lost. He knew he never would.

He exhaled, slow and deliberate, like the breath he hadn't realized he'd been holding, and lowered his arm.

Then he tilted his face to the sky and let out a howl.

Raw and ragged, it came from somewhere deeper than his lungs.

It echoed off the cliffs, wild and wide.

He didn't know when the tears had begun.

He opened his arms and spun slowly, a careless circle beneath the stars.

For a moment, he felt weightless, unshackled from past and future alike.

He lifted his gaze, searching for Filch's constellation, always a watchful sentinel, steady above him.

But it wasn't there.

The sky hadn't changed. The clouds hadn't moved.

It had … vanished.

A weight settled in his chest — not dread, exactly.

More like a strange awareness.

As if something had searched for him in the stars — and found nothing. As if he were missing from a map that no longer knew how to hold him.

Sol frowned, scanning the sky again.

Maybe he was just tired. Maybe the fever was playing tricks on him. But the shift lingered, as if the silence had noticed too.

He stayed like that for a moment, still and small beneath the empty sky.

He thought he saw movement in the distance, figures watching him.

Or maybe just trees.

He held his gaze, waiting.

Then, louder this time, he cried out,

"I AM HERE."

His voice cracked on the last word, but it didn't matter.

This time, someone might have heard.

Wyatt was here.

The people he'd met today were kind.

Shav would guide them.

In. Hold. Out. Repeat.

And maybe, just maybe…everything would be okay. Maybe being stuck wouldn't be so bad after all.

He slipped a hand into his cloak and pressed the button against his chest. He thought of the Wilds, the stag, the silver mark, the hush of sacred breath.

It hadn't spoken.

In the silence, he had been seen.

The weight in his chest hadn't lifted, but it no longer threatened to crush him.

He lifted his gaze to the stars and whispered,

"Let them call me Spillborn. The old gods have answered, anyway."

Note From the Author

This story began with a question:

What happens when the path you're given no longer fits the person you're becoming?

I've walked that path, bent myself to fit, made myself small, stayed silent to stay safe. But silence doesn't save you. It just buries you a little at a time.

So, I wrote a boy who dares to become.

Not because he's fearless but because he's afraid and still steps forward.

If you see yourself in him, even in the quietest ways, I hope this book reminds you that you are not wrong for wanting more. That it is not blasphemy to be whole.

This was never about finding the path.

It was always about lighting your own.

Thank you for walking with me.

— X.K. Westwood

Introduction to Valkiric

Valkiric is a ceremonial language rooted in rhythm and breath. Once spoken openly by the elven seers and the oldest practitioners of sacred rites, it has since become a language of memory and reverence—passed in whispers, carried in rituals, and etched into the bones of the world.

Most Valkiric phrases are structured around breath-based syllables, flowing with intention. Each word carries emotional and spiritual weight, often requiring silence to be felt as much as spoken.

Pronunciation tends to follow smooth, open vowels and soft consonants. Accents fall on the first syllable unless marked otherwise by an apostrophe (e.g., 'Sha'rei' is pronounced SHAR-ay, with a softened second syllable).

The apostrophe denotes either a breath pauses or a tonal break and should be treated gently—not abrupt, but reverent. Many phrases are not meant to be spoken quickly; to rush is to empty them of meaning.

When read aloud, Valkiric should feel like an exhaling intention.

About The Author

X.K. Westwood (he/him) writes stories that live between the lines — between truth and myth, faith and doubt, who we are, and who we're told to be.

A queer storyteller with roots in performance and poetic fiction, he believes in the power of quiet resistance, found family, and the sacred weight of becoming.

The Sibyl's Ember is his debut novel and the first in the *Reflections for Reckless Soul Saga*. When he's not writing, he can be found curating playlists for fictional characters, whispering worldbuilding secrets to his dog, or imagining better worlds — and then daring to write them down.